THE BISHOP'S RING

A Struggle Against God

BY

BILL DEBOTTIS

authorHOUSE™

1663 LIBERTY DRIVE, SUITE 200
BLOOMINGTON, INDIANA 47403
(800) 839-8640
WWW.AUTHORHOUSE.COM

First published by AuthorHouse 04/19/05

ISBN: 1-4184-8447-4 (e)
ISBN: 1-4184-8445-8 (sc)
ISBN: 1-4184-8446-6 (dj)

Printed in the United States of America
Bloomington, Indiana

This book is printed on acid-free paper.

PREFACE

This book is historical fiction, filled with suspense, faith adventure, religion, and mystical moments. In other words, it contains the very things that make up our lives. It's a story about the lengths to which faith in God plays in our lives and what we will do to keep faith while God looks on.

This story began with a daydream I had. It turned out to be a foretelling of a rendezvous that was to come. Little did I know when I wrote a first draft copy of this book I would set it aside compelled by a feeling something was missing. But I would come back to complete it.

I chose to continue to research and write towards another book.

Several years later, out of the blue, my wife and I were invited by Polish/German friends to travel to Poland. In Poland the improbable happened. We went to a Polish Cathedral where I had imagined and mused scenes in this book to build a story. While there, one of our traveling companions, a history professor, told us a story, about the Cathedral's patron saint's martyred death, which was very much a part of my early morning daydream years before. I was stunned! My earlier unfinished book was no coincidence.

The visit in Poland embellished my knowledge of Poland's hate filled Communists, and my desire to connect with the fiber of faith that supported the Polish people in their Catholic faith while struggling against their atheist rulers since World War II. I had to rework and finish this novel. It drove me to make changes. I was left to decide where to cut, rewrite, and add clarity to my not so coincidental daydream. Yes, portions of this book are fictional based on many true facts. But the martyred saint's after death miracle, no small part of the story, is true.

I hope you enjoy my efforts to provide entertainment, food and delight for your soul. Enjoy a modern day thriller born of ages past. God wins!

St. Patrick's & St. Joseph's days 2004
Bill DeBottis

FOREWORD

Two Generals, George Washington, a colonialist, and Thaddeus Kosciusko a Polish Patriot, met with their armies at Valley Forge, Pennsylvania. They shared a belief of changing the world. They fought in the American Revolution to defeat tyranny. A second Polish Patriot, Casimir Pulaski fought with his army, but died in the Battle of Savannah, Georgia. Polish Patriots' names are spread across America honoring their service to American freedom. Other immigrants to the new world joined with them.

The Constitution of the United States ratified on June 21, 1788 established a unique belief in liberty for all people, majority rule, and freedom of religion. Through Kosciusko's efforts, Poland's Constitution was approved May 3, 1791. Poland became the second nation in the world and first in Europe to have a written Constitution. Later, when Russian and Prussian forces entered Poland to partition it, Kosciusko led an uprising from Cracow. Poland lost its sovereignty and he died a hero in a Russian prison. Kosciusko rests now nearby Poland's martyred saint who first wore the **Bishop's Ring.** The legacy of Washington and Kosciusko to fight for freedom of self and others has become the legacy of America: "In the face of tyranny, fight for freedom of self and others."

Chapter 1

Even at 16 years of age Magda Tymanski knew she attracted the eyes of men, and boys giving her a confident feeling. Shy and demure, she was one of two sisters with long golden blond hair, and endowed early on with beauty far beyond their youthful years. Attracted by their enthusiasm, classmates in school were happy to be friends with the sisters. It was no small wonder others would want to form friendships with them living in Poland's town of Wieliczka.

The year was 1957 and Poland's Marxist rulers brought Communism into a land where personal independence and the Roman Catholic faith in God lived for one thousand years. God knows about the evil spirits which plague men's soul. Christ spoke about them as the evildoers. The time was coming when the God of History and Mystery would begin once again to reveal Himself through a powerful saint, St. Stanislaw of Cracow, Poland.

Born in 1941, Magda was followed by her sister Marta a year later. They really never knew anything but poverty. Joseph, their father, lost his farm when it was taken from him by the Soviet Army to be a part of a collective of farms. Their mother Alina, a strong and determined woman, was a caring voice as the girls matured into young women. Poland was in the process of being governed with puppets picked by their Soviet masters, rather than governing themselves with freely elected representatives. So intent was their Communist masters in governing what was on the outside of Polish life in attempts to remake man's world, they failed in giving each Pole

1

a valued self-respect, and an appropriate honor. Contemptuously, their atheistic view of life was to treat each person as a unit in lock step with their political views. God was to be taken out of daily life. Those Poles who gave "unsuspecting cooperation" to the Soviet model became puppets of the Soviet rulers. Governing meant slavish observance to the laws of the rulers in which Polish citizens had no right to dispute. Follow in lock step or be smeared, persecuted, tortured, and killed!

God was the enemy! Soviet armies supplied the force surrounding Poland to keep it from straying. In time, Poland's Communists directed their own Soviet style indoctrinated military, with corrupt powers to take advantage of their own citizenry. Church building was strictly forbidden in a country that was more than 98% Roman Catholic. The Communists took God out of Poland, but the Body of Christ, which is the Church never left. It still remained in the hearts of the Polish people.

Doctrinaire Marxists pretended to want to give social betterment, but what they failed to comprehend when eternal moral and spiritual principles are forsaken, undercutting what lives inside the hearts of people dooms social and economic growth in individuals and society.

Long ago, and a millennium past, the rulers of both State and Church were first found in Gneizo in 966 A.D., and later found on the same Castle grounds in Cracow. History reveals God's voice and action are found in the lives of the ancients, when a nation was formed 4000 years ago with Abraham, followed by the Patriarchs, Moses, King David, through to Jesus Christ and his Apostles. The Poles understood and connected to the reality God is the creator of both the Church and the State.

The Church reminds each person given life at conception has a soul and thus becomes an eternal being, to live in joy with God or pain forever with evil demons. The Church brings solace, healing and hope to the hearts of people. It bears the truth and enlightens minds. It gives goodness, strength and resolution to wills, all of which brings about social betterment. Revolution without God is tyranny and chaos. The Church following Christ offers views incongruent to those Marxist free thinkers filled with evil spirits, who would drive God out from His Right to Rule over human life. The God of History and Mystery once again after seventy years was about to reveal Himself through normal means.

Among their friends, Magda, being the oldest and prettiest sister, was a confident young woman. Without boasting, her demeanor, without speaking a word, cried out, "I have got what it takes." And with that attitude she was able to trigger others emotions in any effort coming forward instinctively to help and support her. Enthusiasts like Magda are not the most cultured people in the world, but they are among the only ones who make history. No one knew but God. And He had designs on Magda to play a part in a dangerous role to bring closure to Poland's slavish miseries.

The God of History and Mystery has a long memory ensconced in what some say history repeats itself. Magda was about to become a symbol, a reminder connecting her to a continuum unforgotten by God.

The story of the Bishop's Ring of which Magda plays a role begins with the great martyred Bishop, St. Stanislaw of Cracow, Poland. His ordered death by a brutal king, King Boleslaw the Bad, in 1070 A.D., began when the king abducted a comely woman against her will. The Bishop protested to protect the woman's right to be freed and was rebuked by the king whose response was to kill the Bishop by decapitation. His body was then quartered; its parts scattered in hidden places. Soldiers loyal to the Bishop found the body's remains and placed them in a plain wood coffin. Later, upon opening the coffin the soldiers were amazed to see the body of the Bishop had been miraculously returned to its original structure.

Today, the remains of his miraculously restored body lie encased in an ornately carved silver sarcophagus, in the nave of the Cathedral of Cracow. His head, a sacred relic, is deposited in a reliquary for special keeping. Proving all things are possible with God, this miracle speaks to the majesty with which our Creator honors and upholds the dignity of each person's body he creates for this world.

What was not buried with the Bishop was his Bishop's Ring, a symbol of his Church authority as a descendant of Christ's Apostles.

In the course of centuries that followed the death of the saintly Bishop, his Bishop's Ring has always been looked upon as a force for unity, bringing differences together to fight against those who tread on the civil rights of the least powerful among us.

In the midst of the small treasures the Bishop's executioner kept, was his sword, and the Bishop's Ring as his booty for carrying out the king's orders. But as time went on, the executioner grasped the enormity of his evil act, and he gave up the Bishop's Ring. Sheer terror was the legacy for those who coveted it for their own aggrandizement. The ring took on a legendary life of its own thereafter, as men sought to possess it, not knowing it served only those in the service of God.

In man's search for his own meaning of life, the mysterious and mystical nature of God is often confusing, and impenetrable. Just as the Bible gives the story of creation and man's ultimate destiny, this story begins with a journey filled with mystery, as time makes its way from darkness beneath the surface of the earth to light and the 20th century.

Those who study the nature of God say He sees all things, past, present and future in a continuum. It helps us to know this, that what we know or experience now, may have deeper meanings, the origin of which go deeper than we can contemplate. But we try, anyway! Follow our journey!

Long before the first words of the Holy Bible, "In the beginning," were written, God was keeping track of the movements of people following the Great Flood. Who belonged to whom, and where they were to settle. While God watched from above, the sons of Noah, Ham, Sem and Japeth and their descendant families parted company. Ham's tribe members headed for the lands of Africa and Arabia. Ham's son Canaan settled in what was later to become the land of Phoenicia (Lebanon) and Canaan (Palestine). Cush's descendants went to Ethiopia; Phut's went to Libya. Sem's son Arphaxad became the father of the Hebrew race; Elam, Asshur, Lud and Aram became the forefathers of the Persians, Assyrians, Chaldeans, Armenians, and Syrians. Japeth's sons, Gomer, Madai, Tubal, Tiras, Magog, Javan, and Meshech became the forefathers of the French, British, Germans, Russians, Medes, Iberians, Greeks, Romans and Balkans.

The time now is 3500 B.C. The period: Neolithic as scientists now call it. It was a time when modern research says salt mining began in the area we now call, Wieliczka, a place in southwest Poland.

1500 years after scientists suggest salt mining was taking place in Wieliczka, with populations expanding throughout the earth, the time had come for God to make good on his promise found in the Book of Genesis, Chapter 3, Verse: 15. He called out Sem's descendant, Abraham, and his wife Sara and their flocks of animals from Ur of the Chaldeans, and chose him to be His prophet, in keeping with His promise made to Satan. God promised Abraham, whose wife was barren he would become the father of a great nation, with offspring as great as the sands of the seashore. Abraham trusted and followed his God's directions to the land of Canaan, already populated with the descendants of Canaan. The Creator, Father of all human life, included all born of human flesh in His plans.

Abraham, by today's standards, would be a millionaire. He bought and paid for his portion of land upon which his claim was made. From this land, God's plan, a people would rise up. Later Prophets shouted God's message of hope and wrote the coming of a Messiah. All Hebrew women held on to the hope they would become the mother of the Messiah to come. The lessons of history are clear. God's Spirit watches over the formation of nation states and the good and evil of humanity. As a good and holy Creator, He rewards holiness and punishes sinfulness. If not in the present, He will administer justice in His kingdom. All of this was made clear in the Old Testament to be followed by the New Testament's New Covenant with God, fulfilling God's promise to Abraham when He included all people spread across on the face of the earth. Patriarchies evolved into territories ruled by kings, judges, and those opposed to being ruled.

Travel in our time and go on the banks of Poland's Vistula River originating deep in its southwest corner, and watch its meandering flow northward, through vast farmlands, meadows, narrow and wide widths, and rising bank sides. Nearby in each village are the vestiges of ancient churches and rich culturally imbedded beliefs. Mark your ways along the path where the river slows, and stop by places where history suffered horrendous blows, places like Oswiecim (Auschwitz). Step forward, advance into a land of mysteries, crushing defeats, and miraculous divine interventions. God was keeping His promise to save humanity.

Poland received its name by defining its people, "People of the Land." But they were much more. Legends abound. Stop off in Cracow, and work your way back to a town called Wieliczka, site of the ancient Royal Salt Mine, a subterranean labyrinth created by God twenty million years ago and once the safe home of the legendary "Bishop's Ring." Upwards of 800,000 to 1 million people visit this site every year founded by Blessed Kinga, who was to later become the patroness of Salt Miners.

As her legend tells us, Kinga, daughter of a 13th century Hungarian King, Bela IV, was engaged to marry the Polish Prince of Cracow-Sandomierz, Boleslaw the Chaste. She learned her fiancée's country was highly populated, but it had no salt. She asked her father to give her one of his salt mines as a wedding present, which he generously granted. After taking possession of her engagement ring, she tossed the ring down the mineshaft of her new gift as a sign of her ownership of the mine.

Later, when she came to Poland, she ordered the construction of a mineshaft in the vicinity of Cracow. In their first recovery attempt the miners found a rich salt deposit. Inside the deposit they found the Princess's engagement ring, which had to pass through underground waters, to follow her to her husband's country. As one reads into this legend, one wonders was this a mere coincidence her engagement ring was found in the vicinity of Cracow, the site of other mystical coincidences defying explanations?

Blessed Kinga then moved to exploit opportunities in mining and salt trading for the good of the working miners of Wieliczka. It became the oldest documented salt manufacturing site in Europe. Later, well digging led to the to the discovery of rock salt. Salt as a commodity equaled economic power and survival. As time moved forward the Dukes of Silesia and Cracow granted Charter Rights to their loyal friends or leased out the parts of the salt mine. The region prospered.

The proceeds from salt under the Piast and Jagiellonian kings provided almost 1/3 of the royal revenue. Poland's influence grew. Roman Catholic King Casimir the Great codified the unwritten law of the country; statutes of protection regulated the rights of the miners who worked in the mines. In the seven centuries where miners slowly came to know the mine, they discovered its secrets, treasures, and used it as a safe haven to hide St. Stanislaw's legendary Bishop's Ring. The difficulty for finding it in the salt mine had to overcome many obstacles.

The Wieliczka mine grew to nine working floors, beginning from a depth over 200 feet to the lowest depth of more than 1000 feet. The miners quarried beautiful galleries, defying death and injuries to beautify their workplace. They constructed drawing machines, harnessed horses to transport massive blocks of salt. Their dangerous work made the miners more religious than other social groups. Their custom was to plant a cross at the spot where a miner perished and celebrate Mass in altar chambers, which they had hewn out of the earth.

The Royal Salt Mine at Wieliczka is a unique human achievement, a testimony to the strength of man's body and spirit to overcome struggles with industriousness, courage, humility and passion. Hidden underground are over 200 kilometers of galleries, 2,040 chambers and uncounted lakes, 26 surface shafts and approximately 180 shafts connecting caverns on different levels throughout the mine. In the 700 year history of the mine 7.5 million cubic meters of salt have been extracted, the equivalent of which equals 20% if the earth's equatorial girth. Yet, it is said that only 3% of the total mine has been used, and 2% has been set aside as a tourist route that will delightfully dazzle even the most cynical among us, especially Blessed Kinga's chapel in which so many beautifully carved religious images represent the love the Poles have for God and the Saints of heaven who mirror the image of God.

The miners also displayed their sense of humor in their artistic sculptures and make many wonder where the inspiration came from in the making of the movie, "Snow White and the Seven Dwarfs" after seeing a carved group of rock salt gnomes, who are believed to be working hard to help the Wieliczka miners.

But the real religious character of the miners reflected the faith and values so widespread in all parts of Poland. An award winning carved rock salt relief of Leonardo da Vinci's "The Last Supper" gives pause and appreciation to other works in Blessed Kinga's Chapel depicting such as "Herod's Sentence" and "The Massacre of the Innocents." The stories of the Old and New Testament are presented in faith and face.

Mining rock salt is dangerous. Miners are threatened by the elements: fire, water and mine gas. Hundreds of water leaks threaten the mine and the town of Wieliczka above it. When fire was used to light the mine, the dangers from explosions due to methane gases in the forms of potassium nitrate were ever present, and fires could last for many months. Potassium Nitrate is a crystalline compound used in the pickling of meats, but also in the manufacture of matches, pyrotechnics, explosives, rocket propellants and fertilizers. Throughout all risk conditions, the Bishop's Ring remained safe in the mine.

The relic ring and legend deserved to be in the Cracow Cathedral Treasury, where other treasured items in Poland's long Catholic history are stored. The three miners, who had taken a vow of secrecy to protect the whereabouts of the Bishop's Ring, prayed for discernment in ways to discharge themselves from the responsibility of secrecy by including a fourth miner. It was time to save an endowed Poland, and its civil rights from a brutal king, called "Communism." Among the silent miners who knew of the Bishop's Ring's presence in the salt mine, a time had come when they believed a new chapter should begin in the legend of the Bishop's Ring based on past miraculous events and warnings for humanity.

1917: October 13th Miracle of the Sun at Fatima, Portugal.
November 5th Bolshevik Revolution, 20th century war
against God begins in Russia.
1945: Yalta Conference, in February. President Roosevelt
gives post-war Poland to Soviet Premier Stalin.
Communists working in the U.S. Department of State were
making policy decisions as undetected Soviet spies.

For an empire, which had never been able to feed its people, the post-WWII Soviet Russian slave machine swarmed over Eastern Europe, robbing nations of their resources, destroying their religious institutions, slaughtering clergy, and imprisoning millions in slave enterprises to help in the construction of their domination of the world. Poland was a rich target. Wieliczka was not the only source of prosperity in Poland. The "People of the Land" were blessed with "know how" and above and below resources, other nations coveted and fought over to control. Poland's Silesia and Breslau region's 66 mines generate nearly all of Poland's energy resources. The same region produces iron, steel, and textiles. Farmers produce dairy products; harvest grains and vegetables, raise hogs, and cattle. Throughout all of Poland, evidence of the Roman Catholic religion is expansive and deeply imbedded in practice. Wars and suffering has brought this people to rely on God to save them from their oppressors.

Andrej Androwitz and his wife Brina met while he served as a military officer in the Polish Embassy in St. Petersburg, Russia. Brina was the daughter of a Russian Minister serving in the Czar's Cabinet. Their love flourished years before the Marxists seized power overthrowing the Czar.

Colonel Androwitz was well aware of the designs of the Bolsheviks, whose actions contradicted their earlier promised words. The Bolshevik view of the world began to emerge three weeks after gaining power with decrees denying the sanctity of marriage by ending the role of the Church to conduct a sacramental ceremony giving God's blessing to newly wedded couples. All marriages were to be conducted by civil authority; couples were to show their consent on civil documents. God was left out of the ceremony. Divorce was easily granted when requested. Abortion on demand was promoted. Promiscuity flourished with concomitant diseases. The first attacks on the order of a well-regulated society were upon the Church, the defender of the family, as the first known unit of any society. Marxism did not recognize the family! It recognized each person as units of production owned by the State. The Bolsheviks set about the task of removing millennial Christianity from all facets of Russian society as their first order of business.

Soon after the Bolshevik revolution stormed over Czarist Russia, Colonel Andrej Androwitz a soldier by profession was ordered back to Poland from Russia. His wife's passport was honored since diplomatic recognition had not been given the new Soviet State at the time. Aware that Catholic Poland was the next-door neighbor, and the Bolsheviks wanted world conquest, Colonel Androwitz, alarmed, held talks with Poland's Josef Pilsudski, Chief of State, on Soviet worldwide intentions.

A year later, 1918, the Bolsheviks, now calling themselves "Communists," at the ending of World War I, the day after the Armistice was signed, German-Communist forces already within the country set out to take over Berlin and Munich but were met with citizen resistance. Germans rose up against Bolsheviks to halt atheism's "Red Menace." The Bolsheviks lost the battles but the war continued in Catholic Bavaria as new assaults were introduced on Catholic religious culture in books, music, and social engineering. Bavarians knew who caused this assault on their beliefs and they resented the intruders forcing their ungodly secular changes on their lives. Polish-German Silesia had much to fear.

The people of Poland believed the Church would never be destroyed based on Christ's words, "The gates of hell would not prevail against it (His Church)." Christ, the Son of God, gave credence to the belief the Church shared a role in authority with "Caesar," over human life, since both authorities, divinely created, unified were to act for the will of God. Christ pronounced: "Render to Caesar the things that are Caesar's and to God the things that are God's." Nation's too, would be judged.

Along the winding Vistula River in Cracow, high on the hill above its banks stands Wawel Hill Castle, where Church and State coexisted on the same grounds in beauty and splendor, and did for many centuries, a testament to the truth, that both can exist side by side; not separated from each other, nor destined to act with opposing purposes. Until Russia conquered Poland at the end of the 17th century and transferred the Capital to Warsaw, both Church and State lead their nation in Cracow in matters dealing with God, and to give help in partnership with civil authorities to guide their nation in unity of purposes in Cracow.

Several years after Poland's victorious 1920 war with Soviet Russia, Colonel Androwitz returned to the diplomatic services and was reassigned to Poland's Diplomatic mission in New York City. In 1925, his wife, Brina, delivered an eight-pound boy, and they called him Grigor.

When Grigor was school age and old enough to comprehend, Grigor was educated and traveled to famous places where Polish Generals, like Thaddeus Kosciuszko and Casimir Pulaski and their troops came to the aid of the American Revolutionary forces under General George Washington to fight battles, for American independence. A grateful nation, America bestowed honors by naming towns and counties across the country, from Pulaski, New York to Kosciuszko, Mississippi, up and down the country across to Stanislaw County, California to respect Poland's heroes. Poland's General Conrad Pulaski was killed at the battle of Savannah, Georgia, fighting for the American colonies to have their independence, which included the freedom of Religion, deeply cherished in Poland.

England's Ruler at the time of the Revolutionary War was King George III. As head of the Anglican Church, he imposed taxes on all other Christian faith Churches within the thirteen colonies. Tithing to one faith and taxed by another was another form of subjugation and reasons for people to seek their independence from oppression, which the "People of the Land" clearly understood was worth fighting against.

A train ride up the Hudson beyond Albany, Grigor learned General Thaddeus Kosciuszko and his troops, working under the command of General George Washington, shared honors defeating the British in the battle of Saratoga. It was Kosciuszko who directed where the battlements would be stationed overlooking the Hudson River, at a place now called West Point Military Academy.

The family's time in America allowed them to see for themselves the contributions Polish immigrants made in the development of industrial strength across a wide swatch of land beginning in Boston, across New England to the Midwest, in steel mills and factories where they settled. "People of the Land" went to work in American mines, factories, and farms, just as they had done in their homeland

and communities grew and prospered, slowed only by the economic Great Depression.

The Androwitz's returned to Poland in 1938. Grigor came with an American Passport, and the family settled in Cracow. His father took a position at Jagiellonian University, where young Grigor desired to enroll someday. The following year Germany attacked Poland, and World War II had begun. In the early days of the war, in the Nazi siege of Poland both of his parents died. Grigor, an American by birth, spoke fluent Polish. Orphaned, he had no time now to search for relatives on his father's side of the family. Friends at the University helped him for a while. Without telling anyone where he was going, at age 14, he sought to hide from the Nazis in the cavernous salt mines of Wieliczka to avoid being taken for the slave work camps the Nazis were building. He had been told the Nazi authorities avoided the salt mines for fear of being ambushed.

Grigor's escape to Wieliczka was nothing less than miraculous, but his acceptance into the mine as a youthful miner, underwent scrutiny. His American passport, his historical knowledge of "Polish America" provided much wonderment to men whose dreary lives underground were uplifted with hope. What he found beyond a hiding place, in the trapped environs of danger were holy men, holier than most, because of their precarious existence. There he found solitude, a prayer life with older men, and God. As the war wore on, the experience led him to think about becoming a priest when the war was over. Meanwhile, he found fun and joy in the crystal caves where halite crystals sparkled in the near darkness of Blessed Kinga's discovery of the mine many hundreds of years before. When Grigor announced his intentions in 1945 to enter the underground seminary to the a fellow miner, the "secret three" holding on to the whereabouts of the Bishop's Ring were informed. The three miners, in their holy cause, had found their champion. They were going to have to wait until his ordination to the priesthood. It meant more time to wait and hope.

Shrouded in secrecy, eight years passed, and Grigor was ordained a priest, and he established contact again with old friends and Oliver Takentur, an American Journalist and his son Gabriel whom he met in Cracow as an orphan. In 1961 Grigor was able to find his father's second cousin, Conrad Kaminski, who by this time was married to Magda Tymanski. For him it was a sign from God to proceed. The Bishop of Cracow agreed.

Years of planning had gone into preparing for the safe keeping of the legendary Bishop's Ring. It was 1965. The question was: Would his cousin Conrad Kaminski and his beautiful wife, Magda, be willing to take on the task?

Conrad, at first doubted. He thought of having to leave both sets of parents, and Magda's sister Marta, to carry out this dream. Magda was Magda, up to the task. They would talk about it, and pray over it.

Like Abraham and Sara, it would become a journey of faith in God.

Chapter 2

An ambulance siren honked and screeched its way out of LaGuardia Airport passenger terminal in a rush to deliver a fallen man to the hospital. The man suddenly collapsed on the reception area floor. Lieutenant Robert Morrison of the NYPD was called by Airport Security to speak to a man who had been waiting for his wife's flight to arrive. He and his wife had a statement to make to the Police. When the policeman arrived the man began his statement in a befuddled fashion.

"I was sitting over there, waiting for my wife's flight to arrive, and watching passengers come and go in front of me, when I saw this man fall down. His right arm was outstretched when he landed on the floor. He was about thirty feet from me, over there," pointing to a spot where the man fell. "He looked directly at me when I saw something fall from his hand. People hurried to go around him. There was confusion. I saw a flick of light coming toward me. But I didn't see anything. When my wife arrived," he turned to his wife and said, "You tell the rest."

She looked at Lieutenant Morrison. "I didn't know what went on. When I came toward my husband, I saw a small sparkle of light reflected from the sun from behind where my husband was sitting. We kissed, and I asked him what he was hiding behind him. He said, 'Nothing.' I reached down and picked up this shining ring from the sunlight coming through the windows. It has a beautiful red ruby setting." She held it out for him to see. "My husband told me it must be connected to the man they took in an ambulance to the hospital.

If he survives or if he was married, maybe he or his wife would like to have the ring back." She handed the ring to Lieutenant Morrison. "On second thought," she said, "we will give you our names in case its just never claimed. It's so beautiful."

She placed the ring in Lieutenant Morrison's hand. He said, "Thank you." Then he asked them to put their statement into writing. The couple completed their statement in Airport Security office and went home.

Airport Security officer Larry Smith updated Lieutenant Morrison. "We found the guy was a designer or something like that. A business card in his wallet says he worked in Forest Hills. The EMS didn't revive him."

Detective John "Buddy" Rogers lit a cigarette, and let the smoke stream up along his face. He addressed his friend, the Lieutenant, with his nickname, "Moe, this isn't just any ring."

"Let me take a look at it again. Nope! Never seen anything like it. It's not a military service ring, or college ring. Looks special though with the coat of arms on the side. I can't read it. It's too small for me. Could it be religious?"

"I went to a Catholic School. That's Latin script." John Rogers said. Morrison took the ring from him, and put it in his coat pocket.

"I got to write up a report on it. Could mean something stolen merchandize or a piece of evidence in a criminal investigation. You never know."

Smitty said, "I didn't find airline tickets in his effects."

"What else been done?" Lieutenant Morrison asked Rogers.

"His family has been informed. They will be here in a couple of hours to make arrangements for the body. Taking a train in from the Syosset. We contacted his office. The guy's boss is on vacation out of town and can't be reached. Maybe the man's family knows something about this ring. The witness statement reads like he wanted to give it up."

"I can ask and fill them in." Lieutenant Morrison answered. "No need for both of us to wait around here. I'll go to the precinct and come back before the family arrives. More to think about! Just hunches." Lieutenant Morrison shook Rogers hand and they parted.

With the information he had been given, Morrison returned to his precinct to turn in a report of the designer's death. Until he spoke with the widow the ring would be kept out of placing it into custody since the ring's finding may have been stroke of good luck for its finders. This very beautiful ring was dropped into small plastic snap locked bag and placed in the Morrison's coat pocket. His hunch was not to place it in evidence. He learned to live by his strong hunches. He headed for the train terminal to wait for the family of the deceased. The deceased man's wife was told where the police officer would stand and what he would be wearing. All they had to do would be to approach him and he would take them to the hospital.

Showing compassion to the bereaved had great meaning for this police officer. The cops at the precinct understood Morrison. They rarely questioned his motives or his due diligence. It had to do with his past. When he started out on the street as a patrolman he knew everybody and everybody knew him. Staggering waves of crime filled the city since his younger days on the force. He saw the sons of the powerful walk free but more disturbing were the arrests of drug dealers and dope pushers. He lived long enough to learn everyone's humanity was on the line when he went out to a crime scene. It was then in his youth that things did not always appear to be as they were in reality. Experiences taught him to play his hunches. Lieutenant Morrison would wait for the family to shed some light on the ring. In the meantime he would live with his hunches, and this time, he had the hunch he shouldn't let this one slip by without some "police questioning."

"Lieutenant Morrison? Are you Lieutenant Morrison?" Magda Kaminski asked.

"Yes, Mrs. Kaminski, I presume."

"Yes, my husband is Conrad Kaminski. This is my son, Thaddeus, and my daughter Katherina." Morrison shook their hands, and then invited them to follow him to his unmarked police car without another saying a word. He opened the doors on the passenger side and closed them when all had been seated. He moved swiftly around the car to his door and quickly placed himself inside and closed the door. He had to tell them Conrad Kaminski had died, a fact that had not been told to them when they were contacted. Inside of the car, they would share their grief. While the family sat on the train into the city they had hope the husband and father would be alive when they arrived. It was only when he confirmed Conrad's death that their hope was lost and sorrow set in. Now they were left to wonder what had brought about his death?

Morrison started the engine and drove toward the hospital. The Kaminski's talked in muted tones. He planned that they would first identify the body, and then he would take Mrs. Kaminski aside to ask her a few questions. It also crossed Morrison's mind Kaminski was the victim of foul play. This was not his first case of an unexpected death on the street or public building. The more he thought about these possibilities the more significance the ring had as if the ring was a clue to something more nefarious. He did not want to discuss his hunch in front of the children. He would have to take Mrs. Kaminski aside, present her with the ring and ask her to explain what her husband might have been doing with it, since Kaminski was not wearing it when he collapsed in the airport terminal.

They pulled into the hospital parking lot.

"The hospital will ask for your signature to identify the deceased as being your husband's body. If the County Medical Examiner suspects foul play an autopsy will be performed. He was not bleeding when he died. If initially he finds something that does not appear to be a hundred percent kosher such as suspicions of foul play there will be a delay releasing the body. An unnatural death sometimes lead police to think something criminal might have taken place."

"How can that be? Conrad is no criminal. He is a just man." Morrison looked at the children and turned to her.

"Mrs. Kaminski, I didn't say he was a criminal. But I think you and I ought to go aside someplace and discuss something I have in my possession. Let's do that. Can we send the children off to the cafeteria down the hall while you and I talk here privately for a few minutes?

Mrs. Kaminski told her children to go to the cafeteria, and she would be by in a few minutes. She came back to Morrison and they found a quiet lounge where they could talk. Morrison pulled the transparent plastic evidence bag out of his pocket and handed it to Mrs. Kaminski. "Can you tell me something about this ring?"

Her eyes suddenly showed signs of despair. He knew the moment she cast her eyes upon the ring she knew what it was. "That ring was kept for someone who someday will become a Bishop. A Catholic Bishop!"

"What's that supposed to mean? I thought those deals were all cut and dry. Catholics never get a clue what's going on when it comes to picking a Bishop. So what is your husband doing with a special ring like this?"

"He was asked by his boss to show it to a priest. He was doing his boss a favor." Mrs. Kaminski said quietly.

"I don't understand." Morrison asks, "So why was your husband in the airport? Is this priest from out of town?"

"Yes, from out of town. I didn't know where my husband was going today. He said he would be back tonight. I know he didn't want to go to the airport for his boss."

"Oh, why is that?"

"He felt strange about doing it. He told me. His boss always sent him on these kinds of trips to show the ring. It was a mistake to tell his boss he had it. No one knew Conrad. He would just show up, show the ring for his boss and return home. His boss always told him it was just part of doing business. Conrad never believed him. We came from Poland, you know. He was happy to have his job as a designer of Churches since only architects are licensed to give design approval. But we don't know American business. We don't know how business things get done. His boss said it was a courtesy." Morrison thought her story had holes in it.

But he was hearing a message. His life was filled with investigating variations of the seven deadly sins. He began to suspect Conrad's boss would go out and find the pious unworldly priest, whose parish pockets were ripe for the picking. When Conrad was asked to show this beautiful ring to a pastor a big question arose, "WHY?" filled Morrison's Catholic mind. He put the ring back into his pocket.

Mrs. Kaminski did not know, nor seem to care about the big events of the city, since she settled two hours away from the busy world of big business. Morrison thought the big fish in this game was going to have to be Conrad's boss if her claim was true. Conrad was the dead pawn!

Years in the police department taught Lieutenant Morrison that every strata of society had its winners and losers. Upstanding citizens have been found stuffed in the trunk of cars while their business partners cooked the books, and the killing is made to look like a gangland killing or a disgraceful affair gone badly. He had to be cautious about this because Mrs. Kaminski may have been a part of her husband's sudden death. Perhaps a conspiracy to make her a widow was in the works. He could think that. Lieutenant Morrison told himself he couldn't say anything until he learned more.

If she was telling the truth, it sounded like a clergyman was innocently or maybe not so innocently involved in a bait scam to get their hands on this ring. Where best to carry out a bribery than among priests who are bound by their ordination promises to keep confessional secrets?

Her comment was the deceased's boss would send him out to show off the ring. Did she say the ring would be given to a Polish Bishop? How do you find the right one to wear it? And how long has this been going on? Was there something more going on than just showing off the ring? If he didn't like doing it why according to the witness's statements did it look like her husband was so willing to give it up? Did the deceased want the police to give it back to his wife so that his boss or someone else could not have it? Or did the dead man want it protected? Morrison had many questions.

Morrison held the packaged ring in his hand inside of his coat pocket. All he had to do would be to give it to Mrs. Kaminski and be done with his interest in her husband's death. For reasons he could not explain he could not go ahead and release the ring to the widow whose husband dropped it. He asked himself, "Why was he connecting the death of the man with the ring anyway?"

As he started to pull his hand out of his pocket, he felt a twinge in his forearm, and his hand suddenly gripped the bagged ring so tightly he could not release it if he wanted to. If he pulled his hand out of his pocket the ring was going to be in it. A feeling came over him this was not the time to release this ring.

Magda began to weep uncontrollably. Conrad would not fulfill Father Grigor Androwitz' wish for this ring to end up on the hand of a Polish Bishop. This ring had again encountered difficulty in its long path to its destiny. Deep within her soul she lived with Father Grigor's warning about betrayals.

"Conrad," she wiped her eyes, "was healthy, too young to die." She was afraid to think about how all this came about and feared more trouble was coming her way.

Chapter 3

Now Magda waited for the words. Just what happened to Conrad? The policeman hadn't been specific. What was going to happen to her and the children? She sat pensive, alone in her thoughts as the policeman strode off to make phone calls. The past came clearly into focus. Memories stirred. Her face was blank as she revisited her life in Poland when she and Conrad first met and the circumstances of that meeting. She thought of her village and the deprivation of her people in comparison to the life she and her husband had built for themselves in America, which they would not have been able to do under Communist rule.

Her thoughts turned to the events, which brought her here to America.

She remembered, as teenage girls, how both she and her younger sister, Marta, were often the target of male eyes as they matured into womanhood growing up in Poland. Their golden blonde flaxen hair was not unusual among other golden blond haired children. And although they were a year apart in age, only their close neighbors could tell who was the oldest and who might be the prettiest. At the age of sixteen and fifteen both girls were very much young women in their physical charms. Not only did schoolboys notice but also so did young soldiers who came through their town looking for girls to meet while on their tours of duty. There was more to life than shiny boots and cleaning rifles.

Magda and Marta grew up in Wieliczka, a very quaint and reasonably clean place. Wieliczka was famous for its Royal Salt

Mine had become a national treasure with its subterranean labyrinth of crystal caves. In 1978 this Royal Salt Mine was named first on the list of the UNESCO World Cultural and Natural Heritage sites. In their youth, under Communists, women cleaned the roadway with long brooms, taking wide swaths of dirt and pushing it to the edges of the curbs, where they would come back later and push the dirt down the street. The streets were walled built before the Soviets imposed collective farms upon rural landowners. On either side of the walled streets, family barns bordered the sidewalks. Farm wagons were stored within these barns at the end of a day's work. When the farmer and his animals came home at night, the droppings and the muddy wagon wheels provided village women with work cleaning the streets.

Neither Magda nor Marta could imagine cleaning streets. Magda remembered telling her mother she didn't want to be a farmer's wife. Her mother understood and taught her daughters how to sew fancy dresses even though they were unable to buy even one. She could make more than one.

She often thought it was her fancy dress, which caught the eye of the soldier, who came close enough to speak to her and that lead to her new life. The encounter abruptly changed her life. Swiftly, her mind focused directly on the time she met Conrad.

Conrad, walking home after work, heard Magda's screams as he passed a door to her father's barn. He quickly ran to the door, opened it, and found a soldier ripping at Magda's clothes in an apparent attempt to rape here. He jumped on the back of the soldier, and began choking him until the soldier almost lost consciousness. Magda was able to climb out from under the both of them as they struggled. Conrad, the stronger of the two when he saw Magda was free, he got off the back of the soldier and pushed him out the barn door along the sidewalk. A crowd had gathered in the street, and witnessed Conrad's forceful shove of the soldier out of the barn embarrassing the soldier, who hid his face. Reporting the incident would bring about troops harassing her neighborhood.

Those were her memories. Little did she know it would become a defining moment in her life.

Her attacker lived with his memories. He would never be embarrassed again in a test of strength. He wanted revenge and vowed to not forget the incident. He went to the trouble of finding out the names of the girl he attacked, and the person who prevented him from doing it. The police had provided information based on an inquiry from his military unit as to who these people were, on the pretext of their civil wrongdoing. It was a memory she later erased so it would not interfere with her hopeful outlook on life. Not so, her attacker, who took pleasure in his anger justifying reasons why he needed to be respected as a soldier. The army had ways for him to seek his revenge. Humbled, he couldn't move fast enough from Wieliczka, carrying a not to be forgotten memory.

As she sat alone in the hospital memories brought her back to Poland and their newlywed table talks. Conrad recounted his days before marriage when he worked in Cracow at a drafting table in a government ministry for building construction. At night he came home on the bus that took him to his family's small apartment. In the summer after work Conrad worked in the fields outside the village tending to farmers crops. It was a matter of survival since the Communists had taken over and applied the Marxist principles of centralized planning and government. He had little time to meet people except on his Saturday night, when people crowded in the bakery/beer hall. Magda, at sixteen was not likely to be found in such a place. She didn't look sixteen more like twenty to Conrad who was twenty-six.

Her memories continued to flash as if she was deliberately being reminded. After she came into the house crying and telling her parents a soldier tried to rip her dress off in the barn, she told her father a young man had saved her when she was screaming for help. Magda's father went out from the house that day and saw people crowded around Conrad congratulating him for stopping the soldier. And she remembered seeing her father approach Conrad with a serious look on his face. She could still hear the spoken words fixed in her mind.

"You have saved my daughter from the soldier?"

"Yes."

"Come with me to my house. You must meet her, and let her give you her thanks. I want to drink a toast to you."

That is how they, two strangers met, and how their friendship began. Conrad realized the soldier and other soldiers could come back to find him for vengeance as he walked in the dark to his home from the bus. He was prudent. He asked the Tymanski's not to report the attempted rape incident fearing reprisal. History would be repeated with a vengeance.

Conrad was young, alert and smart enough to watch what went on at work when the fate of someone, who reported wrongdoing on the part of others, and how those who report wrongdoing are treated after an episode, dies down. Almost always revenge follows. Conrad listened to his priest who explained Christ's meaning of turning the other cheek. The priest advised the one who slaps another on the cheek might find the slap coming back to him in some form as life enfolds. Follow Christ's words!

Magda, surrounded by the smells of a hospital had her arms folded, her eyes closed in quiet prayer. She reached for her Rosary as tears streamed down her cheeks. Trust! She had to trust the Lord. She wanted God's will to be done. A Polish Bishop would wear that ring! She had confidence God would rescue her. It was time to meditate and pray each decade of the Rosary. She found solace in the five Sorrowful mysteries.

When she finished praying, she needed to be uplifted with warm memories.

Her father took it as a special sign when Conrad saved Magda. He invited Conrad to come to the house for a Sunday meal where Conrad could meet Magda's mother and she would cook a fine meal for him. He accepted the invitation as a token of gratitude. From that point on Conrad was on his best behavior waiting for the day when Magda would be old enough to marry. Conrad later told her he believed God had allowed this strange event to take place for a special reason, which he could not define. What did his dying portend? She trusted her father when he said God watched over her. She believed his words and quiet humility pleased God. Living under Communism, her father told her not to worry, God has his own ways. He protects those who call upon Him.

Her parents were now deceased. Her memories now brought smiles and tears as she lived her destiny in this journey of faith.

At her age of eighteen Magda's father gave Conrad permission to marry Magda. Her father feared other men would recognize her beauty and come to him asking for her hand in marriage. In his simple way her father thought her marriage was arranged in heaven, as Conrad, like St. Joseph, would become his daughter's protector.

For several years after the attempted rape incident Conrad was the subject of investigations coming from a government authority. The Secret Police suspected him committing crimes in which his name was always being advanced as the troublemaker. Things were going to have to change. They feared a serious charge someday would be lodged against him and he would be sent to prison without a fair trial. Years later Conrad found a friend in Cracow who could surreptitiously gain the soldier attacker's name from the authorities. Countering false charges they prepared documents for their Church Pastor of times and places when Conrad had been harassed and falsely accused. His priest fought his hidden enemy by proving the charges of crime to be false.

Conrad appeared to be healthy. Magda was left to wonder why their heavenly helpers were nowhere to be found in Conrad's death. Just as quick this thought entered her mind, she quickly dismissed it as a loss of faith if she persisted to think this way. It was no time to lose hope.

Magda continued to wait for some word from the hospital but none was forthcoming. Lieutenant Morrison left her alone with her thoughts as he had done so many times with people caught in a traumatic situation. As in this he had once been where she now found herself reliving the past. He could see she did not want to talk. She wanted to be alone to think.

By the time Conrad asked her father for permission to marry Magda she had much of the mystery figured out. Men, she thought liked to look at beautiful women. And because she attracted so much attention of men then she must be beautiful. She wanted to copy styles of beautiful women and talk like one. Magda's mother a realist told her she would attract the eyes of men. But it would be up to her to study in order to speak intelligently and learn how to sew in order to wear beautiful clothes.

She reminisced about the day years after they had married when a letter came for Conrad's father from his first cousin a priest, Father Grigor Androwitz. The letter stated Gabriel Takentur living in the United States was ready to "Carry out the plan." Father Grigor's letter was also a letter of introduction to meet the Bishop of Cracow. It included invitations to the Tymanski and Kaminski family members to meet the Bishop in the Cracow Cathedral at a time and a certain place.

Conrad's father, Wladyslaw, and his mother, Marianna, knew it was a signal from Father Grigor the time had come. Magda's parents rued the day of this news.The memories of that moment in time swirled now in Magda's head. Only after Magda said, "Yes" did she contemplate the possibility of never seeing her parents again. But she knew she and Conrad were going to take part in something very historic for the Polish people and their faith.

She recalled the Bishop, saying, "Someday with the help of God, a Bishop will wear the ring I hold here in the palm of my hand." And then he spoke of the legend connected to this special relic, St. Stanislaw's Bishop's Ring. Their conversation she remembered huddled on what the Communists knew of the Bishop's Ring's existence and how they would use it if they had it in their possession. They knew what significance it played in the faith of the people of Poland.

Magda was reminded of the Cracow Bishop's comments on that special day. "Father Grigor's been entrusted by the Royal Miners with the safe keeping of this holy ring. He holds a high position of trust in our hearts here in Poland. We are indebted to him for his courage. For now the title and documentation for this ring is given to Conrad and Magda. But your title and protection of the ring is only temporary until the one priest for whom it has been destined has it placed on his hand. You will know when that time comes. We have been told the Secret Police are inquiring among the miners in Wieliczka to see if they know of its whereabouts.

"For that reason, we the Church, are sending the Kaminski family to West Berlin on our Church's business. Father Androwitz

will be traveling with you t[...]
Magda, he said, "You will go w[...]
they will return home without you. I[...]
new travel documents, money and airlin[...] *BISHOP'S RING*
where you will be received by Father Andi[...]
Gabriel Takentur. Father Androwitz will rem[...]nrad and
are safely employed in a Polish Community." [...]a, but

She remembered her youthful response. It seeme[...]n
from so long ago. She shrieked in happiness. It had bee[...]
she told Conrad, to smell perfumes women wore in Berlin
at the clothes, and buy some scented soap. She understood the[...]
being offered to leave Poland for a specific purpose to transport[...]
Bishop's Ring out of Poland, to be kept in a safer place, in America.
Then they would return to Poland. Now the ring was in the coat
pocket of Lt. Morrison. Her thoughts drifted again. Was the ring in
a safe place?

She remembered how startled she was when Wladyslaw's said
it would be best if Conrad and Magda also brought Marta along
with them. Would Magda's parents give Marta up to save her from
being a target? Wladyslaw saw a chance for their young to escape
from a Marxist regime, which controlled their lives. Magda knew
then what her father-in-law was thinking. He wanted them to be
free from Communism, to be free from the harassment Conrad
was getting from the Police, which they suspected had been started
because of the attempted rape upon Magda by the soldier. Later,
when Magda's parents were willing to let Marta go to be together
with her sister to find a new life free from any more harassment
from the Secret Police, Magda understood the meaning of love and
sacrifice. Conrad's father Wladyslaw never spoke to Magda about
the hopes his cousin Father Grigor had to bring the ring where it
could be held in America until the day Poland was freed from its
current slavery under Soviet Domination.

The Bishop of Cracow's interest to send the young Kaminski
couple and Marta to America was a risk, but it provided Church
leaders with a chance to deny the Polish Communists authorities of
finding the ancient Bishop's Ring. They would be the least suspected
of carriers. Magda reacted excitedly to the offer. She remembered her

of the plan to escape
d their daughter's lives
y believed in the power of

parent's sadness and jo...shop's concern for transporting
from Communist P...or and received a long necklace,
Magda's parents ...nally wear around his neck with a
miracles and...ed the clasp on the necklace removed
Mag...ing on the necklace. Modestly, she turned
...ing inside of her blouse and under her bosom
the ri...visible was the necklace at the top of her neck
w...vered the rest of the ring. She then turned around,
...arms as if to demonstrate she was a magician. The
...shop nodded to her ingenuity and looked at Wladyslaw,
We know the ring will be well protected with Magda." She
remembered she gave no thought to her actions she just became a
willing subject. And it was good that she accepted the challenge.

Now, it seemed long ago they left behind, family, friends, small possessions and their homeland to smuggle this ring out of Poland. She knew that when she had to expose the contents of her suitcases to Poland's border inspectors they would not ask her or Marta to undress, at least not in front of Conrad. After they arrived in America, Father Grigor received word Conrad was being sought on a smuggler's charge at a time after they left Poland. One more false charge of a supposed crime was to have been committed, even though Conrad disappeared.

Her thoughts traveled backwards.

Conrad and Magda came to believe their escape from a life of terror at the hands of the Secret Police was due primarily to the protection afforded as the custodians of the Bishop's Ring. Their secret task seemed to cast a mystical spell allowing them to leave Poland and come to America. She wondered, "Who would be destined to wear this ring?"

Father Grigor once mentioned the same priest named Jerzy, who had Cardinal Wyszynski's attention, and who was now laboring in a "Medical Group" helping the sick. Conrad took it Father Grigor meant Father Jerzy Popieluszko, a priest who electrified twenty

28

thousand of the faithful at his outdoor Sunday Masses in Warsaw. The young couple was kept informed on this rising cleric who defied the Communists. The praise Father Jerzy received had the Kaminski's believing the Bishop's Ring would be returning to Poland in the not too distant future. Poland's Primate Cardinal appointed Father Jerzy to organize a voluntary medical help group in conjunction with Pope John Paul II's visit to Poland in 1979. They held out hope then Father Jerzy would be elevated to become a Bishop.

In 1982, Father Jerzy preaching, led the entire Catholic population of Poland, in a vow, to protect and defend every life, every unborn baby, and to view life as a gift as the greatest treasure given to mankind. Doctors were reminded of their Hippocratic oath. The priest preached abortion as a violation of the commandment given by God, "Thou shall not kill." And strongly suggested that any human law that violated God's Law was unlawful since the power of the state to make human law is derived from the powers given to it by God. His defense of this principal was aimed at Polish medical people in particular. His preaching, she remembered from letters, put conscience and government regulation on a collision course toward conflict. Was this the priest who someday would wear the Bishop's Ring? He had courage and the convictions. He stood for God!

After Father Grigor Androwitz' death and having lived in America for a number of years waiting for the day when the Ring was no longer in their safekeeping Conrad remarked, "The Communists could die or go out of business, but the Anti-Christ Litigator's Union here in America would still be working to destroy Catholic teachings in America and destroy the Church. Father Grigor used to say. 'Their efforts run deeper than Communism. We have people in America, who would sleep with the devil to destroy the Catholic Church! What the Church stands for they fight against and that includes all Christians. They have a huge capacity to hate behind their smiling eyes and fallacious rhetoric. They know what they are doing. It's a demonic obsession.'" It was a statement that Magda repeated often in her mind because she knew the depths of hate of people who follow Marxist-Leninist principles.

She now had to wonder about the future. The Polish Secret Police murdered Father Jerzy along a roadside near Bydgoszcz in 1984 and dumped his body into a reservoir. He was Conrad's and her hope to wear the Bishop's Ring. Satan foiled their hopes.

Someday, Conrad once told Magda, the Church will recognize Father Jerzy as a martyred crowned saint in Heaven. But it was no consolation to her now to even care. Was there more to Conrad's death she would soon learn? Was it about the Bishop's Ring?

Since the death of Father Grigor, and their location having been traced to the Buffalo area, Gabriel Takentur, their friend and co-sponsor recommended they move to the greater New York City area where the sheer mass of people would make it difficult for their pursuers to find them if they were still interested after all these years. Oliver Takentur, Gabriel's father, as a journalist knew the meaning of being pursued and threatened by the Soviets in the days of Lenin. They took Gabriel's advice and help and Long Island became their home.

What was life to offer Magda now in Conrad's death? Would she be safe in Long Island? Would she be the Bishop's Ring's last hope of its destiny to be worn on the hand of a Polish Bishop?

Chapter 4

Magda finally called her sister to tell her of Conrad's death and to ask her if she would take the children for the night. Marta, shaken, agreed and Morrison provided a police car and ride for the children. Morrison invited Magda Kaminski to the hospital cafeteria for a cup of coffee. The children went to their Aunt Marta's Queen's apartment off Northern Boulevard, while Magda promised she would come by later to be with them. She wanted Thaddeus 20, and Katherina 18, out of the hospital and with her sister. She sat at a table in the lounge. Morrison came by with two cups of coffee, two creamers and two small sugar sacks. Without speaking he motioned to the creamer and she nodded. He poured the cream into her cup of coffee. He could see she was distraught but he needed to ask questions. She needed to be evasive. She now surmised Conrad's death was no accident. She knew their haunted past.

Morrison stated, "You said the ring belonged to a Bishop and your husband was delivering it?"

Magda responded, "No. I think I said Conrad was sent by his boss to show the ring to a priest. He didn't like to do it. It is private property. But his boss knew he had it and wanted to impress a priest. I know Conrad did not want to do it, but his boss insisted. This coercion would never be done in Poland."

Morrison picked up on her remark. "Oh, what is that?"

"Tell an employee to show off his personal property to a stranger."

He continued. "You consider this ring, which you call, a Bishop's Ring, to be personal property?"

"Yes, it is an inheritance from his priest cousin who died about fifteen years ago. We have it in our family for that long."

"I don't understand how his boss could order him to show it to a priest. What's the priest's name?"

Magda shook her head from side to side. She told Morrison that she did not know the name of the priest but maybe she had his name at home among Conrad's papers in his desk. Before she volunteered any information like that she remembered how Conrad had always warned her someone from the Poland's Secret Police might have found out where they settled in this country. So she didn't know if a murderer was posing as someone who was a policeman or a priest.

Morrison could see this was not the time for deep questioning. He kept his suspicions about Conrad's death to himself. So far, it seemed to him Mrs. Kaminski was not hiding anything. If anything, he was enamored by her good looks. He could have wished he didn't meet her like this, but only when she felt it was time to talk to another man. He wanted her to know he was willing to listen to anything just to get her mind off what had happened to her husband.

Morrison questioned, "Tell me something about Poland. How long have you been here? And do you miss your homeland?" He wanted to free her mind from the fear of upcoming questions. Sometimes, unguarded, a person would give him a clue or a memory which could ultimately solve a case.

She pushed her hands through her long blonde hair and pushed her head back and took a deep breath. He could imagine she was about five feet eight or nine, due mostly to her long, shapely legs. She took a deep breath and exhaled, dropping her mouth slightly as if to begin to say something in responses to his question. She turned her head and looked directly into his eyes, with a look that said she wondered if that was the real reason for the question. He waited. She dropped her head and looked out of the window to the street.

"What can one say about one's homeland? It is a place one loves, because one loves her people. We came here when I was a young bride before we had children. We didn't have children right away. My husband could only get work in a steel mill in Buffalo even though he was a draftsman. Draftsman did not get paid as much as working in the steel mill. He worked with many Polish speaking people." She did not want to tell Morrison Conrad's cousin had suggested they settle in Buffalo because of its large Polish community. In Buffalo, Father Grigor had priest friends who would protect their identity if the tentacles of the Polish Secret Police came looking for them.

Magda continued. "We were friends with a high ranking Bishop in Poland. He wanted us to have the protection of the Polish Community in Buffalo." She stopped. Her body quivered in shock. "Poland is a country that is tortured by rivalries. Napoleon used it as a doormat to go into Russia. The same with the Germans! Bismarck used it. We got back what he took from us at the Treaty of Versailles. Then Hitler came and Russia had invaded us, many times. Before Communism, Russia tried to impose their Eastern Orthodox Christianity upon us. We did not want it. Hitler tried to destroy us as a race of people just to steal our land and rebuild it as part of his Third Reich. I was alive when the war ended, and I know about the spiritual scars left upon us as a people. When I lived there I heard many stories about these tortured rivalries in Poland but people here in America will not be told because the Poles have no power. Only people with money and power get to tell their side of the story to gain sympathy. It is not always the truth, but they get to tell it anyway."

"What do you mean?" Morrison asked.

"Many innocent suffer with the few that are guilty. For the few are guilty of money crimes! Swindlers, you know! Everyone suffers, and the guilt of the few swindlers is lost among the many who suffer."

Morrison stopped Magda. "You seem to be talking in circles. I don't understand what you are trying to say."

"When Hitler came to wipe out Poland, there were many Jews in Poland. They had been there for hundreds of years. Jews were his targets. Polish kings invited Jews hundreds of years ago to live there when no one in Europe wanted them. They were about ten percent of our country. They chose to live separate, in ghettos, like in Cracow's Kazimerz district. This was not unusual for them because they didn't share our faith. They owned businesses in the 1930's during the Great Depression. When some people lost their farms and property to them in the Depression of the 1930's many people believed they conspired to control the money of the country. Poles suffered at the hands of the wealthy. But here, you do not hear the full truth. Just as many Poles died in Hitler's work camps, as did Jews who died. It was horrible for both groups of people."

Morrison responded. "The large wealth of any country is always spread among the few wealthy enough to hire others to work. It stands to reason. Because of it, there is going to be jealousy and resentment."

"True! I agree. My parents knew families who lost their farms to those bankers who carried their mortgages. It's this way Lieutenant in every country the wealthy are always going to be the few. Not all Jews were resented. They also like us had their poor. But before Hitler there was resentment in Poland. Those who survived the war will tell you Poles became the workhorses for Poland's wealthy class in our own country." She turned back to look into Morrison's face to see his expression before she would say anymore.

"You have to understand, for nearly a thousand years as Catholic people we fought religious wars with Turks, Eastern Orthodox, German and Nordic Lutherans, what have you! There are Catholic Churches all over Poland yet again there are wealthy people who ignore and deny our religion when we are the majority. It's happening here now in America. The Bishop's Ring is more than just a ring. It's a symbol of our Polish faith and freedom. It stands for denying Communists from taking God out of Poland and out of people's lives. People are being denied work in Poland because they practice their Catholic faith. Now a small group of people hold Poland hostage to Marxist atheism. Conrad taught me how the Marxists operate in our American society. The Marxists fight their battles on the inside of a nation by taking control of the offices of the government with elections of office holders sympathetic to Marxist goals and themes. They use our U.S. Constitution against the majority to weaken the government. America is not the same America when we arrived here. It too, is losing ground to the Marxists among us."

Morrison listened quietly, allowing her to vent her emotions.

"I am a seamstress at home. I have a small sewing business that keeps me busy sewing dresses for women for weddings, bar mitzvahs, and party celebrations. Word of mouth you know. Jewish Ladies talk when they hear I am from Poland. They brag. They will tell you in honesty the mad man Hitler knew where he could find money by killing the Jews. In Germany and Poland! Europeans know atheist Jews followed Karl Marx and invented Communism. Are the holocaust and Communism related? Does God punish evil with evil? You hear only about their Holocaust! But not the Poles holocaust! The innocent, God-fearing Jew will find God's justice because God is merciful. But I don't pity the atheists who died. God ha___e for them. My husband is dead. I believe a Comm_____ and killed him. When Conrad's killer dies will_____ Or will he repent? Will I be able to forgive tho_____rad's death? I must in order to gain heaven. To_____his killers! Forgiveness brings about peace.

C_____

_____subject. "German Jews who lost their _____und out living here, received big awards _____a patron who brags how her father _____ntant in the Fisk Building on West 57th

_____reparations. Poland got atheistic

_____u blame all Jews for Poland's

_____y. Karl Marx declared himself an _____just as Hitler did. The Communists _____lions of Christian people in Russia _____War II. For Marx's disciples, I can _____uld not have been invaded if Jewish-_____e over Germany at the end of World _____and Munich. After WWII, religious _____side us. As a Catholic I believe those deaths were for redemptions of sins caused by Communist persecutions. God will take the just to heaven."

Morrison stopped her. "I can see you read "The Rise and Fall of the Third Reich!"

"And you too, Lieutenant? My family lived through the war. But here I get a chance to read what others have to say." She stopped to gather more thoughts. "For me, the second world war started fifty years ago. The war has been over since 1945. The American military helps to save the world from the Nazis and the Communists. I am tired of hearing about the Jewish Holocaust. The Jewish holocaust is all over the media. When will the public be told just as many Poles died in Hitler's rampage?" It was a sad question.

"The legacy of that war is that we Poles for all these years still struggle with Marxist murderers left over from World War II, struggling to take back our country. I am telling you about my homeland. This Bishop's Ring is just one of many symbols we hold dear and trust God will end this seventy-year reign of Soviet terror in the world. Did Conrad's killer want the Bishop's Ring?" She stopped to fight back tears welling in her eyes.

"It is well known and documented in the history books that Polish Generals and their armies fought and died for the independence of this nation against a king who believed the early settlers were his subjects and owed him fear and favors like taxes. Poland today has a brutal king called "Communism" who wants us to fear him and give him slavish loyalty.

"If there is anything we Poles are known for besides kielbasa, it is our Catholic faith! It is woven into our culture to defend it, perhaps more here in America now, than in Poland because people have been brought up in Poland without God, thanks to those who gave us Communism. The Marxist ideology is hidden here but is very much a part of social engineering taking place from lobbying groups who have adopted Lenin's decrees for changes to destroy the influence of religion on society. No more Christmas crèches in the town square! We know what I mean. Right?"

Morrison was listening, taking a measure of this widow, still strong and committed, believing in the charted destiny for the Bishop's Ring. She recognized his distant stare as if he was being more curious.

"It's what the suburbs give you away from the city. When I have time to read or think as I sew dresses and gowns I think about what could have been without greed and war. Conrad, in these last few years, always made a living that allowed me to stay at home. I watch TV. You can't get real truth coming from any of those TV talk shows. They are open confessionals without a priest giving absolution from their sins." He smiled at her observation.

He said. "I used to tape those shows, I understand what's going on. I know what you mean. We don't see a well informed, practicing Catholic as a talk show host. TV usually hires nominal Catholics whose views follow secular, elitist viewpoints in an effort to change people to embarrass or shame the Church. It's their war to put religion in the margin to keep it less important in life."

She responded. "Sin and God, are never really discussed. Conrad calls it a `subterfuge'. Most Catholics are not liberal as Donohue."

They talked. She reminisced. The conversation was, at best, an easier way to spend time, and not think about what the doctors were going to find in the autopsy.

"Are you going to be okay Mrs. Kaminski? I do not wish to pry into your personal affairs but will you have a way of making money after this is over?"

"Yes. I sew at home." That's all she would say.

The Bishop's Ring was on her mind. When could she get it back? And now, what was she going to do with it? She had to talk to keep from crying. He knew that much. It was a way of venting emotions, caught up in the horror of the tragedy. He had seen it so often before.

Her eyes glazed when she said, "You know it was Christ's own countryman who plotted to have him murdered. In Poland it has been that way every since the Communists took over."

"Mrs. Kaminski, I hate to have to admit this but I mean, I look at you and I know why we are here, and I see a beautiful woman. Excuse me for saying that, but,..."

"You asked me to talk to you about Poland. But I can thank you for the compliment. Conrad always complimented me. He used to say my looks could get me into trouble, to watch out."

Morrison did not know how to take that last remark. There was yet another side to this woman. She had a human weakness. She knew she was the object of male attention. It showed she enjoyed being a very attractive woman. Morrison thought she was like a doe in the woods, leaving a scent.

This dichotomy of her personality bothered Morrison. It could be the wrong signal and invite others to think she offered more than her good looks. To himself, he thought of her as a "man magnet."

Magda continued. "When we moved into Syosset, on Long Island, my husband applied for a drafting job in fashionable Forest Hills. The long train rides became his new life. I was left alone at home with time to spare so I took up sewing wedding party dresses, and reading books. Outside of housework, sewing has been my life on Long Island." She sat in the hospital lounge, more composed, and talking.

"When can I have my ring back, Lieutenant?"

"Well, Mrs. Kaminski, it's like this. Because we think your husband was murdered, we could hold it for evidence in a murder. You see it could be someone wanted that ring, more than your husband knew. I don't know, I'm just speculating. My bosses on the other hand, may take a dim view of me turning it over to you until we know more about this. If your husband died of natural causes then I see no problem with turning this property over to you after you provide us a proof of ownership."

The proof of ownership! She thought, if I take it out, then when they read that it was part of Father Grigor's will, they will find out what it really is and then an investigation will really begin. It might be claimed, if the word was out, the ring was brought into this country illegally and belonged as all property is claimed to belong to the State in Communist Poland.

She leaned forward and looked up into Morrison's face and with a smile asked, "And what if I can't provide proof, will I still be able to have my ring back, Lieutenant?"

He looked at the heavy gold chain, which hung around her neck and continued down into the cleavage of her bosom.

"That's a beautiful chain you have on." He said.

"When I get the ring back, I will hide the ring…"

Just then, the Medical Examiner, walked into the cafeteria. He recognized Morrison. "This is not a compound we're are use to seeing around here. You can go to work now, and find our killer."

Morrison was given the manila folder. He had the copies. From the photos, anyone could have been the murderer. Including Mrs. Kaminski.

"From this point on Mrs. Kaminski, it is my duty to inform you your husband, in the opinion of the Medical Examiner, has been murdered. The ring cannot be returned to you at this time."

Now her worst fears were coming true. She believed they had been found, and the Polish Secret Police were closing in on them.

She made her point. Fellow former countrymen!

She also wanted to know if Quentin LaFayette had anything to do with Conrad's death.

"Lieutenant. I am going to need some help and maybe protection." Danger awaited Magda. Morrison knew it. He reached into his coat pocket and fumbled the covered ring in the plastic lock bag around in his hand.

Chapter 5

Elsewhere earlier prior events unknown to Magda had already taken place in Upstate New York, which had much to do in bringing about the consequence of her present grief. She had no ideas to share with Lt. Morrison in unfolding the causes of her husband's death. The events began like this..

The women, who came to work at the diocesan Chancery office, knew when they went to work there it was not going to be like any other place they had worked before. Betty Ryan left her former employer because she didn't like her fanny pinched and did not expect anyone in this "company" to do such a thing to her. If they did, she would report such things to her uncle, the Monsignor.

Betty Ryan had black hair and a wide Irish smile. But the back room was ambush territory. When she came to the chancery she knew the money was not going to be the same, but at least she would have her sanity. Besides, priests were above that kind of language and behavior. She didn't know what to expect, but her uncle had always been a straight shooter when he showed up at her house. She heard him use non-clerical language at times in a card game of pitch, which no one would have expected coming out of his mouth. But then she excused it by saying he had his collar off.

Her rescue from the cashier's position at the A & P Store was none too soon. While she worked there, to take a break from her busy cash register duties she had to pass through swinging doors to get to the lunchroom. In the backroom she would be teased about her love life by one of the married male stock clerks. Eddie "the Rabbit" Reynolds worked in the produce department in the back room. When she walked by his work area, he would suddenly lurch at her, grab her, and hold her as if he was slow dancing with her to the 1950 voice of Vaughn Monroe, singing "Racing with the Moon." Eddie would sing in her ear while she would fight him off in a playful way and felt embarrassed if anyone should see them together while he held her in the dance embrace.

The once fast nimble fingers which punched a rack of keys on a chrome covered cash register and eyes that searched for prices on soup cans and cereal boxes, now glided over typewriter keyboards, or placed paper into copy machines, and filled envelopes with the directives which came out of the Chancery to the parishes. Now, through attrition and promotion, she was the Bishop's secretary.

When she turned "fifty" she was still a lady who held up well with age. Secretly, she held out the hope someday she would marry. Each night went home to the empty family home, which she inherited. But for now, she had all she could do to be the "sister" of so many priests who would drop in, give a nod or say hello, and be on their way back to their parish. In her position, she heard the gossip, the jokes, and discussions of men who were moved by concerns of their singular lives. When her uncle, the Monsignor, had passed on to his eternal reward, she lost a friend, one of two confidants with whom she could speak her mind, and gain advice.

Quentin LaFayette walked into the chancery and stopped at the reception desk to ask for a diocesan directory of churches. He had done this before always expecting one would be forthcoming. A printer, who was favored with a steady flow of orders, usually printed the diocesan Church directory of personnel assignments as a courtesy to the Church. To have one was Quentin's first line of attack.

"Yes, I'm new to the area." He said. "I was wondering if you could tell me something about some of the parishes, just in case we wanted to..." He never finished the sentence, hoping that Rosemary, the receptionist, would direct him to his prospect targets by leaving the impression he might be moving into the diocese from out of town. He had not divulged who he was or what he wanted but by having the directory, he would soon find out who served in positions of decision making for his next project.

"Can you help me?" Quentin asked with a look of being totally lost, "I wouldn't know where to begin to find a good parish to..." Just then, Betty came out of the Bishops office and walked across the hall to her own office and caught a glimpse of the stranger at the reception desk. He stood in his London Fog raincoat, holding open the parish directory, which she noticed in his hand. She walked toward him. He recognized her curiosity getting the best of her since she may have overheard him ask for help. Rosemary turned to the telephones to answer the incoming calls and Betty came to this visitor's assistance.

"May I help you?" She said, noticing all at once that he was impeccably dressed down to the crease in his pants and his thin-soled Italian shoes.

"Yes, yes of course." He said, taking a quick full measure of her appearance as she came closer. He made it his point in a non-verbal way to let her know he did see her as a woman, with the eyes of a non-clerical man. "I am new to the area, and I am looking for potential places." He didn't say anymore, but looked at her directly, as if he was charmed by her presence. She inhaled his male cologne and was sure she had never caught that fragrance. He took off his raincoat to give Betty an idea he wanted to stay to talk.

Rosemary took note of his pointed chin and tweed jacket with leather elbows, as well as the salt and pepper colored hair, which seemed to flow like a wave across the sides of his head and fall full to his collar line. His slim chin dropped from his wide cheekbones, accenting his appearance. To herself, Rosemary thought he looked like an artist's rendition of a devil, but then she knew it would not go over too well with her boss if she described him that way. Rash judgments are very sinful! Besides, in her position, meeting so many different kinds of people coming through the door it would be foolish for her to start a name calling game. The Irish and Italians in the building would understand her game but she doubted anyone else would enjoy her ethnic humor attaching nicknames to one's physical appearances. Her attention shifted to Betty who looked at the stranger, Rosemary thought in a totally different way. When he left, she was going to ask Betty what she thought, but by then, others were walking through the front doors, and she had not heard Betty invite the stranger to her office. The quickness of the transition to Betty's office escaped her observation.

"My purpose," he began, "is to get a feel of what is going on in the diocese. That is, you see, I am a designer of churches and renovator of aging church buildings. You are aware of the design latitude given to new church designs since the Second Vatican Council, Ms. Ryan." he said looking at the nameplate sitting on the top and front of her desk. It was a practiced statement he used often when he visited Chancery offices to gain attention of the higher ups. And with that remark, he reached into his side jacket pocket for a business card. He placed it between his index and middle finger and held out for her to take. He knew where he was and with whom he was talking. He did not need to speak with a Bishop just yet, but he did need to know whom the priests were to whom he might offer his services.

"That is out of my field of expertise, Mr. LaFayette," Betty said not wanting to offer information to this stranger in her highly confidential position. She knew he already had the Diocesan Directory, which he walked away from the reception area with in his hands. Just then, Father Lawrence stuck his head into her office, not expecting to see the stranger sitting in the corner, "When is the Bishop going to be free? I have to head out in about a half an hour to talk to Monsignor O'Toole. He called and told me wants to retire. Health has got to him."

She said, "He's been saying that for five years. And of course, you are going to help him do it, so you can put in a bid for his fiefdom."

He said with a smile and wry grin on his face. "Don't you think it is about time, I should be turned out to the pasture, or ahem, the vineyard of the Lord, and be given a pastorate?" It was a look Quentin LaFayette understood. Betty Ryan's uncle used to tell her there would be a big fight to get Monsignor O'Toole's parish. He likened the change to come when the one who ended up with it would probably have to have the speed of a pariah or the patience of a vulture. Father Lawrence was showing his colors, and since he was an insider, he would have the Bishop's ear sooner than anyone else before the word was out.

The memories of dinners with her uncle and Monsignor O'Toole would last long in Betty's life. She had been the companion to both when they took their night off together and they ended up in their favorite restaurants. Now, it was going to be Monsignor O'Toole who was going to put in for a place at the priest retirement home. She could only wonder what Father Lawrence had been saying to him to come to this decision without him first talking it over with her, a long time tested friend. She was after all, like family to him, his last link with his close friend, her uncle. The three of them even vacationed together.

Quentin LaFayette watched the eyes of the two speak an unspoken language and concluded that this priest was someone whom he should get to know and realized that Betty Ryan sat in an inside seat of power. It appeared she had the Bishop's confidence whenever she wished to speak to him.

LaFayette spoke. "I'm going to be in the city for a few days, Ms. Ryan, I was wondering if you would honor me with an opportunity to take you to dinner, either this evening or tomorrow evening?" The sudden bold invitation surprised Betty, who immediately looked at his left hand to see if he was wearing a ring. The impulsive gesture on LaFayette's part was his way of attempting to get closer to his business goals. She was the door through which one had to enter before decisions were made. He, too, noticed the lack of a ring. She could, he thought, be more than a companion for dinner.

How many times had she turned down invitations, she asked herself? In an unguarded moment, when her thoughts of Monsignor O'Toole's retirement was really possible, she said "Yes" to Quentin's invitation for the following night.

When Quentin LaFayette left her office, Betty Ryan quickly called Monsignor O'Toole's rectory. "Monsignor, are you going out tonight for a dinner, or would you like me to drop in and cook a meal?" Betty asked.

"I'd love to go out, but I would rather have a home cooked meal from your hands, my dear, than go to a smoke filled restaurant!"

"Tonight, I'm going to cook Chinese for you. Mostly vegetables. You had cornstarch and soy sauce the last time I looked in your pantry, unless the cook used it up. She'll be surprised tomorrow when she smells the odors left from my concoction tonight."

He responded. "Sounds wonderful."

"Good, I'll see you at six o'clock. I'll stop and pick up a few things." Betty hung up the phone and went back to her paperwork wondering what Father Lawrence was going to say to her long time friend. How many times had her uncle and Monsignor O'Toole talked about the times when they would give up their parishes? She wanted to be there because she knew this was something more than closing a door on one parish and moving to the next. This was his final parish. His days were going to be spent with the older gents, and she had a glimpse of his thoughts on that aspect of his life. Father Lawrence was never told of her family friendship with the Monsignor, which started with her uncle many years before. She kept that part of her life private.

Come to the kitchen Monsignor, while I clean and cut up these vegetables. We can talk."

"Good idea." He responded.

"Father Lawrence came out to see me today. Told me, since I was putting in for retirement he needed to get the paper work ready and to ask some questions." Betty listened as she put the vegetables under running water to clean them in the sink. Monsignor O'Toole took his time expressing himself. "Your uncle, The Lord rest his soul, was quick to speak out about us clergy when things were not one hundred percent. He was very generous to all priests. He was a priest's priest, Betty. I miss his friendship. I'm going to miss it even more when I retire and look at those faces in the retirement home. He was spared that agony."

"What are you talking about, Monsignor? You're going to love it up to St. John Vianney's. You can play cards, watch the tube, play golf when you feel like it." Betty gave an optimistic look into his future. She wanted the evening to be a pleasant. She knew she was speaking to a priest with spiritual depth, who was very much like her uncle and she knew that as long as he lived she wanted to be his friend. In terms of their friendship, they were beyond the stages of discussing how she was going to spend the rest of her life and with whom she was going to spend it.

"Your uncle and I would talk at night over the phone and speak about the crop of priests behind us. I've got to give him credit. He knew quality. He was tough on young priests. One thing the Bishop did not do to him was to send him less than a good speaker. They had to tow the line in his house. Sermons were written by all of his assistants. He was a model for them. He used to say from time to time, it was not the priest's first responsibility to celebrate Mass, but to preach the Word of God. It always inspired me. That's how strongly he felt about the Sunday homily." Betty listened over the noise of running water in the sink. "You can't give what you don't have inside of you," he would say to the younger priests." Betty nodded as if in agreement, having heard the same remark from her uncle. "He was right you know." Monsignor O'Toole continued, "He required his assistants to maintain a spiritual life, so when they stood up in the pulpit on Sunday it wasn't going to be a vegetable patch sermon, a lot of 'Let us' preaching."

"So what did Father Lawrence want from you, so much so he had to rush right out here to pick up so that you couldn't supply me over the phone to give to the Bishop?"

"I think he was on a fishing trip. Really. He didn't seem to be so much interested in me. He wanted to know about finances, the physical condition of the Church. It's not what I had in mind when he asked to come out to talk to me."

"He asked to come out to talk to you?" Betty responded with a question. "I had the feeling from what he said you asked him to come out to see you." Betty added. "Father Lawrence is not scholarly. I'm only saying he thinks he's ready to be turned out to pasture as he put it. I've heard him at the Cathedral for the 12:15 daily Mass. He is more a bureaucrat, for sure. That's not to say he doesn't have the same kind of aggressive tendencies businessmen have. Speaking of one such, I have a date tomorrow night. We're going out to dinner." He failed to comment.

"It's up to the Bishop, not me. You'll know before I do." Betty knew, by her uncle's standards, Father Lawrence needed spiritual depth growth. Her uncle's spiritual depth and her critical Irish wit placed Father Lawrence's sermonizing coming out of the Boy Scout Handbook. She didn't care to bring that fact up and spoil Monsignor O'Toole's dinner.

"The next fellow is going to have some fun around here after he arrives, looking into the writings of Father Dwyer. He left them to me. He was here from 1945 to 1971. He was somewhat of a history hobbyist. Fascinating things he wrote about the Russian Revolution and how the Communists weaved their way into power even in this country. Alger Hiss and Harry Dexter White were no flukes. Father Dwyer believed Communist conspirators were making inroads into the National Democratic Party! They paid back Nixon and McCarthy for bringing it up there were Communists in the Government! Nixon was wise. State and Defense departments were filled with thousands of Soviet spies. But both men were smeared constantly. Nixon paid big proving he did have enemies!"

"My uncle believed the Russian Revolution was created, in part to destroy the Church. With all their contrary denials he would say, 'It's not what they say but what they do. Look at Europe, the results!'"

The Monsignor countered, "Communism is Satan's gospel of lies. His followers hide behind patriotic front organizations to insert their anti-God, secular agenda." She agreed, saying, "And some media help them." He responded, "Lies have been inserted over time into our society for many years by an elitist left minority." In a moment of deeper thought, he came forth with this response.

"Ancient Israel split into two nations, the land of Israel to the north where the tribes fell into idolatry; and the land of Juda to the south, from which the Messiah would be born. America may be splitting into two nations someday. It's going to take a firm resolve of the religious people of this nation to hold off the ACLU with their Nativity lawsuits at Christmas. There will be more challenges coming."

He changed the topic to talk about Father Lawrence.

"Father Lawrence is pretty aggressive." She said.

Monsignor O'Toole put his fork down on his plate, and said, "The whims and fancies of new pastors can be their own undoing. I may have provided him with the answers on how he could take this parish over when I leave."

She offered her comment, "You left him an opening a mile wide. He'll run right into the boss with his new idea to fix up the place. I shouldn't be talking this way about him. But, I hear him talking about new architectural changes in churches allowed by some Bishops."

"Maybe I shouldn't retire!"

Chapter 6

Betty Ryan it seemed settled long ago, to be a rigid-frigid woman. Smoke? Yes. But that was a while back. She gave up smoking one Lent and never returned to the "filthy habit." She liked the added weight she gained after she quit smoking. Now she could claim to have a bust line, and her hips were rounded. She seemed to have become prettier as the years passed. She wondered: Would I be a pretty bride?

When most women her age dread the facial lines, which considerably set off the eyes, Betty's eyes sparkled without such worry. She did admit to herself while putting on her creams at night might have had a good effect of keeping her skin young looking. But she also attributed it to the fact most of the women she saw with lined flaccid faces were smokers. If she ever did allow herself to think of herself as married she would have to keep herself presentable as a lady of rare substance to attract the right kind of gentleman.

As she drove home she wondered why she told Monsignor O'Toole why she was only interested in companionship. She was not over the hill, as her uncle used to kid her about happening to her because she had never married. She just thought she waited too long. But there was more to it she had to admit to herself. It had to do with her money.

Though she never made much money working in the Chancery, she never lacked for things. With what money she was able to save, she found someone who watched the Diocese investments to advise her where to put her money to work in small stock investments.

49

He gave her advice. And she profited to the extent that, at age fifty, she did not have to work any longer and could live off the interest and stock split growth from those investments of thirty years. While she never bragged about how much she had, her Monsignor uncle, told her to be wise about men who come looking for a woman with money. She lived by her rigid rules and frigid attitudes. She reflected Monsignor O'Toole knew she had her own mind when it came to being in charge of herself.

Quentin LaFayette used his "Southern Drawl" when he thought it was to his advantage, although he lost most of it by the time he passed into manhood. He left Louisiana in his teen years when his father set up an office in New York.

In New York he marveled at the tall buildings and decided that someday he would like to become a designer of buildings. It was the kind of youthful thought everyone has when they are growing up and free to daydream about their future. He knew he did not want to sell oil to the spot markets, like his Daddy. The money was great. He lacked for nothing, but he wanted to take a step up the ladder in life.

St. Patrick's Cathedral impressed him. There it stood with so many modern buildings rising around it to dwarf it. Across the street, Rockefeller Center! Somewhere in his cavernous mind he kept thinking not everybody was going to be a specialist in Church design, so he would have little competition if he would follow his instincts and take up building design as a career.

In that way he was like his father. He liked to corner the market, command a price, and be his own boss. He heard his father talk to customers on the phone and watched him operate. Everything was for sale, at any price, at any time, in and out of season. Nothing was sacred. He heard his father brag about this one and that one and who won and who lost on the deals that were made. He saw how the market fluctuated and how his father could be up and then down like a roller coaster. His emotions spread out on the table when he finally arrived home at night. It wasn't going to be a way for him. When people have to come to you and you are one of a few who do your special kind of work, it is they who need your service, he thought.

You can get your price. He carried that thought with him when he left high school. He still held on to that belief.

But Quentin's circumstances were different. His father did not have to deal with unions. Unions control the prices with the kind of wages they demand and ultimately get for their people. Contractors always have the excuse of blaming costs on the unions. Quentin found out "favors," better known as bribes and payoffs, worked well in getting contracts, and in completing jobs on time and under budget. He also knew people who did not play the right game or sing the right tune ended up with trouble.

Quentin knew good times and he knew bad times. He found out clergy enjoy tickets to St. Johns games in the Garden, or watching the Knicks, or seeing the Giants play football. Catholic Clergy may remain unmarried but they usually go to games with friends. He himself was a sports fan. So he would buy the tickets and have one of his staff pick them up and then deliver them in person or send them in the mail to the rectory. That's the way it started.

Now it was beyond that, because as a designer he lacked the credentials of a Licensed Architect. Caught in an awkward position of offering a design service, he had to depend on Architects to sign off whether his designs were correctly conceived, and in order with local government authorities. Architects could take business from him. Quentin was bound to be his own man. He added Construction services to his Design firm, and offered both design and construction in search of new customers. He lined up marble cutters, painters, plasterers, stained glass window artists, stonemasons, steeple climbers, and copper roofers, the kinds of tradesman uniquely qualified for the construction or renovation of a church. The contractors, who paid Quentin a percentage under the table, also padded their work costs in their charges to him. He would then add a charge to the Church for the contractor's service, hidden within his percentage of the general contractor's bill. Neither a trusting priest nor his own contractors knew he profited twice from those who hired him.

It was the semblances of the appearances of the man, which threw people off. Money had paid for his dignified look. But underneath his richly tailored clothes he fought hard to gain business. Quentin could be as persuasive as a slick car salesman when selling his services. Many clergy were taken in by his velvet charm. The list included some church trustees, who looked on their positions as trustees more as something of personal recognition, rather than one of safeguarding church funds. A long time had passed since Quentin had been to confession.

But, in the middle of prosperous times for others, Quentin's well was running dry. He needed business to meet his office payroll of fifteen employees. The staff included a compliment of another senior designer, a junior designer, draftsmen, secretaries and an office manager. He had to take to the road to drum up business. The ongoing projects would soon be finished, and without more projects, what he had managed to build would quickly disintegrate.

Quentin was not one to set aside his money in the company treasury, but removed most of it except what was needed for payroll, taxes, rent and his credit cards.

Betty Ryan gave Quentin directions to her home where she could be picked up at 7:00 P.M. for their dinner date meeting. Quentin traced the path on the city map he had picked up in the hotel lobby newsstand. He assured her he could find her home and would be prompt in picking her up. During the day he mapped out places he would like to go to and make visits. The falling leaves had made the drive around the city easier to spot churches as he drove through neighborhoods with his right hand holding his pocket tape recorder, while speaking into it describing the neighborhood, churches, schools and other signs of connection to life within a parish boundary. That first day, he found several Catholic churches.

At the exact moment when he rang Betty's doorbell, her grandfather clock began to chime seven times. This, she thought was the sign of a man who was not only prompt but out to prove he was someone special. She was ready to leave, but asked him in, feigning she had just a couple of things yet to do.

"Shalimar, isn't it?" He asked as he walked over the threshold and followed her into her living room."

Betty responded, "I like it. But I don't wear it at work."

Quentin countered, "It's a 'man trapping' fragrance. You would drive the priests crazy when you walked into their offices.

Betty mused, "Well, thank you for the compliment. They are used to me. And hardly do such things move them as a woman's perfume. She said smiling, "I get away with a lot around there, but they kid me a lot. I would be sending a message if I wore this fragrance there and I would hear about it every time one came into the office from their parishes. The word would spread around I am man hunting." She paused. Then asked, "Are you married? I don't see a ring on your finger?"

"I'm not married. I'm a widower."

"I'm sorry." She said.

Quentin responded, "I'm not ready to talk about it...yet."

She turned and began walking away. "I have a few things yet to do. Make yourself comfortable. If you want a drink, the cabinet is over there. Help yourself. I'll be right back!"

Quentin was dressed in a dark blue pin striped suit, French cuffed starched shirt and blue and white striped tie. Betty went to her closet and picked out a short pink dinner jacket, cut above the waist, to compliment her dark blue dress, which was pleated below the waist, and flowed as she walked. She felt his eyes following her as she walked to go to her bedroom.

When she came back into the living room, he quickly jumped up from the chair. "Your place is lovely. I can see you have a flair for decorating."

Betty smiled, "Coming from you, that is a compliment. Thank you."

"I asked one of the good Fathers yesterday, where there was a good restaurant to take a lady who wanted to be discreet about her date. One priest told me, the one that turned up the most in the confessional, when he would ask where the sinners first met, the good Father recommended Henri's French Restaurant. We have reservations!"

"Sinners? Are you expected to sin on this date?" She asked with a wry grin. "I often wondered where it all started in this town. Henri's is the place? Hmn! You'll have to tell me what the priest looked like who told you about his research." She nodded her appreciation and turned to look at her house as they departed.

As they sat with the French Menu in hand, Quentin took the initiative. "Do you have a favorite?"

"Actually, as you know, living alone, I don't do much cooking for myself in the exotic categories. Being all-Irish we are not like the French, famous for our cooking. We Irish are from potato country. We make cooked ham, cabbage and potatoes, an Irish delight. Simple food."

Quentin responded, "That being the case, then I know you have eaten from brother pig, who so willingly gave of his life, to make life so rich and promising. I was thinking we could improvise and give us something from both the pig and the chicken, like, coq au vin. That's very French. They use the drippings from the bacon or salt pork to fill into the sauce mixture of burgundy wine, cognac or brandy, which they pour over the chicken."

"Do you like to cook?" She asked.

"We are French, originally. I really never knew what other food tasted like until I was out on my own. But every chance I get to come to a French restaurant when I'm out of town, I look forward to the experience. I feel very fortunate to have as my guest a pretty dinner companion. Thank you for accepting my invitation."

Betty smiled and thanked him for inviting her. She was watching him and listening to his remarks. She was trying to pick up something about him, which attracted her to say yes to his invitation. There had to be more to this man than just a chance opportunity to take her to dinner. She remembered how much he wanted the Diocesan directory of parishes and priests. She also knew she could spoil her evening if she looked for a clue for any purpose he might have more than a dinner companion. As a widower he could be lonely and she experienced that feeling herself perhaps more than he ever did. If he did have more on his mind, it would soon be evident.

She liked what she saw, and could easily find him to be the kind of man, that she could finally fall in love with. He had charm, elegance, wit and an appreciation of the finer things in life. He was not just an observer in life but a man who made things happen. He was the hunter and she the hunted. It was not too late for the mating

54

ritual to begin for her or for him. She told herself she was ready to really look at herself ready to be changed. This man was 180 degrees from being an "Eddie, the Rabbit," the supermarket lothario.

Betty was tired of being cautious about men. She did not like the idea others might think she was in the closet as a lesbian since there was no man in her life. It had been that the only man whom she liked was the kind she was more certain would never want to touch her.

When the evening came to an end Betty was ready for human warmth and romance. Up to that point she thought Quentin had been moving in that direction as he walked up the stairs and to the front door of her house. She was ready to invite him in for a nightcap. Instead, he took her hand into both of his and bent over and kissed it, as if he meant it, and looked into her eyes and thanked her for a lovely evening.

He saw the expression in her face. It was filled with signs she really enjoyed being with him and the evening. He knew she would go out again with him if he asked her. So he did. And yes, she accepted.

"I'll be back in a few days. I'll call you again."

When Quentin turned and went toward his car, she was suddenly the same old Betty again. She wondered how much of what she said that night would come back upon her, and whether the information was helpful to him or was just job talk. She was just going to have to wait for future developments.

Chapter 7

The parishioners knew they had someone special in Monsignor O'Toole. His sermons were so well prepared, filled with Church teaching covering matters of faith, morals and scripture. They had countless examples from human history that were skillfully dispersed to make his points, within the content of his subject in the sermon. He was such an overpowering speaker people knew, in order to speak this way, he had to have a deep spiritual illumination filling his soul. Such ability to talk about the Lord and his teachings came from his commitment to Christ and prayer in his life. Among priests Monsignor O'Toole was the priest's choice for spiritual advisor and confidant of so many priests. It was a source of pride to his parishioners that he was their holy priest.

His fiscal ability to live within the parish means and still save money was a source of happiness. He did not have to resort to begging, extra collections or bingo games, which he considered to be a failure in his ministry if he had to do anything other than to teach and preach the word of God. He practiced Faith, Hope and Charity not gimmickry. These theological piety virtues would help his people into heaven.

Monsignor O'Toole received a call from Betty that night. She informed him that a letter was sent out from the Chancery to him, accepting his resignation as pastor and retirement. She knew it was going to be a shock to him when he received it. And she wanted to be sure the blow was gentle when he eventually received it.

He asked Betty, "The Bishop didn't even call me to discuss any of this with me. What's going on down there? Don't they have feelings for people who worked for them? Am I wrong to expect a call from the Bishop would have been in order?"

"No you are not Monsignor. I thought he would get to it. He dictated the letter. Then Father Lawrence went into his office and closed the door. They talked for more than an hour. It may have slipped his mind. So much going on! When he comes in the morning I'll ask him if he spoke with you, sort of a reminder to give you a call."

The Monsignor asked, "Was Lawrence called in or did he invite himself into the Bishop's office?"

Betty responded, "He invited himself in. He wasn't scheduled."

"Betty, is there something you should be telling me as a friend? I mean, I didn't expect this so soon. The parish will be shocked at the quick turn around. We should have a month or more to prepare people for the change of command here. I would like to have discussed what I think the parish needs in the form of a pastor. These people have been my flock for so many years. I do have some insights in that matter, do you understand my position?"

Betty answered, "I don't think it was going to matter Monsignor. All you had to say was the word 'retirement', and Father Lawrence was ready. He loves to spend other people's money. I've noticed it around here."

The Monsignor continued. "I'm hearing you. Our Dwyer Trust fund is set aside dedicated for the education of Children. From what you said earlier about his architectural interests of course. I gather our trustees are going to be put on the Chinese waterwheel. Any new man is going to want to set his own style."

Betty answered. "Yes Monsignor. But your parish is one of the few that has an excess."

"I never had to beg, nor shame people into giving. What they gave was enough to give us the surplus." He sighed and said, "I guess I'll have to get Arthur and a few others to help me clear up and out of here."

"If you want to you could come over here." She said. "There's plenty of room. That is if you won't find enough space for your stuff up at St. John Vianney's."

"There won't be enough space for my stuff, that's for sure. Maybe I will take you up on your offer to store things until I can sort them out and give them away. It would be nice to have a place to go to when I don't want to sit around becoming bored. I appreciate your offer for the use of some space." For a moment he seemed tired. Betty awoke him.

"It's the new Betty. Betty that has love on her mind, I think about catching a man even at this stage of my life before I dry up and become a prune."

He frowned and said, "You got it that bad, huh?"

"Monsignor," she hesitated, "my friend, you are not going to be around forever. I'm not a 'man hater.' Never was. I'm not a lesbian. Never was. Marriage was always on the back burner. But now I am ready for a man."

"What ever happened to your date? You have kept me in the dark about him."

"So far nothing's happened that is a matter for the confessional. But we are seeing each other when he comes to town. He's made a few visits to Father Lawrence I have noticed but he did not discuss anything with me. I am left to assume, he's looking for parishes in need of his services. Father Lawrence would know about that stuff. I think he has been scouting for a parish for a long time."

He said, "I will have enough time to collect my things and put them into boxes. Later and then I will have the time to sort them."

Betty asked, "And what are you going to do afterwards?"

"Well, I'm still a priest. I never really thought of myself as being retired, except I did think I would like to become a roving priest, helping out in parishes. My voice is still okay. I can boom when I want. People still tell me they love my sermons, so I guess I'm okay, in that department too."

"You know, Monsignor, it would be great if you could go around the diocese and give talks and sermons to the parishes on the need for vocations. Since vocations have slowed down you might be able to pick up some interest."

"When I was a boy, the priests were out there talking to us like missionaries. I'll never regret being a priest. But I guess I told you before, maybe, sometime. Maybe your idea will work. If the Bishop does call me, I'll bounce it off his noggin to see if he goes for the idea."

Betty said, "I'll remind him to call you in the morning."

The parish retirement party came and went so quickly! The gift of a new car had been quietly engineered among the men of the parish who had been Monsignor's eyes and ears in times of trouble. When it ended Monsignor O'Toole did not leave without tears in his eyes and a soft spot in his heart for the more than five hundred people who came by to wish him well in the parish hall. He had time to enjoy it now.

Father Lawrence waited a few weeks then blamed weather for low attendance after his announced plans to make some physical changes now in the parish plant. Change came later in the church building, in order to conform to the ideals set out in Vatican II for church structures. Faces in the pews turned to stone.

People were anxiously waiting to hear a sermon, a homily, a teaching about the Ten Commandments and living a virtuous life. They waited. The Monsignor taught them what faith offered in a world beset by turmoil and fear. Soon the church seemed to have less parishioners attending Sunday Mass. The pews that once were filled to capacity now had wide spaces between people. It was a bad beginning.

The new pastor erroneously thought in the beginning that people had come out to see the new pastor. Now that he had been there awhile, it appeared to him, they slipped into their old habit of not showing up on Sundays. The parish was losing attendance.

As people became more discouraged, parishioners made calls to St. John Vianney's Retirement Home of the Diocesan Priests, for Monsignor O'Toole. Men in their fifties who made their First Holy Communion in that Church were now leaving it for reasons they could not speak about without bringing forth anger and disgust at what the recently retired Bishop had done in appointing this priest to the pastorate.

Father Lawrence was Pre-Vatican II when it came to his unwillingness to share authority with the Parish Council. He lacked the kind of experience that came with years of sharing heartache and triumph while working with people of a parish. Almost from the beginning of his priesthood he was brought into the bureaucracy of the diocese and given desk jobs. He had never had any real full responsibility of being at the rectory at night to welcome parishioners in for a discussion of concerns, which affected them. His day ended at the diocese at 5:00 P.M. and he went home to a residence built for diocesan priests not assigned to parishes. His days were filled with people coming in off the streets with proposals, entertaining him with their dog and pony shows, smoke and mirror acts, that all were designed to make symbolic changes. But had little to do with the substance of faith, which the Church had maintained through the centuries, and used as doctrines of teaching.

Father Lawrence sold himself to the soon to be retired Bishop, as an agent of change in a parish he said needed extensive physical changes to the church plant. The Bishop, wishing neither to confront the aging Monsignor about stewardship, nor decline to offer Father Lawrence a worthy assignment, was easily swayed out of loyalty to Father Lawrence to give St. Catherine of Siena parish as his first pastorate.

The people of St. Catherine parish knew they had a surplus in their treasury. It was not long when they began to see physical changes taking place on the property and in the church in the form of landscaping. Paid staff replaced volunteers. People who knew the success of the volunteer efforts were appalled at the unprofessional appearance of paid services formerly run by male volunteers. Worship services were changed in the way Masses were celebrated. It all appeared to take the mind of the parishioner away from the substance of the faith in favor of the new symbolism of liturgical thought. The Gospel of repentance was dead.

People excused it at first as part of the ritual of getting one's feet wet. But all of the changes taking place cost money. Parishioners became confused and some angry because money was being spent for useless and trivial efforts that were designed to give the appearance of a lot of activity while the church continued to turn off many of its supporters. The activities, which had been the backbone of the parish, such as children religious training, including the Upper Grades suffered. By the time people began to realize what was happening to the parish in losing its parishioners, the Bishop, who made the choice to replace Monsignor O'Toole, was in retirement himself.

Who was there left to complain to?

Monsignor O'Toole kept his mouth shut. He was wise enough to know how the Holy Scripture values time. Scriptures remind when it was time to be born and when it was time to die.

Quentin LaFayette made his call to Father Lawrence. He had been around clergy long enough to know feelings get bruised when priests do not get appointed to parishes they feel they deserve when vacancies occur. In making his calls upon pastors, he found out by listening to what others may have surmised took place in Father Lawrence's appointment. It was music to his ears when he listened. Other priests thought Auxiliary Bishop Sullivan, even with health issues, should have been given Monsignor O'Toole's parish. Quentin saw the appointment of Father Lawrence not so much as loyalty to the Bishop, but for his ability to seize the moment.

Later, when Rome did not follow through with the appointment of Auxiliary Bishop Sullivan to the position of the Local Ordinary Bishop being vacated due to his retirement, the Vatican selected another Auxiliary, Bishop O'Farrell from Scranton, to step into the slot of the Ordinary Bishop. When that happened, Bishop Sullivan, the Auxiliary Bishop, told his new superior, Bishop O'Farrell, he thought, due to his health, he would stay on until a suitable replacement could be found.

There was no way, Monsignor O'Toole thought, that Father Lawrence could be so clairvoyant as to see these changes coming before he was appointed the new pastor.

Quentin wanted to interpret these changes could improve his own wealth if Father Lawrence was seen as someone who could move up as a future Bishop. The feeling among the local clergy was such that the new Auxiliary Bishop would be of a more conservative heart, and more aligned with the Pope's thinking. They also saw Bishop O'Farrell in this light.

It was money in Quentin's pocket to know as much as he could about the internal politics of the dioceses he called upon to sell his services. Father Lawrence's position was abundantly clear to Quentin. He proved to Quentin he "competed" for recognition. A priest who loved to show off his Church meant money in the bank for Quentin.

He selected innocent Father Lawrence to play his game.

As a matter of course, it has always been the policies of all faiths, to keep their keep their churches, temples, synagogues, shrines, mosques in the best possible repair. Their buildings were valuable resources to the faith people. But Quentin knew unless he created the desire for change in the physical plants with a highly developed sales show his chances for becoming involved would be limited. He had to overcome the thinking that local talent and skills could do as good or a better job. He had to depend upon finding priests, trustees and others who accepted his subtle subliminal suggestion game to gain contracts.

Not all parishes in the diocese lent themselves to appear to be showcase church properties. In the poorer sections of the diocese the physical deterioration of the churches could be clearly seen. Northeast winters created water damage to roofs and ceilings of churches. Exteriors in some cases needed cleansing from accumulated soot and wind driven dirt. Pointing and repairing steeples usually made the newspaper photos. Quentin always made certain of that because it fed his hunger for recognition. The publicity helped since his name would be published as the designer in charge of changes being made to church structures.

Now that Father Lawrence had the prized parish, Quentin was ready for making a statement about change and his abilities to do dramatic things. An eager Father Lawrence was ready to talk to Quentin LaFayette.

Chapter 8

It took a while before Monsignor O'Toole made the connection that Quentin LaFayette and Betty were seriously dating when the designer came into town. He was also well aware Quentin had formed a friendship with Father Lawrence and wondered why Betty had not told him about the news. He had to hear it from a parishioner. She had plenty of chances to tell him. He came over to her house often to sort out his books and enjoy the quiet of her home while she was at work.

For the first time in recent memory, he was in a place where the phone did not ring often during the day and where he could take a snooze, read a book, watch television or make himself a lunch. Betty allowed him to use her home as he wished. The neighbors knew his car and the arrangements because Betty made sure they knew so as not to draw wrong conclusions. He was usually gone when she came home so she would not feel obligated to cook for him unless she had invited him to stay for supper.

Monsignor O'Toole knew something was taking place. Betty seemed more detached and pre-occupied. He knew she was going out to dinner when LaFayette came to town but she kept this part of her life quiet; at least for now. He also heard from time to time LaFayette had been at St. Catherine's Rectory because the parish busybodies always seemed to know what was going on. But Betty kept silent. He surmised something was being planned for St. Catherine of Siena parish. Betty was not telling him anything. And he understood if she had to tell him a story about St. Catherine's it might upset him emotionally, so for that reason she avoided the subject.

Monsignor O'Toole was in a quandary how to figure out where Father Lawrence fit into this picture of new construction work. The parish plant was not in any physical decay when he left as pastor of St. Catherine's Church. Was the Parish Council being left out of the loop, as well as the parishioners? Gothic Churches such as St. Catherine's represented history and beauty and a devoted purpose of the craftsmen who built them. They are irreplaceable, defining a society where the faithful baptized their children and worshipped long years before entering into their eternity.

He had time to think now how he spent his priesthood and what fruits he would be bringing to the Lord for the gift of life given to him, and how he had carried out his duties.

Monsignor Francis Jeremiah O'Toole had come to believe that all human acts, meritorious and moral, debased and sinful, played a part in the big purposes of God. His job was to bring sinners to Christ. What had all this talk to do with changing the Church? Changing the Church began in the confessional! He knew he was as an instrument of God's Grace.

The people of his former parish at St. Catherine of Siena Church were not rich as a group, but there was some old money among some of the families. Their money kept the parish solvent and the Church normally maintained. By standards that seemed ironic for an Italian saint, the Church was designed as a gothic structure laden with leaded stained glass windows and shaped in the form of a Cross. It had a white marble altar and a marble communion rail sitting atop a black marble floor.

When Vatican II changed the way Mass was celebrated, with the priest now facing the people, Monsignor had a simply designed altar table installed, covered with normal alter linens. Mass was no longer a private devotion, but a community celebration, all in Communion with Jesus. The Vatican Council reinforced the Truth; that in this Church, founded by Christ, all are welcomed as "One with Christ" as a Body in the Eucharist (See New Testament, John 6:51). The Tabernacle, in the Catholic Church sanctuary, is the repository where the "Body of Christ is present in the Holy Eucharist" and is held in Holy Reverence.

As the Monsignor sat back in Betty's soft living room chair, he wondered what force drove the new Pastor to make changes at St. Catherine of Siena parish plant? He wondered: Would the patron of his former parish think now of events at the parish where she is venerated as a saint?

This saintly 14th century Italian woman, he thought, a Third Order of Dominicans member, and Doctor of the Church, devoted her life to the poor and sick. The Monsignor imitated her in the virtues and austerities she practiced. She was a foe of extravagant living, an attitude, which he copied. She brought about the return of the Papacy, which had been held captive, in Avignon, France. For her role restoring the Papacy to Italy she earned the title Papal Ambassador, which later helped to bring peace between Florence and the Papacy. But what was most spiritually illuminating to him was her mystical relationship with Christ and the Blessed Virgin. As with other stigmatics, she too claimed she received the five wounds Christ received in his crucifixion, visible only to herself until after her death. Patron saints are well known to Catholics to grant favors, to interfere in causes, to perform miracles to shine forth the light of God. He thought in this 20th century who, besides the Pope, or Mother Teresa, gathers such respect to influence others of high rank as St. Catherine once did, with her work with the poor? Popes bowed to her commands! He told himself, "I would like to meet him or her!"

The Monsignor could only speculate if the Italian mystic was observing events at the Parish named in her honor. She played a big role in bringing about changes in the Church in her time. While he had difficulty understanding why all of the changes, his prayers to her asked for revelations to calm his heart. Would she answer him?

His mind turned to Father Lawrence as pastor. It was going to be a while before he adjusted to parish life. Usually Bishop's appointments looked for leadership, parish needs, skills and abilities, personal spirituality and preaching as a necessary skill. In these days a priest needed to have an ability to explain Church teaching on morals, beliefs, laws, scripture and history. In view of what a seminary taught in his day the priest's responsibility was clear. They were fishers of men chosen to save souls. The vocation of the priest would always be, regardless of how it came to be a duty where souls were to be saved for Christ. Any priest would feel honored to be picked to serve in a parish under her patronage. How did Father Lawrence fit into her role at St. Catherine's?

How many thousands of hours had the monsignor sat in his confessional box and listened to the sinners confess their sins? Often he had to caution the penitent not to form rash judgments about others and their motives for behavior. Rash judgments would lead to the moral danger of mortal sin as a sin against the virtue of charity. Worse, if one brought a falsehood or a truthful statement to destroy someone out of malice they too, one could be judged harshly by God. People had to be holy including himself. All had to be one with Christ, as a member of His Body.

Still, he often recognized people did not know when they offended God. They didn't recognize their actions or hardness of hearts. For these moments he would take the time to soften them with an understanding of just what sin was and how it offended God. In a world where sin had lost its moral sting upon the conscience Monsignor O'Toole kept reminding the faithful to go to confession, receive absolution from sin and the grace of God. He feared such advice passed away from the pulpit of St. Catherine's when he retired.

So now he was placed on the horns of a dilemma. Father Lawrence, it appeared to many, was the kind of priest who did measure his successes by the Sunday collection and not by the number of sinners he converted to a holier life from his place in the confessional.

As the Monsignor left Betty's home for St. John Vianney's Retirement Home, the atmosphere there reminded him of a time when people from all over the world came to Ars, France to have the humble village priest hear their confessions. How the world had changed! St. John Vianney became the patron saint of all diocesan priests worldwide for his holiness. People who forgot or held back a sin to confess, illumined by Christ, he told them sins not to forget before proscribing a penance and absolving their sins.

Monsignor O'Toole, to rise above the fray to avoid moral lapses linked to changes at St. Catherine's Parish remained silent.

Phil Flask his onetime altar boy when he arrived at the Parish called the Monsignor at his new residence at St. John Vianney's Retirement Home. Phil said, "It's his ideas, Monsignor, now to renovate the Church and build a new rectory. People are leaving. They don't think it is necessary, now, at this time. It's a slap in the face to you. It's like he's come in here and now has to make a name for himself. You were never 'show business'. He's show business. People who lived here all their lives, thirty, forty or more years, are going down the road now."

It was the complaints against this priest, which bothered Monsignor O'Toole the most. He had never been in such a situation where people rejected him. Before he began to draw any hasty conclusions he wanted some time to settle the news between what he was hearing and the actual results of what Father Lawrence was doing.

Monsignor O'Toole did not know much about Quentin's planned scheme. Nor did Father Lawrence know he was about to be dragged into something, which would seriously damage the good will of the parishioners.

Quentin LaFayette's long-term scheme was to capture the interest of Father Lawrence in a renovation process of St. Catherine of Siena Church. In so doing commit first to start paying for services before anyone on the Parish Council could question what was being done. Quentin's scheme suggested the service begin without telling the trustees. He had all of the answers ready for Father Lawrence when asked how to pass his services off to the trustees, gather a new retainer and begin the process of redesigning the Church. As he did with other clients he never asked for the business, he just assumed he had it, and the priest-client who was inexperienced and embarrassed about his lack of worldly expertise usually allowed him to proceed. Quentin carried an arsenal of information in the beginning of the relationship to impress until he had the priest's confidence. Then he exposed the full package of plans down to the fundraisers. All a priest had to do was sit back and wait for the money to roll in. The years at work had taught Quentin what usually worked when approaching a new "client." Like his father, Quentin learned everything was for sale, even his soul.

Lo and behold, it worked again with Father Lawrence. Quentin asked for and received a referral whereby he could get another parish involved in a project so he could cut travel expenses. That ruse worked well. No one would know double billing was happening because at the present time and without Parish Council approval, he still would be paid. The fee would be covered. Besides, he thought it's rare that a parish is ever told how much is in the kitty or if the cupboard is bare.

The new program idea Quentin brought to the Parish Council for approval he emphasized reconstructing a Church that had to be more with the times. When his designs were shown, a red flag was raised, a warning to the elder faithful. The designs were absent of any dignity, respect, love and what was faith. Something was missing in the sanctuary. The Tabernacle was missing! Potted tree plants surrounded the circular wall of the sanctuary. The huge canopy above the tabernacle and crucifix was removed. The very notion of removing the central focus within the Church shocked the parishioners. When questioned, Quentin said it was required now in changes of the liturgy to remove the Tabernacle. He was either lying or poorly informed. Father Lawrence did not object to the design.

The word "tabernacle," a derivation of the word "tent," taken from the Old Testament served as a covering (the tent) wherein God resided in the Ark of the Covenant so as to be near His Chosen People as they traveled from place to place until when the Ark was placed in the Temple. The Ark was a chest made of acacia wood overlaid inside and outside with gold. Its cover was pure gold and inside it contained the Decalogue, the Ten Commandments, as a lasting testimony of Moses' Sinaitic Covenant, between God and His people. The Ark was simply the "Throne of God."

What characterizes Roman Catholic Churches throughout the world is they have one thing that is uniquely common. As one enters the Church, straight ahead, the eyes of the person are directed to the Tabernacle, which sits upon the Altar in the center of the main body of the Church. The Tabernacle, spiritually affirms the offer Christ made of himself at the feast of Tabernacles, to eat his flesh in the New Covenant. It is the place where the Holy Eucharist, the Body of Christ, is safely kept.

Central to the theme of Roman Catholic worship is the belief in the true presence of Christ Himself, who resides under the consecrated species of bread and wine. Christ's presence is manifested at Mass when using the words Christ used at the Last Supper, a priest consecrates bread and wine to become the Body and Blood, Soul and Divinity of Christ. The moment it happens, "Transubstantiation" takes place. Christ is truly present, in a mysterious way, under the both species of bread and wine. After Mass, His Divine Presence under the species of unleavened bread is reposed in the Tabernacle, atop the altar in the center of the Church.

In the days following Second Vatican Council, the American Catholic Bishops had been persuaded to allow for the change of location of the Tabernacle within the Church. It has not been a popular move with Catholics, who see any other location of the tabernacle of the true Divine Presence as an act of "Divine Absence."

The Mass for the faithful was always viewed as reparation of sins, in participation with Christ in a non-bloody sacrifice to God. Quentin's radical designs usually placed the Tabernacle out of view of the Main Altar on a side altar. His senior designer disagreed with his placing the tabernacle on the side altar. The Divine Presence, he argued, should never be taken away from a central view. Quentin claimed in his presentments the Bishop's "ordered" the changes. Parishes had to follow the new changes. His claim was all part of a greater scheme.

But many Archdiocesan Cathedral's leaders had not changed the tabernacle locations in churches because people complained. "Out of sight, out of mind!" A loss of belief among future Catholics in Christ's presence in the Eucharist did not seem to bother Quentin. With Father Lawrence's help Quentin LaFayette sold his "package" to another church. Quentin told Father Lawrence, "You will be remembered as the one who brought St. Catherine's into the 21st century." Monsignor O'Toole was upset when he learned changes were underway. To him, he believed the changes were more about symbolism than substance of faith. Narcissism over Worship! But he kept his private thoughts to himself.

The parts of Vatican II Documents called for change, LaFayette clearly adopted. He dismissed the parts of Vatican II Documents, which called for lay partnership in decision-making processes. Parishioners were left out of the voting process, even though they were expected to pay the bills. The Pastor made a final decision. Employees were allowed to vote at Parish Council meetings for the projects to gain approvals. Slick!

Father Lawrence explained the work went ahead based on receiving permission given by his predecessor. Phil Flask told Father Lawrence there would be uproar in the parish if the tabernacle were removed from the center altar. Fund raising fell short of the total cost of renovations. Father Lawrence quietly transferred "Dwyer Dedicated" funds into the General Fund to pay Quentin's design and construction fees. Lafayette's top designer made changes to the design and produced a masterful change in Gothic tradition. Quentin however, shifted the Tabernacle to the side altar. All that was left was for Father Lawrence to accept the kudos and listen to the comments on the changes.

Quentin said, "You know Father, some of my priest clients have gone on to bigger and better, if you know what I mean?"

"You're suggesting?"

"The pointed hat and walking stick."

"And? What are you saying?"

"The Auxiliary is going to retire soon, I hear, because of ill health. You're going to look good on paper. Someone will sit up and take notice. I know how those things are." Father Lawrence just looked at him and said nothing.

"It might be too much to mention, but someone who works for me, has a Bishop's Ring, he said it's more than nine hundred years old. He's has papers on it. I saw them. It's beautiful. It would look good on your hand, when that day comes. And I know it's coming the way we are preceding here. You're moving mountains that's for sure."

"It will be a long while before that happens."

"But do you agree with me, it can happen? Because, if you think it can, I might be able to talk my employee into making it a present to you since it can't be sold, and it can only be worn by a Bishop."

"There will be time for that to think about. It has crossed my mind, I will admit."

"Let me know when your ready. I hope soon, before he sets it aside to give it to someone else." Father Lawrence looked over at him but said nothing.

"I know it might be against protocols, Father, but I am appreciative of all you have done, considering what you have been up against. I have arranged a vacation for you." He put an airline ticket on the desk. "I could arrange it so my employee would show up at LaGuardia in between your flight to St. Thomas. He could show you the ring and you could be on your way, is that agreeable with you?"

Father Lawrence nodded his approval.

Quentin LaFayette went forward with his seductions. But his best-laid plans did not foresee the consequences entering into his sneaky swindle.

Betty Ryan was oblivious to Quentin's deviousness. Father Lawrence wanted a new aura for St. Catherine's Parish. He innocently bought into the snake oil salesman's tales of grandeur. And Monsignor O'Toole, wise by his years remained silent. He knew when he heard the Tabernacle had been moved to the side altar; Quentin LaFayette did not share in the unity of thought around the world where the Tabernacle should be located. That faux pas spoke loudly about the man and his avant-garde approach to spirituality. Deep in his soul, the Monsignor expected a future disaster. Something happened which would test Monsignor O'Toole's beliefs.

Unknown to Quentin his top designer lay dead in a hospital, and his widow and the police were certain Conrad was murdered. Quentin's scheme failed so far in its purpose to make him richer. A patient police detective, skilled in finding answers, listened and looked for clues as he drove Magda to her sister's apartment in Queens.

Elsewhere, there were uprisings in Poland. Magda knew the legend of the Bishop's Ring. Her optimism turned to fright. The ring would become even more valuable to the communists if they possessed it.

Chapter 9

Magda sat silently in shock in Lt. Morrison's car as he proceeded to drive her to her sister's apartment. Not only had she lost her husband, but also on this dark dreary night rain cars in traffic glistened setting her into an even more silent and somber mood. She did not want to talk, but she had lingering fears connected to the secret of the ring.

She had suspects in her mind, who might want to kill Conrad, not the least of which was his boss, Quentin LaFayette. He could hire somebody. He made no secret of wanting to sleep with her. If his eyes could suggest a rendezvous, as they had more than once to meet with him, she could believe he could plan a moment like this, and then after, pursue her. He could plan to be the shining knight that comes to save her. Yes, she could believe it. She put her head into her hands and silently prayed for Conrad's soul, which by now appeared before God in judgment. Each told the other a day like this might come as safe keepers of the Bishop's Ring. Her mind drifted.

She strongly felt Quentin's interest in her but she kept it to herself. Conrad did not need to think that everyone she came in contact with was a spy or a sexual deviant ready to cause harm to his marriage. She knew Quentin was a person who failed to take in all considerations of his actions she based this on what she could see in the behavior that served his self-interest. Quentin could be both hurtful and uncaring towards others and charming to those who advanced his causes or filled his pockets.

With Conrad, LaFayette knew he had a find, a professional on the staff. Conrad afforded him proper and courteous respect but kept his distance uncomfortable with his boss's double sided personality. Conrad liked designing churches or working on renovation plans. Quentin seemed always to be able to find work and had the final say before showing the drawings to clergy clients. At the beginning of a project discussion the firm's owner set the policies and gave Conrad freedom of design. Conrad stayed within the boundaries of liturgical thought. When flamboyant Quentin stepped up to the worktable to draw his sketches it would be Conrad who would bring him out of the clouds and point to a sense of reality about cost and application. Conrad provided a balance while Quentin searched to find parishes where he could have carte blanche.

It was Conrad who thought about the ability of people to pay for the kinds of work, which would then be performed. This practically was born out of his rooted past in Poland where suffering and sacrifices people made for their Church allowed for his sense of thrift.

In one respect, Magda knew Quentin appreciated Conrad as a stroke of luck to have in his business. And, while not giving him a partnership in the business he did set up a financial plan where Conrad was being rewarded with a retirement program, which included life insurance. The amount of life Insurance was four times the amount of his annual salary. When Quentin told Conrad what he had done for him several years back, Magda remembered him telling Conrad that Magda would not have much to worry about for a while if anything ever happened to him. Conrad was surprised by Quentin's gesture and then was suspicious at first of someone who would want to provide for his wife. When Conrad found out it was a normal business practice to provide life insurance coverage for key employees he understood Quentin's concern for his family. But then again Conrad did come from a world where the threats to life were real. He, more than Quentin knew, could well be in danger because of the Bishop's Ring. But he never told Quentin of the danger connected with the ring.

Magda remembered the evening when Conrad told her about the financial package Quentin put together at work. He joked with her then telling her that Quentin wanted to make her a wealthy woman if he should suddenly die. He continued and joked with her that she could marry Quentin since he was not married. When Conrad said it she remembered how he looked straight into her eyes looking for a response. Both had fears caused by a reality that someone would kill to get the Bishop's Ring. Conrad's joking was a warning, to Magda, that if something did happen to him, she should be very careful about Quentin's intentions. He might come after her to get the insurance money! She understood Conrad's fears.

Now what was Quentin going to tell Magda about Conrad being at the airport? Why was it necessary for Conrad to take the ring from its secure place to show it off to a priest at Quentin's insistence? She knew Quentin deserved watching. But he was supposedly out of town but was he really? Should she have mentioned to Lt. Morrison that it was Quentin who requested her husband bring the Bishop's Ring into the airport? Should she reveal more to the police on the importance of the ring? Did she have to give the police enough information to let them know that she, her children and possibly her sister's family could become targets of killers? Should she speculate Conrad's death was related to the work of the Polish Security Service Police looking for them?

"Lieutenant," she said, "I must tell you this. This ring, the Bishop's Ring, the Polish Communist government would love to have this ring. If it is to leave my possession, it's future belongs to the Church. It does not belong to the People's Republic of Poland. The Communists may be looking for it. Can you imagine what that would mean if they had it? They would not give it to the Church, but keep it as a symbol of their power to control my Church. They would like to show it off and say not even a Pope from Poland can stop them from getting what they want. You cannot know how my people have suffered. The Communists would put it in a public museum under a glass dome. They would post guards with guns to watch the people who came to see it. Their way is to tell a phony story about the ring, with its evil powers to enslave the masses. All lies!"

Morrison said, "It is my Church, too, Mrs. Kaminski. I know what they did to Poland. But, now, we'll just have to wait and see."

Stressed, she responded, "If the word comes out in the newspapers about this ring and where I live, the "People's Republic of Poland" embassy will declare it stolen merchandize and will seek to get this ring back as a national treasure. I need to have protection from publicity from anyone knowing about this. I am surprised Conrad had the ring with him today. Please, no publicity. I will be dead too. My children will be sought out..."

Morrison replied, "I can understand how you feel Mrs. Kaminski, but I do have to file reports of my activities. Reporters do come in to snoop around to see what to report on. But I'll see what I can do to hush this up and to see if we can get you some protection. We have people who can move you out and on to other places where it is safe, if that is what we need to do. You're also going to have to think about protection for your sister here in New York. You're going to need a make over. I don't know what to tell you about funeral arrangements, but they can be delayed. We can hold Mr. Kaminski at the morgue until you make for a proper Catholic funeral. Do you have a priest that you can confide in about this ring?"

She said, "A friend Upstate. But I can't go there. We were traced by the Polish Secret Police to be living there and..."

Holding back her tears, she said, "We are here, Lieutenant."

Lt. Morrison looked for an address on a building in the low-lit lights of the street as a misty rain covered the windows of his unmarked police car. He looked around at the apartment buildings.

He asked, "Can you give me an apartment number, so that if I have to come back to see you in a day or so, I'll know where to find your sister's apartment?"

She replied, "It's Building "B", Apartment 302. Klementowski."

He wrote it down. She watched, and then volunteered her sister's telephone number.

She said, "I will be here until they give me Conrad's body. I will have to get away from this place. I don't know where I will take the children."

"You have a lot to think about Mrs. Kaminski. Here is my card. I'll put my home phone number on it if you want to call me with a question or if you need to have help. If you call the precinct sometimes it might be delayed. You can leave a message on my answering machine. I'll be able to tell by your accent, but leave word you are "Mrs. Chopin," that way if anyone who happens to stop over, and listen to my messages while I am not there, like one of my buddies, Rogers always does, I'll be able to tell him you're a music lover. I listen to highbrow stuff when I get home. It takes the edge off the day. With our work we need reassurance that we belong to the human race."

Lt. Morrison could see she was anxious to leave. He reached around the front seat of the car and picked up an umbrella came around to her side of the car and opened the door for her. It was as if she expected he would act in this gentlemanly fashion. Although, he could not say he would do this for everyone to whom he gave a ride to a destination. They stopped at the door of the apartment building and she gave him a warm smile and thanked him for being thoughtful and courteous. As he walked back to his car, he told himself, she is a "Lady with some class."

On the drive back, Morrison took his time getting to the precinct. He needed some time to think what he needed to do to prevent this matter of the Bishop's Ring from screaming out headlines in the New York Post or Daily News. This would sell newspapers. Plenty of them and for quite a long time! Mrs. Kaminski would become a hunted celebrity whose life could be in a lot of danger, if, as she said, the Polish Security Service Police were involved and looking for the ring. He made a decision to protect the ring at all costs.

Morrison tried to see how Magda might be thinking. Police may have murdered her husband. And police here, would control what her fate became. Will she think the governments of both countries will cooperate and ask for the New York City police to turn over the ring to the Polish Embassy?

Morrison's Precinct Captain, Alfred Antonnucci, was going to have to be informed about this killing. The Captain liked to think he went by the book when dealing with murder cases. Going to this "AA" meeting, as it was called using the Captain's initials, was not about discussing the twelve points of personal power to strengthen one's resolve against the evils of alcoholism. Going to meet Alfred Antonnucci was like walking into a forward moving steamroller.

Morrison always blamed Antonnucci's aggressive tendencies on his "Napoleonic Complex." He thought it must be because as short as the boss was, five feet six and one half inches, holding up a two hundred-twenty pound frame, hiding behind the darkest five o'clock shadow in the City of New York, the Captain behaved as though he was leading an army into battle. Morrison knew him when he was a patrolman. Al hadn't changed when he was promoted up the line. He was still gruff and short with people. Morrison wondered if Al would behave that way if he stood six feet tall?

Morrison carried the ring in his pocket. Rogers and Smitty knew about the ring. No one else he thought would know about the ring, except as Mrs. Kaminski pointed out, the Polish Security Service Police. The thought entered Morrison's mind to conceal the ring from being put into official evidence file with the other evidence with the death of Conrad Kaminski. But it would deny a motive for his death attributed to the Polish Security Police (UB) if he did that. Morrison also considered putting the ring into evidence so it could save Mrs. Magda Kaminski's life by letting the NYPD know foreign police agents were operating in this country with the intent of killing naturalized American citizens.

Morrison pulled up in front of the precinct and jumped out of the car and ran into the building. At the entrance of the precinct, looking at him jump over puddles of water collecting on the sidewalk was Captain Alfred Antonnucci.

Antonnucci said, "Well. What do we have here tonight, Lieutenant? Rogers tells me you have been out collecting Captain Video's secret decoder rings. Any luck?"

Morrison asked, "Do you still go to Church on Sunday's, Captain?" The police captain gave him a puzzled look. "I'm going to need your Sunday behavior on this case. This is going to be different. I think we are both going to be surprised this time. We're going to have to work something out here. This is something that Clark Kent, Lois Lane and Brenda Starr should keep away from if you get my drift."

They walked into Antonnucci's office. Morrison closed the door and checked around through the glass windows to see who might be staring back at him before he began to speak.

"So you have something against the press doing their work, Lieutenant?" Antonnucci said sarcastically.

"Captain, we are not in the business of selling newspapers. We solve crimes or we like to think so, anyway. I got something here where five or six people or more could be put in danger. The fellow who was killed had something somebody else wanted. He was from Poland originally. His killer may be going after his wife, his kids, his wife's sister and her husband. And somewhere a priest in this is mixed up in the dead man's business. I will have to dig some more. If the press gets a hold of this you know how they love to tell about scandal in the Church. The front pages will be filled with stories that cannot be proved, but will be written anyway. The widow's for sure a target. We are going to have to get her some protection."

His boss asked, "How do you know she didn't have her old man killed off? It wouldn't be the first time. How can we check out her story?"

"Don't discuss it with snoopers. The widow seems to think the Polish Security Service Police did her husband in on orders from abroad. I have the item, a ring; she says the Polish government wants. She claims the ring is a personal possession. We could be in some deep crap if word were to get out this man's death was over the ring it would then list her as a possessor of the ring and we would have more killings on our hands. Capisce?" The Captain nodded, closing his eyes in silent agreement.

Al said, "This is the juicy stuff alright, 'Moe.' Some guys would put this story on hold but there is always someone who needs to prove he or she is a Pulitzer Prize candidate. They look for this stuff and throw caution to the wind to get their story. I get the message."

Morrison added, "Right now the widow, Mrs. Kaminski and her kids are staying with her sister. Her husband's killers might think she has the ring. I have it. If we turn it over to the D.A. and remember this is an election year, the crime could take on a life of its own. You know what that means to secrecy protecting that family!"

"You are sure that she needs protection? Or is she using you for a shield against being indicted herself?"

"Captain. It took her two hours to come into the city. She was pale when I met her. Scared. Silent. I think she has been living with this possibility of death for a long time and now it is real. Parts of her story have yet to be filled in but she has been open and I guess scared. If you think one set of police killed your husband how much do you want to tell another set of police about what you know about the murder?"

"Makes sense!" The captain picked up his phone, dialed, and said, "Murph, get in here. I got a job for you."

Marta saw the torn and worried look on Magda's face as she walked around her apartment. Marta knew the secret of the Bishop's Ring, but she did not live with the same kind of secret fear Magda and Conrad lived with everyday. The Embassy of the People's Republic of Poland in New York was a reminder to these sisters for as long as Poland identified itself as Communist. The "People's Republic of Poland Embassy" was going to be their point of danger. The sisters were naturalized American citizens and needed their new country to save them from their hostile native land.

Chapter 10

Investigator Murphy had the look of anticipation on his face. His eyebrows almost reached his hairline as he waited for Antonnucci to tell him about the job.

The Captain ordered, "Contact Rich Marvan in Connecticut. Get a rental price on a trailer from the TIP boys. Could be two weeks or two months, I don't know. We got a job coming up. We might have to store a house full of furniture. You still got those borrowed Real Estate signs?" Murphy nodded. "Good. We're going to need them, maybe. Depends upon what information Morrison comes up with about the homeowner. We may have to use the 'sold house-moving routine.' We got a hit on a guy. Now his family is in danger. We think foreign sources."

He continued. "I've got to make a call over to Manhattan. We are going to need the 'B' team. No gun fights. Just camera surveillance on the People's Republic of Poland Embassy! We need pictures of people coming and going. I've passed the place. I think its over on East 49th or someplace nearby. Manhattan would know. We're going to need 8" x 10" black and whites. We're going to have to identify people by faces. Need close-ups of faces, hands, attaché cases the works! Put a video camera on the entrance. Tape the comings and going. If you tape little old ladies getting travel information to go back home for a visit, we're not interested. You'll recognize the traffic."

Al, steamrolled, "I presume you have that unmarked tractor available in case we need to pull everything out of the house at a moment's notice. Need four of your muscle flexers from the gym to move the furniture." He turned to Morrison. "You're going to have to tell the lady if she suspects the out of towner's the only way she's going to be protected is if we put up a smoke screen until there are some answers. We can move the furniture or we can store it and she can move back in later. Who knows, maybe she will not want to move back in with her husband out of the picture? You better check with her. We need to be drastic. You know yourselves these guys don't play games. They move in, take what they want and are gone on the next flight out."

Al turned to Murphy. "Those photos better be good. We'll have to alert the guys at JFK with them. The hit man may be gone already or he may be sticking around to finish the job. He may have something he wants to get before his trip back home. You got all of this, Murphy? Line things up. Let me know when you're ready to deliver the tractor with the rental trailer. It won't look like a moving van from Mayflower, you know. I'm calling Manhattan about the stake out. Take your equipment along just in case we get turned down. Use long distance lenses and microphones. Take 'em to the Polish Embassy. Let me know your arrangements. Soon!" Murphy left the office.

Al asked Morrison, "You got anything on the murdered guy's boss? Where was he when Kaminski was killed?"

"Out of town, his secretary said." Morrison responded.

Al continued, "Follow up on that to see if it was a necessary trip. You got any more on this case?"

Morrison added, "The widow is staying with her sister here off Northern Boulevard. She lives out in Syosset. I have the feeling this is something she and her husband have been dealing with for quite a while, like since they came here or even before. It's just a feeling. Oh, she told me the employer took out life insurance for the deceased. Is murder covered as a double indemnity? Would make a tidy sum to start all over again."

"Does she become a suspect in your mind?" Antonnucci asked.

"She's different. Besides being beautiful she has an old fashioned quality something you don't find around here. It's not because she lives out on the Island. She's not like those fire spitting dragon queens just dying to get on one of the "man hater" TV shows. She's different."

"When do you get time to watch that stuff? What brings that up?"

Morrison reacted, "I tape it. You can learn a lot about character and how some people get even without ever getting caught. The widow's been silent almost resigned to what's happened to her husband. I'm not use to that. Hey, you ready for this?" Al's eyes began to roll up into his forehead, as he folded his arms. He continued.

"When I was a boy in Catholic School, I remember the Sister telling us one of those saint stories. I never forgot it. It's about a woman who went to confession to this priest." Antonnucci indulged him with a bored look on his face. "Anyway, the woman goes to confession to the priest, Father Philip, and this woman tells the priest she has an enemy and the enemy has done very spiteful things to her. So she tells the priest she was angry and spread bad rumors about a woman in the village. For her penance the priest tells her to go to the market and buy a chicken, and then break its neck to kill it for a meal. Then he told her to walk home from the village market pulling the chicken feathers and tossing them down. When she was done, he told her to go home and cook the chicken. But to come back and see him the next day! So she did." The Captain waited for the ending.

"The next day, the priest tells her to go back where she ended the day before and start picking up the chicken feathers. She complains they would all be blown away in the night. The sainted priest then says, 'Starting slander travels fast and spreads to others and can never be brought back. The injury to someone's name can never be brought back any more than the feathers could be returned.'"

"So, what's your point?" Antonnucci asked.

"It was a story about St. Philip Neri who was the patron of our church. Sisters like to tell those stories." Al's eyes rolled.

Morrison hurried, "Every time I think of the news media, there are always those who thrive on slander, or are excited by gory crimes which in a case like this could injure reputations and get people killed. I know how you love the newsies, Al. So we got to be careful, Al. Once the information is out, there is no way to retrieve it. Good people get hurt. God only knows. I think about Sister and her little story often, seeing people getting hurt and causing pain in so many lives." He stopped.

"Ah, isn't that sweet? Save your sermons for the priest the next time you see him. Let him repeat it. We don't have time to worry about that stuff around here." Al said.

"Anyway, the reason I brought up that little story from school days is I think there is something in the past of the Kaminski's that caused them to leave Poland. They went to Buffalo first. Then they hid from the Polish Security Police and came down here. Mrs. Kaminski is not saying much but I would bet she would not want to go back to Poland even for a visit because something is hanging over her head or her husband's." Al listened. Morrison became serious.

"When we were in the hospital waiting for the autopsy report, she did tell me how bad it is over there, and the great need for hospital supplies, and how her husband used to be a part of the underground smuggling in supplies from Germany from hopeful expatriates who live there. I gathered from her, her husband was some kind of hunted man and got out of Poland with his life. Just a hunch that goes beyond the ring thing."

Al asked, "Let me see the ring." Antonnucci said with authority. Morrison reached into his coat pocket and brought it up to his hand and looked around the window walls of the office to see if anyone was looking at them talk. Antonnucci saw his actions and responded with a deft retrieval. He pulled out the top drawer of his desk and set the ring in the thin drawer where he kept his envelope opener and printer's lens.

Al said, "There's Latin on the sides of this coat of arms. I don't understand Latin. Beautiful Ring, that's for sure."

Morrison answered, "She says it is a Bishop's Ring. Her husband inherited it from his cousin, a priest in Poland when the Communists took over Poland around 1950's. It's supposed to have quite a history. She thinks her husband was killed to get this ring. It's what the People's Republic of Poland government would love to have. If the D.A. gets his hands on this, she and her kids are dead meat. She knows it Al. She knows what goes on here in the political world. Moving her out of here may be the best idea you came up with, er... this week."

84

"Yeah, yeah, I know, Morrison you guys still think I came off the boat yesterday. Give me a break." He handed the ring back to Morrison, without looking through his office windows and said, "We got some time on this ring before the A.D.A. moves in on this killing. We'll probably have to baby-sit the Rich Kid on this so that his political career is not hurt if this goes to a trial. Don't know how this one is going to end up." Morrison quickly put the ring into his suit coat pocket.

Al remarked, "I hope you have a place for it, when and if we need it back quick." Morrison nodded he had a place. They both knew that for some strange reason they were breaking rules they would not ordinarily break. And the looks, which came across their faces to each other, indicated to both of them they were breaking with strict police procedure. And they knew either one could end up in deep trouble for what they were doing. But somehow they were ready to risk making the decision.

The ambivalence of Captain Antonnucci's attitude about the ring not being put away in the evidence room struck Morrison. The Captain was with him on this and was going to allow some latitude. But it did not stop Morrison from wondering whether some unseen force had an over powering influence upon what was happening in this matter. He had been around police work all of his working life and it never ceased to surprise when coincidences occurred which no one would have expected. Or that, criminals changed their story for no apparent reason and confessed or implicated others! But in this he found there was no compelling reason to expose this ring, which had been in "hiding" for centuries. He wondered about his own actions.

When Lt. Morrison reflected more on it he began to see there would be more to this than just the desire of the Communist Regime in Poland to have the ring. That's why he kept the ring! He knew it had to have a mystery attached to it. Enough had been told to him to know this ancient ring had a destiny and many lives would be changed in ways people would not understand. For that he looked forward to the events, which were certain to follow Mrs. Kaminski's claim the ring belonged on the hand of a Bishop.

Chapter 11

Police detective Murphy took a reconnaissance trip over to Manhattan in an unmarked police car, with a plain clothes officer, and a police photographer, to investigate the street where the People's Republic of Poland's embassy was located and to establish a stake out. The police car drove slowly down the street as Murphy scanned the upper floors of buildings on the opposite side of the street from the Polish embassy. His eyes were lifted skyward. As they approached the embassy he noticed that two men were about to enter the embassy. "Shutters," the photographer sitting in the back seat of the police car, with the window down, using his long lens, quickly snapped a picture of the two men. They looked at the car as it came toward them, but when Murphy did not show interest in them, one put his key into the door and turned it and casually entered the embassy through the double door.

Murphy heard the winder advance the film as he sat behind the wheel of the unmarked car. When the car had passed the embassy he asked. "Did you get those guys?"

"Yes. Got one of them good. I got a close up."

"How close?" Murphy asked.

"I saw the boogers up his nose." Shutters said.

"Good. You know the lens. How close do we have to get to take rolls and rolls of people coming and going?"

"I can take a 500 millimeter lens and count the hairs on your hand, from a block away Sergeant."

"No wisecracks, Tomato Brain. The captain will grind you up and put you in with his home made sausage, if you screw up on this one."

"What's up this time?"

"He'll tell us when he's ready. I'm going to circle the block and come back. You keep your eyes out for a location to shoot film.

The two men who entered the embassy walked directly to the staircase instead of the elevator and proceeded to walk up the stairs to the second floor. They sat at a desk near the front window. They were well hidden behind the lace and draperies that covered the windows to the street. They could look out but in the daylight it would be difficult for anyone to look in. The conversation changed. Now they were behind secure walls.

Polish Security Service Police Colonel Janus Piotrowski said, "I have not seen anything in the newspaper about our comrade traitor's death," while pulling the cellophane string from the top of his American cigarette package. He cut the top corner from the pack and forced the corner of the pack from the bottom to yield one cigarette. He lifted his Zippo lighter from the inside lower pocket of his suit coat and lit his cigarette. He had studied and copied the American way of lighting cigarettes so as not to be detected as being different. He even held his cigarette the same way Americans held one between their index and middle finger, not pinched between his thumb and forefinger as that would be a dead giveaway the smoker was foreign unaccustomed to American ways. He took a puff and inhaled blowing smoke away from the direction of Waldemir Wilk, his chauffeur.

Wilk asked, "You did not say Colonel, why it was necessary to kill this man," hoping to understand what his superior had in mind.

"The man has something that belongs to the State. I came here to bring it back with the least amount of notice from anyone. It has taken us years to find this man. It has taken us years to find where he keeps the treasure we seek."

"And what is that, sir?"

The Colonel looked at Wilk and turned and puffed on his cigarette and blew the smoke toward the window. "If I tell you that Wilk someday I may have to kill you, too. It is best you do not know. Right now, only I know why I am here. Only I know my mission here is not really to push papers, and grant visas to homesick grandmothers and widows looking for their families in Poland, before they die."

Wilk could see the Colonel's eyes close as the smoke from the cigarette drafted upward around his face. He had breached the wall of separation by attempting to be familiar with the man who came with "Special Orders," from Poland.

"I did not mean to invade your thoughts, sir."

The Colonel turned and looked at Wilk. "I like you Wilk. I want you to live. If you have this information, it can be taken from you or it can be sold. I could die because you have this information. I will share many things with you. You are new on this assignment with me. First time we are together. You were not supposed to see the man die. We think he died but we are unable to find if it is so. It was unfortunate you saw me use the weapon. I know you know what it is from your training. But I don't know if you ever saw it used. The comrade traitor must have had a weak heart to drop so soon. I thought we would be out of there with my prize and in the embassy limousine before the poison would take over. But he fell to the floor. I had to leave in order not to be seen."

The Colonel was being intentionally vague to Wilk. The chauffeur had only recently met him with a change of embassy staff. The most Piotrowski felt like revealing was that he was a Colonel in the Security Police but he did not use that information. For all others, he was a career embassy employee, a trade envoy who was sent to English speaking foreign assignments. "You already know enough to get yourself killed Wilk."

It was a sobering thought for Wilk to think about and the man with whom he had been assigned to protect. His job as a chauffeur was awarded to him while he served in the enlisted ranks of Poland's Army. He drew recognition and attention as a willing and energetic soldier. He had scored well in weapon target drills and served as a driver for a battalion commander. Wilk was the man Colonel Piotrowski had requested. He was taken out the personnel pool of Polish army soldiers who drove for colonel or general rank officers.

Detective Sergeant Murphy circled the block. "These embassy types, they are a little paranoid, you know. They see a van parked in their neighborhood they think the State Department is spying on them. I guess if we go to the second or third floor of this building on the left you could shoot down the street, couldn't you, Shutters?"

"Yeah, I could get them from there, but I don't know about the angle until I put a glass on the door and see what comes into range. Then you know I'm going to have to blow up the shots to 8″ x 10″'s. Then you have to figure only a short time for the sun so that's going to be a problem."

Murphy squinted, "Shutters, just take the pictures. That's your job. No crying. No whining. The captain isn't going to stand for it. Tell me where you need to be and I will set you up. We've been here twice. How about the last block? Can you take it from that corner, third floor? It looked vacant. I'll go around again. Check out the place with the management. But I'm going to cut right and park up the street, and walk back to the corner. Play tourist. Take pictures out of sight of where I park. I won't be long so don't stay away."

Captain Antonnucci stood behind his desk with his hands in his pockets looking down at the Daily News in the center of his desk. "Nobody's got a whiff of this yet, Moe!"

Lt. Morrison, sitting in the couch in his office, nodded in agreement. His eyes were downcast, almost closed.

"Tell me about these people we are sticking our neck out for, Moe."

Lt. Morrison lifted his head and looked at the Captain. "Well boss it's like this. I know its foolish for a policemen to get emotionally involved but I see a lot of fear in this lady, who now has two college age kids. But it doesn't come from the money angle but it comes from fear that she and the rest of them are next."

Al asked, "What does she look like, I mean?"

"She looks like," Morrison hesitated, then spoke, "She looks somewhat like Hollywood, you know, like she's been in movies or on TV. She's got high cheeks, pretty blond hair. That's the only way I can describe her looks. She's as pretty, I'd say. That's what scares me about this. You take someone good looking the newsies are going to sell newspapers with her picture on the front page. Foreign sounding name, exotic looks, you know Al, and her looks could be her death sentence!"

"You must be enjoying your work then, Moe. Anybody that looks that good should make it to your "hall of fame" list for most beautiful babes..."

"That's it Captain bring her in here looking as good as she does and you know there is going to be questions. And if you clam up, some sex starved fiend in here is going to make you pay the price by divulging there is a hush-hush going on and maybe the reporters should look into it kind of thing. There is always someone who pulls the plug and let's out the story because they have a pernicious sense of what true justice is. They think it is served by exposing secrets that only belong in a priest's confessional."

Al stared, "I told you before, Moe, you're not going to get anywhere with that crap around here. These younger guys don't follow the Cross! They grew up in the counter culture. It's the 'Not what you do, but what you say that counts,' philosophy. You come here and you have all of these anti-establishment lawyers, the hate mongers, the grandchildren of Bolsheviks bred from the Russian Revolutionaries who came here to cause trouble seventy years ago. They're here just to muck up the system. You just want to quit."

"That's the thing, Al. Freedom of the press get others killed and who will own up to it if she is harmed?"

"You are getting emotionally involved, Moe." Al looked at him closely. "I know you could retire from the force, but I can see this one case, is enough for you to want to stay a little bit longer, is that what you are telling me without telling me?" The Captain had a look in his eye of questioning what Morrison's motives were, and if his police job was going to get in the way of sleuthing the case."

Morrison smiled through his half closed eyes, and dropped his chin when he said, "The lady is going to need protection. Who better than a policeman with expert handgun skills, eh, Captain?"

Murphy stood in front of the manager of the building with his hand in his pocket ready to pull out his police badge. "Would the corner suite on the third floor be rented or vacant? I can't tell from the street." The manager gave a discerning look at the six foot four inch man in his blue pin stripe suit and yellow tie with blue polka dots. Murphy could see him waiting to see if he wanted to answer his question. He drew his jacket aside to reveal a holstered weapon. He quickly drew attention to the gun, to get the man's reaction.

"Who did you say you were?" The manager asked Murphy.

"Sergeant Murphy." And with that he flashed his badge. The man wasn't impressed. Murphy moved toward the manager. "There's some activity going we have to keep some tabs on. You hear those fire trucks? You could be next? We think we got us a crazy S.O.B. Arsonist! So is that place rented?

"No. You want to rent it? Follow me." The view was ideal as Murphy glanced down the street toward the People's Republic of Poland Embassy.

Murphy said, "Can't tell how long we'll need it. Lot of weirdoes out there! We're here to see no one gets hurt."

The manager looked at Murphy. Was this a threat? Or was there something going on and this cop was giving a friendly warning?

Morrison came back to the Captain's office. "The deceased's boss is back in town. He claims not to know that Kaminski went to the airport. His story doesn't corroborate Mrs. Kaminski's story."

Chapter 12

Colonel Piotrowski had been to America once before as a trade envoy. Now in this current assignment he served in a dual capacity as a trade and cultural envoy. As an eager member of the Security Service Police he had convinced his superiors that a national crime had been committed when the ring, a treasured national artifact was removed from the country. Piotrowski said he was the only man who could return it. He had other reasons, for revenge, which he did not reveal to his superior, General Koslowski. The Colonel loved going to the movies. Since movies were America's second largest export, second behind Boeing airplanes it was his task he convinced himself, as a cultural envoy to become an expert in this form of American culture. The movies, he told General Koslowski, were very subtle forms of mind control. Movies directed and distracted minds away from reality. They assisted in educating the masses to be violent and unpatriotic toward the State!

He reminded the General that Hitler used movies for his propaganda purposes in order to distract the German people. His argument was that Poland should have a watchdog against imperialistic propaganda. The General understood. He signed orders and sent Piotrowski to America. It was a task Piotrowski asked for and received all with the purpose of recovering the Bishop's Ring. But he also had other personal motives.

Piotrowski's grandmother brought him up after his parents were killed in the war. She thought he was still the same boy she rescued from the Nazis. She did not know he had adopted the mentality of a conqueror and never knew he dropped his faith. In her innocence, she remarked without thinking to whom she was speaking, when she spokes of a rumor of the holy relic, the Bishop's Ring, was in America, near New York City. He kept his calm, and when he returned to duty, Piotrowski asked his superiors for a new assignment. America!

After coming to America, the Colonel learned of his grandmother's death, true to her faith. She would never learn in this life what her daughter's son would become.

Janus Piotrowski entered the Polish Army, baptized in the Catholic faith. But his Army life was anything but faith filled. His grandmother would have no knowledge of the kind of indoctrination he would receive in military training. Or how much of the re-education was designed to destroy any behavior, which gave credence to a power beyond the muzzle of a gun or the power of the state to control the destinies of mankind. Janus accepted the secularism he was taught and left his Catholic upbringing home when he entered the Army. He never went back to the "Church." From the day he entered the military he could remember only once anyone ever getting the better of him. But, he thought that person was several years older and at the time, physically stronger.

While in the Army he grew in stature and in physical strength. So much so he knew other soldiers admired his muscular arms and his square shoulders. He could hide his expressions easily behind eyes that smiled but nearly closed as his narrow face skin taught revealed charm. But his face easily withheld any thought of what he might be thinking. Other soldiers gave him his space. Few would challenge him to feats of strength such as arm wrestling because they expected to lose. He held out hope that someday he would be allowed to take up officer training, and become a leader of a group. It happened and he was quickly promoted up the line of command.

The first time he came to America in 1972 he went to see the movie, "Dirty Harry" five times. He liked policemen who used guns to settle disputes. But more, he was told, he looked like the movie star who played "Dirty Harry." He liked that. Later on, his looks offered him the opportunity to masquerade like the Elvis Presley impersonators.

When he went back to Poland after his assignment was completed, he brought back a new persona. It was one he identified with earlier. It added to his aura as being tough minded and ruthless when he had to be. He long remembered the day when he suffered a humiliation over a girl. He vowed then he would not be shamed again. He would get even. Even if it took a while, he would get even. The "Dirty Harry" persona fit him. He wore it like a badge of honor among other officer colleagues. In his Security Service Police circles the persona helped him rise above others for promotion. It also helped him forge a role that he was the man with the weapon to do the job. American movies, he told himself, taught him how to really behave with revenge.

Back in Poland his mind would travel back to America and the darkened theaters where he would go to study the culture of the society so different from his own poor nation. Yes, he belonged to the powerful army but he was not unaware of the primitive countryside. In the cities people worked all of the time but the living conditions were so bad people could not imagine anything more. But he didn't worry about the political arguments that separated Communism from Capitalism. Now he was a tactician, skilled in military maneuvers hired to find The Bishop's Ring and bring it back to Poland. Those were his instructions.

Janus learned to speak English without an accent before he came to America. He viewed films where he saw the landscape of America, and was able to discover the great natural wonders of the land and to see how people lived. He used the movies to separate the propaganda of the various groups demanding power, position, or privileges. It was part of his indoctrination. Class envy, he understood, was exploited in American films to cause disunity in society. This was acted out on film screens. America did not need any other enemies. There were enough enemies exploiting their own system for their own special selfish interests. He believed the Polish Secret Police when they said the Soviet KGB Front Organizations in America backed films with money to inspire turmoil. Cynically he would laugh at the attack on Senator Joseph McCarthy's name when it was used as a reminder of what was wrong with America! He understood the formula for creating class turmoil. The attack on

McCarthy was always the bait in the ploy used by sympathizers to distract and then destroy the enemies of Communism.

American movies provided him with a depth of research on one American culture he would not have to learn by studying its secular culture on his own. In less than two hours he could go to a movie and learn how a murder was committed, how the police worked to solve the crime, and how much blood had to spill before the movie ended. He went to the movies a lot to see who went and what they went to see. He noticed the younger people attended a lot of movies with sex and violent scenes. Although moviemakers could make more money by attracting more audiences, the family films were infrequent. Family troubles were exploited. It was a cultural education to see how Americans were being educated with a cornucopia of films. The movies had long ago escaped from the story telling which inspired the Wizard of Oz. The Wizard of Oz, a film he actually enjoyed because all of this information about differences among the cultures of interest to him and his superiors.

It too, was a part of the "Psychological Warfare" conducted by members of the Soviet Block to weaken American moral resolve in the war to gain control of men's minds. What better way to unsuspectingly change the moral composition of a conscience and the culture of a country, he thought, than by making movies that portrayed morality irrelevant?

Piotrowski attended the cultural envoy sessions in Moscow conducted for the Warsaw pact nations. They were sponsored by the Soviets in which the lessons of the past were unveiled. Soviet research revealed that following the Soviet Revolution of 1917, the new government engaged in cultural and religious changes. Changes included a divorce by decree and a liberal legalized abortion policy. These changes brought about a moral collapse of the country. The Soviets learned valuable lessons that decadent moral behavior allowed in any society will destroy that society and the government's ability to control it. The Soviet swift action to destroy the Church in Russia by taking away its moral authority over people's lives almost brought about the total moral collapse of the country. The Soviets encouraged children to be defiant and spy on their parents to see if they were opposed to the new government. The Soviets turned to nationalism, to gain support in a new era. But change was slow and many years behind European economies.

Piotrowski learned that when the Soviets found out that divorce by decree and legalized abortion impacted harmfully on their own society their social experiment of abortion on demand ceased. The Soviets learned they would suffocate in their own vomit if they continued such radical practices in their society. In their perverse thinking those lessons provided valuable help. They used those anti-God decrees, as weapons of destruction, exporting their social declarations to destroy families knowing it would cause conflicts when life was devalued. The Warsaw cultural envoys were told why social turmoil and conflict was good for the West, but not good in their own pact nations.

The Colonel understood fully why he liked going to the movies. He had been briefed as a part of his days of instruction in psychological war techniques. In America the task of destroying the Church was left to supporters in Soviet supported front organizations operating in America. They operated patriotic sounding names whose purposes were defined to influence the lawmaking process to bring about an atheistic society.

While Communist governments would not tolerate pornography for their own citizens they knew the power of it to destroy the spirit within a person. Pornography was America's moral blind spot. Now he was back a second time in the U.S. This time he came as a Security Service Police officer with the rank of Colonel. He was a leader and expected to bring back the Bishop's Ring. All of the prior investigative work led to the conclusion of the possibility that the ring was smuggled out of the country. The censored mail going to the Church authorities as well as incoming mail from America, suggested the ring could be found in the Buffalo area. On his first assignment when the trail became cold in Buffalo he returned to Poland. Now years later, the leading suspects were found again this time living on Long Island. For Piotrowski that moment was filled with excitement to return to America. Revenge would be sweet.In uncovering this information, it led Piotrowski when he arrived to target a church designer. He wanted to see if the designer could be bought for a hefty price. Information was sent back and forth to

Poland via a locked mailbag. This time he was ready to take care of business personally in the persona of a policeman. The sooner he finished his business he could go back to Poland, where the Party would award him with another medal for his uniform. He wanted to be an honored hero of the State. His arrival at the Polish embassy in New York went unnoticed.

Piotrowski closed the Playboy magazine he picked up at the newsstand while out of the office for a quick lunch in the sun. He placed it on the corner of his desk where he knew his secretary Wanda would be sure to see it when she came into his office. Americans, he told himself, would be surprised to find that in Communist countries, even in China it is forbidden to produce or sell pornography. One did not have to read the language to look at pictures. He deliberately left the magazine on the corner where she would sit when she took dictation.

He could imagine what Wanda looked like twenty-five years ago with her blonde hair. She was still somewhat pretty but the box of chocolates she consumed for herself every week had taken its toll on her body. The once attractive waist now bulged. Each of her arms had collected a hanging slab of soft loose fat. She was not unattractive. But her problem was she still thought she was as beautiful as she was at twenty-five. At forty-five, she became a widow when her husband was killed in a coalmine accident. She improved her secretarial skills to gain a better position with the government. When she was selected to work in the New York Embassy Office, she knew her preparations paid off.

Piotrowski wondered what it was she had done for the Party to put her in the ranking position of being his secretary. She sat next to his desk while he stood behind it looking out the window as if to be creating a letter in his mind. She waited for him to begin. And while she waited her eyes focused on the cover of the magazine. She looked up at him, as he caught her looking at it. He motioned to her to look at it if she wanted. He continued his formulating thoughts and walked to the next window. She turned the pages slowly looking at the young women posing naked before her eyes.

"You like young, beautiful, naked women, Colonel?" He nodded as, looking back at her, as if preoccupied with his thoughts. Then he added. "I like women. Even better when they are naked!" It was a remark she caught. He would not discriminate based on a woman's age. He gave her his "Dirty Harry" smile. Wanda Zabinski was not used to seeing other women staring back at her in provocative poses in their natural skin. She could feel heat rise in her body, a sensation she always welcomed when her basic urges needed to be satisfied. She looked up at him and saw him staring at her, with intent in his eyes. "I don't know if I should ask you to take a letter, or take your clothes off."

"Whatever you please, Colonel."

"The magazine excites you?"

"The girls remind me what I looked like when I was their age."

He called for a taxi and invited her to join him. She put her pen down. He waved her out of his office and joined him in the taxi. In Poland there would be no porno magazine to excite them to a mid-afternoon tryst. She wasn't the one he wanted, but he would keep taking her until he got the one he wanted.

In America, where all can worship God, its citizens are free to read this in the New Testament, in 1 Corinthians, 6th chapter:

"The body is not for immorality...Every other sin a man commits is outside of his body, but the fornicator sins against his own body. You must know your body is the temple of the Holy Spirit, Who is within - the Spirit you have received from God. You are not your own. You have been purchased, and at what a great price! So glorify God in your body."

Colonel Piotrowski knew in his heart of hearts, as all men do, he would be judged by God. His grandmother loomed over his thoughts. His Catholic conscience was imprinted with divine sacraments. He was confirmed in the Holy Spirit, who waited for his confession and repentance. And soon!

Chapter 13

Captain Antonnucci called Magda and convinced her his bogus moving company would only take her furniture and put it into storage until the threat upon her life ended. She asked for, and received protection to go to her home to retrieve her belongings. The Captain assigned Morrison to take her with an unmarked car to Suffolk County. From there she could pick up her car at the train station in Syosset. Morrison would follow her to get the description and photos of the neighborhood. Shutters would develop them. Other police agencies were not going to be called in to assist on this because of the high risk of security leaks.

With no written account of Conrad's death in the newspaper, the lack of any signs of life at their house did not alarm their neighbors. The Kaminski's lived at the end of a long street. They bought this particular house because of the privacy. A prior owner had lined a very tall wall of bushes between himself and his neighbors after a silly dispute over territorial privileges. The prior owner liked his privacy and he told the Kaminski's that had been his reason for growing the tree wall. After ten years his firm transferred him to Pittsburgh. The Kaminski's liked the house and bought it, for the very same privacy reason. But unlike the former owner they made certain they met their neighbors so as to not appear to be hermits.

Without their knowledge Colonel Piotrowski had found them living in Syosset. He knew when Magda took Conrad to the train in the morning and when she returned to pick him up. After dropping off Conrad in the morning he trailed her to the shopping center where she went to pick up groceries. He watched from a distance in the all day parking lot when Conrad returned and followed them to their home. Each time he followed with a different rented vehicle so as to not let her think she was being followed. Each time he used different rental firms and a false driver's license for identification.

When she took the children to the beach in the summer, he took photos of her. When she bent down to kneel on her blanket his long lens filled the screen format of his camera with bursting cleavage coming out of the top of her bathing suit. All he had to do was imagine. His fetish for female nudity filled his mind constantly as he awaited the day and the time when he was going to have her to himself.

Magda never knew she was being stalked. She never knew he had taken a special close-up photo of her. While napping on the beach and her top loosened a draft of wind lifted her top off her bathing suit exposing her full breasts. While her daughter scattered to retrieve her top, Magda's pursuer enjoyed his small victory capturing a most alluring photograph. He had that photo to remind himself someday he would not have to look at it because he would know her. He did not keep his photographs of Magda in his office, just in case his secretary might find them in his file or for his driver/bodyguard to learn about her. That kind of information was enough to point a finger and get Wilk killed.

Shutters long lens was focused on the front door of the People's Republic of Poland Embassy. Few came and went. His assignment was clear. Take rolls and rolls of film if necessary. A photo might, Morrison told him might turn up some kind of clue to Mrs. Kaminski belief she had that Polish Security Service Police were involved in her husband's death.

Suddenly a car stopped along the curb in front of the Embassy. The make of the car, license plate were framed. Shutters took the photo. A tall man with sunglasses got out of the car. It was the Colonel. Wilk came out of the Embassy, got into the car, and drove it off. Piotrowski went to the Embassy door, but not before looking up and down the street, squinting his eyes to see if anyone was paying attention. He quickly used his passkey, and entered.

It was time for Shutters to close up and go back to the photo lab to develop his pictures. When he arrived at the lab he found Morrison had dropped off a couple of rolls of film to be developed. The "NO ENTRY" sign went on after he entered the photo lab. Shutters unpacked the film inside a black box and prepared it for processing. After both sets of film were printed and air-dried, he started looking at his work. Something caught his eye. Morrison had taken the picture of a street with cars parked on it as a general view. Shutters discovered a car that Morrison photographed earlier in Syosset as the same car that he photographed in front of the Polish Embassy, when one driver turned the car over to another, just before he quit the stake out.

Morrison said, "It's the same car, Captain. Same license. No one in it! But in Syosset! It's a lucky break for us. We can place the car in two separate places, connecting the embassy with Syosset. So, now we know we have something to worry about." At first the Captain said nothing.

"The furniture's out. She got what she wanted from her desk and some changes of clothing. Now this guy knows the house is empty. But we don't know if he trailed the truck taking her furniture out. He's got to be wondering about Mr. Kaminski. No obits published." The Captain remarked to Lt. Morrison.

Morrison added, "I spoke with Kaminski's boss, LaFayette. He says Kaminski has disappeared. He said he doesn't know where he is. He already told us he didn't know Kaminski went to the airport. I don't think he knows how much his secretary already told us. There might be another angle to look into for us."

"What's that?" The Captain asked.

Morrison answered, "LaFayette took a cruise with a woman companion. She's from upstate, the secretary says. I asked for her name and telephone number. The secretary was scared when I spoke with her; it was like she had expected the police to come in any day. She had a 'ready to cooperate' sound in her voice. She wanted no trouble. But she was the type I don't think would give out this kind of information, like his companion's name, unless she knew something was up. She said they went on a seven day cruise almost a week before this happened to Kaminski. My question is, did they go on a cruise? Maybe she was led to believe they went on a cruise. I kidded her. I asked for proof that her boss's companion was a real person and not a made up one. She produced a photo. It was the two of them together. So he does have someone, who, if the secretary is telling the truth, can corroborate his story of being on a vacation cruise with him."

Al said, "So, you know what to do next. Call her."

"Yes, but I also got other information. LaFayette took out a Key Man insurance policy on Kaminski for a half a million. He is the beneficiary. Took another one out on Kaminski, the secretary tells me, making Kaminski's wife the beneficiary. You get the picture? If he is only missing, no one is to collect. LaFayette could want it to appear that way at least to us for now. And later collect on the policy. Or he may have designs of wooing Mrs. Kaminski into his bachelor pad. Together they would have a lot of bucks to live a good life for a while."

The Captain responded to Morrison. "You have been a cop too long."

"I learned to talk this way hanging around you, Al."

His boss whispered, "But no one is talking about the ring you picked up. Call that companion of LaFayette. Find out if she was with him during that week. You may have an accessory to murder if LaFayette is the guilty guy who paid someone off to do it. We don't know anything about this woman. He may be two-timing her. Play it. Ask questions. Dig in!"

"Ms. Ryan? This is Lieutenant Morrison, New York City Police. How are you tonight?"

"Well, I'm fine, Lieutenant." Betty said with caution. "The reason I am calling, Ms. Ryan, is to investigate a police matter and I need some information to verify some stories we have been told."

"I'll do what I can to help, Lieutenant." A cold sweat covered her forehead as she had been sitting at home alone reading a book. The shock of getting a police call from New York made her just a bit leery of what she might be hearing next.

Morrison queried, "Is it true, Ms. Ryan you were on a vacation cruise with a Mr. Quentin LaFayette recently?"

She corroborated, "Yes, its true. In separate cabins! Is there something wrong with Quentin, Lieutenant?"

He responded, "Not to my knowledge. We are just calling to establish some people's whereabouts." With a chance to continue the conversation, Morrison wanted more information. Information as to whether she knew anything about LaFayette's connection with a priest, who may have come to meet Conrad, LaFayette was not talking about his business to anyone. She may reveal, as the secretary did, without their knowledge, a bit of information that could fill in some of the information.

He said, "I know Mr. LaFayette is a man whose business is involved in dealing with clergy. Was there a chance you were supposed to meet a priest before going on your trip?"

She quickly responded, "You must be thinking about Father Lawrence. No, that was not the plan. Father Lawrence was going on vacation to St. Thomas but stopping off in LaGuardia. If that is some help. But I think that was supposed to be after we went on the cruise. Mr. LaFayette would not be in trouble would he?"

"Just investigating, Ma'am," He replied.

"Mr. LaFayette is a gentleman. Why, he gave tickets for Father Lawrence to take a St. Thomas vacation. You know, the laity tries to do their share. Our priests are not overly compensated for their work. Occasionally someone comes along and splurges and lets them live a little get some Caribbean sunshine. They need it too, you know?"

Morrison coldly said, "I don't know if he is a gentleman, Ma'am. We can't say yet if a man has been murdered or not. But if you say he gave tickets to a priest for a St. Thomas vacation, you and the priest could be charged as accessories to murder, if Mr. LaFayette is charged with a crime." She was terrified.

"What? What you say...? Accessory to murder?"

He said, "I can tell you are shocked. If you did not know about what is going on here, you'll be cleared. So will the priest. What is your connection to the priest?"

"He's a pastor Mr. LaFayette has worked with on a few projects. They have a friendship. Have you spoken with Father Lawrence yet?"

"No." Morrison gave a small laugh to soften the conversation and reduce the apprehension in her voice.

"I work for his boss, the Bishop. I know the concerns of the Bishop and the last thing in the world he would want to hear about is that his priest is caught up in a crime mess. He doesn't need the publicity. You know the tabloids! The next thing you know, every priest will be labeled a criminal. The secular media loves to shame the Church. It's a devilish thing they do with half truths."

Lt. Morrison noticed how calmly she took his call except for the insinuation of LaFayette's involvement. He thought he would milk the conversation a little more.

"If you work for the Catholic Bishop then it won't be hard to find you. I don't know how to say this Ms. Ryan, since you went on a cruise with Mr. LaFayette but I'll just have to be blunt." He continued to question Betty. "Is there any chance you would believe he was having an affair with the wife of one of his employees?"

Quickly startled, she erupted, "Whoa! Lieutenant. You want me to answer that question after I told you we went on a cruise together?"

"Ma'am, I did not mean to hurt or insult you. You are upstate. I am here. We need to cover a lot of ground. You may be called down or we may come up to see you to get a statement. The same for the priest."

"Lieutenant. I have an idea. Would it be all right to send someone to you to vouch for my character? I can't leave work with the stacks of work on my desk after the vacation. I have done nothing to be ashamed of but I would not want police coming here. I have a friend, Monsignor O'Toole, who is a retired pastor, someone who actually preceded Father Lawrence in his present job. If I send him down to you would you talk to him?"

Morrison responded, "It won't do any harm. Don't talk with LaFayette about what I talked to you about so you can avoid a complicity charge."

She said officiously, "Give me your name and number and where you can be reached, Lieutenant. I will speak with Monsignor as soon as I hang up here."

Lt. Morrison came back to the Captain's office. "There is a priest involved. Ms. Ryan admits LaFayette gave a Father Lawrence vacation tickets for St. Thomas before she went cruising with LaFayette. I played her for the last one to know by suggesting LaFayette may be two-timing her. Now she wants to send a retired Monsignor friend down to see me.

Al speculated, "I wonder what LaFayette is going to do or say now, especially if he finds out another priest has been involved in this mess. It looks bad for the priest who thought he was getting a Bishop's ring. Doesn't it Lieutenant?"

Morrison gave a quirky grin, "It could be. Her Monsignor friend knows Father Lawrence and what he might be up to. I don't want to call this Father Lawrence yet because I don't want to tip too many off as to what's going on."

"Okay. Good work,... so far this week." The Captain replied.

Chapter 14

Betty put the phone down. She was shocked. Her eyes glazed over and for a moment she could not think. She felt betrayed. What had Quentin done to her? How was it that she was involved in a man being murdered? Somehow, the stereo easy listening elevator music seemed to sound like thunder and lightning crashing down upon her. The book that she was reading when the phone rang was now pushed aside. She neglected her customary bookmark placed in the last page of reading. There was only one person with whom she could talk now. She would have to divulge what she hoped she never would have to say to another person.

Monsignor O'Toole answered his phone with one eye on the television screen. All he heard was a faint, "Hi."

The Monsignor asked, "Betty? Is that you Betty? Are you all right? Betty? Betty speak to me!"

"You can tell it's me by just hearing a "Hi"?"

"Yes, my dear. Just that much! What can I do for you?"

She said, "You can run an errand for me."

"Where to?"

"New York... to see the Police down there."

"Is this a joke?" He asked.

"I wish it were but it isn't. They called me to tell me a crime has been committed, and my name came up in connection with the crime. I think a man has been killed. For some strange reason they are connecting Quentin LaFayette with the murder. As you know, he was with me on the cruise. I was in a separate cabin I want you to know.

"Uh huh? Likely story." He said with a jocular tease.

"It's true. FRANCIS!" She raised her voice to him.

"I see I got your Irish up Miss Ryan. So if you were away in the Caribbean how does that connect to New York? I don't understand."

"I guess I'm his alibi, if he needs one. I was with him. We were seen aboard the ship together."

"Tell me more."

"That's going to be a difficult story to tell. Just trust me. I hate having to tell this. Lord knows how I hate having to tell ..."

He asked, "Is this a matter for confession?"

"I hadn't thought of it that way."

"Are you interested in putting on a pot of tea? If you are I'll be over, say twenty minutes."

Betty felt a sense of relief. The priest could see the pained expression on her face. He would know that it was not easy for her to tell him all she heard on the phone. If the police detective told the truth she had better prepare the Monsignor for the worst if he goes to New York on her behalf. She could hardly believe Father Lawrence was a suspect involved in a man's murder.

Betty had come to see another side of Quentin. It had not been evident when she first met him and went out to the French restaurant on their first date. What she had failed to recognize was she was truly very fortunate to be around religious men, who were very conscious of trying to improve their behavior on a daily basis and be less of this world and more for the next. It was not this way with Quentin. He lived for the "Now." Quentin's pride and ego to prove he was better was the moving force for his competitiveness. She realized his work in parishes was strictly a way to make money in an area where there would be few competitors offering this service. She had come to terms with the fact that he was carrying on a very elaborate "dog and pony show" for the clergy. They were less educated in the ways of the world, but at the same time the clergy were truly influential members of society who made decisions and had access to find large amounts of money. She heard Quentin say once it was like "robbing children's piggy banks."

When the doorbell rang she didn't know if it was the Monsignor or the local police with a warrant for her arrest. She become shaken since talking to Morrison. She was relieved when it was the Monsignor.

He gave her a kiss on the cheek and said, "You have me wondering my dear. With all this talk! I forgot to bring my Superman cape, tonight, just in case I needed to fly off to New York." He settled in a chair opposite her couch and noticed her hands were held together in a prayerful form and her head held down.

She began, "About a month ago, Quentin drove through and stopped at the Chancery to see me and to take me to lunch. He said he was on a business trip. When we finished lunch he handed me an envelope and told me there were some cruise tickets in the envelope. He winked at the time and said it was kind of a repayment of a favor."

"It's easy for that guy to turn a carved Michelangelo into a potted urn." Monsignor O'Toole said sarcastically.

"I knew you would say something like that. I know how you feel how the Dwyer Children's Education fund was used."

"The rascal," he said, "turned a filet mignon into hamburger. He didn't know what he had. Old Man Dwyer spent a king's ransom to build that Church. Everything in a Catholic Church is there for a religious purpose. That guy is a butcher."

"Please, Monsignor. I've heard you say it before. I know he is not your favorite person. And now I think he's got Father Lawrence hooked into something." She stopped.

He remarked, "I can believe it. I've heard the rumors ever since Auxiliary Bishop Sullivan took a flip and fell on his can. He took three months to recover. He's been going to retire for a long time. I'm getting the picture, Father Lawrence is setting himself up for a slot."

She agreed. "I think you guessed right. Father Lawrence comes around, and peeks in to let me know he is still here. I never got that treatment when you were Pastor."

"I wasn't looking to become a Bishop. I had a job among my people."

"That is the other thing. Father Lawrence flew to New York when he could have had a connecting flight in Atlanta and on to St. Thomas. Quentin wanted him to come to New York. He wanted him to look at a ring."

"What kind of ring?"

"Quentin did not tell me much. He has so many contacts with so many clergy. There is a Bishop's ring that has an exquisite design on it. Quentin thought that if the day came it would be a fitting gift for Father Lawrence on being ordained a Bishop." She spoke softly.

"You know so much of what is going on, and yet you have never told me this much about Father Lawrence. Your insides must be bursting with this kind of knowledge. I only heard the Bishop Sullivan rumor in the last week." He acted surprised.

She countered, "This has been an active situation ever since Father Tim Ryan retired." She stopped momentarily.

"I think Father Lawrence thinks he's got a chance. Bishop O'Farrell likes him. It's the others around the building who see him as an interloper encroaching on the process. Your feelings are not misplaced. There are jokes going around quietly making fun of Father Lawrence in his count down to the nomination. Everybody seems to think that Bishop O'Farrell is going to nominate someone but if I were to have an answer I don't think it is Lawrence. O'Farrell doesn't owe any big favors. He has no court vying jesters."

The Monsignor turned serious. "We haven't talked about this before. You kept all of this in, about Lawrence. Why? Because you thought it might upset me? I respect O'Farrell, ever since he came on board, I see a Bishop who treats all of us with the same sense of charity. The Pope did the right thing. He was the best man for the job. He is a theologian. I like that. Not political I like that! I think the Bishop can see through the fancy dancy stuff. Lawrence has pulled off his act, but not without a lot of harm and complaints. And for that, confidentially I would not vote for his nomination to the Auxiliary spot."

"You see why I don't talk about Father Lawrence in front of you."

He responded, "Who do I see in New York? And what do I do there?"

"Here is Lieutenant Morrison's telephone number. Please call him. He'll give you details of where to meet and you can vouch for all that I know. I can't leave the office right now. My vacation backed up a lot of work." As an after thought Betty added. "I know about the Bishop's Ring. If Quentin says he knows nothing about the Bishop's Ring, then he is lying. Morrison did not sound like he was kidding when he almost accused me being in some plot to cause harm to someone. In a way I feel used. Morrison also suggested that Quentin may have been having an affair with the dead man's wife and he was out to collect insurance money."

He said, "Be careful not to be taken in with such suggestions. It may be a trick to have you turn on Quentin. You know him. Out of his own mouth, he will either convict himself or free himself from any blame or crime. I'll call Morrison tonight. Let's have some of that tea."

The next morning, Morrison was at LaGuardia Airport to meet Monsignor O'Toole. Each had described their physical description. Monsignor wore "civvies" on his flight. He was expecting to be taken directly to the police precinct to clear up the matter who Betty Ryan was, and the mysterious priest who had entered the scene. When Monsignor O'Toole presented identification, Lieutenant Morrison did the same. Morrison led him to his waiting car and they then drove to the precinct.

Morrison started talking, "We are trying to keep this case under wraps. We think a killer is at large. He has one victim. He may seek another. We are not sure. Ms. Ryan, from what I understand, enters into this because she is a good friend of Quentin LaFayette's. Our suspicions right now are he may be tied up in a conspiracy to commit murder. From what Ms. Ryan said she could be an accomplice."

"That's why I am here, Lieutenant. I don't know Quentin LaFayette other than he has done a lot of work around my former parish. My successor hired him to redesign the Church. I do not wish to speak ill of another priest but his ways are not mine. We operate from different time zones. I'm twenty years older. He is just coming into his own while I am awaiting the big crossover. I may think many things about my successor, but I can't think of him as a person ready to commit murder. He is a priest like I am. We don't murder people."

Morrison asked, "Ever been to Israel, Monsignor?"

"Once. Years ago," the Monsignor responded.

"The clergy over there carry weapons and kill people. They say it's for self defense."

"I'll pass on that." The Monsignor replied.

"What, you don't believe those clergy Monsignor? Then why should I believe ours here? I've seen a lot I wouldn't have believed possible when I became a policeman. You're right. People do cover up their motives. That's why you are here too maybe to cover up for Ms. Ryan?"

"Not cover up, Lieutenant. You and I have something in common. Both of us have questioned sinners most of our lives. I do it for eternal justice, and you do it for man's justice to be served. I want to see justice served. I have known Betty Ryan since she was a very young woman. She is a niece of a very good priest friend of mine."

"She's got one thing in her favor." Morrison retorted. "She told me something that corroborates something I had heard from another source. I can't tell you yet. We are just now lifting the ban on press coverage of this incident."

"Why are you doing that? Won't you be putting people's lives in danger?" The priest asked.

"The pieces of the puzzle are beginning to fit. You coming here opens up some possibilities for me, I'll have to admit. Ms. Ryan would not have sent you if you have been friends for so long, I can't imagine, you came to cover up a crime. I mean she would not want your life's work to end on a sour note, would she Monsignor?"

He responded, "I don't think so."

Morrison continued, "I don't either." Then with second thoughts he said, "Ms. Ryan said a Father Lawrence went to see the ring at the airport. That also agrees with the widow's remarks. Maybe the widow's husband went to the airport with the ring because his boss insisted upon it. I took note of it because I couldn't imagine a boss insisting on any employee to display his personal belongings to strangers. The widow, Mrs. Kaminski told me the ring was supposed to be given or worn by someone who was to become a Bishop. Does your Father Lawrence have a shot at making it to be a Bishop? Is that what all of this fuss is about? Obviously, someone does not want him to be a Bishop."

"I am retired, Lieutenant. I don't keep up with the politics of the Chancery. Father Lawrence might think he would like to be nominated, but if you asked Betty Ryan, who works for the Bishop himself, she would not even give you a definite answer because the Bishop has not made up his mind. We first have to see if our Auxiliary Bishop is going to take a retirement or keep working."

"I'm going to level with you Monsignor. I would like you to meet the widow, Mrs. Kaminski. I'm going to propose something to her. It is going to have to meet with her approval because it will be her life on the line. As much as I would like to think we could protect her all the time from a possible killer we do make slip ups. Currently, her house has been emptied. We suspect her husband's assailant knows that the house is empty. He may be looking for her. Most of her furniture except for some clothes, tables, beds, and personal items, has been stored away until we can bring her husband's killers in. We don't limit this to a one-man operation. Mr. Kaminski's body is in cold storage until it's released."

He cleared his throat. Morrison continued. "Our problem, Monsignor, is that we can't withhold this information forever. The killer is going to see through our schemes because we are not saying anything. I'll bet he's looking for Kaminski's obituary information right now in the daily and weekly newspapers delivered in and around Syosset. We've got to think the worst about this guy. Ms. Ryan may have spent a vacation with his accomplice. This is a frightful situation for Ms. Ryan and Mrs. Kaminski and family to be in. Ms. Ryan, right now is Quentin LaFayette's alibi, but she is also the person who can corroborate Mrs. Kaminski's word that Quentin LaFayette arranged for Father Lawrence to see the ring."

The Monsignor had a question. "I'm missing something here, Lieutenant. If LaFayette had arranged for Father Lawrence to see the ring, why was this Mr. Kaminski killed in the process?

"Somebody wanted the ring, Monsignor. It wasn't Quentin LaFayette. But with Mr. Kaminski dead, someone would profit by the experience, someone like his boss, who carried a Key Man insurance policy on his life. He also carried another policy on Mr. Kaminski's life, for which he paid a premium, in which Mrs. Kaminski would be the beneficiary. He is a bachelor. And when you see Mrs. Kaminski, it would be easy to understand, why he would hope to get lucky. Well, I don't have to tell you what I mean, with all of the confessions you have heard in your life. If money is a motive, there is a motive for him to have put Father Lawrence at the airport scene, as a pawn, maybe, to allow the killer to carry out the deed so he could collect the insurance money. There is another angle to this, the killer wanted the ring but he didn't get it."

"How do you know that?"

Lt. Morrison reached into his coat pocket and pulled out a plastic bag with the Bishop's Ring in it. He held out his clenched fist, which held the bag. Monsignor O'Toole reached his hand toward Morrison's hand to have Morrison place the plastic bag into his hand.

"You now have the Bishop's Ring, Monsignor!"

Monsignor O'Toole stared at the ring inside of the small plastic bag. He did not take it out of the bag. A sense of awe came over him as he read the Latin inscription."

"What's it say, Monsignor, in English I mean?"

Soft spoken, the Monsignor said, "Go, teach all nations."

"That's a shepherd on its side, isn't it?" Morrison asked.

"Look's like it Lieutenant. There's no doubt about this one. A Bishop would wear this ring. As a Catholic Bishop or Orthodox prelate equivalent, one is the lawful successor to the Apostles. They pass on their office to their successors. When I say lawful authority, I mean only successors to the Apostles have been given the Rite of Sending, to ordain other Bishops, and have teaching authority and pastoral rule over the Church, from St. Peter to the present time."

Morrison offers, "You can understand then when a Communist tries to get a hold of that ring, he has a treasure he can use to deny an intended receiver of the ring."

"What are you saying Lieutenant?"

"I think we have a foreign government that wants that ring. Poland to be exact! If I have it, or if it is found out that I have it, all hell, pardon me Father, could break loose. I'm sure you know what I mean. You listen to the news on TV. It's not that the media really are interested in what we do as police, as much as it is, I'm convinced after my career length the media want oversight and call the shots. It provides the place and space for police haters to vent their fire. They are in the business to sell and profit. Justice sometimes takes second place." He continued looking at the priest.

"I'm trying to save a family from being killed. That's why nothing has been printed or said about this murder. That is why our precinct is not in chaos right now." He looked for affirmation. The Monsignor waited.

"Anyway, I'm going to ask my boss, this is the proposition, if Mrs. Kaminski goes along with it, to have you take the ring back home with you, until we get this matter squared away. If your Father Lawrence is going to become a Bishop and this is the ring he wants, Mrs. Kaminski's will have to give her permission. She said she has the ownership papers and the inheritance papers on the ring. It's her choice to give it away. Get my drift, Monsignor?"

"You want me to take the ring home with me, and hope the killer doesn't follow me to my room at the retirement home. Is that what you're saying, Lieutenant? Isn't this evidence in a murder?"

Morrison responded. "Yes, to both questions. I don't think the murder can be proved based on unfounded claims causing Mr. Kaminski's death. If given Mrs. Kaminski permission I suggest you put the ring in a secure place. Mrs. Kaminski has no interest in keeping it. I get the impression she would be happy if it left her possession so she could get on with her life. Once we catch our killer or killers she'll be free to make a life for herself and maybe by then this matter of who gets the ring will be settled."

A smile came to Monsignor O'Toole's face. Morrison looked over to him, as he neared the precinct.

"What's the smile for, Monsignor?"

"I was just wondering about the day I show up with this ring and Father Lawrence questions me how I received it. It should prove very interesting."

Chapter 15

Monsignor O'Toole was dressed in a wool plaid shirt underneath his goose down jacket Betty had given him for Christmas. It was cold outside of Lt. Morrison's warmed and heated car. Both stepped out of the car and avoided the puddles of water and snow in front of the precinct. Once they came inside noise and racket filled their ears as drug dealers were being hustled through the precinct rooms to meet with detectives. Captain Antonnucci sat at his desk in a sealed off room reading reports. On the corner of his desk was a copy of the New York Daily News, as a reminder to every cop, without exception, that they were not above sordid review by these kinds of publication headline writers.

The two men passed between chairs lined up along detective's desks as they made their way toward the Captain's office. Morrison gave a thudding rap on the door. The Captain looked up and motioned to the two of them to come in. He set aside his paper work as Morrison closed the door to the glassed in cubicle.

"This is Monsignor O'Toole. He is Betty Ryan's character reference. Her story corroborates Mrs. Kaminski's about Quentin LaFayette's knowledge about a ring and LaFayette's involvement with the deceased in having the ring shown off to a Father Lawrence. Monsignor O'Toole knows Father Lawrence. As a matter of fact, Father Lawrence replaced him as pastor of the same church."

"How do you do, Monsignor? I'm not used to seeing you priests dressed like you came off a trip to the lodge." Antonnucci said to the priest and turned back to Lt. Morrison.

115

"I discussed the idea of relieving us of the Bishop's Ring with the Monsignor. He has agreed to take it back with him when he returns home. But we will need Mrs. Kaminski's permission. I think she will be happy to get rid of it. Then, we can truthfully say that we don't have the ring."

The Captain asked, "But does that plan throw out a ring connection to Quentin LaFayette? You get my drift? Are we throwing out our way of getting someone connected to this killing by giving the ring away? That's the only thing that bothers me about your suggestion."

Morrison responds. "First of all, LaFayette is not going to be told we got rid of the ring. He will still think either of two women can nail him. I might suggest to LaFayette there is a lady upstate who, will be told he killed his employee to get to his employees' wife. Let him stew over that. But he's got bigger problems. If the killer wants the ring and we don't say anything about it then the killer might assume that Quentin ended up with the ring and Quentin is looking for a bigger price for the ring."

Monsignor said, "So this is the way you deduce and come to your brilliant crime solving conclusions?" He heard how the two veteran cops might employ a variety of workable ploys in the course of turning up the heat on their suspects. The two policemen laughed.

"Lafayette is going to be easy in comparison. Getting to the people in the Polish Embassy, without enraging federal agencies or tipping them off and keeping it local could damage police future relations with other government agencies. Too many chefs in the kitchen could raise the consciousness of the killer." The Captain said.

Up to this point, the officers did not know who Piotrowski was. They knew he might be housed in the Polish Embassy. They were almost certain of one thing; Quentin LaFayette knew the man, his physical appearance and how to contact him.

The Captain said, "Shutters dropped these off. Does someone look familiar in this photo? It's only a side view. Have you seen that chin on a certain church designer?" He continued.

"The shot is the front of the Polish Embassy. Shutters took it."

Morrison added, "That's a pretty good make on Quentin LaFayette even though it's a side shot."

The Captain remarked, "Shutters took it when Murph was cruising. He's has more here you should look at. Get used to the faces! He's singled out the repeaters. That one is their limo, tagged. He's the driver. Here's 'Polish Harry.'" He used quote signs with his hands.

"Looks like I should be in contact with LaFayette again. The sooner the better! If this tall guy is the killer he could be out of here and we wouldn't know it, if he stayed inside the Embassy and never came out."

The Captain commented, "I'll have Murphy bring LaFayette in here for a little questioning. That way we will see him up close and watch his mannerisms. We'll hold him a while so you can talk with Mrs. Kaminski about the ring option plan. But you've got to get back here before some lawyer comes in here wanting to spring LaFayette loose."

"That could take several hours, Captain."

"Any excuse staying back and attending to the grieving?" Antonnucci fired back, with a wink in his eye toward the Monsignor."

"What kind of shape is this woman in?" The Monsignor asked.

"That lady is in fine shape, Monsignor, but I don't know how she's bearing up with the rest of this stuff." Morrison said. "You'll see she is in fine shape."

"Apparently, I had used a bad choice of words fellows for what you have been able to observe. I meant to ask about her mental condition. You say she has children? She just lost her husband. Some time has passed. And there is no burial? This is not normal from my years as a priest."

Morrison commented. "This is not a normal situation Monsignor. I think she's ready to see this thing through. The press will be given a statement after we interview LaFayette. If we book him it will go out to the press. It will depend upon what he tells us and how we take it from there. It will be up to her after the Medical Examiner releases Mr. Kaminski for her to make arrangements for the body. Her neighbors will be shocked. She knows that. They are going to be even a little bit more concerned when her house shows up empty and they come by to offer condolences."

The Monsignor asks, "So what is next?"

"We are going to visit her at her sister's apartment. There, we will talk about the ring and what she wants to do with it. My thinking is she would be better off not to have it than for someone to take it from her and we lose the evidence."

The Monsignor asked, "But you are willing to let me walk off with it?"

"I know where to reach you Monsignor if I have to come looking for you. I don't know where to go to look for our killer. I don't know what it would take to arrest him as of the moment. I have to find the weapon that was used to kill Kaminski, to collect samples of the poison compound that was found in Mr. Kaminski's bloodstream. There is the thing about diplomatic immunity if the killer is from the People's Republic of Poland. So we are going to have to play this one by ear for a while to see if we can find a way to get our killer to reveal himself. Right now we are thinking that our killer is here in America. The coroner says the compound is of foreign origin. That leads me to think that our killer is from the Polish Embassy."

The Monsignor asks, "Then what about LaFayette?"

The Captain responded, "Conspiracy to Murder."

Monsignor O'Toole took a back step with that remark. Morrison waved off the Captain to go to his police car. "Follow me, Monsignor, at least one of these guys we're tracking is usually found in a church." The clear implication of the remark to Monsignor O'Toole did not leave out the possibility that Father Lawrence may also be connected in the complicity charge of murder.

The two men went into the high-rise apartment building and found the "Klementowski" apartment. Marta, Magda's sister, answered the door and let the two men in. First, Lieutenant Morrison introduced himself and then Monsignor O'Toole whom he told her came along for a special reason.

Magda asked they be excused and they went into the bedroom her sister provided for her. The air was stuffy and smelled of perfumes, not something either man were use to smelling at least for a while for Morrison.

Lt. Morrison explained his idea to Magda to allow Monsignor O'Toole to hold onto the ring for security reasons. It was not, he admitted, police procedure to do this but he somehow felt compelled to make an exception in this case. He said he couldn't explain it but that is what he wanted to do with the ring. She smiled. And for a moment she pondered and finally nodded, yes.

Magda spoke up. "That is the way it is with those who hold onto the ring. It is as if it wants to have its own home. I know and understand your feeling Lieutenant. From time to time, the ring has always made us wonder when it has been a very bad time for us. Something urged us to make a change. That is why we left Buffalo. It is as if St. Stanislaw, the first Bishop who first wore it is watching over his own relic."

"Did you say, a saint's ring?" the Monsignor asked.

"Yes. St. Stanislaw of Cracow. I have the papers on this ring. I made a copy, if you want to read what my husband's cousin, a priest, translated into English. The belief is that it belongs on the hand of a Polish Bishop. But it really belongs to the Church."

"I don't think that is what someone had in mind when they invited Father Lawrence to look at it." Morrison said.

The priest spoke up. "I don't think Father Lawrence is Polish. Could be? Maybe his name was changed when his forefathers came to the country. To answer your suggestion, yes, I would like to read about the Bishop's Ring. Yes, I will take care of it if it is released to my custody."

Morrison said very little as he watched the two of them talk about the ring and she pointed out the paper she had with the ring and its importance to the Church of Poland. Morrison could see she was willing to take the chance upon a prelate member of the clergy as the best person to watch over the ring. When she stopped talking Morrison could see the happiness and relief in her eyes. He quickly rose from the chair in room and said he had to leave to go back and wait for LaFayette to be brought in for questioning.

In a very short time, the two of them were gone and Magda felt a weight had been lifted from her shoulders. She looked at her sister and said, "We should pray for the priest who now holds Poland's treasured relic ring. He will need our prayers. The devil is close by, I know that feeling."

Quentin LaFayette did not like being brought into the precinct. He was expecting some kind of formal conversation with the police. He knew they were not sitting around knitting. Sergeant Murphy's voice was firm. He hoped that Mr. LaFayette would cooperate in the investigation of what appeared to be a murder.

In the meantime, Morrison returned Monsignor O'Toole to LaGuardia. He called ahead to see if he could get the priest a return flight home. He was told an express flight was leaving in forty minutes so he stuck his emergency light out on top of his car and made his way through traffic in plenty of time for the priest to catch an upstate return flight. Morrison said he would be in touch, and returned to the precinct.

Captain Antonnucci was impressed with Morrison's timing and speedy return with his mission accomplished. Morrison was told LaFayette was being held down the hall. Morrison knew now timing was going to be important. He also knew he had throw a scare into LaFayette to get him to come clean. The killer was not going to wait and he did not know how long the police could hold off on the moving ploy before many questions were going to be asked.

"We got our work cut out for us." The Captain said. The man's got to have a weakness. All killer's do. See if you can pry his weakness out of LaFayette. Put the burden on the Pole. We need twenty-four hour surveillance on both men. We have to see what he does outside of that building. We've got to see where the Pole eats and what he does for fun."

Chapter 16

Lieutenant Morrison began, "Mr. LaFayette, let's get off to a good start. We are here to ask questions and if everything is satisfactory you will be able to go back home or to your office depending on the time we finish. Is that understood?" Quentin LaFayette nodded sitting in the chair looking at the tape recorder wheel turning as Morrison spoke.

"We are recording our conversation because we want to have a statement when it is all over. You are not being placed under arrest at this time. We are investigating the homicide of one of your employees. We appreciate your willingness to come in and discuss what you think happened to Mr. Kaminski. We'll let you begin."

LaFayette asked, "Do I need an attorney here? Now?"

"If you think you do I will read you your Miranda Rights. Before arresting you can have an attorney present. I can't decide for you. You tell me, what you want, and we will go with that."

LaFayette noted the casual attitude of Morrison. He did not want to be arrested because his name would appear on the Police Blotter for reporters to see. So LaFayette decided to cooperate. The police, he reasoned, might think he was guilty of being part of a crime if he needed an attorney. He looked at Morrison, and shook his head, "No."

"Just tell us what you know. If we think of a question, we'll ask it, and hope to get a response from you. If you think you want an attorney to represent you, at that time we will cut off all conversation, so your civil rights are protected. Do you understand us?"

He nodded. "You'll have to answer loud, so the tape machine operator can later take your responses off the machine."

"Tell us your name, address, occupation, how long you have been doing what you do." LaFayette complied.

"Tell us who Conrad Kaminski was to you."

LaFayette looked up, "He was my employee for many years. He worked on some of my jobs, like the foreman. He did some design work but some of it was left to the younger fellows. He was a key guy in my company. We had design differences. He was more traditional and safe. If you know what I mean."

"Does it mean he was treated like a 'Key man' in the company? Did he have privileges? Come and go as he pleased?"

"Yes, I treated him well, as best I could afford. He worked for me for at least eight years. We talked and shared experiences."

"Did he ever tell you about a ring he had that had special significance?"

LaFayette spoke, "He was not a showy man. Very modest. Made the best of his money. He could not afford to be a jewelry hound. You know what I mean?"

Morrison stayed on course. "That wasn't the question, Mr. LaFayette. Did he tell you about a ring he had?"

"Yes. He showed one to me once. Very beautiful."

"Did he tell you anything about the ring of a significant nature?"

Quentin could see the Lieutenant had some information and should be careful how he answered Morrison's questions. "Yes, I believe he did say that it once belonged to a Bishop, or something like that. He said he got it in an inheritance from a cousin who was a priest."

"Is that so?" Morrison acted astonished in order to put Quentin off guard. He let Quentin think this was a new revelation and he fished for the next question; hoping Quentin would fill in the blanks.

Morrison continued, "Well, if it belonged to a Bishop, it was probably blessed wouldn't you say? As a blessed object it could not be sold in a transaction say for money according to church rules. Right? I mean you would know more about that stuff in your line of work dealing with Churches and their sacred objects."

"That's about right Lieutenant."

Morrison noted his attitude. "So if a person killed to get a blessed religious object, which happened to be a ring, and then tried to sell it, well, what would he be doing?"

"The Church would call it a sacrilege, first."

"That's the Church talking. I'm thinking the person would be killing somebody for some good reason beyond a fancy religious ring. Wouldn't you agree?" LaFayette said, "Yes."

"And for someone to do that it's has got to be important to him or her to do this beyond the value of a ring which wouldn't get much in a pawnshop."

LaFayette disagreed. "Conrad's ring was special. It would bring in a good buck."

"No, I'm not thinking like that. This killing for a ring had nothing to do with the melted down value of the gold. He did it for some other reason then. I'm struggling with this Mr. LaFayette because I can't think of a man giving up his life for a ring. Especially one that has no other useful purpose than to sit on someone's hand, excuse me, a Bishop's hand. It doesn't make sense. Don't you agree that would be a terrible reason for Mr. Kaminski to give up his life?"

"Yes, of course, yes. I feel terrible about it. I was away on a cruise when it happened."

"Yes, your secretary said so when this thing happened to Mr. Kaminski. So you were nowhere in sight when his killing happened. Out of the country so to speak." He stopped for a moment, but only to switch to another line of questions.

"Mrs. Kaminski tells me, she does not have the ring, and Mr. Kaminski left her a note telling her you had asked him to bring the ring in to show to a Father Lawrence. She's grieving badly, you know. At least I'm sure you can imagine. She seems a little confused about all of this because according to Mrs. Kaminski she said her husband always took great care over this particular ring. So, did you tell Mr. Kaminski to show his ring to this priest you knew?

Quentin LaFayette began to squirm in his chair as a bead of perspiration came forward on his forehead. He tried to appear to be relaxed but now the questions were not so simple to answer. He did not know what the Lieutenant had uncovered or how much work had been done to come this far. Was the officer trying to trick him by saying she said she did not have the ring?

Surprised, he asked, "She doesn't have the ring?"

"No, Mr. LaFayette, I ask the questions. Did you ask Mr. Kaminski to show his ring to a priest friend or client of yours?"

"I may have casually mentioned it to him in passing. Father Lawrence is a very astute priest when it comes to the particulars of rubrics, er, explaining decorative art and ceremonies. As I remembered the ring had a beautiful red ruby in the center setting. We discussed it was the color to signify the rank of a Bishop in the Church. You can imagine from our work we would pay attention to such matters because our job when consulting is to inform pastors of the more sublime forms in sacred art."

"So, this Father Lawrence was a priest who took more than an average interest in such things? He would fly down here just to look at a ring, Mr. LaFayette?"

"Well, this wasn't just any ring, Lieutenant. Conrad said it was a Bishop's Ring. Father Lawrence is a client of mine. He was interested in seeing the ring."

"But a dead Bishop's ring is a dead Bishop's ring, Mr. LaFayette. It can't be sold as you say. So, was Conrad Kaminski expected to give this ring to Father Lawrence?"

"I think Father Lawrence had a genuine interest in the ring for its ecclesiastical value."

"Mr. LaFayette, I am investigating a murder. A man does not get killed because of something he owns which he cannot sell morally according to his conscience. He had it a long time. Do you sense my frustration here, Mr. LaFayette? If all you did was to put him in touch with this Father Lawrence to show him a ring that would be okay. But in the process Mr. LaFayette, your employee was killed. The ring is gone and Mrs. Kaminski has a note telling her you sent her husband to the airport to show off the ring to a priest."

Quentin sat silent. Did Piotrowski lie to him? Did he pick up the Bishop's Ring and now he was not going to pay? The promise was five hundred thousand dollars. Did Piotrowski set him up to take the fall? With Conrad dead and no one in sight according to the questions the police were firing at him was the Polish Government lying about the half million-dollar offer for the ring? Or was it all a set up? Why did Piotrowski kill Conrad? He didn't have to kill him! He was only going to drug him and mug him in the men's room and take the ring. This is not the way it was supposed to be. Now Conrad was dead and he is the man who sent him to his death. It was becoming very clearer now to Quentin he may have been a part of a very elaborate scheme to get the ring. The Poles could slip their man out of the country and he, as the police have framed it, would be the only connection to the ring and Conrad's death.

Quentin did not respond to the last statement. He kept his head down. Morrison moved on in his questions.

"You said Conrad Kaminski was a key man in your organization." Quentin nodded. "And so you took out life insurance on him in the event of his death, for a period of time you would need to replace someone. You purchased Key Man insurance on him!"

Quentin, looking down, without much movement, said in a low tone. "Yes." "Did you have an intention of offering him a partnership portion of your business?"

"Not at this point. But it was feasible. He was not an outside contact person. In this business you need to travel to find the work. He was not interested in traveling so it made it difficult for me to see him in a role where he could bring in business."

Morrison continued to probe. "Couldn't you hire someone to make the calls on your clients and still offer Mr. Kaminski a partnership because of the worth of the man's work and the time he spent with you developing the firm's reputation?"

Quentin raised his eyebrows, and shrugged. "It was possible, I suppose. I traveled a lot. I was concentrating my thoughts on contract sales building the business."

"Did you have any other life insurance on the man's life? Like, did you offer his wife and family protection if he should suddenly leave this earth?"

"Yes, yes, of course."

"And Mr. LaFayette, how much did you carry on Mr. Kaminski's life that benefited you, and how much would his family get as a benefit?"

"It was term insurance, no cash value. It was just something to have just in case. The Key Man policy was for five hundred thousand and the widow insurance was for four hundred thousand dollars."

"So you are saying he was sufficiently insured. You and his wife could start new, fresh should he die."

"She would have something until a transition took place. Maybe she would... I don't know what she would do. I would need that kind of money to be able to stay back from the road for a while until I trained someone to take over Conrad's duties."

"Do you like, Mrs. Kaminski, Mr. LaFayette? I mean do you really like Mrs. Kaminski to the point you might have a romantic interest in her? She is an attractive woman. When this story hits the newspapers and it's learned that you set her up with an insurance policy you know how people are, Mr. LaFayette. Some will question your intentions."

"Lieutenant, it was not expensive to do. It was for Conrad's family. It's not extraordinary. You just do it because it is the right thing to do."

"But don't you see, Mrs. Kaminski and you are going to be paid an awful lot of money and the insurance companies may get a little suspicious about your motives in all of this. You have to think of those guys back there at the insurance companies cutting a couple of checks totaling nine hundred grand. Would they be suspicious about the two of you getting together and sailing off into the sunset for a while? You get my drift?"

"People are going to think what they want to think Lieutenant. Mrs. Kaminski is a very fine lady." He said nervously. "If you knew her well you would see that about her. Besides that she is pretty. I'll admit to that. I'd be a fool not to it's too obvious. Any one looking at her, would say, yeah, the guy had the interest in her and maybe... but it wasn't that way. I didn't see her that often. She stayed out on the Island. She never wanted to come into the city. So let's not start something here that isn't in the picture. I'm not your killer if that is what you're leading to with your questions."

"Too many coincidences, Mr. LaFayette. We police have to look into every avenue for answers. Do you have any suggestions as to who might be the killer?"

"I think you put your finger on it, Lieutenant."

Morrison quickly responded, "What's that?"

"It may be someone who wants a beautiful woman and is willing to kill her husband to get her?"

"So you are suggesting the motive for killing Conrad Kaminski is to get to her? It doesn't make sense. You said yourself she is a housewife who stays out on the Island. They aren't flashy people."

"But, she's beautiful. I would think someone who fills his head with fantasies about beautiful women is a likely candidate for your killer."

"You are not much help. Mr. LaFayette. The world is filled with men with fantasies about beautiful women. Look at the circulation of the girlie magazines. Look at Playboy Magazine and how many copy cats are there now?"

"In my business Lieutenant I look at angles. Lots of them! All the time! I try to shape and mold columns and pillars and create forms. I look at a lot of angles before I settle on the right one which fits what we want to achieve. Sometimes I have to reach beyond what I am doing to come up with a unique answer. That is what I am saying to you. Look beyond. Mrs. Kaminski may be the real target of your killer."

"I'll think about that angle Mr. LaFayette."

The new direction suddenly startled Lt. Morrison. Could it be true the killer wanted to get to Mrs. Kaminski and the ring had nothing to do with it? Was that the killer's weakness? Was LaFayette diverting attention from himself by cleverly suggesting the beautiful lady was the source of the trouble? If that were true then the photos he and Shutters took and connected to the rented car from the People's Republic of Poland Embassy may be an angle to explore. But why a Long Island housewife when in Manhattan hundreds of thousands of beautiful women work within blocks of each other if all the killer wanted was to find a beautiful woman to dream about?

What else was it about the Kaminski's that attracted the attention of the Polish Government's embassy? Of course there would be the normal denials if they were questioned about the interest. Going that route would end up with a closed door in the face.

A frustrated LaFayette asked, "Is that all, Lieutenant?"

"Almost. This will be typed up. You'll have to stick around to sign this statement. Don't leave town for a while. Call me if you have an out –of-town business appointment. I can tell you are not in the best of shape on this thing. I've got to meet with the Captain. A statement has to be released to the press. Your company's name will be involved in the statement. So expect the press. I would talk this over with your lawyer. I'll be honest. It looks bad for you unless we find a killer." Morrison could not place him at the scene of the crime and he did not have a co-conspirator to corroborate LaFayette's role with the crime.

He wanted to say more to LaFayette to rattle him but that might force the designer to make statements to the press to cover his butt so he could not be linked with Magda Kaminski. The Lieutenant wanted Magda kept out of the publicity cycle.

Morrison's last words, "Oh, by the way if you're concerned about Conrad Kaminski's family don't mention anything about them if the news hounds come calling." The Lieutenant was firm in his advice to LaFayette.

Chapter 17

Quentin LaFayette's suggestion there may be more for Lt. Morrison to look into for a motive did not deter the policeman from continuing to think that LaFayette and the priest had an involvement in Conrad Kaminski's murder. The priest may have been an unwitting accomplice, nevertheless, involved because he was the link, which brought a killer and the deceased together. Morrison didn't swallow LaFayette's explanation about Father Lawrence interest in sacred art as his reason for the stopover in New York en route to a Caribbean vacation.

Morrison walked into the Captain's office. "You're right, Captain. Again. It's the second time in, a... week. LaFayette came up with another pearl. The killer was out to get Mrs. Kaminski. That's what LaFayette thinks. He got my attention. He makes sense, to kill her husband to get to her. He thinks the killer had a romantic interest in her. It makes her vulnerable. He makes it look like she needs protection. A stalker? It's possible."

Morrison said to Al, "From Shutters' and your photo prints we have a make. We found our movie look-a-like in two places, Manhattan and Long Island within a close time frame on the same day. I didn't let on to LaFayette we had a photo of him with our movie look alike. Saving one just in case we need to spill it on him."

The Captain dropped a bunch of photos onto the desk. He said, "We got our "Porno Pole" here with a long lens camera getting into the limo. Shutters used his 210-meter lens. Brought him close up."

"Why did you call him Porno Pole?" Morrison asked.

Al laughed, "Last two nights the boys followed him to 42nd Street. He dressed like a cowboy with a Texas ten-gallon hat. He stood in front of a porno theater and watched the women as they walked by. The guys were up the street in an unmarked car. They think he wanted to be noticed with his Hollywood looks. He went in to the dump got his fill and came out. Got in a cab. They followed him to Queens. That's right. Queens! Northern Boulevard. Then lost the cab in traffic. Got his cab number. We're checking to see where the cabby dropped him off. The guy lives a double life. By day, he works in an embassy. By night, he's a foreign cowboy, riding the 42nd Street range, looking to be a cow poker."

Morrison countered, "the Klementowskis live off Northern Boulevard." Morrison said with a sudden sense of seriousness. "My guess is he knows where the Klementowskis live and he probably keeps a glass or a camera lens on their apartment. Do we have any more shots of this guy other than with LaFayette? We ought to have a sketch made up to look like him and circulate it along the street but put the guy in a cowboy suit. We'll see if anyone recognizes him. If word gets back to him he'll think he got one over us thinking we are looking for a cowboy. He won't know what it's for. It might also keep him in Manhattan and not in Queens. He might have an apartment in one of the adjacent buildings to spy on the two sisters. Who is on this recon?"

The Captain said, "Rogers. By the way, you have a problem with him and the guy on Airport security when Kaminski was hit. They know about the ring. Rogers asked about it. Wanted to know what we did with it. I jokingly said you tossed it in the river. Rogers looked at me like I lost it. Talk to him. His tongue could slip, and he could let out a wrong word to a reporter, without even realizing it.

"Okay. I'm going to detail Rogers to the boulevard with the sketch." Then Morrison asks, "Is it okay to talk to Joe Mancusi?"

The Captain asks, "The psychologist?"

"Yes. We have to find out who and what we are dealing with here. The guy leads a double life. He murders in a suit, but dresses in cowboy clothes. I think he can't make up his mind who he is!

The Captain shrugged, "Go ahead, the cowboy's a weirdo."

The receptionist opened the door to Dr. Mancusi's Office. "Come in, Lieutenant. Your call sounded urgent. I had a cancellation so I can fit you in. What can I do for you?"

"I appreciate you taking me on such short notice, Doctor. Send the bill to the department for the consulting time." Lt. Morrison shifted in his seat as he tried to make himself comfortable. "You haven't read about this killing yet. We got a situation where, we think the killer's a diplomat. But he is not really a diplomat. He masquerades as one. A guy has been murdered. A person we've talked to says the murder motive may not be as we might think it is. Our source is under the gun to come up with some answers because he could be fingered in the hit. The guy who did the killing, our source says, killed for a different reason than steal from the dead man. Our source says the killer wants the dead man's wife. Sounds like a diversion?"

"Could be, go on."

"Our suspect may be hiding something. What I am looking for is some kind of motive that would send a sex fiend to kill a man so he could get to his wife. The dead man carried an art object on his person when he was killed. If our informant is telling the truth with the woman angle the art object the killer was supposed to have killed for is his diversion. If that works, then we will be looking for a sex fiend."

Dr. Mancusi asks, "Are you talking about the guy killed at the airport? I heard it over the news in the last hour. That one?"

"That one." Morrison did not reveal news of the killing was delayed.

"You move fast. You have a suspect already? It didn't sound like that from the radio report."

"A phony diplomat can skip the country in a jet plane and never come back. We don't want to give out too much information. Just enough to keep reporters happy."

"Tell me more. But first, based on what you said, she must be beautiful, right? Nobody risks arrest unless the prize is worth it."

"Oh, she worth it all right! We also have reason to believe he is someone who may have photographed her, even stalked her. He's like a 'KGB' type. The guy who died was injected from a sharp instrument with a poison compound not used around here, the coroner says is, meaning the U.S. We also think the killer may be holed up near where the widow is staying until this thing blows over. She has a sister here in Queens, and she is staying with her. She's got her two kids with her. It's tight and they are cooped up."

"So little to go on. The dead man, is he foreign born?"

Morrison responds, "Yes. Poland. Other than our suspect, we think the killer wanted the murdered man's one of a kind art treasure. His attack was foiled. He failed to steal it. We also think he is still active in pursuit of it and the wife."

Dr. Mancusi interrupted, "How long have these Poles been here?"

Morrison says, "More than twenty years, I would imagine."

Dr. Mancusi continued, "Do you have an age on your suspect."

"Fifty, somewhere in there. Close to her age if that is what you are driving at."

The doctor responded. "You don't know what goes on in those foreign embassy offices. You think they are there for trade purposes but I know from my patient lists foreigners living here are regularly checked out. The government is looking for spies. Foreigners get pretty paranoid because they have relatives back home. Or, they don't know if it's our government or their former one which is doing the checking on them. Those foreign grudge matches can last a lifetime."

Morrison asks, "Help me out on this, please."

"I had a patient give me a lesson years ago. He was a German immigrant who came here with a couple of degrees in electrical engineering. He could only get a gardener job when he started working here. He told me what went on in Germany after World War I and the rise of Nazis. Germans had no money. Widespread starvation. Germans lost their property to wealthy investors who had the money. Property transfers were 'sub-Rosa,' but on the books of what we call county government. To live up to his political promises Hitler went to people who had the money to have them loan money to the government. He failed.

"He went to the biggest, the Rothschilds, a prominent German family famous for supplying European governments with vast amounts of money, and spy information services. The Rothschild's, for example, spied for the British and provided vital subsidies for those who opposed Napoleon, and brought about his defeat. I checked out my patient's story.

"It appears it's the Rothschild flair to profit from either victory or defeat. The original Rothschild, Nathan, aside from being financially very smart benefited from his spy network. In Napoleon's day, carrier pigeons carried news back to London in one day of the allied victory over Napoleon at Waterloo. Frightened London Stock Exchange investors, worried over the war, sold all of their shares. Old Nathan bought them up preventing the stock exchange from collapsing. His methods of intrigue brought about his successes. The family prospered. They had a family monopoly for the flotation of large international loans.

"More to the point, this patient told me when Hitler approached the Rothschild's for loans to prop up Germany, the Rothschild Bankers wanted 15% interest on their money, when the going rate was 3%. The banker wanted five times more! This enraged Hitler, who by then knew who were the wealthy people with businesses, art and treasures, and land holdings. Unlike the average person, the wealthy business people were less inconvenienced by the long standing economic Depression in Germany when Hitler came to power. A banker's greed invited heavy consequences to follow. Those who seek revenge will stop at nothing to destroy an enemy who would deny them. The point of the story relates to that art object you spoke about. Obviously, your killer suspect has a mission other than diplomatic. He serves a purpose for Poland. The art object, if it is something important, may have value beyond money, something more intrinsic, which the government wants, in the hierarchy of motives, I would say, for its own protection."

Morrison was left to wonder with his conclusion. "We have spies among us, traitorous men working in U.S. government offices like Jonathon Pollard who spied and provided vital secrets for Israel. We give them billions every year to provide for their protection. Why does Israel spy on us? Why?"

Mancusi smiled and said, "It's a simple answer, really. Men do two things in their motivation. They act to either make a gain or avoid a loss. Stealing secrets, like patents, weapons, art, political policies, have great value. They can be sold, bartered, used for bribery and graft and many other purposes for a spying nation. By these examples, the art object you say the murdered man owned obviously is worth killing for.

"What's the state of the killer's mind now?" Morrison asked.

The doctor responded. "News will awaken the community to this crime. He's got to be alert. He could become violent if he thinks he is a caged animal. Maybe he will hide behind his credentials! Then we have a different breed of animal. If he is a KGB type he is trained in cunning. He knows how you operate more than likely. He knows what to look for as signs if he thinks he is being trailed, because he is, one of you. He is trained, perhaps better than you.

"Now given that set of circumstances, there are the inner fears he has as a human being. He's also an animal with self-preservation instincts. Behind one's anger is fear. If the fear is dealt with sometimes the anger goes away. People who have anger problems who recognize them as problems can sublimate them. Some have cured themselves by turning inward to prayer if it is appropriate. Or they can find a space away from everyone and shout out the fear and anger by admitting it. That is a first step. He does not want to be cured."

Morrison interrupted, "Let me tell you, it is a religious object which is in play here. It's represents power to those who have it."

"Are you talking about a holy relic?" The doctor asked.

Morrison responded, "Yes."

The doctored waited and said, "Let me finish what I was saying. Now, you said he could be fifty years old. Fifty years ago, we were in a war. People got killed. Life was certainly abusive in the worst sense from the war and what followed. Fear propels Communists to want power. Power is driven by competition and egotism. If he is a Communist playing the party line that ideology has been his god. But you don't have to be a Communist to want power."

"How about a priest? Does fear propel him to gain power?"

The doctor asked, "Want power? A priest has all the power he needs. He brings Christ incarnate down upon his altar everyday!"

Morrison suggested, "You know what I mean. The power of success?"

"Ah, that kind of power!" The psychologist responded. "It may fulfill the need to overcome a failure or to compete or for not being forgiven. Fear as we know will propel the motion to succeed. When Catholics go to confession to a priest in the act of forgiveness the priest offers absolution. As a Catholic I know Grace comes with confessing sins. It is a way of curing oneself of many hidden fears.

"On a personal note, I lost weight by confessing I overindulged in food. I knew the problem, but Grace wiped away the desire to overeat."

Morrison said, "I'll have to remember that when I retire."

The doctor continued. "Confession takes away fears of punishment. Every priest knows that. The forgiveness of sin in a confession to a priest takes away large guilt burdens. The priest is dealing with them on a higher level, the soul, helping the sinner justify himself before God. A priest has all the power he needs. He offers certainty of forgiveness, which the Son of God, Christ, understood. I can't remove sin. I help people overcome their problems on a human plane. If sin is involved only God through his ordained priest acting for Christ has the power to forgive a penitent's sins."

"It's nice to know you don't play God, doctor." Morrison remarked. The doctor looked at his watch to check his time. He went back to talking about Communists.

"Communists are abusive of human rights. Secret Police, KGB types, don't believe in forgiveness of sin, because they neither believe nor fear God. You see, sadly, they need a way to get some satisfaction, and that way is to see others suffer or to becoming a hero."

Morrison picked up one his statements. "So, our killer and potential killer is a person who might want to get even for something he might think has been done to him personally or to Poland, or both?"

"It's a possible theory, Lieutenant. You may know something about the man who was killed. Maybe in this warped mind of the killer the deceased did do something the killer thought deserved his

135

death. People take out their revenge in warped ways." He stopped and magnified his point.

"The anger one carries inside may kill oneself with a heart attack. Anger is self-defeating. So is the plotting of evil against others. It does terrible things to the psyche. Look at the Middle East! Anger and greed set people to go off the deep end. It's why the rest of us think they are crazy."

"Does he have to kill again?" Morrison asked.

"It may be counterproductive if he does. But if his feelings are strong enough it may be his only avenue of release in his warped view of life. He or she may wear an expensive suit but is capable of very sinister behavior. On the other hand, tormentors enjoy tormenting victims with all forms of harassment. I don't have to tell you how many ways people are victimized this way."

"I think we have talked enough doctor I've got work to do. You struck a nerve. I've got to see the widow. Maybe she can fill me in some background."

"Good luck. Call me, if you need me."

Chapter 18

The Captain grunted, "Lieutenant Moe," the F.B.I. is in on this."

"Who is in charge?" Morrison asked.

"We are. They called and will cooperate." The Captain responded.

Morrison quickly reacted. "We need a make on the 'Cowboy'. Can they get that? We need to know how long he has been here. Is he someone who comes and goes or someone with a semi-permanent status? We need to know his access to flights in and out of the country. Maybe they can tell us if they have anything on him. Did Rogers get that sketch out of Fred Heymann, yet?" Morrison was full of questions.

"Yeah. It's good, too. Last time I saw Rogers he was off to the copier to make copies. He should still be here. We made up two sketches, one to show the street and one to show Mrs. Kaminski. We're are going to give the stores the cowboy sketch but they will know he's a 'suit.' In case he catches on and goes to his suits then they will also have a chance to identify him with a shirt and tie. That shot of Shutters' close up his nose is clear as a bell. But it's been sketched to make it appear that it's a drawing. We're telling the stores around Mrs. Kaminski's sister's apartment building to keep a watch for a limo in the area. They'll see limo's but not too many dropping off passengers."

"Thanks, Captain. That's a ... three this week. Keep up the fair work!"

"Get out of here, Moe."

Morrison stopped by Buddy Roger's desk. He was sitting looking at the composites Heymann sketched. "Is this what the suspect looks like?"

"One of them." Rogers said without looking up.

"You mean there is more than one." Morrison queried.

"Don't know yet. Did Smitty say anything about a priest being in the area when the deceased collapsed on the floor over at LaGuardia?"

Rogers responded. "Didn't say anything about a priest. Where'd the priest come in? If a priest was there, don't you think he'd come over and look at the body? I mean, it's part of their thing. Last rites, and all that stuff."

"Yes, your right. But if the priest was wearing vacation clothes, who would know if he was a priest? That's another angle."

Rogers asked, "What's with the priest business?"

"Don't know myself, Buddy. Listen get those out as soon as you can. We are going to need some men dispatched to the area. Get with the captain on that. Let me know on a private line on how you make out. I'm going to see the widow to see if she can draw her own sketch. Maybe I'll find out something." He hesitated.

"Oh, by the way Buddy, before I leave. The Ring?"

"Yeah?"

"You didn't see it! I'll tell you later. Shut Smitty up too. I'll tell you about it when this thing get unraveled. Right now say nothing, especially to the Feds. We'll save ourselves some time and worry. Got that?"

"Yeah."

Morrison came out of the precinct and looked up and down the street to see if he was being watched. He walked to his unmarked car opened the door and slid in. Within seconds he was gone and away from the police station. As a security measure he drove around Queens with what appeared to be no apparent purpose hoping to see if he was being trailed by anyone. The cars that followed him appeared to have destinations. He pulled up to a pay phone located in the parking lot of a convenience store and rolled down his car window. He called the Klementowski residence. Marta's husband Maximillian answered. Morrison told him he had to speak with Magda. She came to the phone. He was brief. He had to see her and ask her some important questions. They had to be alone he told her at first and then maybe she could include the other adults, but keep the children out of this.

Then he called into Rogers to have some security force with the unmarked cars pulling duty in the Northern Boulevard section where he was going to be parked to keep an eye on the area to see if anyone was following him. When he arrived near the Klementowski apartment building, he plugged in his earpiece to the police radio inside of his trench coat, picked up an attaché case where he kept his files on the case, and quickly moved toward the front entrance. His eyes were on the adjoining building's upper floors.

Mr. Klementowski answered the door quickly. He looked through the peephole and unlocked the door and let Morrison inside. Klementowski did his customary nodding and handshake. Then he directed Morrison to the living room where Magda was waiting. Morrison asked for privacy with Magda for a little while and then they all could talk, he said.

She directed Morrison to the perfumed bedroom.

Morrison asked her, "Are you okay?"

She nodded, her face saddened by the reality she was now alone and for the first time in her life she was vulnerable. She was without someone to protect her. While he lived, Conrad was her protector. When he walked with her or talked to her he was her friend, advisor, lover, husband and strength. Their coming together, so strange as to how it happened, had a knowing long lasting bonding character to their relationship. They sensed, as the years passed, the bond went beyond the physical realm of having intimate pleasure onto the metaphysical realm, they recognized more than love kept them together. Together they held something precious. It had meaning. They felt God's miracle would be worked. The day was coming when the Bishop's Ring would be placed on the hand of a Polish Bishop.

Above all Magda had in the years since leaving Poland become a realist. There was nothing romantic about being sought or hunted.

Buffalo was where the people of St. Casimir's parish greeted them with open arms. But Buffalo was also the place they had to leave because as they were told by sources they trusted inquiries were being made and suspicious circumstances were noticeable. The Kaminski's were not alone. Other Poles who left Poland often suspected "trailers" were watching and reporting on their fellow Poles to the godless rulers back in Poland.

Morrison began, "Mrs. Kaminski we are looking into some new information about your husband's death. So you understand..."

Magda looked up at him, and nodded.

Morrison began, "For a moment let's forget about the Bishop's Ring. Let's concentrate on the killer who wanted to harm you or your husband. The ring is only secondary. Is that something I would be right in assuming?"

"My husband and I have no enemies, Lieutenant."

He reminded, "But you left Poland, and you said something about the Security Service Police to me and how your husband used to work in the underground movement."

"That was so long ago. I know Communists have long memories and they like to punish people but..."

"Didn't you leave Buffalo because you were being chased out of there?"

Magda was suddenly jarred from Morrison's cryptic questions. "Yes, we were."

The detective reached into his attaché case and pulled out his manila file folder. "I have a picture of a man I would like you to tell me see if you can identify him." He slid the 8 x 10 glossy prints out and laid them on her lap as she sat in the chair. "Think about Poland and the past, does he have a familiar look of someone you may have known in the past?"

Magda stared at the picture. It was a clear shot of a man who had lines on his face, a strong jaw and a muscular frame. Suddenly and without warning, she let out a roaring scream, throwing the photo prints on her lap. Startled by her screams her sister and her brother-in-law came running into the bedroom. Morrison could see that he had found a hidden secret of terrible pain and wondered if she was going to continue to scream. Her screams would alert neighbors something terrible was going on in the apartment. Morrison needed security, and he did not need any additional police coming to this address.

Quickly, he gathered the photo prints as Marta grabbed her sister and hugged her. Morrison put his index finger to his closed mouth and signed to her brother-in-law know there should be silence. Maximillian Klementowski moved toward his sister-in-law and put his hand over her mouth. She looked at the detective her eyes bulging over his hand on her face while her body heaved back and forth as she tried to gain her breath. Slowly the four of them settled down. Magda looked at them and pointed to the pictures.

Morrison handed the pictures to Maximillian. His wife looked at them and tears formed quickly in her eyes. The detective could see they knew this man and he had either a good suspect or a killer. He did not know if they thought he was the killer or if they actually knew the man in the photos. No words had passed for several minutes as Mrs. Kaminski calmed herself down and the neighbors heard no additional screams coming from the apartment.

Magda's fear that Morrison had witnessed was not irrational. How was he going to leave the apartment building without people peeking from behind closed window drapes? His efforts to arrive and leave without notice, so as to not alert others about his activities, were now in jeopardy. He was going to have to think of a way out of this predicament.

"This man," Magda began, "I believe it is the same man, who was not a man, I mean, he was a soldier in Poland. I remember the face, he... tried to rape me in my father's barn. But it was so many years ago. I tried to forget. I remember the face, yes, the face."

Marta blurted in, "It was Conrad who came by coming home from work and stopped him from doing it."

"He tried to rape me but he did not succeed." Magda said. "Conrad was older and stronger. And the soldier was probably scared of what the people would do to him if they caught him. It happened in our small village. But that is also how I met Conrad for the first time."

"Mrs. Kaminski are you sure this is the same man?

Now she was defiant. "How is it you have a photo of this man?"

Morrison responded, "You said the Polish Security Service Police might be after you. We are just taking photos of people we know about are operatives of the Polish Embassy. This face turned up as one of the photos. We pieced a connection through a process of elimination. You have to be absolutely sure this is the man. For your sake we can build something around this case without involving the Bishop's Ring in the investigation. If the killer's superiors did send him here to get the ring and they connect him with a murder for something in the past then they might let him hang out to dry. We can establish a motive for the killing. The ring does not have to enter into it. The only bad part of that is that it might take LaFayette out of the case. I am not so sure about how much he is involved. He stood to collect insurance money for your husband's death. But he did make provisions for you to collect as well."

"What happens next?" Maximillian asked. "I have two women here who can identify this man. Are they in danger?"

The Lieutenant pulled his file out again and took the sketch of the cowboy out. "Does this man look familiar in this neighborhood?"

"It's him, isn't it?" Maximillian asked. "Yeah, he looks familiar. A guy who looks like this lives in that building over there." Maximillian pointed to the closest apartment building. "I've seen him come around here at night. What got my eye was his cowboy outfit. A Texan lives in New York? That's what I the first thought when I saw him."

"Clever masquerade disguise. That's all." Morrison said,

Morrison looked at Magda. "Stay inside the apartment. We are moving you again. We are going to keep an eye on that building putting a security watch on it and on this one. Get ready to pack and move again. I'll be in touch soon."

Morrison packed up his attaché case. Then looked at Maximillian. "I'm going to need your help to get out of here without people wondering what went on here a few minutes ago. I want you to start laughing loudly as I start to leave and pretend everything is happy and wonderful in here. People may not have caught on who is staying here yet and why she is staying here. But they would understand laughter as a sign everything is okay in here."

Magda looked at Morrison with a smile. She had calmed herself down. She knew this policeman had her best interests at heart. Although now she had much to fear he seemed to be taking this one step at a time and she had to trust him.

Maximillian laughed heartily as he closed the door on Morrison. If they did look out people might think he was a salesman with his attaché case. He was parked far enough away that maybe they would not see the small antenna coming out of his car trunk. It would be a dead give away that he was a policeman.

Now Morrison had a clear make on Conrad's killer. The man got his revenge on Conrad. What next? Morrison could only pray to God Magda was not going to be the target of another murder connected to him in his life. He wanted to retire in peace when he retired.

Chapter 19

Monsignor O'Toole knew he could not in good conscience keep the information about the Bishop's Ring from Bishop O'Farrell. There was going to be a lot of news stories. Morrison left him with the distinct impression that Father Lawrence may be called in on the investigation if Morrison was unable to solve the mystery of why Conrad Kaminski was killed. When that news of the murder hit the papers or airwaves questions would come up. Perhaps someone would find out about the ring. Morrison didn't know if Father Lawrence was going to be able to escape scrutiny. What the Monsignor did know was that Bishop O'Farrell did not need to be surprised or embarrassed by Father Lawrence's attempts to prove he was a sacred art scholar.

Betty Ryan was certainly going to be disappointed and hurt by the unfolding events exposing Quentin LaFayette's motives. She was going to find out she had been used by him. She had been the first to help and find a "Father Lawrence."

The drive back from the airport to the Prelate's residence at the retirement home allowed him to wonder what brought Father Lawrence into this mess. O'Toole's spiritual insights taught him God allows evil to take place. But for those with faith and trust, God can turn evil into good. Father Lawrence wouldn't be the first priest who was motivated to build the parish plant, for the recognition and maybe even power. LaFayette would be faulted when people were asked to make sacrifices and pay for unnecessary changes in the Church plant. O'Toole's mantra has always been Christ requires that the gospel be preached. All other things take second priority. Had Father Lawrence forgotten?

Monsignor O'Toole saved his own judgment. It was for the Bishop to make a judgment on Father Lawrence's behavior. Perhaps others would be this way if they had inherited debt free parishes. But many parishes were in debt or had very little money to deal with. While St. Catherine of Siena parish, thanks to the generosity of the Dwyer family Education Trust Fund, it earned enough income to pay for extraordinary expenses associated with the parish school, thereby allowing Sunday collections to be used for the parish maintenance. Now, the prelate wondered about the fund. Had it been used for God's greater glory and honor?

The question Monsignor O'Toole contemplated since he had been a Diocesan Consulter and while he served as pastor, was whether this priest would be so free and easy with other people's money if he had been placed in a less wealthy parish. St. Catherine of Siena parish was not by diocesan terms on a week-to-week basis for operational continuance. How would Lawrence behave among the truly poor? How would he behave among the places where Christ worked? Or for that matter, how would he, O'Toole, himself, behave?

The Monsignor locked the door to his car and walked around the back of the retirement home to enter through the kitchen. He waited for a sandwich a staff Sister had offered to make, and went over to the corner of the kitchen and ate it. Without saying a word to anyone, he walked to his room hoping not to have to meet anyone along the way. He picked up the phone and called Betty Ryan.

He said, "Betty."

"Yes, Monsignor."

"When you go to work tomorrow I want you to find a free spot on the Bishop's calendar, and jot me in for an hour. Please do this as soon as possible. This is an urgent priority. It takes precedent over everything.

"Do you want to tell me if I am involved in your conversation with the Bishop."

"Now that would be telling you something, wouldn't it Betty?" The Monsignor said with a smile in his voice. "Please do not fret my dear. I won't turn you in."

Betty asked, "Is Quentin in trouble?"

He responded, "Up to his eyeballs. The police think he is involved in that man's death. The man who had the ring."

"No, that's not possible!" She shrieked.

"Betty, you do not know everything that is possible about him and his business. Be cautious! Before you begin to defend him. Remember, it was you who gave him Father Lawrence and your reward was a cruise. It was an innocent gesture on your part. But by doing it LaFayette has brought you into this mess. I don't think the police will bring you into this. Lieutenant Morrison is on top of things and smart enough to see through people who set others up to share the blame."

Betty was shaken. Her voice lowered. She shivered, thinking about what this could mean to her. What would others think of her if they had discovered she was linked to a man who was a criminal?

"I can get you in tomorrow. I'll call you in the morning first thing, about eight thirty."

Nothing was said about O'Toole having the Bishop's Ring.

Bishop O'Farrell warmly said, "Monsignor O'Toole, come in, come in. It's so nice to see you again. How's retirement treating you?"

The prelate responded with hearty handshake. "Retirement's fine, Bishop. I stay very busy with research papers my former predecessor willed to me at St. Catherine's. He was a wonderful priest. He had a great sense about spiritual matters involving the Blessed Mother. I've been pouring over his writings. I think he was a prophet for our coming times. He saw a lot in the conspiracies we have come to visit."

"Yes, well, Betty said that you had something important to talk about. I would like thank you for your weekenders at the parishes. It's good to stay active. I'm sure the Lord appreciates it. But, what can we talk about today?"

The Monsignor had a look of exasperation on his face wondering how he would break disturbing news. "I come somewhat disadvantaged by the fact I never had a chance to serve under you. We really have not had a chance to get to know each other very well. I think the gents up at St. John Vianney's are very happy about your appointment. But they haven't seen much of you up there for visits. May I make a suggestion for your consideration, Bishop? They have a wealth of wisdom you could tap into for your edification and enlightenment. I know they would love to see more of you since you came to us from the outside. I would hope you could make a night of it some time. I think they need it."

Bishop O'Farrell looked at Monsignor O'Toole and quickly took measure of the priest. The Monsignor was not afraid to come right out and directly address what he had on his mind. He set the record straight. No, the Bishop had not been to the retirement home very often. This was not a scolding by the older priest, but it was a gentle reminder he should visit this very valuable resource. Monsignor O'Toole was setting the atmosphere. He would listen to this man.

The Monsignor began, "Bishop, I am spiritually conflicted about what I am about to tell you. I know it is going to cause pain to you and to others. But not to tell you, would be a lack of loyalty, a vow I took on the day of my ordination.

"There is no simple way to tell you this except to say a man has been murdered in New York City. The police have made a connection to the Church. One of those suspects is a priest connected with the case. That priest is Father Lawrence."

The Bishop gasped and pulled himself back in his chair. His eyes opened wide. At that moment, Monsignor O'Toole realized the door to the Bishop's Office was still open. He was not certain if Betty was going to be able to hear the conversation or not from her office. He got up and walked to the door to close it. The Bishop took this momentary lapse to gather his thoughts. Strangely, the Bishop behaved like he did not hear what had been said to him.

"You were pastor before Father Lawrence at St. Catherine's?" It was a question the Bishop already knew the answer to, but he was stalling for time. O'Toole answered, "Yes."

"How do you get along with him?" It was another question the Bishop knew the answer to. But this time he wanted to hear Monsignor O'Toole's response.

"Bishop, I get along with just about every priest in this diocese. I think I have their affection and respect. I have been in a position to be of assistance to many pastors over the many years of my priesthood.

Father Lawrence is someone who came along who has not needed my assistance. To put it bluntly, I think he would not like it if he would be compared with me. I think he is trying to make his own way. At their instigation, I have had many conversations with former parishioners. They grumble about him. I have always listened, and tried to avoid saying anything that would be derogatory about him. Although I often wonder about the Church patroness how he sees her church family. Her life was dedicated to the poor, and abhorred extravagance."

"You think he is corrupt?"

"He is not corrupt. He's on a mission to make many changes he believes are necessary. He lacks the required time in parish work. Father Lawrence seems to think he has to make a name for himself. I think he has been swayed by his contractor's rhetoric."

How?"

"I don't know who to hold accountable. Throw out the role of the laity and Vatican II. My sense is that he needs guidance. Only you can do that. My complaint is that he does not listen to what is said to him by the parishioners. It appears his contractor has him dreaming about his future possibilities."

The Bishop asked, "Did you close the door when you left St. Catherine's?"

The Monsignor shook his head. "I tried. But people continued to call. First, it was out of friendship. I enjoyed their calls. Then I began to hear complaints. Then, I did not like taking their calls. Then, thankfully, they knew I was not in a position to change anything. When you were appointed Bishop they let me off the hook. I know in my heart many are hurting. They tell me a whole new group has replaced the old standbys."

The Bishop responded, "Well, that is going to happen, anyway."

"Oh yes, I agree. New blood can be good, sometimes."

"Nobody ever disagreed with you? You served more than what twenty five years?"

"Never as vocal, or controversial. When I became an honorary member of the Pontifical household, in the Monsignor ranks it was a reward for my services with Bishop Williams. I was his confessor. I have conducted myself cognizant I am vested with greater authority and responsibility. I would have been open with you about the Church reconstruction. I am still a loyal priest, and happy to be one. That is why I am here."

"Thank you Monsignor. If we can depart for a moment from the concerns you brought into me about a murder, I would like to tell you I am struggling with a problem. And since my predecessor felt comfortable discussing their sins with you, I would lose an opportunity if you walked out of here without discussing not sins, but a problem I have."

"Yes, I would be happy to help if I can."

"It's the matter of Auxiliary Bishop Sullivan. He has told me he is willing to retire. Health, you know. I'm going to have to make a nomination to Rome and soon. It's a quiet secret around here. I know some would like to be considered for the Auxiliary Bishop's position. There is no right of succession attached to the nomination. I have the feeling Father Lawrence has been actively seeking support from other priests. I've only been here a short while but..." The Bishop stopped speaking.

The Monsignor reminded, "Pope John XXIII suggested to us to open the windows and let some fresh air into the church. Didn't he?"

"Yes, he did." The Bishop agreed.

The Monsignor continued, "You are in the wonderful position Bishop of letting some fresh air into the diocese." The Bishop inquired, "Do you have someone in mind from outside the diocese?"

"Someone from the diocese, someone working outside the diocese. Actually, I thought he would have been a good replacement for me when I was about to retire but that situation never presented itself. He was sent to our mission church in Tennessee. It surprised everyone at the time because he has great talent. He is very spiritual. He gives great instructional sermons and he is a great teacher. I've heard that from many other priests. I have heard the gents at the residence speak well of him, those who knew him when they were active."

"What's his name?"

"Anglicized, it John Piorek"

"What do you mean, Anglicized?"

"John came to us as a gift from Poland. His Bishop wanted him ordained. The conditions were very difficult for young men in his country to get an education and training to become priests. They usually ended up in the military first then the coalmines. So after his military service John managed to come here how I don't know, but he was ordained here. He has been a part of our diocese ever since. He probably escaped your attention down there in Appalachia. But he is one of ours."

"He's not Irish!" The Bishop said, half jokingly.

Quickly the Monsignor added, "He's a priest of Jesus Christ!"

"Oh, yes, yes, by all means." Their eyes met with a knowing glance.

"I have the feeling Father Piorek has had more than his forty days in the desert and is ready to begin a ministry that would be everything you would need or expect of him as your side kick. I think he got shoved out of the diocese and into the woods."

"Let's talk about murder. How is Father Lawrence connected to it?"

"Good. I have a ring in my possession I want to show you." The Monsignor pulled the Bishop's Ring out of his pocket in its plastic bag where it had remained since it was picked up off the floor in the LaGuardia Airport terminal. He showed it to Bishop O'Farrell without taking it out of the bag. The ring belonged to the man who was killed.

"This ring is said to have been St. Stanislaw of Cracow Bishop's Ring. I have papers on it. They tell of Roman Catholicism's early days in Poland. It was being kept for the hand of a Polish Bishop. See the Latin inscription on the side! Father Lawrence went to New York to see the man who was killed. He never saw the ring."

Bishop O'Farrell looked at him with a startled face.

"The New York City Police suspect Father Lawrence's designer-contractor is involved in a scheme. The police are protecting the widow. She says he plays con games on priests. He apparently had Father Lawrence interested in it for himself. You may guess why. The widow-owner of the ring wants me to keep it until this matter of her survival is cleared up." Monsignor O'Toole said without further comment.

Chapter 20

Father Lawrence's suntan was still a slight bronze color when he received a phone call from the Bishop's office the same day Monsignor O'Toole's visit with Bishop O'Farrell. The mini/vacation still gave him a few days of sunshine. Sun is not so plentiful in the northern climates during the winter months.

Father Lawrence still had the memory of the face of that man looking up at him as he fell to the floor of the airport in his mind. It was a horrible memory. For the first time in his life, it seemed to him he walked away from someone who needed help. But he knew instinctively if he went to the aid of the man, there would be questions; some of which he did not want to answer. Father Lawrence panicked. If it were learned he was the one who came to meet the stricken man about the ring police would speculate about him. He wanted it all to fade away as a bad dream. Now he was sorry he ever listened to LaFayette in the first place.

Did he think he had an opportunity for the next nomination to the Auxiliary Bishop position? Well, frankly, he thought he did, and told Quentin that much. The ring idea was Quentin's. He reminded that fact to himself. Although the idea of being a Bishop with an ancient ring which once belonged to a Bishop centuries earlier did excite him for its antiquity value. Father Lawrence recognized Quentin could be fickle. Maybe this was one of those times when Quentin could not deliver on his promises. Lawrence just hoped the man would be taken to the hospital and given help because the man looked in pretty bad shape when he went down. The priest could not explain to himself why he did not come to his aid. Any day now, he thought, Quentin would call and tell him he had the ring and would stop by and show it to him.

When Father Lawrence showed up at the Chancery for his visit with the Bishop he stopped by Betty Ryan's office to give a thumbs up sign before going in to meet with the Bishop. When she saw him in the doorway she looked at him and waved him off. She returned to her keyboard and the stack of correspondence she was working on. She said nothing to him nor asked him about the vacation. Or even discussed whether he got to see the ring. He thought nothing of it because she seemed swamped with work.

He knocked briefly on the open door of the Bishop's office to break the concentration of the Bishop.

The Bishop said, "Come in Father Lawrence. Close the door."

The surprise for Father Lawrence came when he was asked to close the door. This Bishop rarely closed his door Father Lawrence had come to notice since visiting at the Chancery on a regular basis. This was significant. The suggestion had meaning. The call to meet with him had meaning. Had the Bishop come to some conclusions about what was going to happen with Bishop Sullivan's situation? Father Lawrence went in and sat down comfortably in the chair closest to the window. The Bishop got up from behind his desk and walked to a circular table in the corner of the room and invited him to the table. The Bishop smiled and stuck out his hand to shake Father Lawrence's.

The Bishop spoke, "Welcome back from the lands of sunshine. You look like you got a good tan."

"It was great. The weather was great, lying on the beach. It got up to 85 degrees some days. So different from our weather here."

The Bishop did not comment on the remark. He looked down at the file folder on his desk drawing the eyes of Father Lawrence to the file. He said nothing. But turned toward the window and then turned back to Father Lawrence.

The Bishop said, "A Bishop's task Father is not always a pleasant one. He has to choose to do things he would not like to do, as well as when he chooses to do things that he very much likes to do. Sometimes he is not satisfied with the results." Father Lawrence sat

153

straight in the chair looking into the Bishop's face for signs of what may follow.

He continued. "We Bishop's take our episcopacy very seriously. We share our actions exclusively with those of Christ. Our function, I do not have to tell you, is apostolic. We minister as Christ and the apostles ministered. We have a three-fold function as a teacher, a sanctifier, and as a priest. A Bishop is both the sign and the instrument of Christ the eternal priest. The Apostles the first bishops, I do not have to tell you, at the Last Supper received the commission to act for Christ as His person."

Father Lawrence listened to these opening remarks as if they were meant for his instruction, and hoped the end of the remarks would conclude with him being nominated for Bishop Sullivan's soon to be vacated position of Auxiliary Bishop.

"We are the shepherds of the Church and charged with ministering to the whole flock. The Holy Spirit has placed us and together with Christ we affect the work of salvation for souls. Our first role is to teach about the kingdom of heaven! Bishops are charged with the responsibility for the salvation of the souls of the people over with whom they are placed. They are responsible for the souls of the priests who minister to their flock."

"Yes, Bishop." Father Lawrence said emphatically.

"You are aware that Bishop Sullivan may be taking his retirement soon."

"It has been mentioned. I mean I have heard this."

"Now that I have mentioned the role of a Bishop, can you mention something to me which you think is significant in conducting one's self as a Bishop?"

Father Lawrence seemed to have an answer to that question if it ever came up. "He should obviously have the qualities of a leader."

"I had something else in mind, Father. Al Capone had those qualities." He said with a smile. "His Holiness, the Pope, would want me to be more specific about someone I would recommend to him for elevation to the level of a Bishop. I have not known you except for what you have been able to accomplish. When I look out among the priests of the diocese, I also see them doing extraordinary work. Different, but extraordinary." He continued.

"It is not easy being a priest in a nation that is changing, a nation becoming more pagan in its practices. The best part for me is to know that my priests are doing a wonderful job. The worst part is when one of my priests gets caught doing something wrong. The rest of the priesthood is held up to ridicule by Satan's finger pointers. The good we do is rarely praised or recognized by them."

"Yes, I know. It must be very difficult for the Bishops to keep track of bad things priests are accused of doing. The media loves to focus on us because of our vows of celibacy. They look for those kinds of stories, I guess."

"A Bishop has to be aware of those things, for sure." Bishop O'Farrell responded. "But there are other things we must watch as well. There is no doubt priests have enormous responsibilities. They must take them seriously, and they can, err in the course of ministry. I'm speaking in ways that are not sexual sins, which the media likes to focus on with its attacks on the Catholic Church and Christian values in general. While it likes to point out the sins of a few priests, the false pride of media fails to recognize its own sins as promoters of acceptable levels of violence, sex outside of marriage, fornication, drugs, near nudity on TV, promiscuity, illegitimacy, foul language, and the lowering of social morals. How many have been unjustly smeared, or delivered up to embarrassment? The media hails its role in delivering news, but accepts no responsibility for the changes taking place in families, where this culture of horror and death is promulgated. It was not always thus. Television feeds this culture of immorality. Our Church is of divine creation. The media is a money making enterprise, sometimes without a conscience in the issues it supports!

"They sell advertising, not morality. Media sources sometime act as if they have divine authority from God as well. We know what the Lord would say about looking for the splinter in another man's eye when one has a 'log in your own eye.'"

Father Lawrence felt as though he was being instructed as to how to look upon the administration of the ranks of priests within a diocese.

"We are in the world, but not of the world. We are here to save souls for Christ. I am not going to take the time here to focus on

155

those subjects because they are not the purpose of this visit. It is my responsibility to offer His Holiness a nomination to replace Bishop Sullivan. I have been listening to what others have been saying and whom they think would make a fine candidate for the position of Auxiliary Bishop. Your past service here in the Chancery allowed you to see many priests file in here. The primary challenge for me is to focus on the spiritual life of the person who will hold a Bishop's staff. As a practical matter I can't get around to all of the Confirmations I should get to and sign off on the books of the parish." The Bishop explained.

"In our first discussion, Father, I think I caught you off guard. You were not ready for questions. Our vocation calls us to be holy. We are priests. I know it is easier to say, than it is in practice. Sometimes if we could just get away we think our life would be better, like the vacation you just returned from sunshine. It was but a mere respite. After we come back we are refreshed and ready for new challenges.

"The difficult thing for a Bishop to do is to send some priest off to his next assignment, and then, for what might seem an eternity, leave him there. A Bishop has to be sensitive to his fellow priests. He has to make sure they are happy, challenged and a part of the diocesan family of clergy. That is not easy, even for myself. Vatican II tells us we must have the "missionary spirit." Well, thankfully, this diocese had the missionary spirit before I arrived. We have men in South America, and Shady Trail, Tennessee."

The Bishop watched Father Lawrence's expression when he mentioned Tennessee. On his desk in the file was Father Lawrence's letter to his predecessor recommending the appointment of Father John Piorek to the mountainous village mission established by the diocese when he served at the Chancery and before he was sent to St. Catherine of Siena parish. There was no comment coming from Father Lawrence, which the Bishop found to be unsympathetic toward his fellow diocesan priest. Maybe Father Piorek was shoved, as Monsignor O'Toole had intimated so that Father Lawrence could be the one to get St. Catherine of Siena parish.

"Speaking of Shady Trail, Tennessee, it has been recommended to me by other priests, which I find strange, that Father Piorek come home, and another priest be sent to replace him. We could ask another diocese to send someone but I don't wish to prevail upon my brother Bishops to do something that we can afford to do."

"Did he ask to come home?" Father Lawrence asked, hoping the Bishop would answer his bold impertinent question.

"No. But there are others who think he should be replaced. I have spoken with him. He said he would do as I saw fit. We had a wonderful conversation. He said he lost some of his harsh Polish accent and picked up some Southern drawl. He enjoys the people. They are friendly enough but a little bit slower than New Yorkers. He's had an outsider's perspective, even now, seeing us, as different. Of course, he is one of us and still expects to someday comeback and serve here. I can tell you, Father, I did not know him before. But speaking to him I find a nobility of spirit. It's rare even among us priests.

"He told me he has had the opportunity to look at the heavens at night. While praying he sensed the presence of the Lord at his side. You can't imagine how wonderful that sounds to have one of my priests tell me that. Shady Trail has been a good place for him to grow in the Spirit. What a gift! It is especially so for those who still search for meaning and happiness in their ministries. Are you happy in your ministry at St. Catherine's, Father?"

"Yes, Bishop, I am. I have a great sense of achievement being at St. Catherine of Siena parish."

"But do you feel the presence of the Lord in your work? I hope you understand the importance of my question. I know it is an open question to phrase it like that, but…" The Bishop stopped his words, and waited for a response. He continued. "I have noticed reading between the lines there have been fewer confessions heard since you have taken over the parish."

Father Lawrence responded, "I think it is due to the changing times. People have lost their sense of sin."

"Yes, we know. It's our job to tell them God has not lifted the Ten Commandments from his requirements to get into heaven. They must be told to seek forgiveness. We have the troubles we have in society because people are unwilling to forgive others! Yet, we expect God will forgive us without repentance for our hidden sins. We are likely to be more compassionate and more sensitive to the feelings of others and therefore less likely to offend others by bringing up the matter of reconciliation with God. As one who acts for Christ, as I am called to do, my first task is to make sure all of my priests have an understanding of compassion that Christ had for us sinners. We trespass deliberately against others often in commission and in omission because we have things to do." The Bishop chose his words carefully for Father Lawrence to hear.

The Bishop continued. "We need to be forgiven. Like Christ we offer ourselves up to do penance. If not for ourselves for others and the world we live in which breaks God's laws. There is so much spiritual power in acts of forgiveness for the graces that flow from it empowers us to do great things. I was amazed at the conversation I had with John Piorek and what he has had to overcome in his life and how he has had to forgive others who trespassed against him in his native land."

He said, "Forgiveness, was something he had to learn. It helped him overcome many internal battles. Of course you could hear it in his voice. He says Shady Trail has been a marvelous spiritual experience for him. He says it changed his life. I am grateful he was able to overcome the long lost trauma of his past. It gave him peace of soul. Shady Trail provided him with such great opportunities to become closer to the Lord." Then shifting his focus, he continued.

"I know you like the brick and mortar projects. They're important and certainly important to you. What did the Lord say? "Destroy this temple, and I will rebuild it in three days!" He wants the resurrection of the 'just' to help them save their souls. Saving souls is our vocation above all things beyond our brick and mortar projects.

"I now ask myself: Is what I do helpful to saving the souls of those entrusted to my care? Those are my primary concerns. They should be yours as well, Father. As the Shepherd of his flock I must help you to save your soul. And you help save the souls entrusted to your care. Those are my primary concerns, Father. In other words to come back to your concerns will you be holier for all that you do or just more recognizable?"

Father Lawrence looked at his bishop and could see he had been given a penetrating question that no other Bishop had asked him before. This was not a question about his value to the diocese. It was about his value to himself. Apparently, the Bishop was looking at one's worth to the diocese more in a spiritual sense than in physical appearances of the churches. Suddenly, it was becoming clear to that this Bishop was not like his predecessors who put brick and mortar interests highest on the priority list. Father Lawrence was slow to answer. The Bishop saw he wanted to say something but failed to offer a comment. The Bishop continued.

"The reason for my questions, Father, is quite evident to you, I am sure. Saving one's soul is more important than becoming a Bishop. It serves no one to carry the apostolic mantle of responsibility; if for instance, one is void of teaching the meaning of the scriptures, or void of applying the moral or dogmatic teachings of the Church to daily living. What we send the flock home with after the celebration of the Eucharist is also important. The faithful must have food for their souls. 'Woe to him who fails to teach the Gospel, and the commandments, as a shepherd of souls,' the Pontiff said to me."

Father Lawrence nodded in agreement as if he understood. But Bishop O'Farrell wanted to take it up to the next level.

"I think the people of St. Catherine of Siena parish need a change Father Lawrence. You have been there for a short time but you have accomplished a lot. You are, and I can see this, a tireless worker. But an intense man who I am told wears blinders. For you it's a horse race. That's not necessarily a criticism. We could use more action on the part of some. But I think it also tells me you need to gain a wider perspective. I sense you see yourself in the office of the Auxiliary."

Father Lawrence shyly nodded, "It's true." He answered.

The Bishop spoke slowly. "I have given that some thought, as well as others for the position. Someone is bound to be disappointed, but we priests know that and live. I've had disappointments in assignments under my former Bishops. The worst parish can bring out holiness in the priest. The best Diocese can just as well send a Cardinal or Bishop to hell, if he fails in his mission and is unrepentant. Those are our ironies."

Father Lawrence was not his usual self. He waited for a final word of what was to become of his life.

"I hope you will understand in this appointment, there is no nomination for you to advance to the office of Auxiliary Bishop. I have recalled Father Piorek to the Diocese. He will replace you as pastor of St. Catherine of Siena parish. And you will replace him as pastor of our Shady Trail mission parish in Tennessee."

"This comes as a shock to me, Bishop. I thought I."

"I know it does Father. Just as I was today, shocked to speak with the police in New York City. I found out you have been linked in the murder of a man. If they find cause to have you brought in I will pay the expenses from Tennessee. Before this startling information I had already determined Father Piorek was going to replace you. Will you need a defense lawyer?"

"Bishop?" Father Lawrence's eyes turned steely gray as he squinted to look into the face of his Bishop. "I don't know what you have been told by the police in New York, but I am not involved in a murder."

"It's a sermon for you to preach. Presumption is a mortal sin! It can send the proud to hell by thinking all are so worthy of the Lord's blessings. We know what the Lord said about the self-righteous Pharisee who gave his honored dues to the temple. He counted them as nothing in comparison to the poor woman who gave more, from her substance, little that it was.

"From what I now know I think you presumed you would be appointed the Auxiliary. At Shady Trail you will have no church to refurbish. You will have time to work on your spiritual life and find greater assimilation with the Lord. I want you to continue to teach the commandments and about virtues. I know that you are disappointed. In your desire to be recognized a man lost his life. The police may never indict you for murder Father but a soul has entered eternity it appears because of the unscrupulous behavior of your designer friend. He will no longer be given work in this diocese, regardless of the outcome of this matter.

"There are things Father, we would all like to have happen for us. But in your presumption you may have brought disrepute upon the work of too many hard working priests who have no ambition other than to serve the Lord. This time listen to the people at Shady Trail. We all need a 'change of heart' to pursue holiness. I am

160

offering you a chance to be among God's favorite people, the poor. Father Piorek spiritually prospered in holiness among them. You can too. In ancient times, when the Religious Prefect of Rome asked St. Lawrence, whose name, incidentally you bear, to assemble the treasures of the Church. The next day, St. Lawrence brought the poor people of Rome to him.

"Sunday notify your parishioners you are being transferred. You will leave in two weeks for Tennessee. You will be surrounded not by a beautiful church but by the real treasures of the Church, the poor. The New York City Police have warned me not to have Father Piorek's name ever mentioned as your replacement. Be ready to return if called to come to New York.

"I suggest you contact your confessor. I pray that you are innocent of complicity to murder another man. May God be always with you."

Chapter 21

There was no cheerful wave good-bye when Father Lawrence left the Chancery. Betty Ryan wondered how much the Bishop knew and how much Monsignor O'Toole told the Bishop the day before. The Bishop did not tell her of his decision to transfer Father Lawrence to Tennessee. No one was talking to her. She waited for Quentin to call. He hadn't called her at the office or at her home.

When Father Lawrence arrived back at St. Catherine's parish the look of disappointment on his face was obvious his parish secretary noticed it right away. He told her, "I will not be taking calls for a while. However, I will be in my office."

He called Quentin LaFayette. "Why did I have to hear from my Bishop that he spoke with the police in New York about a murder and they think I am involved in it?"

"Hello, to you to Father. How was your vacation?"

"Don't give me that Quentin. Answer my question."

"Yes Father. Can I call you back in a short while? We're short handed here because we lost one of our most important staff people. I know you'll understand. I'll get back to you in a little while." The phone line went dead.

Quentin couldn't talk, that's why he cut me off. Father Lawrence thought to himself I can't let this get to me. I must compose myself. This is the first time anything like this has happened to me. I never thought anything like this would happen to me. When this gets around it's going to be embarrassing. But what happened to the ring? No one is talking about the Bishop's Ring. He sat at his desk waiting for the phone to ring. Finally, his private outside line phone line rang. Few people had the number. It had to be Quentin returning his call.

"Father when you called I had a detective in here. I probably would have liked to talk to you about what you knew about Conrad Kaminski's visit to the airport. We have not talked since you came back. Now, I have a question. Do you have the Bishop's Ring?"

Father Lawrence responds, "What? Do I have the Bishop's Ring? No, I don't have the Bishop's Ring. Why would I have it?"

LaFayette countered, "Well, you wanted to have one, the last time I talked to you, and so you had an appointment with a man, remember, who just happened to have such a ring, remember?"

"No I don't have the ring. I wanted to tell you. The man collapsed on the floor. The man was no more than twenty yards in front of me. I think he recognized me. But I was in civvies. I didn't want to let the cat out of the bag so to speak so I kept on going. People muddled around him until a security guard came to see what happened and he called for an ambulance. I got out of there before they started asking people questions in the area and I would be detained."

Quentin asked, "If you don't have the ring, then who does?"

Lawrence answered, "Maybe a bystander robbed him? I don't know."

"Don't be funny with me Father. I got a maniac after me looking for that ring! He knew Conrad had it with him and somehow well, I think he killed him. He said Conrad died before he could mug him to get the ring. Now he thinks I have the ring. If I don't show up with the ring he's got a very embarrassing plan to kill my business. The trouble is I think, he knows about you and your desire to see the ring. If I don't produce it he may come after you. Or Betty Ryan or all of us."

Father Lawrence asked, "How did Conrad Kaminski die?"

"A chemical compound was shot into his leg with one of those spy canes that act like a long barreled rifle. The maniac stuck Conrad in the leg at the airport. The dose was too much for Conrad and worked faster than 'Killer' thought it would. Your plane was late. By the time you arrived the chemical had gone to work and did major damage to Conrad's system. 'Killer' counted on taking him to the men's room and stealing the ring."

Father Lawrence hurried, "How do you know all of this?"

"Because the killer told me. He thinks I have the ring or Conrad's wife has it. He might think it was passed on to you. He has been looking for the ring for years, he said."

Father Lawrence asked, "Have you talked to the police about him?"

Quentin hesitated, "Not quite. They might think I was in cahoots with him, they may even connect Betty and you in on this murder!"

The priest was outraged, "Surely, you can't be serious?"

Quentin shifted the burden, "Who knows what they will do? They will work every angle of the case hoping to lay blame onto someone."

Father Lawrence shouted, "Why don't you just come right out and tell them who this guy is?"

Quentin replied, "I think they know who he is. It's a little bit more complicated than just nailing him. He's a Polish diplomat."

Father Lawrence revealed, "The next time you talk to him, tell him to take me off his hit list. Tell him I said I do not have the ring, and there is no chance I will ever need the ring."

An alarmed Quentin asked, "What are you saying, Father?"

An angry Father Lawrence whispered, "I'm saying I just got fired by the Bishop. The New York police have been in touch with him and he is sending me to a mission church out of state. Where I'm going the killer would have a rough time finding me. He also told me as of now your services are no longer required in the diocese. But I am sure you will hear from the Bishop yourself. Just think how Betty is going to feel when she types that letter!"

"Father, I tried to do something nice for you. I am sorry it didn't work out." Father Lawrence interrupted, "Right now, I have a soul to save and it's mine. I'll have plenty of time to think about the fast lane when I'm working in the missions."

Lt. Morrison brought an envelope into Quentin LaFayette's office at the same time Father Lawrence had placed his first phone call to LaFayette. The designer led the detective to his private office to discuss the envelope's contents. Quentin knew when he saw the photographs he was going to have to do some heavy duty explaining.

The envelope was addressed to WABC radio. Its contents had been removed and copied by the radio station. A special delivery messenger was sending the originals to a Queens's police precinct. When Quentin saw the photos contained in the envelope he explained, "I should be so lucky!"

There before his eyes was an 8" x 10" glossy photograph of him lying in the sand and sleeping beside him was a bare breasted Magda Kaminski. The clear implication of the attached note was the radio station could help the police if they announced the deceased designer's wife was having an affair with his boss.

Quentin smiled, "It's blackmail Lieutenant. You can see that for yourself. Sand makes a good background to splice two negatives together and make it appear as one background. I'm surprised the guy got a shot of her. She's a modest lady for what I know about her."

"You better be right about that Mr. LaFayette. We don't know who else received one of these but be prepared for questions from the media. I don't have you completely figured out in this deal yet but I do think some innocent people are going to be hurt by this kind of stuff. Our guy said this looks like a frame up on the photos. He put it under magnified scrutiny, and says the sand in one photo is larger in the distance than the sand closer to you if that is any consolation."

Quentin smirked, "With all due respect to Conrad I never had this kind of luck with his wife."

Morrison looked serious. "Just to let you know what is happening out there Mr. LaFayette, you have enemies going on the offense."

"Who are the others?" Quentin said absentmindedly.

Morrison noted the attitude. "You're not out of the clear just yet Mr. LaFayette. Complicity, remember? The infighting may get worse we just don't want to have any additional loss of life."

Quentin asks, "Has Magda Kaminski seen this farce?"

Morrison said, "Right now I don't think she would be in the mood or could handle such a photo. It worries us that it might be published without her corroboration. You're going to have to tell it's a fake when you're questioned. And if newspapers print it tell them you can prove it is a fake in a court of law. But don't tell them how you know it is a fake. It may force them to examine it more clearly than just for what it is."

Quentin remarked, "What I see there, though, is not a fake. She's all woman." Morrison picked up on the remark. It has a tone of disloyalty to his dead employee's memory as he spoke about Magda's body in a faked photograph. It also spoke about his lack of character in other ways. It was a reminder of another painful time in Morrison's life when his life was turned upside down by men with callous disregard for his deceased wife.

The smear campaign was on. Morrison was unsure if anyone in the People's Republic of Poland Embassy would admit one of their own was involved in a murder and other related crimes.

When Morrison got back to the precinct, the Captain called him into his office. The Captain held up a telegram. "What's this? From F. O'Toole. Sunshine traveler will next go to Tennessee. 2 weeks."

Morrison answered, "It means one priest is transferred to a location out of state and will be leaving in two weeks. I asked Monsignor O'Toole to keep me posted as to what's going on. He assured me Father Lawrence for whatever this appears has the heart of a good priest. He's has a rare style. Driven yes, but no to complicity to murder."

Bishop O'Farrell called Monsignor O'Toole to invite himself up to the priest's retirement home, at which time he wanted to tell him of his decision to bring Father John Piorek home and appointing him to be the Pastor at St. Catherine of Siena Parish. On this news from the Bishop about Father Piorek coming home the Monsignor could only wonder if St. Catherine of Siena was once again working her miracles. Time would tell.

Monsignor O'Toole quietly wondered what financial shape the Dwyer Education Trust Fund was in. As a contributor to the Trust Fund maybe now he could find out if LaFayette benefited from the Fund's money.

Chapter 22

Father John Piorek stayed long enough at the mission to introduce Father Lawrence to his parishioners and to say good-bye. It was a sight Father Lawrence had never witnessed in all the years of his priesthood. These people were poor, no doubt about that. Many carried Irish names. But he had not ever seen that type affection for a pastor ever in his priesthood. He witnessed the mountainous parish of St. Thomas Apostle saying good-bye to their departing priest. The church was named after the martyred Apostle known for his doubt about the Resurrection of Jesus, but who later died a martyr's death. There was little doubt about the love and affection these people had for the priest who came and spread love of God into their lives.

The week before Father Lawrence departed St. Catherine of Siena parish. The suddenness of his departure left many wondering. The faithful who always came to a reception for a departing priest were thanking him for his service. And with them came envelopes expressing their financial good wishes. The curious came to find out where Father Lawrence's new assignment was going to be. Lastly, the committee people who took his direction felt obligated to see him off to his new assignment. There were smiles and laughter and good wishes. And then it was over. Lawrence had packing to do, and storage. He did not know how much of what he possessed would really fit or be of any relevance in the place he was going. When he arrived at St. Thomas Apostle parish, open arms greeted him. A big smile came from the six foot four, slim framed priest who never really lost his Polish accent completely. He felt very strange seeing the priest whom he recommended to be sent out of the Diocese to this mountainous village. Now he himself was sent there.

"It's wonderful to see you, Andy. It's especially wonderful to see somebody from back home."

"It's great to see you, too, John. Whew, so many trees! I never saw so many in all my life. It was a good drive. I enjoyed it. I almost got lost along the way but I made it."

"This place is God's secret. You're going to love it. People are not 'New York' here. Poor, there is no doubt about that. The collection on Sunday sometimes comes in with brown bags of garden vegetables for you to cook up. They give you as well as they have. Sometimes even better than they have for themselves! Maynard Bowles comes by to take care of the coal for the coal stove. Keep the fire stoked, as they say, because the nights can get chilly. Maynard will come by to take out the ashes from the stove every day when it's real cold. You could do it yourself, but he likes to be around. He's a cross over from the Baptist persuasion. I think he is still wondering if he did the right thing. He's a good man to have around. He will keep you company because as he put it to me, 'You're a bachelor, too, Father.' Maynard loves to hunt wild turkey and he loves to tell stories about his success tracking those big birds."

The two priests exchanged stories for a couple of days as Father Piorek made Father Lawrence comfortable with his new surroundings and then Piorek was gone. The people would pay for his cable TV if he wanted it installed. "I never got it because I was too busy." Father Lawrence could only wonder doing what and for whom.

Maynard Bowles was quick to meet the new Father. He looked him over and took his measure. Father Lawrence was quick to notice the scrutiny. In the morning quiet following his celebration of the Eucharist Father Lawrence sat in the corner of the log cabin residence and drank coffee and wondered what God had in store for him. He wondered if he should start with asking the women to sew new sets of vestments, or would that be a return to an old habit.

A month had passed while Father Piorek reoriented himself to life in a large parish. On this particular Sunday morning in spring, Bishop O'Farrell was there to officially install Father Piorek as pastor of St. Catherine of Siena Church. The priests were vested in white with the Bishop wearing the garments of apostolic times complete with miter worn on the head and crosier carried as a walking staff symbols of an ancient time to mark the authority of the office of Bishop. The procession of altar boys was led by one carrying the portable cross and followed by several, two of which, carried candles which they placed on each side of the altar. Three priests walked in the procession led by Monsignor O'Toole, followed by Father Piorek, and Bishop O'Farrell.

The church was packed. A choir sang out with glorious "Alleluias." Outside the birds chirped and the sun filled sky made it appear it was a celebration not unlike Easter when new life comes forth.

Bishop O'Farrell stood before the altar and looked from side to side and then forward to the congregation. "We are here today to install a new pastor for St. Catherine of Siena Parish. I am sure, you will find Father Piorek to be a very friendly priest but that is not the reason for this choice to serve you now. It was his time to rejoin our diocese after serving faithfully in the Church missions of our country. Before he left he worked at several churches in the diocese. But I will leave those stories for him to tell as he acquaints himself with you.

"You know it was the decision of the Vatican Council II to have Dioceses like ours to extend themselves to do mission work. For many years the Church in America sent priests overseas to foreign lands to convert the poor and underprivileged and to teach the Gospel of Jesus Christ. Well, the Diocese honors that request of the Council Fathers. We make our contribution. Priests who have served the poor have come back, if not enlightened about the differences in the quality of life but spiritually enriched by the experience. I'm sure that is the case with Father Piorek as I have listened to him tell us of life in Appalachia.

"Father Lawrence has been reassigned as some of you already know to a mission church. We hope he will find the kind of riches there for his faithful service as Father Piorek found among the less fortunate in the missions. We do not have to look far to find poverty and the lack of the gospel. The years of Father Piorek's service to the poor have also brought him closer to the Lord. It is where the Lord himself served in His ministry among the poor. And so, our prayers go out today in gratitude to God for returning Father John Piorek back to us filled with love and faithful service. We pray when Father Lawrence eventually comes back to our diocese he too will be imbued with the same energy and desire to serve as when he left. Now let us begin the liturgies of the Word and of the Eucharist and the installation of your new pastor. In the name of the Father, and of the Son and of the Holy Spirit, Amen."

When Mass was finished the people roared with their approval.

Outside the Church after Mass, Father Piorek met with his new parishioners. Monsignor O'Toole visited with his former parishioners and Bishop O'Farrell stood along the side standing in the sunshine talking to and greeting his flock. When all three went into the rectory a breakfast had been prepared for them in the dining room. The women's brigade of kitchen help went about the task of cooking and cleaning.

In the front office the money counters were counting the mostly silent contributions as dollar amounts were entered into the registers and the amounts were tallied. Father Piorek walked through the rectory where several parishioners were on hand to make short work of the financials. It was not a sight he was used to seeing. He went to the lavatory and washed his hands in preparation for breakfast. When he came out the Bishop came over to him and took his arm. "After breakfast, I want to talk to you and Monsignor in the study."

Father Piorek was elated at his new assignment. He went on to tell stories of the people of Shady Trail. What it was like while he was stationed there and the kinds of characters that come out of the hills to get a smell of the person who was running the Church. The two visitors listened intently with open astonishment and tried to visualize Father Lawrence in that environment.

"I won't be used to rich food for a while and I won't be used to having so much help. But, I guess I can get used to it." Then turning directly to the Bishop Father Piorek said, "I don't know why you brought me out of Tennessee with such suddenness, Your Excellency. I am truly surprised. I am also surprised you replaced Father Lawrence. He has done a wonderful job it appears with the renovation of the Church. It's unfamiliar for me to see the Tabernacle so far away. I'll have to get used to that, I guess." Father Piorek was trying to figure out what the sudden interest in him had been since he felt he did not deserve the recognition that should perhaps go to another priest. The Bishop wanted to wait until all three entered the study and the door would be closed. He would tell Father Piorek what was on his mind and not worry about parishioners hearing it and spreading rumors.

When the breakfast was finished, the three priests quickly departed for the study and let the parish women clean up the dining room and do the dishes. A ham was put into the refrigerator but the smell of it permeated the whole house. The Bishop was the last to enter the room and closed the door. "Food odors. I prefer to stay away from them or I will gain weight," he said. The three of them sat down in leather chairs and commented on the furnishings of the rectory. It was not the same, Monsignor said as when he was there. It was just an idle comment filling time waiting for the Bishop to open up his remarks to Father Piorek. When the small talk ended, the Bishop looked into Father Piorek's eyes.

He said, "I have spent many hours on my knees praying over this decision, Father. Bishop Sullivan was hurt in a fall a while back. As it turns out his health is not good and he is going to retire. Your name came up not just once but several times. Priests who studied with you at the seminary as well as priests you have served with here in the diocese have come forth with your name I might add as a possible replacement for the Auxiliary. Of course, I did not know you since I only arrived here a little more than a year ago. I trust my priests. What they were saying to me was something like, 'Don't forget John Piorek. He may be gone but not forgotten.' Frankly they told me it wasn't a good move to send you to Tennessee when you were sent."

"It worked out well, Your Excellency. I was happy there."

"That's just it, John. You were happy there but some people might think it was banishment."

"I had no family here so I didn't mind." Father Piorek responded.

The Bishop assured him, "Well you have family here among your fellow priests. They thought maybe you were banished."

Father Piorek did not comment. The Bishop continued.

"Today you were installed as Pastor of St. Catherine's of Siena. Now," the Bishop stopped and looked at Monsignor O'Toole and returned his glance to Father Piorek, "with your permission I would like to nominate you to become the next Auxiliary Bishop of this diocese."

The new Pastor slumped in his chair. His eyes welled up with tears. He could not speak as his throat suddenly became dry. His eyes watered as he blinked the tears to the side and down his cheek. A lump developed in his throat and he was speechless. He looked at the Bishop and the Monsignor, brought his hand up to his mouth, and mumbled as if to tell them he could not talk. For a few moments, Piorek just looked down until he was ready to speak.

"I could never imagine myself becoming a Bishop in my whole life. I am a simple priest. I have simple desires. I have no interest in ruling."

The Bishop laughed, "Auxiliary Bishop, Father. No right of succession. You will not have to rule." He said with a large smile, "unless, later on that right is granted to you, here or somewhere else. 'Holy Mother the Church' needs priests with the missionary spirit today more than ever. It needs to have men who know the worst of times because our society is becoming pagan. You are an apostle. You have been born among atheist rulers. You have worked with the poor.

"In a way this is something many priests will not agree that life has become too soft for them. That is why the Council wants the Bishops to re-ignite the missionary spirit among the clergy. The wisdom is to take priests out of their rectories and put them back on the street where they belong. It's where the Lord worked his ministry. My own vocation to the priesthood came by the example of a priest who made himself very well known to a group of teenagers. It must have been the same way for you, back in Poland when you were encouraged by your Bishop to come here."

"Yes, I thank God for him every day. But, now I will have to get used to the side altar Tabernacle."

Monsignor O'Toole responded, "Pardon my shortcomings. The liturgists would have you believe that the priest is a "presider," as if Christ was the master of ceremonies at the Last Supper! Deeming the priest a presider carries no theological weight for me when I was ordained I was called a priest according to the order of Melchizedek. He offered bread and wine to his guests as the Lord did. I am not comfortable with being introduced as a "presider" on Sunday. There are many presiders in life for functions but very few priests who have the oils of ordination covering their hands to heal the sick and comfort the sinner."

The Bishop listened but did not respond. Father Piorek asked, "From what you say I take it you do not like the way the church has been renovated Monsignor?"

Monsignor O'Toole just waved his hand as if to say he did not want to comment. Then changed his mind. "Father, if I were here I would have spent much less money and the people would have been very happy with my decision."

Bishop O'Farrell added as a comment. "The pledges for the payment for the changes must be paid. I'll expect you will form your thoughts along those lines. We cannot default on our commitments."

Father Piorek felt somewhat overwhelmed said, "It is kind of a shock to go from a poor parish to a rich parish practically over night. It will be a new adjustment. And so now you want me to accept the nomination of becoming the Auxiliary when I have yet to meet with my fellow priests whom I haven't seen in years to get their feeling in this."

The Bishop asked, "Did the Lord ask the apostles to check with their buddies to see if they cared whether or not they leave the group? A Bishop is a direct descendant of the Apostles. What I am asking is: do you want to carry on the apostolic authority and tradition, to share with me in the teaching magisterial functions and to do the Lord's work as an Apostle for Christ?"

Father Piorek responded. "Your Excellency, I understand the importance of the offer. I come home, and this happens to me." Father

Piorek paused. He put his hands in prayer and hid his face from the two awaiting his decision. When his face emerged there were tears again in his eyes. He looked at the Bishop and nodded his approval. Monsignor O'Toole saw the unseen, a holy hand intervening in a larger struggle.

Father Piorek stood up, and looked out of the window and upon the spring flowers, and the trilliums which seemed to still blossom in the yard, while one, he noticed, was red. Was this a sign?

"Now tell me the bad news." He said.

Monsignor O'Toole said, "There is a killer on the loose, and he may be coming after you. But he's looking for Father Lawrence."

"Are you certain, Monsignor? Please don't tell me that. If you knew why did you take me out of Tennessee? I don't understand. And you want a dead Bishop?" Father Piorek responded.

"You speak Polish." The Monsignor said. "We think the killer is from Poland and he is looking for something he thinks Father Lawrence has. But we know Father Lawrence does not have what he is looking for."

The Bishop assured him, "For now, Father, we don't think you have to worry about anything. I will submit your name to the Vatican for the Auxiliary position. I think the Holy Father will be quite pleased to find that we nominated you to the rank of the episcopacy. In fact I am certain of it." The Bishop concluded his remarks with, "Thank you, Father. You will be hearing from me."

Chapter 23

The suddenness of changing seasons from cold and rain to sunshine could not come soon enough. Several weeks passed and the suspected killer kept a low profile. Meanwhile Magda and her children had been moved.

It was obvious to Morrison that Magda should not stay with her sister. She needed to have her own space and her own furniture along with her children. Both children were out of high school. Her daughter wanted to attend the Fashion Institute of Technology but was waiting a year. Her son had completed two years of Community College but was waiting to enroll in an architecture school for the fall semester. He had been employed when his father was killed but felt now it was better to stay close to his mother until there could be some permanency in their lives.

As it happened, Morrison told Magda to wait until a police safe house was available for her to move out of her sister's apartment. Captain Antonnucci took the trailer of household goods and brought it out of storage. He put them in a home in Queens that had been vacant but was for sale for several months. The "For Sale" sign remained but it was listed under another broker's name. The telephone number was actually a line used by the Police precinct for their "sting" operations.

Magda came to her new house at night and parked in the garage under the house. Like so many other attached houses it gave the appearance of being a street designed by an accordion manufacturer. "If you did not know which specific house to come home to, even on a clear day you could easily pick the wrong one, even if you only had a slight amount of alcohol to drink." Morrison joked with her she could wind up in the wrong house if she climbed the wrong stairs.

He did not tell her was that he lived directly across the street. He waited until she moved in. Then he would tell her. As soon as this situation was over he promised her she would be back in her own home. Conrad was buried, unreported, in a private Catholic ceremony.

Earlier, Quentin LaFayette called his insurance agent to put in a claim for the beneficiary proceeds on the life insurance he had taken out on Conrad's life. He was told he would have to supply a death certificate from County Vital Statistics, show them his policy, and proof he was Conrad's employer and named beneficiary on the policy, the records clerk would then consent to his wishes. But later he became nervous when the insurance company notified him that there would be a delay in payment of the proceeds.

The insurance company said they could pay the proceeds to Conrad's wife, as a named beneficiary, since she was not the owner of the policy. He considered it a stupid rule to pay her, and to have to make him wait when he owned both policies. He wondered if the insurance company had been in contact with the police since the cause of death on the death certificate was listed as a probable homicide. If it had the police must have cleared Magda but still held out reservations about Quentin and anyone else connected with Conrad's death and the Bishop's Ring.

The insurance company death benefits section had sent Magda her benefits check through the mail but it came back from the post office with a "Return To Sender, Addressee Left No Forwarding Address." stamped on the envelope. The Insurance Company sent a letter to police agencies on Long Island asking for help in locating Mrs. Conrad Kaminski.

Morrison told the insurance company his precinct was involved in investigating the death of Mr. Kaminski. He wanted to know what kind of information the insurance company needed to have to reach Mrs. Kaminski. He instructed the clerk who is in charge of the insurance case file to send the letter to Mrs. Kaminski, in care of him, to a Queens Post Office. When the letter had been received she would contact the insurance company and provide whatever identification was needed for them and information as to where they could send her insurance check. Morrison's mind moved rapidly toward the future.

Morrison surmised the killer would like to know where she was hiding. LaFayette would like to know as well and for reasons less than honorable. There was the matter of Mr. Kaminski's personal effects, which had to be returned to the family. But it was most important to deny any supply of information on the whereabouts of the Bishop's Ring.

If LaFayette found Magda the detective thought and either schmoozed, cajoled or tortured the information out of her and then turned her over to the killer the chance of stopping another death would almost become impossible. It was his years of working homicide cases and police instinct that convinced Morrison that LaFayette could be working both sides of the street. Without being able to come up with the ring to save his own skin Quentin could be dangerous to either Magda or Father Lawrence. More dangerous if he had already received a bribe or part of a bribe if the ring could not be delivered!

When Morrison met Magda at her new house in Queens he told her to open up two bank accounts in two separate banks. He instructed her to follow the directions of the insurance company in supplying information to identify her as the person who would be the proper beneficiary recipient. When the insurers felt satisfied everything was okay he told Magda to have them send a wire transfer of funds to the bank where she had established the first bank account. When that money was deposited there she was then to have that bank notify her and then have that money wired to the second bank to her new account number. The reason for this action, he explained to her, was so that she could make these transfers in case someone would be bribed to follow the money trail. Morrison suggested to her the last account be a numbered account in which only she knew the number.

Morrison didn't know if "The Cowboy" had connections. But the Lieutenant wouldn't put it past Quentin LaFayette to have made those connections somewhere down the line to someone who knew someone working in the banks or insurance company people who could come up with Magda's name and address. Magda was in deep grief. She could go back to a normal life as soon as these things were cleared up. He promised her.

Colonel Janus Piotrowski was not satisfied with the results of his attempts to have a story about a tawdry love affair between LaFayette and Magda printed in the New York news media. But the Police's effort he suspected to pull Magda out of the spotlight and move her away prevented reporters from getting a juicy story to print. Magda was not at home to deny the allegation or to be photographed and tell her story. The killer had not expected that particular police tactic of her removal. He was not deterred by the NYPD in his pursuit of Magda and the Bishop's Ring.

Piotrowski did know Magda was at her sister's apartment. He had a glass on her and a camera on the bedroom where she slept. His camera lens could peer through the sheer curtains and capture Magda's movements as she moved about the room. She always turned out the light though when she undressed for fear that someone would be watching. But now she was gone. A fire burned deep within him. Revenge had not been enough. He wanted her. He could understand like an athlete who struggled for years and felt the twinge of excitement long after he had left the field of play. The thrill of two opposing forces meeting a challenge to prove who is superior.

The spy remembered the day when he was denied his opportunity with Magda. He wanted Magda when she was a young flower, blossoming in beauty. When Piotrowski was finally overtaken by the older, stronger, man, she was lost forever. He felt he had lost the only real battle he had entered in life. And now he now had a measure of revenge. But it was not enough.

Piotrowski's life had been turned upside down because of her. He had turned Conrad in to the Security Police for subversive activities against the State. He changed physically from the scrawny soldier, to the muscular marvel envied by his peers. In time, he joined the Security Service Police, and applied for a spying trip in Buffalo, New York. He was found out and returned to Poland unsuccessful in bringing back the Bishop's Ring. Now was his opportunity to turn wasted years into fame.

This effort was going to end. If this time he did not succeed he promised himself he would quit his attempts to change the one hated moment for sexual conquest he had spent his entire life trying to achieve. He had long realized as time passed his desire though still strong for her had mellowed. He was ready to give up the hunt and chase. But now she was vulnerable and alone. Now was the best time to try again.

Piotrowski's real mission was to bring back the Bishop's Ring. His atheist superiors did not care how often or when his secretary satisfied his whims. But they did care whether he brought back the Bishop's Ring. It would be such a coup to have the ring with all of the labor unrest in the country. The Polish union leader Lech Walesa would call for more strikes. The Polish Communist government wanted to embarrass the Pope by flaunting its possession of the Bishop's Ring. The State hoped to put the Catholic Church in a subservient position as the Soviets had done to the Christian Churches in Russia. He dreamed capturing the Bishop's Ring could lead to the rank of General in charge of Security Services.

The whereabouts of the Bishop's Ring had to be found. The Colonel knew that as much as he watched the movements of American police, on television and in operations in New York. They were not as dumb as television often portrayed them to be. The woman was gone. His collaborator did not know where she was. The ring was missing. LaFayette claimed he did not have the ring. Now what?

Piotrowski had been in touch with LaFayette and LaFayette told him what the priest told him. He did not have the ring. If the dead man had brought the ring to the airport, which was the original plan, the Colonel surmised, and neither the priest nor his collaborator had the ring, they were the only people on the scene that would have any knowledge about it. Did the Police give the ring back to the widow? Did a traveler swipe it?

The Polish Colonel could afford to play the waiting game for a while. At the same time he quietly waited for leads to turn up by remaining in contact with LaFayette. He thought holding out the half million-dollar bribe for the ring still excited LaFayette. Upping the price might bring more action. If LaFayette was really interested in helping but he knew LaFayette was also being considered a prime suspect in the case because he himself had tried to set him up as a suspect. If LaFayette knew that he would not so gently tell him to take a walk. But so far LaFayette had said nothing to him about a photo of Magda and himself laying together in the sand.

Driven by his dream of promotion rewards Piotrowski made contact.

"I know Mr. LaFayette you are a busy man now that you have less help but my sources are willing to pay one hundred and fifty percent of their original offer for your services in securing this treasured piece of art work. This is their offer. In the event you have to make concessions along the way to those who may have information leading to the location and eventual recovering of the art piece there must be someone in your circles who can satisfy my client's interests in this art object. Do we have your attention?"

LaFayette responded, "My sources have been specific in telling me that they have not seen nor know of the whereabouts of such a treasure as you seek, sir. You are quite right there may be added costs to finding such a treasure. Your offer will be considered favorably. But as you can tell from the magnitude of art collections, some of these discussions and the people involved want absolute silence about their participation in finding such artifacts. They do not want to be compromised. I think you can understand that."

Piotrowski agreed. "Certainly, but unless we are able to acquire what we want your commission in this transaction cannot be paid. Remember the contract. Payment was based on delivery of the service."

"Understood." Quentin placed the receiver on the hook.

A few moments later he ended his silence. He dialed long distance to a private number.

"Betty?"

"Quentin. I was wondering when you were going to call."

"I would have sooner, my dear, but I feel so bad about all that has happened. I just couldn't get myself to talk about it. You know what I mean?"

"It's terrible." She said.

Quentin had his alibi. "When I spoke with Father Lawrence he was just blubbering away making absolutely no sense. He says he doesn't have the ring. How could he not have the ring? Conrad promised me he would bring the ring to the airport. I could always count on his promises. If Conrad said he would bring it he would bring it. You could trust him to do just exactly what he said he would do. I think Father Lawrence is lying to me. What's with this priest, does he lie?"

Betty was careful. "No, he doesn't lie. Quentin, I have no idea where the ring could be. It hasn't turned up here."

"I called him back. They said that he was no longer at St. Catherine's. They wouldn't give me his new address. The little snot probably recognized my voice and wouldn't tell me. But you can tell me can't you?"

"Quentin I have a letter I typed out today, from the Bishop addressed to you. In effect your services are terminated in our Diocese. If word got out I gave Father Lawrence's number to you I could lose my job on the spot. You know how much I love my job. I love it so much and you must have seen that because you never in all of our time together asked me to marry you. I always thought it was because you thought I was married to my job. But, anyway, you still never asked. Well, it's the only spouse I have right now. I am not going to throw it away for a fling with someone who comes and goes when he pleases and never makes a commitment to me. Father Lawrence is not the reason why I won't give you his number its because its just you I guess."

"Do you know what you are saying? If the police see me involved in this they can see you involved in this because you gave Father Lawrence's name to me and we went on a cruise together. You knew about the meeting at the airport. So I guess we are all caught up in this thing, Betty."

"You are Quentin. I'm not." She hung up the phone.

Now Quentin was calling in his cards. He reached for his Rolodex and spun it. He adjusted his glasses and picked up the receiver again and started punching numbers.

"Father Norman. How are you?"

"Good, Quentin. And you?

"Fine. I just heard about Father Lawrence being transferred. Did you know about that?

The priest answered, "Oh yes. He went to Shady Trail and Father Piorek came here. You'll probably be dealing with Father Piorek from now on with any work you want to do over at St. Catherine's."

Quentin continued to question. "Shady Trail? Where's that located?"

"It's our mission parish in Tennessee."

"Was Father Lawrence a bad boy or something like that to get sent down there?"

"No, no, no, nothing like that at all. Father Piorek is quite a priest. Well liked.

"What's his name again?"

"Father John Piorek. I think he left here about eight years ago. Polish, I believe. Anyway, this news will be coming out in the Catholic Register soon. They will have a story on him. Good choice. I don't have the Tennessee number but it's in the Diocesan Directory. Do you have one?"

"Yes, I think I do. Thank you for your help Father, and it was nice talking to you again."

In a parking lot across the street from Quentin LaFayette's office a light colored Ford delivery van was parked. Inside two men sat at the controls of an electronic eavesdropping device monitoring LaFayette's phone conversations. After LaFayette hung up, the crew leader said, "Morrison is going to love this tape. Better get it to him, quick!"

Chapter 24

"Monsignor O'Toole?"

"Yes."

"This is Lieutenant Morrison. This is not good news. We have it on tape that 'QL' has found out how to find out where 'L' is. One of your own, was contacted, and he, well he was conned out of the information, not realizing what he was giving away."

"Who was that?"

Morrison said, "A Father Norman. 'BR' refused to cooperate with 'QL.' She sent him packing."

The priest said, "Good."

"I don't know if anything will come of this, but 'L' should be notified right away and take proper precautions in case someone thinks he has the merchandize. His life could be in danger."

"Did we do the right thing Lieutenant?" There was silence on the other end of the line. After a long pause, Morrison responded.

"There are going to be risks Monsignor. I'm sure you're trying to look out for the best interests of the Church. One life has been lost. Another may be on the line now, I don't know. I don't know if 'QL' is going to do him in or our other suspect will go after 'L.' I think 'QL' may. He may think that 'L' does have the artwork. What we do know now is that 'QL' is in this with our other suspect. We know the stakes have been raised to one hundred fifty percent of the original offer to get the artwork. So that suggests that 'QL' was not so innocent right from the beginning. LaFayette was onto something and he needed players to bring out the artwork and to do the heavy hauling and to get the merchandize out in the open. 'L' was the pawn. Get my drift? 'L' was set up with a con man's pipe dream."

The Monsignor responded, "Yes, of course. It speaks volumes to me now. It shed's light. 'L' was taken in by a con man. Who says it can't happen to the unsuspecting?"

"There's another consideration here. I want you to know the phone tappers know there is some merchandize involved. I just thought of that. I'm going to have to get them to keep quiet about this. The place already around here realizes there is a hush-hush deal going on here. That only drives the curiosity level up and people talk. As my father used to say a remark left over from the Second World War days, 'Loose lips sink ships.' It's true.

"In case someone is ready to make a move and take a trip south I think you ought to be warned first so that security can be in place if it is needed. You might want to have police protection for 'L' You can call for it from where you are and more effectively without bringing us into the picture because that might blow our cover here. I don't know much about that part of the world. I'd hate to think a Sheriff Deputy like a Barney Fife was put on the case to protect a 'pawn.' Barney would really screw it up." The priest listened and waited for more direction.

"'QL' has stretched himself out on this one. I'm waiting to see what his moves are. He's been instructed to stay close to home. But a private jet flight back and forth from might be too costly. But with the stakes moved up he might think he can afford to take care of the situation himself and be back before anyone suspects he left town. I have the feeling he has the connections to get that kind of quick service. For that matter have it done for him."

The Monsignor reacted, "I'm very disturbed by what I'm hearing."

"This is New York. Two thousand homicides plus a year! People stop for a second then go about their business. Life is on the cheap seats. The only grievers here are friends and families. Life goes on. This is just one of the two thousand homicides. I can't explain it, but something keeps driving me. That's all I can say. It's like a feeling the widow had about the merchandise, the need to protect it. I got that same feeling, and I can't understand why."

"I fully understand you. I think I can explain it to you the next time we meet or when this is over."

Monsignor O'Toole said good-bye and hung up. He had to ask himself if he had blundered. Morrison was telling him Father Lawrence's life was in danger and that either one of two suspects could show up at his rectory and thinking they are going to get the Bishop's Ring. Would they just kill him if they didn't get it?

Monsignor O'Toole called the Bishop. The receptionist had left for the day. The phone continued to ring without being answered. He had to reach someone. Betty had gone and was on the way home. He tried the Bishop's residence. He was in luck. The Bishop's housekeeper answered the phone. She saw the Bishop stepping out of his car so she asked Monsignor O'Toole to hold and he would be right with him.

"Yes, Monsignor," he said, holding the phone in one hand and taking off his coat with the other.

"Bishop, I just spoke with New York."

"One moment please, I want to take this in my room. Please hold." He put the phone on hold and went to his room to resume the conversation. He picked up the phone handset.

"Yes. Go on. I'm here only to shower and change and go out to a meeting."

"New York said they have information that the suspects know the whereabouts of Father Lawrence. They may be en route to pick up the merchandize. When they don't find it they may take an inappropriate action. The suspect familiar with Father Lawrence may have connections with contract killers but New York was not sure."

"I see the hand of the devil in all of this I don't mind saying." The Bishop responded.

"New York suggested we make arrangements down there to protect Father Lawrence so as to not 'blow their cover' was the way he put it on what was going on up here."

"Yes, I think they are right. Listen! Call Father Piorek! He has the phone number in Shady Trail and the contacts. Have him get in touch with the authorities before he speaks with Father Lawrence. I haven't spoken to him about the holy relic yet. I think he's heard

185

enough for now. Then tell Father Piorek to call Father Lawrence. He should tell Lawrence we received information he should expect trouble any time soon. You've got to keep out of this Francis because you'll be connected to the merchandise if Lawrence thinks you know something. You better make clear to Father Piorek that under no circumstances is your name to be mentioned, under my orders in his conversations with Father Lawrence."

"Yes, Bishop." The Monsignor responded.

"I heard from Rome today. They are delighted to accept Father Piorek's nomination to become our Auxiliary Bishop. This is very interesting, indeed. They would like to see the ceremony conducted in the National Shrine of the Immaculate Conception in Washington. His Holiness, it seems has taken a personal interest in our nominee, and will be sending a representative from the Vatican to be on hand to welcome him into the brotherhood of Bishops. What should we think of that?"

The Monsignor shrugged. But he knew more. Magda had told him how the ring came to be in America and its manifested destiny to be on the hand of a Polish Bishop. With this news he knew more was coming. It's part of the mysterious ways of the Lord, His wonders to perform, which he would share with Morrison when this was over.

"They want us to include invitations to all of our Cardinals and as many of the hierarchy as we can reasonably afford to house. They will solicit funds for the occasion in order to cover all of the expenses that we cannot cover with our delegation's expenses."

The Monsignor commented, "It's quite special. I've never heard of such effort for an Auxiliary Bishop."

"It is because they told me Bishop Piorek represents a missionary zeal. His evangelization among the poor and service to them they feel so strongly attached to his spirit as an apostle of the Lord. This is what Vatican II called for among the Bishops. John represents the letter and the spirit of those Vatican II documents."

"I believe I am getting a picture." Monsignor O'Toole said.

"I think we are both getting a picture, Monsignor. Let's keep the devil out of it."

"Father Piorek. This is Monsignor O'Toole."

"Yes, Monsignor, how are you?"

"I'm fine. Listen, I have something to tell you. Bishop O'Farrell probably would have called you himself but he is out to a meeting so he asked me to call you."

Father Piorek answered quickly, "I'm listening."

"Father Lawrence is in deep trouble. He does not know I know this. Bishop O'Farrell has instructed me to call and tell you that you should not breathe a word or use my name in conjunction with this information because other people including myself could get killed. The Bishop wants you to call the local sheriff in Shady Trail. Tell him Father Lawrence needs police protection because he may be getting some unwanted visitors ready to do him some harm. Even kill him!"

Piorek responded, "It sounds like he should be very concerned."

Quickly O'Toole became seriously concerned. "We need law enforcement in on this. Now, is Sheriff Deputy Barney Fife in charge or is Andy Griffith?"

"Sheriff Barney is in charge, Monsignor. Jim Barney is his name. But he's of another persuasion. Died in the wool Baptist. Always called me 'Mr. Piorek,' because he told me he called no man Father except God in heaven. But he's got a cousin named Maynard Bowles who is a good pal of mine, a convert, who probably has Father Lawrence wrapped up in his war stories by now. I can call Maynard, and he can deal with his cousin. He'd love to do that, he will act as the protector for the good Father."

"What are you talking about Father? Can't we get police for Father Lawrence? My God! Some devils may be on their way right to the closest airport to that place. They could go out, murder Lawrence, jump back into their jet plane and high tail it to New York and be there before the sun comes up. Now, what are you talking about?"

In a voice sparkling with mountain chatter, Father Piorek announced, "I'm talking about Maynard Bowles, a Vietnam veteran, the best hunter in the mountains down there. He's twice the man the sheriff is if you need someone to protect you. Besides he will whip his cousin's rear end if he doesn't protect Father Lawrence. He wears a seven-inch bladed Bowie knife strapped to his side. He walks around in camouflage clothes. He can hit bull's eyes with his 45 automatic handgun at fifty yards. You'd feel sorry for any bear that wanted to wrestle him. Some times I feel he thinks he's still in Vietnam!"

"Would he protect Father Lawrence?"

"Absolutely. No questions asked. But will it come to that? I mean, you just told me not so long ago a crazy killer is on the loose and wants to kill me. He hasn't shown up here yet!"

The Monsignor warned, "No not yet, but the rest of the picture has not been filled in with color. You know enough to set your friend Maynard straight. The Bishop wants you to call the sheriff. Just tell him the priest is not cooperating in a conspiracy if the sheriff starts to ask questions. Tell him the request for protection comes from your Bishop. Alert Father Lawrence to call his friend Maynard. The guy sounds like he is a one man SWAT team. The Bishop would have called but he had to rush to go to a meeting. But please keep my name out of this."

Monsignor O'Toole advised Father Piorek, "Lawrence should be very concerned but he does not need to send any non-verbal messages should some visitors arrive in the next few hours or days at his rectory."

Piorek responded, "It's a log cabin, Monsignor."

"That's different from what he's been used to."

"The parishioners built it. It's the best around."

"I know he will appreciate going first class."

Father Piorek moved quickly to follow the Bishop's orders to call Father Lawrence and Sheriff Barney.

Chapter 25

The Cutler Construction Company twin engine Lear Jet taxied down the long ramp to the takeoff runway. Two pilots inside waited for clearance from the LaGuardia terminal tower before taking off. They checked their gauges to make sure everything was in order. The fuel tanks were full and they were ready for take off. The signal was given and the throttle was pushed forward. The privately outfitted jet screeched down the runway gaining momentum and rose upward in its climb. It then faded from sight of the airport in the clouds.

"Crude" Cutler picked up his nickname in high school trying to get dates with girls. It stuck when he fractured the language in conversation using curse words working on construction jobs. He took to the nickname as a badge of honor among his associates. Cutler, crude and greedy, was able to build a financial empire among Real Estate speculators tearing down and building skyscrapers.

Crude and two of his company vice-presidents sat in their swivel chairs looking at Quentin LaFayette. Quentin's eyes stared at the cabin wall, vacant, as if he was in a dream. "It's a pleasure to do something for you, Mr. LaFayette. Now I can return you a favor. You sent me so much work it makes me feel good to repay you. You don't look too comfortable." Crude handed Quentin a mixed drink. "Here, its a good way to fly. Takes off the edge."

Quentin LaFayette nodded. "Where do we land?"

"Near Nashville. It's a private airport. Ever been there?"

"No. The closest I've come to Nashville is to flip through the channels and I just keep on clicking through till I find something of my taste."

Crude asks, "Do you watch Hee-Haw?"

Quentin smiles, "I like sports. I follow what's on in season. I don't have to think. It's lazy I know but I like to shut down when I hit the door of the apartment."

Crude wanted to get personal. "Have you got a penthouse yet?"

Quentin shook his head. "I'll buy a house and pay to have someone cut my grass before I get into penthouse living."

"So, ah, the boys here, ah, got us a limo waiting when we get there. One of my associates arranged for it. We should be there after dark, maybe ten thirty." Then cutting to the quick, LaFayette asked, "You got any problem with this? I mean he is a priest."

Crude assures him, "Only if he gives you a problem, do I got a problem with him. The boys will take care of everything."

"What if he has the merchandize stashed away some place what do I do then?"

"We borrow him for a while until he gets it for you and then we bring him back."

LaFayette asks, "Unharmed?"

Crude responds, "Of course! You got what you came for. I'm happy."

LaFayette questioned, "If he can't produce, then what?"

Crude said, nonchalantly, "The boys will waste him. We will be on our way, jump in the limo, head back to the airport and jet back to New York. Tomorrow morning go back to work like nothing happened."

LaFayette squirmed, "Just one, dead priest. I don't know if that solves my problem. I need the merchandise not a dead priest."

"The dead priest is the message for the next in line to wake up and turn over what you want. It sends a message."

Quentin sipped his drink and wondered who the next in line would be. Betty Ryan knew about the showing of the ring but she was with him on the cruise. Magda must be under Police custody because she's disappeared thanks to the stupidity of the blackmailing dumb trick artist who offered him one hundred and fifty percent, a three quarter of a million dollar deal. If Crude knew how much money was involved he would want a cut of it.

LaFayette thought Magda must have told the Police about the Bishop's Ring. His mind wandered into possible circumstances where the ring could be. He knew Conrad had talked to Father Lawrence on the phone but had never met him. Nor had Conrad discussed the ring with him. He wondered if Father Lawrence found a way to contact Magda to find out what happened to Conrad. Piotrowski said she moved quickly to get out of her house. LaFayette's thoughts drifted.

Maybe Conrad decided not to bring the ring in and she had it all along. The Police are not mentioning it. Should a priest be killed just because she kept the ring? Quentin was having problems. He made good money being connected with Father Lawrence who supplied him with names of other priests from his seminary. They were all pastors. Those leads led to other work. He sat there and looked at the pillows of clouds and continued to think this through.

All of this could lead to a reverse in business if Father Lawrence put the word out he was involved in a scam operation. He would be ruined. One diocese shutting him off was going to be bad enough, but many could bankrupt him. Would silencing him save his business?

He hoped God would understand his motives for trying to keep so many employed. They would be put out of work if he failed. It was not just his employees but also all of the craftsmen in the trades who would be out of work. Those families needed him and his sources so contracts could be awarded and the work continued. With his erroneous thinking the truth of murder eluded him. His conscience had been compromised to kill a priest!

Crude caught Quentin daydreaming. He said. "We had the food service pack filet mignon and chilled wine for supper. Any time you're ready to put your napkin on and slice into your juicy filets, let me know. I'm kind of getting hungry here. I was thinking we could eat now and then take a little nap before we set down. Then if it's a bouncy ride at least the food and booze will be down the hatch and won't be coming up on us. You know what I mean? I got this hiatal hernia right here under my heart and I get the worst heartburn when my food's not settled. I should make commercials for those antacid pills."

Quentin said, "Sure, let's eat." This guy is going on a killing mission and all he can do is think about his stomach. But that's not all he thinks about. This plane is outfitted like a roving brothel!

The four men sat together at the dining table behind the wing section of the plane. They enjoyed the gourmet meals prepared by the dining service at the airport. They had taken off their coats. Quentin saw the two "Vice-Presidents" with automatic pistols strapped and holstered to the side of their chest. The reality began to set in they were on a killing mission.

Crude Cutler watched his eyes as they first came in contact with the weapons. "I like to watch what my boys do in these things."

"Is that why they call you, 'Crude'? I think my stomach is going to roll over just thinking about this."

"If you got to puke, hit the head. Ha, ha, ha, ha." Crude looked at him seriously. "Hey, don't let it spoil your dinner." Then he laughed again. When he stopped, Crude said.

"Today, it is a church we work on, tomorrow, it is an office building, or apartments. I have to be connected to where the money is. The billionaires in the towers! They own the government and they keep me in business. They're into extortion and kickbacks. Big stuff! Nothing like the little stuff you're involved in. And they got the government diverted to the mafia while they rake in the billions. I give them the lowest price because its what they want and I get the business. They are not like the Mafioso. Those gumbas will all be in jail someday. But the billionaires won't. You want to know why? Because they make what they do look legitimate!" With that remark, Crude pulled in his left cheek and winked to make his point. Quentin listened.

Crude continued. "Nobody cares. They own the freakin government. The little guy will be their freakin slave and they won't say a freakin thing about it because the billionaires are connected to their tribes out west. Get my drift?" Quentin nodded. No comments came forth.

"I'm going to take a snooze. Wake me five minutes before we drop down." Crude said.

Traveling West, Quentin watched the sunset below a wide ocean of fluffy white clouds. Later, the seat belt bell and light went on as they made their way through the bumpy clouds and were prepared to land. The city of Nashville was lit up. Off in the distance he could barely see the hill country.

The plane taxied over to a hanger and a waiting limo suddenly turned on its lights and pulled up along side the plane. The hanger crew manager of the airline service walked out of his office to check the plane in and collect landing fees. He directed the pilots to a waiting cab and told them where they could catch a sip and watch a good show while they refueled on their short visit.

The four men slipped into the limousine and were off to the mountain country to make an unscheduled visit.

Sheriff Barney told Maynard he would keep an eye out for the priest. But Maynard didn't trust him to be too concerned. Father Piorek's phone call sounded urgent and something must be done. The new priest's life was in danger. He let Maynard know he trusted him to stick by the new priest, just as if he would have helped him if he needed help. Maynard promised he'd do his best.

Sheriff Barney always complained about not having the money to hire enough deputies to slow down the crime in the county. But people thought he just wanted more electronic stuff and didn't feel they had to look like a police hardware distribution center. He would just have to make do like the rest. No frills in life. For that reason Maynard didn't really expect much help from his cousin.

On a hill behind the log cabin home of the priest of St. Thomas the Apostle church, Maynard used to sit and with Father Piorek and talk late into the night glancing at the stars. If the phone rang the priest would take off and in a sprint make it through the kitchen side door in time before the fifth ring. When all of the lights were on, they would look into the log cabin as a focus, and Maynard would strike a pose with his forty-five automatic and tease Father Piorek he could hit anything in his house. Even something as small as a book on a table! Father Piorek never took him up on the challenge as Maynard tried to prove to him what a good shot he was. The bullet would later be found in the pages of the book.

On this particular night, Maynard, without Father Lawrence's knowledge made camp on the hill. He brought his sleeping bag, pup tent, camouflage gear and a Special Forces sabrelite to cut the dark with 400 percent more candlepower. He was also armed with an assault weapon and his Biretta 9mm handgun. Of course, he had his trusty Bowie, sharpened to cut facial whiskers, if he needed a cold shave.

Maynard couldn't understand why anyone would want to hurt a priest. What could a priest do that people wanted to send someone to get him? Maynard waited in the darkened night for signs of a car pulling into the driveway in front of the log cabin. Maynard was ready to use his night vision binoculars and check out to see if the visitors were friends or foes.

In the early part of the evening the cars came and left as he figured Father Lawrence held a committee meeting at his home. The last car left about ten-thirty. Then, the road became silent in the night. He used his binoculars to look into the log cabin and saw Father Lawrence reading a book.

At 1:30 A.M. a lonely car came down the road. It slowly approached the church building as if to look for identification. The driver saw the driveway and turned in and turned off his lights as the car moved toward the log cabin with its engine still running. Maynard could see Father Lawrence get out of his chair and look out the window to see who was coming. But, in the darkness Father Lawrence could not see the moving car. Then it stopped.

Father Lawrence went to the phone but the line went dead. The priest blessed himself, and lowered his head in prayer. Maynard scoped the highway with his night vision binoculars and did not see a sheriff car in sight. It made him fearful and angry that Father Piorek was right about cousin Barney. Maynard checked the chambers of his assault rifle and his handgun. They were loaded. He knew that but he wanted assurances. The safeties were on. He felt for his knife and nervously retied the scabbard strapping the knife to his leg. He was ready to go to war. His mind traversed the years. Sweat covered his forehead. He was now on a hillside ready to raid an enemy camp.

Maynard watched as four men climbed out of the limo. He saw one return from the area of the telephone lines. He figured the telephone lines were cut. Maynard knew they were working fast. He could not wait. Maynard had to get closer to the house.

Suddenly, the front door was pushed open. Two men walked in. They had suits on. Then Quentin LaFayette walked in, followed by Crude Cutler.

"I figured it out Father," Quentin said, "You have what I need. You know what I am talking about."

Father Lawrence looked at the four men. "Are you here to go to confession, and confess your part in one murder? Or are you here to commit one more? I told you I do not have what you are looking for. I never had it. I think the whole thing was a hoax to get one of your employees murdered. I can think of reasons why Quentin."

As Father Lawrence spoke, Maynard could hear his remarks loudly spoken as he moved toward the back porch. The back door was closed but the kitchen window was open and Lawrence's voice traveled.

Quentin smirked, "It's not for you to think Lawrence. We did well together but you screwed up. They dumped you. You are no good to me here in this swamp. I've seen the merchandise and it's real. I've tried to think who might have it and it still comes down to you. So either you give it to me or tell me where it is so we can go get it, or say your prayers. Which is it?"

The two men standing in front of Father Lawrence opened their coats revealing their handguns. Each pulled his weapon from its holster. From the kitchen doorway Maynard opened fire on the four men with his assault rifle cutting them down in a hail of bullets. Father Lawrence fell to his knees and reached toward them. Seeing they were dead he began to recite the prayers of the last rites. Maynard did not stop but went back out to the kitchen and around the corner of the house to see where the driver of the limo was located. The man sat relaxed in his seat waiting for the return of the four men. He did not know what happened in the house.

Maynard came up along the passenger side of the car and stuck his weapon into the driver inside. "Get out," he demanded. The startled man pushed the door open. Maynard went over the top of the car as he was waiting for him to get out. "I got a job for you." He pushed him into the log cabin living room and searched him.

195

Maynard kicked the handguns off to the side and said. "I want you to put this trash back in your fancy car fellow and I want you to take it back where it came from. Do you understand me? I have your car keys."

Father Lawrence objected. Maynard looked at him and said nothing. He then looked at the limo driver and said, "Start packing or I will have one more to take back to where I think you all came from." Then he looked at Father Lawrence and said, "Your telephone lines have been cut by one of these varmints. You can't call my cousin Barney. I don't know what he would do if he found out I took decisive action. Whatever he'd do, I know he would try to make it look bad for you. My idea is the best. I want you to follow us in your car so that you can bring me home."

The driver loaded the bodies of the four men into the limo as Maynard looked on. He never so much as touched one. They drove to the airport and up to the Lear Jet. The night clerk gave the driver the key to the airplane's door and went back inside to the office. Maynard put one a pair of gloves he had concealed in his trousers. The driver and Maynard moved the four bodies into the plane's back cabin where two beds had been installed. They pulled back the sheets and covered up the dead bodies.

All this time the driver said nothing scared that Maynard would turn on him and leave the driver in the plane. When they finished, Maynard asked to see the driver's license. Maynard took down the number, name and the address of the driver on a sheet of paper, folded it and put it in his uniform pants.

"I know who you are. If you ever speak of this and it gets back to me, I will visit you. You know the rest."

Maynard closed the plane's door and marched the limo driver to the office. He threw the plane's door keys back to the clerk. "When the pilot comes back tell him his passengers are sleeping off a good one. He can take off when he's ready and take them home. They won't even remember this good old country brew when they're dragged off the plane."

The smiling clerk said, "Gave them some of your own stuff, huh?"

The limo driver looked bug-eyed at Maynard. Maynard responded, "Yes, my own stuff." He and the driver walked out together and walked to the limousine. "You got a mess to clean up in there. It's best you start on it real soon, because somebody might be asking questions after those boys land back where they came from. The pilots are not going to know until they land. I don't know what they are going to say on his flight report. But you better clean up this car and act dumb if you know what's good for you."

The limo driver put his hand to his mouth and closed his eyes and shook his head from left to right. He said, "I got y'all."

Maynard waited till he saw the direction of where he was headed and then climbed in Father Lawrence's car.

"I could use a beer right about now. Do you have any at home because I'm a little thirsty? We got some work to do cleaning up you living room. It got a little messy and I might have to dig out a few bullets out of the walls."

Father Lawrence pulled away from the hanger's side parking lot and screamed at Maynard. "You just killed four men and threatened a fifth!"

"I killed a lot more than that in Viet Nam, Father. I don't have a problem with what I did there up at your place. Should I? You want to trade places with that trash? They came to kill you. I defended you. You know it. I know it. Cousin Barney didn't want to know it. And he's the law around here. Why if it got out how do you think he'd feel if people knew he wasn't taking care of business? He wants to keep his job. No, he won't tell. I'll make sure of that."

"That's what I am afraid of." Then Father Lawrence thought about what Maynard had done and how he was going to get to tell Maynard what he had done was not to be passed off as nothing. But he himself was confused and needed to seek spiritual guidance for himself.

Father Lawrence said, "You're going to have to go to confession."

"What, you want to hear about May Belle again, Father? Hey, I got to go out and see if I can put your phone back in service. That's what you get when you call a telephone company man to be of service."

197

Father Piorek listened to Father Lawrence's account of the night and Maynard's commando mentality toward protecting his person. Now, the problem was what to tell the police authorities when the bodies show up, in New York?

Father Piorek said to Father Lawrence, "I believe the Bishop is in contact with the police authorities in New York. Everything will have to come through his office anyway. I can't for the life of me understand this madness now swirling about us." Father Piorek said. He added, "I think the New York police will have answers for what happened. Remember they clued in our Bishop.

A stunned Father Lawrence could only say, "Please pray for me John."

Chapter 26

Crude Cutler's pilot dropped the twin-engine jet to ten thousand feet, called the control tower, and waited for landing instructions. Off in the distance the pilot could see Manhattan Island. The sun glistened off the walled glass and the two pilots knew they were coming home. They were given instructions and inserted into the flight patterns of arriving and departing planes. When he cut the engines, he looked at his watch.

Hank Short, the Pilot, said, "Ten-thirty. We made good time." He looked at Chuck Edwards, the co-pilot. "Why don't you give those sleeping beauties a rap on the door. I can't believe they slept this long. They were here before we came back from Nashville. Maybe they brought back some babes. Check on them. I'll check to see if the limo is here."

The Co-Pilot, Chuck, gave a wrap on the door. No answer. He opened it and looked at the bodies neatly covered under blankets. He went over to Crude's body and shook it. "Mr. Cutler, Sir." Suddenly he realized there was no movement at all, among the four bodies. He pulled down the covers and saw they were still in their suits and then he saw the blood. "Hank, come here. You got to see this."

Blaring sirens filled the roads to the private airport hangar at LaGuardia. Captain Antonnucci led the homicide contingent of police cars rolling into the parking lot across the street from the airplane hangers. He waited for the light to change and walked into the office and out of it without saying a word to anyone. Police were already on the scene. He climbed the narrow stairs of the jet, and walked back into the back cabin sleeping quarters. No one had moved the bodies. He recognized all four faces. Without saying a word to anyone in the plane he departed and walked back into the hangar office.

"I'm Captain Antonnucci. Police." He showed his badge. "I want to speak with the pilot."

The shaken pilots were in the small lounge drinking coffee. The office manager, pointed to the lounge. The two were dressed in blue airline uniforms, with the Cutler Construction Company cloth insignia stitched onto the vest pockets of their coats. The Captain walked into the lounge. They were alone. He flashed his badge again and told them who he was. They nodded but said nothing.

"Tell me from the beginning!" The police captain said.

Hank opened up. "I'm Hank Short and this is my co-pilot, Chuck Edwards. We work for Cutler Construction Company. We take the execs to and from their business appointments mostly out of state. We are on call all the time. Nothing normal about our work hours! They finish work at the office and we then fly them to appointments. We could stay a day or two or return after a one-hour business meeting. It's crazy but that is the way the business is conducted."

"So where did you go? Or come back from?"

"We went to Nashville. The bosses left us at a private airport outside Nashville and we took a cab into the city and caught a show at a club. And then came back. The boss didn't care. He said he would go to bed but make sure he was back here by ten thirty, this morning. We were here."

The Captain said, "I lost you."

"When we come back to the airport the clerk said that our passengers were drunk and they had to be helped on board. Mr. Cutler likes his booze and women so we didn't think anything of it. We just thought he went to bed, which is normally what he does. Sometimes he sleeps in his clothes. So we didn't think anything of it and took off and came back home. When we found them, we called you."

The Captain asked, "Nothing else? You don't know who helped them onto the plane?"

Hank responded, "This was in the wee hours Captain. The clerk was half asleep when we got there. He said something about a national guardsman was good enough to give the limousine driver a helping hand then he took off with a friend. That's all I remember. He gave me back the keys I had dropped off with him and we went aboard. The clerk cleared us for take off and Chuck put us back on course. We counted stars and watched the sun come up and flew the rest of the way to New York. It's a great job. Paid well. I hope I still have it after this."

"Leave the particulars with the officer. I'll send someone in here to take down information. We might want to talk some more to you. Oh, did you know Mr. LaFayette?"

"Never saw him before in my life until this trip. Of course I have only been with the company six months."

"Do yourselves a favor. Try to avoid reporters on this one. Reporters are out there in the office. If you want to stay healthy and alive the less you say about this the better. You'll expose yourselves to a killer who thinks you know something. I am pretty certain you know nothing this time. It won't be worth it to get your mugs on the cover of The Post or The Daily News. Someone might come looking for you. Someone wanted LaFayette and your boss was taken out with his two bodyguards. LaFayette was not the first. But the news media knows about a silent killer. When they start to fit the pieces of the puzzle together they may think they have to talk to you two guys. A killer may want to cover his tracks and you two know where all of this took place. You know more than you think. The killer might think you know too much." He turned, walked out of the lounge leaving the two pilots scared and sweating in their uniforms.

They got up and went out to the waiting limo and never answered reporter's questions.

When the Captain returned to the precinct, Morrison asked, "What do you think Al?" The Captain's face showed a pained expression. "It hurts to think. But I will say this. It happened in the jurisdiction of Tennessee and it was dumped on us. This one is going to hit the newspapers and radio and TV. Four bodies showing up on a plane with a flight log is going to send this investigation back to

Tennessee. Might hurt the country music business for about a half a day or so. That's what I think."

Morrison seeing he was being relaxed said, "No, come on now."

The Captain waxed eloquently, "Can't you just hear a country singer, coming up with a knee slapper about the four dudes from New York who came to Country Music town and left loaded with lead. It'll be a big hit with the Folsom Prison crowd. Pick any one of those honky-tonk, glad or sad warblers and they will be singing the Nashville blues.

Morrison said, "Captain, we just lost a witness."

The Captain looked at Morrison. "Yes, and you just lost one more S.O.B. whose been mucking up the works. Now the Cowboy is left alone. He doesn't have what he wants, which we assume is the merchandise."

Morrison updated the Captain. "I think he wants more. I think he wants Mrs. Kaminski. In Poland many years ago when he was a young soldier she said he tried to rape her. She thinks he may still be trying. Those photos of her on the beach are more than he got of her before. So he still has his sights on her. He's probably looking for her now."

"That deal he worked out with LaFayette yesterday went sour on him, huh?" The Captain asked, and added. "And we probably had a hand in it by telling your Monsignor friend. What I think is the alert sign went up, phone calls were made and low and behold the National Guard was called in. They were called in to protect one relocated priest who had been sent away for the prideful sin of trying to impersonate a Bishop." He momentarily stopped to laugh adding, "And, if he never prayed that hard before, there is one scared priest down in Tennessee. How is he going to explain to Jesus his involvement in this scam which ended in five men dead?"

"Captain, you're making light of this whole thing."

He looked at Morrison, "I've got to or I will go bonkers." He raised his voice. "Moe, we're counting five dead, and holding our breath about more all over some little treasure. As it turns out, will not ever be awarded to the priest who got us into this whole mess. We are not out of this yet. I'm just waiting for the next shoe to drop. In the meantime, go ahead with the case. We have enough now to proceed. The FBI wiretap taped conversation from yesterday connecting LaFayette with the Cowboy will seal a conspiracy issue and more. The prints of both the Cowboy and LaFayette in front of the embassy! Awesome! They are timed and dated from the camera to establish contact was made just after Kaminski's murder. The tape doesn't mention the ring or the priest, just the merchandise and the offer of the increase in the fee, which links the Pole to LaFayette. You have LaFayette on tape from the statement you took from him, so the voices can be matched up." The Captain shifted his thoughts.

"I don't know what the Assistant D.A. is going to do about this latest bloodletting. He hasn't been talking to me lately probably figuring when I had something to talk about we would get together. I'm going to let him ride this one out on his own and see what direction he's heading. So far, there doesn't appear to be a spot where a discovery could be made to the ring."

Morrison smiled, "That's good news."

The Captain asked Morrison, "What's next for you?"

"I've got to snoop around to see what's going to happen to the money that is supposed to be paid to LaFayette on Kaminski's life, where that is going to end up since he is no longer with us, and if the proceeds will revert to the widow as a secondary beneficiary. She could pick up another half a million, making nine hundred grand!

"Always thinking, Moe, you are always thinking!"

The afternoon newspapers carried the story about the flying corpses across the nation as a fever developed over a gangland hit which sent four New Yorkers back to New York. They were killed for trying to muscle in on Tennessee's entertainment and record business. The papers and news media each copied each other's stories, reporting Mr. Quentin LaFayette went along to design a new opera house based on his business in restoration and construction of churches and other entertainment facilities.

The news account speculated Tennessee entertainment interests saw this as a message to send outsiders looking for new pastures. The New York newspapers even speculated what was done had the help and blessing of the Branson, Missouri entertainment cartel. Further speculations suggested the killings were to keep New Yorkers from producing sexually explicit shows while the rest of the country shifted to more wholesome entertainment fare.

When that story hit the inside pages of the tabloids, Captain Antonnucci roared his approval at the "defense of the fortress and sewer mentality" taken by the news media. With a big smile on his face, he held up a copy of the afternoon paper with its gaudy, bawdy headline. Mocking he said, "**GIVE THEM HELL, NEW YORK**," to which the Captain added, "those Tennessee redneck gangsters!"

The Captain held up another headline, "**DAVY CROCKETT, STILL KING OF FRONTIER.**" Underneath the sub-headings read, "**Takes No Prisoners, Sends Four Home In Flying Sleeper.**"

Over in Manhattan, in the People's Republic Of Poland Embassy, Wilk went into Colonel Piotrowski's office and walked over to the radio and pressed the "ON" button. The news reporter came on with urgent news. The reporter sounded as if what she had to say was going to change the lives of the citizens of the entire city.

"Special Report. This morning, at approximately ten-thirty, a plane pulled in to a corporate airport hanger at LaGuardia, loaded down with four dead bodies. Crude Cutler, Chief Executive officer of Cutler Construction Company was found slain in the rear cabin of his Lear Jet. Three others were killed with him, and were found in the jet plane, including two company Vice Presidents. Their names are being withheld pending notification of kin. A fourth person, one Quentin LaFayette, a building designer, believed to be escorting Mr. Cutler to a Tennessee location for a business meeting, was also killed by an assailant, whom police speculate is at large now in Tennessee. There are only rumors and speculations why the four men were murdered. More news on the half hour."

Chapter 27

Father Lawrence called Bishop O'Farrell to tell him what had happened and to ask if he should he remain in the position as pastor of St. Thomas the Apostle Church.

After the initial greetings Father Lawrence began to give the Bishop a report of events of the previous night. "Father Piorek called to tell me he alerted the Sheriff that I might have unfriendly visitors. He actually said they were killers. I... I could not believe my ears. I had a committee meeting scheduled for last night so I went on with it. I figured no one would show up with a parking lot full of cars to kill me. Then John told me he called Maynard Bowles. He's a local outdoorsman type whom he befriended while he was down here. I already met him in the coffee shop. He works for the telephone company. Anyway, Father Piorek converted him to the faith."

The Bishop eager to hear said, "Yes, Father, go on with it."

"Well the Sheriff's deputies didn't show up. I don't know why. But Maynard told me the Sheriff is actually his cousin. He said the Sheriff was a little ticked off because Maynard joined up with us. I also know Maynard is sort of a legend in this area, a Paul Bunyan type of guy. The Sheriff and his cronies are afraid of him but people here all love him." The Bishop was silent, listening, as Father Lawrence related his experience. The Shady Trail Pastor took a deep breath and continued.

"Maynard told me he called his cousin and told him to make sure to protect me. Well, he and his cousin had words and Maynard told me as we drove back from the little airport he wasn't sure his cousin would send anybody. Maynard decided to take things into his own hands. Then Maynard told me his cousin sort of conned him into protecting me because he said he wasn't sure I was worth protecting. They had a family feud on the telephone. I didn't know about it. I thought the Sheriff was going to be close by." Father Lawrence took a drink of water nearby to overcome a dry mouth and continued.

"When Quentin and his three cohorts arrived with guns without being stopped I was concerned about living in the next few minutes. Then Maynard started blasting away with his rifle and I went blank for a second. Then I gave all four of them the last rites on my living room floor. It happened all so fast. I couldn't believe it. Maynard got a hold of their limo driver brought him into the house and quickly stuffed the dead men into the limousine. I followed them to the airport in my own car. Maynard and the limousine driver put the bodies on the plane and I drove Maynard back here. I was in shock the whole time. I couldn't believe this was happening. It was like out of a war movie."

The Bishop interrupted, "Do you think the law enforcement authorities refused to protect your life after they had been called?"

"I don't know what to think. I think, Maynard probably told his cousin to keep everyone away and he would take care of things once and for all. He wanted to send a message to anyone coming down from New York who thought they wanted to do me in. He fought in the jungles of Vietnam. I think he thought he was back there. He talks about it a lot to get it out of his system. But he's the kind of guy you want around. Believe me Bishop, I felt God sent him to protect me. I believe that."

The Bishop after hearing Father Lawrence said, "I want you to call the Sheriff and report what happened in your living room. I want you to tell him personally who was responsible for the defense of your life. If he wants to take it from there, it will be up to him. Please let him know I, your Bishop, am very disturbed that he had been warned and that it appears his department refused to protect you. The rest is in the hands of God."

"On other matters, Father, I have received word from the Vatican that Father Piorek will be elevated to the episcopacy and join me as my Auxiliary Bishop. They are calling all of the shots on this. I don't understand it yet, but he will be elevated to the rank of Auxiliary Bishop in Washington, at the National Shrine of the Immaculate Conception. We are going to be allowed only so many guests. I would like you to be present for the installation."

"I would be happy to be there, Your Excellency."

"I would also suggest you bring your new friend along. Does he have a regular suit of clothes? I'm sure he must have a suit he wears just for funerals. If he doesn't have a suit take him to a men's store and get him outfitted. Send me the bill. And 'Bishop' Piorek will be very happy to meet him again, and thank him personally for helping to protect you. Anyway, we will arrange for your airline trip after we find out whether your new friend can come to Washington for the ceremonies. Later, we are going to have to get this other matter straightened out with the authorities. Be in peace with the Lord."

Sheriff Barney always said he liked being a policeman the second best thing in life. He then would roll his moustache hairs and grin when he said it leaving them to guess what he preferred as the best thing in his life. But the worst thing in his life always had always been competing with his cousin Maynard. He hated that. Maynard always won. Then Maynard would put his cousin down by saying he'd hate to depend on him if he ever needed him. Even when Maynard, could out do him in just about everything. That included guns and bow and arrow hunting.

When Maynard called the Sheriff to tell him he needed to send out deputies to protect the priest it seemed to be too much and too personal for Sheriff Barney to take orders from Maynard. So in the heat of the argument, and without thinking Sheriff Barney told Maynard to protect the priest because he probably could do a better job of it himself. Sheriff Barney reverted back to a lifetime of competition and allowed his ego to emotionally get the best of him again.

But Sheriff Barney knew that he would face a storm of criticism if word got out that Maynard actually took out the four men the Sheriff had refused to protect the priest. When the Exec Air Service clerk in the airport nearby Nashville said it was a National Guardsman who helped the men onto the plane and then Nashville reporters reported his story on the TV news, the people of Shady Trail knew it must have been Maynard because the guy practically lives in his military and adventure clothing. But Sheriff Barney refused to say a word about it to anyone.

Finally, a Nashville TV news reporter found a limousine and took a trip from the airport to Shady Trail. The reporter called the County Sheriff and began asking questions. Sheriff Barney granted her an interview. In the interview she irritated the Sheriff with her questions. But he knew he faced an election in the fall and needed all the support he could get. He gave this statement to the news:

"Everybody knows that New York likes to throw its garbage on a barge and send it someplace else. It's been all over the news. You've covered it yourself! Now there's a report circulating some human garbage was sent down here and went to a county east of Nashville. The suggestion has been made the human garbage went to a processing plant and then was taken back to New York. We can't confirm garbage processing took place in Tennessee or back in New York. What we can confirm is that the human garbage came in and left the same night but where it was processed we have no idea. We are glad it is back in New York where it came from originally."

Score one for Maynard's "Redneck" cousin.

The excitement around St. Catherine of Siena parish was building as the count down had begun and their new pastor was actually going to become a "Bishop." Now they felt a little better about the fact Father Lawrence went overboard and spent the money because a Bishop should have a beautiful church for his home. Monsignor O'Toole assured Bishop-Elect Piorek some parishioners would come forward with money to return the Tabernacle back to the center altar of the Church, if he wanted to go back and do it. Bishop-Elect Piorek said he would think about it after the celebrations had ended.

Bishop O'Farrell invited Father Piorek and Monsignor O'Toole to his office. The Monsignor came with Magda's text of the Legend of the Bishop's Ring. Seated in the Bishop's office he said, "The moment has come. The Bishop and I have read this document. It is a legendary account of the life of the Bishop's Ring, which will be given to you at your ordination. We suggest you read this tale thoroughly before your ordination. The only thing I can say is, when I have prepared all of my thousands of homilies in the course of my priesthood, I always looked to find the hand of God protecting, and guiding events to come to a holy and satisfactory conclusion. You yourself, I am sure, have done the same."

The Bishop interrupted. "Read this legend. You will understand your calling as a Bishop far beyond our selection of you as our Auxiliary Bishop. God will work through your hands to perform miracles."

The Vatican sent a Bishop from the Vatican Secretary of State's Office to Washington to be in contact with the organizing committee to watch what arrangements were being made on Bishop-Elect Piorek's behalf. Names had to be submitted to the Organizing Committee for those who could attend the ceremonies in the National Shrine of the Immaculate Conception.

The Organizing Committee gave special consideration to inviting officials of Poland, Bishop-Elect Piorek's native land as matter of diplomatic courtesy. A copy of the invitation was originally sent to the People's Republic of Poland Embassy in Washington. It was passed to New York to see if there was interest on the part of the Staff to attend the meeting. Trade Envoy Thaddeus Sobleski, staff person at the New York Embassy responded he would attend the Mass and the reception for the new Bishop. His name was forwarded to the organizing committee which included him as an attendee for the celebration. It would be held on the feast of Pentecost. When all of the names on the guest lists were returned, the members of the Kaminski and Klementowski families were also included.

Chapter 28

It didn't take long for Magda to find out Morrison lived across the street even though he had said nothing to her about it. From her darkened front bedroom she saw a car shut off its lights as it came around the corner and the garage door in the house across the street from her, would rise and the light in the garage would come on. And while the light from the garage door opener was still on she saw Morrison get out of the car as the door rolled down the channels to close. Magda wasn't looking for him. She was just sitting and thinking about her future. What she had once feared had come true.

Conrad had told her a long time ago that if the Polish Security Police would harass him in Poland, then they just might come after him again in America. And they did. But this time she suspected it was because of the Bishop's Ring. Up until she saw the face of the one man in her life who, brought her out of her experiences and made her realize being pretty attracted men in a way she could not comprehend. Older and living in America, watching television news, Magda knew much more.

What did she know of men as a teenager and about sexuality? Back then it was not like now? There were no movies or magazines. People where she came from said little about sex although they obviously knew so much about it because they had children. The boys would tease her, but as far as they knew, they knew less than girls, who at least experienced a female monthly curse. Some boys were more aggressive to find out what adults knew and she knew she drew stares because she was the first among her classmates to begin physically developing as a young woman.

All the girls congratulated her when they went swimming and it became clear she could not hide what the others only hoped they too would develop. That was the way it was then. While teenagers craved to know more and some may have experimented no one would say. The Church warned everyone to live according to God's laws. But it was not like now here in America. Teenagers could ingest a diet of sexual content every day after school on network TV.

The soldier who, tried to rape her she had come to believe as she matured, was as scared as she was. He may have been a little clumsy about the whole matter but as she recognized, men were very much attracted to her and his attempt to have his way may not have been as bad as it all appeared, as Conrad told her. He, too, served as a soldier. He knew how soldiers talked and what was on their mind. The fear of dying in a war, he told her, without ever knowing what a woman could be like may have driven her twenty-one year old attacker to take this chance and try to find out. The soldier did not know how things were going to work out. He may have thought he could end up marrying her after the experience. How could he know someone older, stronger, like Conrad was going to chase him out of the barn? When Conrad reasoned with her, and told her these ideas, she thought he was the smartest man in the whole world, then. She knew she could make a life with him.

When Morrison pulled into his garage she was reminded how Conrad was also there for her without ever letting her think she would have to worry about another forceful attack upon her person by an unwanted stranger. The policeman had said nothing to her that was out of line in his work. He understood her fears.

Now she had to make a life for herself. But she was not going to have to start from the beginning. Her old world sewing skills gave her a start in the dress making business when she came to the country. She made dresses for women at her parish church. As time went on she was asked to sew wedding dresses. She found McCall's dress patterns in the Sewing Center and had them on display in her sewing room. It was not an activity Conrad discouraged. Both knew when they came into possession of the Bishop's Ring, should

211

anything, God forbid happen to him, she would at least have a small business to earn an income. That's the way it all began.

When Conrad was murdered, Magda had a full-blown sewing business working out of her home. She made wedding dresses for entire wedding parties. She took advance orders only when the weddings were at least six months away so she could have the time to complete them before the wedding. She made special order and party dresses as well.

When Captain Antonnucci packed up her house, he took away her business and placed it in storage. She had to contact her customers to let them know that there was going to be a slight delay. She hoped they would understand the delay because of the death of her husband.

Conrad had encouraged her, but remained concerned she would be a target in her business. Now he could rest in peace knowing she could survive and be relieved of the task of custodian of the Bishop's Ring. She did not know where the feeling came from but she knew the Bishop's Ring was now in the proper hands. For all of the years they held it together they had similar feelings of danger and relief over the ring. It may have been Conrad's death, which gave her the feeling of completing a journey. But she sat there gazing through her thin curtains to the street. She told herself since Conrad's burial, she was protected by Lieutenant Morrison and wondered if he too had something to do with being the protector of the Bishop's Ring. When she needed protection, someone was there for her.

Across the street the lights came on in Morrison's house, but his drapes were drawn. Magda thought she heard a piano playing but when an orchestra followed she knew he must have been listening to a compact disk on his stereo. As concert music filtered through the windows and into the nighttime air, she recognized the music as being "Chopin."

Morrison went upstairs into his bedroom. The light behind him followed him into the room and much to her surprise as she looked across the street she thought she saw a telescope on a tripod directed at her house. When he closed the door, the room remained dark and she knew he was there and more than likely looking through his telescope at her house.

At first she thought it was outrageous. But then she said to herself, he was a policeman. They do eavesdrop on criminals in the TV movies. Maybe he is watching the house closely just in case Conrad's killer found out she was living there. She wondered if he could see into her bedroom if Conrad's killer was attacking her in her bedroom. She could settle it all and let him know she knew he was looking at her and she knew where he lived. She could let him know she appreciated the special protection she was receiving. If he was watching her house even while off duty she could find out how much he was involved in protecting her.

She walked back to the entrance to her bedroom and closed the door to signal to the children she had gone to bed. When door was closed she turned on the reading light on the wall behind her bed, which gave off a small amount of light diffused throughout the room. Then she proceeded to undress taking her time as she did it and walked across the room in the nude to the clothes closet to put on a negligee. Before she did she stood in front of the full-length mirror and did some exercising gestures. Then she put on a negligee and walked back around the bed and pulled down the covers and dropped into bed out of sight of Morrison's telescopic lens.

In the morning when she awoke she stayed in bed wondering about what she did the night before. Why did she do it and for whose benefit? It was not something she ever thought she would do. Now, awake, in the dawn of a new day she told herself it was a foolish gesture, sinfully tempting another to lust for her, something she should never have done. But she was curious about this man, who seemed to be there when she needed some kind of support to keep her from falling apart even though she thought she would be prepared for this type of tragedy should it occur in her life.

When she got up she went to the window and looked out for signs of life across the street but it appeared he left home already. The trashcan was placed outside and tire watermarks from his garage to the street indicated a car had left the garage.

An hour after she had her breakfast, the phone rang. It was Morrison. This time he told her he was checking into some more details on the case. But her mind was not listening to what he was saying. She wondered. Did he sit behind the telescope watching her while she undressed? She could not imagine herself behaving as she had for anyone but her husband. She could not see herself do this again, ever, she told herself, as he talked.

She was half listening. Half curious! When they finished talking she said to him, "I think I know where you live."

There was a long pause. Magda waited for him to say something.

He responded, "I know you do. And thank you for telling me. You let me know what I had to know."

She continued on, "I had to let you know how much I appreciate your help and protection. It was my way of telling you I know you are there for me. It was stupid of me to do that, but who is sane in these times?"

"I know we can talk honestly about our feelings. I understand your loss and your fears about someone attacking you. I'll be there when I can. But I also lost my wife due the careless negligence of someone else. But I know differently. To get to me, because of my work they killed the person I loved. I can feel for you because I know the pain. I am there for you because I am working out my own pain, which has not left me. It has been several years since my wife's wrongful death. I see what happened to you and I want justice for you. I want to see it to the very end. I want to catch your husband's killer in the worst way. It is almost as if my wife is here cheering me on." He stopped, revealing his emotions.

"But she isn't here, but you are. And when I saw you last night I was reminded of so much beauty has been lost in my life. I can't speak for what you and your husband had Mrs. Kaminski but I had a good marriage. It ended tragically. When I saw you I could not take my eyes from you. I didn't mean to intrude into your privacy but I admit I am taken into this case. With my own head full of emotions my actions are unexplained. They have little to do with you in this case, even as pretty as you are." He could not say anymore.

She understood him for the first time. When they would meet again, it would not be as it had been before.

"What was it we were talking about when you first called? She asked. He laughed. "You too, are stretched out, emotionally. I can tell. I was telling you, that the insurance company said, that as secondary beneficiary, you are entitled to the proceeds on the Key

Man Insurance policy, which Quentin LaFayette took out on your husband. This should change your life a bit when you add the two policies together."

She squealed, "Oh, thank you very much! I should have been listening to that, shouldn't I?"

He laughed, "Yes. I hope you feel protected."

Quietly she whispered, "I do."

Suddenly he changed his manner. "The Police are on top of things here, Mrs. Kaminski."

She had not caught on. She said, "Magda, please."

"Yes, as you know there are officers standing right here, ready to finish this case. They are waiting for me to put this guy where he belongs. I'll get back to you." She understood the signal. "I expect I will see you, one way or the other."

She laughed. It was the first time in a long time.

Conrad was every woman's dream husband. He was there when she needed him. He would understand her anxiety about her future. They had a wonderful marriage and she thought the Bishop's Ring played no small part in it by focusing themselves on the faith in God, which kept them together. Even now as a spirit, Conrad would love and understand her.

Chapter 29

Magda had not been told Monsignor O'Toole had given the text of the Legend of the Bishop's Ring to Father Piorek to read. He thought it only honest for Father Piorek to read its history should he accept the responsibility as the bearer of the relic ring. The prelate did so believing she would be relieved to finally have found a Polish priest to wear the ring as a Bishop. If she disapproved of Father Piorek because she favored a Polish priest in Poland, the Monsignor's plan was to tell her how favorable the Vatican was to toward Piorek's election to become an Auxiliary Bishop.

Meanwhile, secrecy over the ring's location remained intact. Magda had no telephone contact with Monsignor O'Toole. Still she wanted to know what was going to happen to the Bishop's Ring. She realized her thoughts were not clear. She had relied on Morrison when he told her Monsignor O'Toole would take good care of it until all matters were settled. She called Morrison at his office. She wanted to talk about the ring.

"Conrad and I protected that nine hundred year old ring for so long. Our whole lives were wrapped around it. We had the Bishop's Ring before the children were born. We always had to think about someone was looking for us. If they found us they would do something to us because we had what they wanted." He listened. Her life had been taken from her. Still, at forty-eight years of age she had her beauty and memories. She grieved. And life would go on.

"Now the Bishop's Ring we held for so long in search of a wearer so far has failed. Conrad is gone. It feels like my life is being carried in a boat out into the sea. That is the way that it feels to me right now." Morrison could tell she was having difficulties. He himself had those days after his wife was taken suddenly from him.

"I'll be off on Thursday and Friday this week. I offered to switch shifts with someone. If you are not against it we could take a ride to go see Monsignor O'Toole. You and he could visit. Instead of settling for restaurants along the way we could pack up a picnic for the trip. I could call him. He could pick places for us to stay for the night and we could drive back the next day. On the way back we could stop for a meal." The suddenness of the suggestion struck her as only something a gentleman would do.

"Yes, I would like to talk to this priest who has the Bishop's Ring. Maybe he could tell me about the priest who wanted the ring in the first place. What happened to him? I mean, if he had not wanted the ring I might not be a widow today." And with that remark anger boiled up in her as she thought about what had to transpire between Quentin and Conrad before Conrad could accept the idea that the Bishop's Ring could go to someone other than of Polish ethnicity.

Morrison could hear Magda's muffled rage and how her husband lost his life. She knew his boss. If Quentin had not taken a role in the process he would also be alive. The company in which he founded would not be teetering on bankruptcy. Someone was going to have to do something about keeping the firm going, protecting the interests of the clients whose drawings needed a permanent residence.

Magda said, "I want to hear about that priest! I want to see his face. I want to scream at him!" She wanted to know if Morrison knew anything about the people who were killed with Quentin. Morrison promised Magda they would talk and she would start to get answers when they met with Monsignor O'Toole.

The long ride along the Hudson River and the New York State Thruway was the first feeling of freedom Magda had since Conrad had been killed. The sun was shining. The car windows were rolled down to deliberately allow the fresh air to filter through the car. They packed a picnic. The Lieutenant hoped he would find a panoramic view of the Hudson River along the way. Both were nervous about being in the same car for so long a time. He knew he needed a change of scenery from the homicide detail. She needed to see a world beyond what she had come to know since Conrad's death. Within a short time, talking about themselves and what they seemed to like and dislike and what their interests were the detective needed to focus on the speeding traffic out of the city. As they spoke they came to realize getting out of the city was a little more complicated than they expected. The Lieutenant had been to the Catskills on several occasions for conferences or for vacations in days past. Magda claimed her ignorance of such places as Concord, Kutcher's, Grossinger's, The Pines, Browns or the Nevele. Magda only said she enjoyed the ocean and the beach and getting a good tan.

When they stopped for their picnic, after they had set out the tablecloth on the rest stop table, and set up their little lunch of sandwiches and fruit and ice tea, the Lieutenant kept the conversation light knowing he had a photo to show her when they finished the lunch. There were soft remarks all casual in tone. She let him know how much she knew of what was going on. Perhaps, now she was ready to hear more of why this happened to her.

What neither of them realized was the face of the man she saw in the photo at her sister's apartment, which Morrison had shown to her was known to each of them by a different name. She never said his name. She thought the police knew who he was. She did not know Conrad's killer used an alias. What Lt. Morrison knew for certain beyond a reasonable doubt is that all criminals think they are too smart to be caught. And in this thinking they outsmart themselves becoming statistics in prisons because habits are so hard to break.

Magda said, looking out to the distance hills. "I don't understand how all of this started." Morrison responded.

"When our number one suspect found out where you lived and where your husband worked. He probably checked out Quentin LaFayette. LaFayette's habits, his likes and dislikes, and whether Quentin was taken in by big money. That's usually the way these things begin. The killer is looking for a flaw in LaFayette's character. Quentin LaFayette liked the travel circuit, doling out money, making contracts and being paid handsomely for his services. Where to look first? He had to go no further than Conrad's boss."

Magda said, "Quentin liked women, I know that. I would be a rich woman if I were paid a dollar for every time he checked me out.

He checked out women, all women. But, what kind of person could have killed him and the others?"

"I think Monsignor might have some answers for us on that question." He stopped talking. She was calm looking off in the distance.

Morrison snapped her to attention when he said, "I have another theory about all of this Magda. I think our killer wanted to punish you. It may even go farther and he may want to kill you. He appears to be a cold, silent, and efficient killer. No weapon was ever found. If we did not do an autopsy we might have thought your husband died of a heart attack. He was at an age where those things happen. And he knows we didn't find him when it happened. So he might think he is in the clear. Or we can't bring him in. We don't take these guys for granted. They aren't operating on all fours cylinders, as we say."

Morrison added more. "Quentin and those others guys were accident victims caught up in this thing about the ring. We know the killer does not have the ring. It leads me to think the killer is looking for you, now. He's been intense about this. He has already followed you to the beach last year. It had to be last year."

Magda responded quickly. "How do you know that?"

"We have photos. I mean he tries everything! He even tried to get LaFayette implicated in your husband's death."

Magda was confused hearing this. "What? How?"

The Lieutenant got up from the picnic table and walked to his car without saying a word to Magda. She waited as he pulled out a file from his attaché case and walked back to the picnic table where she was seated. He opened the file and let her stare at the topless picture of herself with Quentin. They appeared to be together.

"Is this supposed to be me?" She asked. He shrugged.

"I never take my top off. I loosen it. I remember, last summer, the wind... yes, the wind gusted,... and it flew away... and my daughter went to get it... and I was asleep... yes, my eyes are closed, ... and she got it... and came back and covered me ... and woke me up."

Morrison answered. "He has a long lens camera, and close enough to get this photo."

She protested, "But I was never alone with Quentin like this on the beach!"

"The picture is a fraud. Our photographer told us the guy in the photo was magnified up because he said something about the graininess in the photo. See, you are so much further when the picture was taken."

She asked, "Did your guys enjoy inspecting this photo, Lieutenant?" She asked with a curl of her lip.

"Police work is rough, Magda. It can be very difficult. There has to be some compensations."

She asked, "Did you enjoy inspecting this photo?"

"I can honestly say it gave me a lot to think about." She grinned and turned away hoping not to reveal her face.

He remarked, "Piotrowski has been schooled in spy tactics."

She asked, "Whom are we talking about now?"

He looked surprised at her question.

"This guy, the one who took this picture." He said pointing to her beach photo. He's the one whose picture I showed to you at your sister's apartment, and you screamed when you saw it."

"That face in the photo I saw at Marta's apartment was the reason we left Buffalo. Where did I get the idea that photo you showed me was of Sobleski? Was it Conrad?" She questioned her memory.

This new bit of information stunned Lt. Morrison. Now it was plain why Interpol and other police agencies were unable to find a file on Piotrowski. Was Sobleski using "Piotrowski" as an alias? This was not uncommon but now someone from this man's past could identify him as someone other than whom he said he was. The rental agent at the apartment complex in Queens said his name was "Piotrowski." And the Piotrowski name was given to the F.B.I. Could it be a man once named Sobleski had actually entered the U.S. and worked at the embassy as Piotrowski?

Certainly! The cowboy outfit, the "Hollywood look-a-like" was a cover up deliberately staged to throw the police off. There were no "Piotrowski" names on the flight rosters coming in or leaving the airport the day Conrad Kaminski died.

Morrison looked at her. "Mrs. Kaminski, I think you gave us something much more than a look at your day at the beach!"

Chapter 30

"Come in dear friends," Monsignor O'Toole said as he invited them into a large library and sitting room at St. John Vianney's Residence Hall. "It is so good to see you. Mrs. Kaminski you are as pretty as he said." She looked at the detective with a smile on her face and turned and offered her hand to the Monsignor. "It's nice to see you again, Monsignor. It is so rare to hear a priest compliment on a lady's appearance."

"I am older now so I am free to speak the truth without too many fears. I only reveal the obvious of what tells me is true." The two visitors were escorted to the corner of the library where they could hold a conversation without being overheard. Other retired priests frequently strolled into the library looking for something to read.

"I have good news for you Mrs. Kaminski. I am thrilled to tell you a priest of Polish heritage will be elevated to become a Bishop in our Diocese. For me it is one of the greatest thrills of my fifty-two year priesthood. The Bishop-elect has asked me to be the homilist at his ordination. It will all take place in the Archdiocese of Washington, D.C."

"That sounds wonderful Monsignor. Then that means I can give him the Bishop's Ring. Praise God! This is music to my ears. Now I know Conrad can rest in peace. I can go on with my life. This was our dream." It was unexpected. Her face was filled with happiness. While they sat there an elderly priest wheeled a teacart over to them covered with a tea set and cookies. They thanked him and he went back to the kitchen.

"Yes, he will be given the Bishop's Ring at his ordination." He repeated her statement of relief, then said, "From reading all of the notes which Mr. Kaminski's cousin Father Androwitz translated in case the ring became the possession of an American bishop, which I believe was his motive for the translations, it appears the history of the Bishop's Ring was filled with risks and adventure since Bishop St. Stanislaw first wore his ring. Many have died over the ring since 1070 A.D. in their attempts to own it. What has happened in this era is no different than other eras as I read the Legend. Passing the Ring on to Bishop Piorek is a time of restoration and new beginnings. In researching tales of saints' lives over many years for my homilies, this tale has all of the drama and risks, which show the hand of God."

Magda said, "Yes, that is true. It always made us nervous about keeping it. The devil has made us pay this price!"

Monsignor O'Toole reminded, "But when a Bishop wore the ring I understand from Father Androwitz' writings the unholy events ceased and human rights were returned to the people."

Magda listened and then asked, "What has happened to the priest who wanted the ring from my husband? Is the Bishop punishing him because so many people died?" It was a brutally frank question the aging Monsignor did not expect from her. He looked at her. He did not know what the intentions of the Bishop were. The departed Bishop never revealed his intentions but she deserved an answer. He looked straight into her eyes and moved forward in the chair as if shutting out the entire world and they were alone.

"May I call you Magda?" She nodded in the affirmative.

"There are defining moments in all of our lives, when the unhappy and unholy events seem to overwhelm us and we are lost. It was that way with Our Lord. One week he is hailed as king of the Jews and by the end of the same week he is crucified on the Cross! His human nature was not separate from his divine nature. He had feelings in his human nature. He wanted the cup of his crucifixion to pass from him because he could feel pain. But his divine nature knew His Father in heaven would accept the sacrificial gift of his life as atonement for the sins of humanity. In the Hebrew Torah an innocent lamb is required for sacrifice to atone for sins. Christ was humanity's innocent lamb sacrificed to atone for sins. Your husband's death was an unholy event in which an innocent man died trying to bring glory to God. Men who want to stay in power caused Conrad's death. Not Father Lawrence." She held her head down.

The Monsignor whispering continued. "Father Lawrence would want the cup of this pain to pass but he will live with a reminder every day of his life. We learned from this didn't we that even a priest can cause pain to others or even death. That is a heavy burden to carry. That will be enough punishment for him. Father Lawrence will have reminders for the rest of his life. It will be there in the back of his mind like so many of us who wished what we had done once in our pride, ignorance, stupidity or lusts, never happened. He could not have known all of the extenuating circumstances that would come about because of the ring.

"I can admit to you I personally believe there is a flaw in the character of a priest to be so aggressive as to want and pursue becoming a Bishop. He puts himself above other priests. The Lord himself spoke against the desire of ranking oneself higher in the coming kingdom of God."

Morrison added, "Especially since so many have died because it appears he wanted the Bishop's Ring. She fears this is not the end of the unholy events."

"Even a priest can buy into the symbolisms of power in society. Father Lawrence appears not to have been careful. A devil has entered in to obstruct God's plans. The devil tempts by using promises of power and control. Pride is the cause of competition to be more and to have more of this earth's treasures. Father Lawrence is only human. I don't subscribe the idea but some do that one has to be a little bit of a showoff to catch people's attention. Such behavior violates our Christian spiritual ascent. Bishop-Elect Piorek is far from a show off. Our Bishop chose him as his Auxiliary because he is a genuine person who lives the vocation God chose him to live. We can read more into his selection on a spiritual level! God is faithful, he keeps his promises" She remained silent.

He continued. "As I read into the Legend of the Bishop's Ring, it would have been a tragedy for anyone but a Polish born priest to be the wearer of the ring. There are time-honored traditions the Polish people expect from the Bishop who would wear this relic of holy St. Stanislaw of Cracow. Father Lawrence would not be able to perform them because he does not speak the Polish language. It makes sense, unknown to all of us why Father Piorek was singled out. Unrelated to Mr. Kaminski's death, when the Bishop asked for a suggestion as to whom I thought would pass the muster, my first thoughts were Father Piorek. Forget about the call for a Polish priest as the Legend specifies. I knew nothing about it."

To assure Magda all was not as it appears he said, "Don't judge the priesthood by this one incident. God needs our sincere best efforts so He will be recognized in our crumbling moral society. That's what we are here for and very little else. Please accept our apologies. We priests are of a human estate. Some of us make larger mistakes than others but we do a very creditable job for what we are given. Society is filled with men devoted to evil and changing the moral compass. What happened to all of us, myself included, had a purpose for which we will have to wait for answers to come in eternity."

The two guests listened to the priest unravel his views while they relaxed after their long ride. The Monsignor's mood changed.

"Listen, this is a time when we will be putting on a big event for Bishop Piorek. And of course, you both will be on the invitation list to attend. Magda, you will have to tell us how many from your family will be attending. Those invitations will soon be in the mail. We will be inviting your whole family, which so richly deserves the invitations.

Magda replied, "Thank you Monsignor. Can I ask a question?"

He responded, "Surely. Ask!"

She inquired, "Will this Father Lawrence be there?"

"Yes, he will be there. He will be located among the rank and file priests who will be in attendance. Oh, and coming with him is a parishioner from his new parish. It just occurred to me, while you are going to be with your family maybe Father Lawrence's guest should meet up with the Lieutenant. Yes, that should be a very good idea I'm sure."

Morrison commented, "I didn't know this, Monsignor until driving up here. Our killer of Mr. Kaminski has been using two identities. One identity would make him a respectable career officer in the Polish diplomatic service. The other disguise is one dressed as an urban cowboy with Hollywood look-a-like features. I will give you both names." He wrote them down. Magda checked for the accuracy of the Polish spelling. Morrison continued. "I know these "big shows" always attract a crowd. I also know our killer is capable of doing everything in a devious manner. People among us do strange things even to the best. Someone shot our Polish Pope didn't they?"

A look of horror came across the Monsignor's face.

Morrison added, "I will need a personal letter of introduction from you sent to the Washington D.C. Metropolitan Police to take to my superiors so that I can get out of town for a few days." He said. "I will need to talk to someone and establish contact to make them aware of what is going on. It's their ballpark, and the game is out of town."

"I have taken the liberty of finding you a hotel. You will stay as my guests in separate rooms. Of course." He winked at the both of them. "We priests are so old fashioned. I have invited soon to be Bishop, Father Piorek to join us for dinner. I thought you would like to meet with the priest who will wear the Bishop's Ring. To meet him at the installation ceremonies would be a very bad breach of etiquette, don't you think?"

Magda joyfully erupted, "Yes, oh dinner would be wonderful! Thank you for your gift and hospitality to us, Monsignor." She said. And then in a quiet turn towards him she said, "I have terrible thoughts towards Father Lawrence. Can you hear my confession? I need to tell you something that has been going through my mind. I have not been in my parish for a while. I need to talk to you about my strange behavior." She said it in a whisper out of earshot of Morrison.

Monsignor O'Toole said, "Yes, of course. It is time to check in at the hotel. I'll get my confessional stole. After confession we'll go to the hotel and meet Father Piorek there. Yes, let's do that."

The priest left the room. Morrison asked what was coming next. She told him she was going to confession and the Monsignor went

225

to get his confessional stole. "Remember I gave you a show one night? That was not the real Magda! I need to confess it."

"Tell him to stick around. That was not me either! I'm not use to peeping but I enjoyed it."

Then Morrison added, "A priest explained to me in confession long ago. It's not always just what we do but how we think that does offend God. He quoted the Lord, 'He who looks upon a woman with lust in his heart has already committed adultery with her.' So if people take joy in dirty jokes, he explained, they are no friends of God. One who does not understand biblical spirituality does not understand sins of thought. I get laughed at in the precinct. I know sin can be committed in the mind. We put people prison after their well-planned crimes and conspiracies fail them and they are caught? So will God!"

She responded quietly, "I know."

He continued. "When you're police and you carry a gun you have to take care of the moment not to die without a parachute. That photo at the beach puts me in mortal danger of lusting for something that is not mine. It's been a long time."

Magda waited to remark, "You went to a Catholic school I can tell." She said. "If I ever remarry I would like a man with a conscience. Conrad had one. It would be important to me. "

"Yes, I went to a Catholic school. Thank God for those Sisters. They always set a good example." He said and turned and walked away as Monsignor O'Toole came back and heard their confessions.

At the dinner meeting that night Morrison let it be known it would be important for the invitation list to be scanned to see if the name of Thaddeus Sobleski had been entered.

He announced, "We have no weapon to inspect for Mr. Kaminski's death. This is a killer who uses unconventional means to kill his victims. He could spike a bowl of punch at the reception or a glass with a killer poison. The coroner said the amount of poison compound in Mr. Kaminski's system was meant to kill. A lesser dosage would only have temporarily caused him to feint. So, if he should show up in the reception line we must be ready."

The policeman was thinking out loud as if they were not there planning in his mind how to prevent Thaddeus Sobleski, a career UB type killer hiding behind the mask of a Polish diplomat from reaching the newly ordained Bishop. Morrison needed some answers.

"Can you tell me what will take place at the Bishop's ordination?" Morrison asked the waiter for some paper to jot a few notes down since the hotel only used cloth napkins. He was given a general idea of the ceremonial ordination of events that would take place. The Lieutenant took his new information with him when he went to Washington.

Magda Kaminski went to her safe house with the assurance that much had transpired in the history of the Bishop's Ring, that these events, unholy as they were, might not have been much different from other unholy events, which helped to protect the Bishop's Ring for its eventual wearer.

Her question about Father Lawrence stirred others in Monsignor O'Toole's mind about Father Lawrence's role in the renovation of St. Catherine of Siena Church. Even the unconventional and frenetic behavior of Father Lawrence may have been driven by motives and a timetable no one had discerned. She and Conrad may have been players in the role of protectors but how many protectors did the Bishop's Ring have in the course of its legendary history? Was Father Lawrence motivated by forces friendly to the eventual coming events? The Monsignor could only wonder.

From reading the legend of the Bishop's Ring, Monsignor O'Toole knew that history was about to change. Everything happens for a purpose. It's what he believed. He had to rethink his thoughts about how and why Father Lawrence behaved in the renewal of St. Catherine Of Sienna Church. Did Christ promise a "Renewal" when he was to come back? Was Father Lawrence an instrument of new life in a renewal?

Chapter 31

On the Feast of the Pentecost three separate seminary choirs convened in the National Shrine of the Immaculate Conceptions in Washington D.C., for Bishop Piorek's Ordination Mass. They added their voices to the sounds of piped organ music, violins, blaring horns, trumpets and trombones. Members of the Fourth Degree of the Knights of Columbus led processions of ceremoniously regaled Bishops from dioceses all over the United States to take their places upon the altar. The chorus of male voices sang Alleluias selected from Mozart's *Exsultate Jubilate*. It was a sound unsurpassed even by the beautiful magnificent choir of St. Patrick's Cathedral in New York City. Members of Congress, Foreign Embassies with ties to the Vatican joined the procession. Father Piorek's seminary classmates followed. Parishioners from St. Catherine of Siena parish church and lay apostolate leaders of various Church organizations were seated in places designated by Church protocol standards.

The Cardinal Archbishops of New York and Washington, D.C., concelebrated the Mass with Bishop O'Farrell. The Ordinand, Bishop-Elect Piorek took his designated place in the open sanctuary. There he would remain alone until the ordination ceremony. After opening prayers and songs of glorious praise to God the Liturgy of the Word readings from the Old and New Testament and the Gospel were presented.

Now Monsignor O'Toole stood high and alone in the pulpit, vested in a violet colored cassock. A white lace surplice hung loosely on his shoulders and arms covering the lower sleeves of his cassock.

He wore a long white stole hung around his neck on both shoulders like a yoke to signify the calendar feast day of this celebration. His frame stood erect and he was for this moment as the famed "LaCordaire," the great 19th century French orator priest who spoke in the great churches of France.

He looked out on the crowded sacred shrine, breathed in its magnificence into his total being and with all of his oratorical abilities at his command he opened in a strong voice mastering every syllable resonating clearly and distinctly and with a power he sensed had graced him for this occasion as he addressed the dignitaries and all other people present.

"For even us members of the clergy, and friends of God, this day seems so extraordinary and packed with mystery. As we look around here in the sanctuary we see Cardinals, Archbishops, Bishops, and other Monsignor members of the Papal Household, and our equally respected brothers from the Eastern rites of the Orthodox Church, and the Protestant Faiths, and Judaism. Throughout the Basilica the faithful come to witness an event in Church history with monumental historical significance.

"We would not have recognized this day, had we not been told by Moses in the Book of Genesis, Chapter 3, Verse 15, that God spoke to Satan after he caused our first parents to commit the original sin of a coming time when the 'seed of the Woman would crush the head of Satan.' And as we know God does not lie! He fulfills his promises.

"That prophecy came to pass. All other prophecies in the Old Testament about a coming Messiah were fulfilled. Christ, the Messiah to come, was born, lived, died, and returned to heaven. And he left behind a divinely created Church to fulfill the prophecy made to Abraham that his legacy would be a nation numbered as large as the sands of the seashore. Just as the ancient Israelites were instructed to slaughter a lamb as a sacrifice and put its blood on their doorposts and eat the flesh of the lamb to avoid the angel of death, we eat the flesh and drink the blood of Christ, the sacrificial Lamb of God who takes away the sins of the world.

"I shall move on in teaching moments what this day means to us now.

"No, this day will not compare with the Church being the savior of Western Civilization in the Fifth and Sixth centuries. Nor does it compare with the evangelization and conversion of France, Germany and England in those centuries. But in some sense it may rise to the perils associated with Mohammed's followers attacks upon Christianity in the East. Take away the schisms, reformers, the suppressions against English monasteries, and the tests of the Church's Divinity and focus upon the lives of the Saints, holy men and women whose lives have meaning for us even to this day. How did all of this come about in a world when brute hordes rampaged in Europe?

"Jesus Christ established his Church, selected Peter his Apostle as the leader the other Apostles would follow in his absence. Before his death and after it, he came back to establish his continued presence among us beginning with baptism. He gave the Apostles the power to forgive sin and to continue his presence among us through the Holy Eucharist. He confirmed them to teach the Gospel and through the Holy Spirit he ordained them and established the Rite of Sending to establish a line of apostolic descendents we call Bishops. He promised it would last to the end of time. Since he is the Son of God and his Church was of divine creation no power on earth will be able to destroy it.

"Today we celebrate the Feast of Pentecost. It is a day when the world was changed for the better when Christ breathed upon the Apostles, confirming them with the power of the Holy Spirit as the Church's first Bishops. It was on that day the Church was born and three thousand Jews in Jerusalem became baptized believers in Christ. From that day forward under the source of all human life and truth, the Holy Spirit has guided the Church from its beginning from St. Peter in an unbroken line of Popes and Bishops through the centuries spreading the Catholic faith throughout the world. Human endeavors alone have never succeeded like the Church has succeeded. Today, here in this shrine we continue the legacy Christ gave to the Church with the ordination of Bishop-elect John Piorek.

"It is a fitting moment when on this day of Pentecost our Bishop-Elect John Piorek is ordained to become an Auxiliary Bishop to take his place as a duly commissioned descendant of the holy Apostles of the Church founded by Jesus Christ. It is a special day with meaning, like so many non-coincidental events in history when God intervenes in our human affairs to put an end to Christian persecution and suffering. For us in this time this is a day when God intervenes to give hope to the faithful that their days of suffering are coming to a close. A sign of renewal is coming to pass and is upon us in this ordination today.

"Signs are what humans have come to expect from their Creator. Those signs come in the form of love, warnings, protection, healings, and the list goes on as we live our daily lives. While we live out our lives God tests our love in so many ways. Satan does as well. More than we know, God knows the works of Satan and the need for secrecy. Let us take a look at history of an example when God intervened to protect the faithful and end persecution.

"The time is 312 A.D. The struggle is over who would become emperor of the Roman Empire. Constantine and his army stood ready for battle on Rome's Tiber River Mulvian Bridge and faced his enemy's army. The battle was about to ensue. In a moment when lives are to be lost in battle and Constantine's survival is in doubt, like a man of his time, he asks for a sign. Suddenly a cross appears in the heavens and written in the background of the sky were the words, 'In this sign you will conquer.' When Constantine conquered his enemy he became Emperor. Christian persecution was put to an end and faith in the true God was established in the Roman Empire. The gates of hell did not prevail over this divinely created Church!

"For people then and for us now, Constantine's triumph over his enemy is a very teachable moment in the history of the Catholic faith. Yes, certainly there have been those who came along in our Church's history, who have preached false doctrines, invited heresy, behaved poorly, and fell to the wicked temptations of the devil. Yet the Church has continually grown as God desired. Men and women all over the world, of varying ethnic strains and cultures have found the message of Christ through this Church to be the Truth. That there is life beyond death, and Christ came to save those who desired life with God. He proved we live again after death by rising from the grave. Christ intends for all of humanity to live forever. He gave us his Church for as long as life continues on earth it will continue to live forever. That's his promise.

"The God of many miracles passes down through all centuries proof of his continued active participation in our lives. In Europe there are many shrines where the presence of Christ, his Blessed Mother, and holy saints have brought about healings, comfort and a cleansing of the soul.

"On this feast of Pentecost Christ appeared to His apostles through locked doors and stood in their midst. He showed them his hands and his side. He greeted them in peace. I shall repeat once again the original words to the Rite of Sending the first Apostle-Bishops found in today's Gospel reading:

> 'Peace be with you. As the Father has sent me, so I send you.' And when he said this, he breathed on them and said to them, 'Receive the Holy Spirit. Whose sins you forgive are forgiven them, and whose sins you retain are retained.'

"Today the Church will authoritatively perform once again the Rite of Sending as Christ performed upon the Apostles on the first Pentecost.

"Christ said, 'I will not leave you orphans.' He meant for the Church to continue guided by the Holy Spirit in a continuance of generations of apostles committed to teaching his Truth. "Thomas, the doubter went to Iraq and India. Others traveled to Ethiopia, Egypt, Greece, Turkey, Persia, Babylon, Spain, Italy, and Galatia. Those whom they conferred the office of Bishop followed in their footsteps, developing community groups, and incurred persecution, even from their own fellow Jews. The Jerusalem Sanhedrin tried to destroy the new Church wherever it was found in cities where Jews lived. All Apostles suffered a horrible martyr's death. The promise by Christ for a better afterlife was an attractive message to converts all over the world. It still is.

"Christ said on one occasion, 'A seed has to die in order to bring forth new life." And we say in light of so much persecution, "the blood of martyrs is the seed of Christianity." A hidden message was imparted to the killer for him to ponder its meaning. For Magda, these words were consoling knowing Conrad was martyred in their cause to protect the Bishop's Ring and that good would come from his life.

"It is fitting for John Piorek, himself an orphan, to be among the descendants of the Apostles. This too is a teaching moment. He left his home diocese like an apostle to work among the poor in a mission church in Appalachia. These people were the same kind of people to whom the Lord gave his message. John taught them, blessed their families binding them to Christ. He baptized babies an early practice of the Church as well as older children and adults. Penitents came regularly to the sacrament of Reconciliation to restore any broken relationships they may have had with God. In his slight Polish accent he preaches beautiful homilies and offered Christ in the Holy Eucharist as a daily gift of Love. He confirmed the faith of the youth and converts. He bound men and women to Christ as one body in marriage. He offered the sacrament to heal the sick and those dying." The Monsignor stopped for a moment to let his words stand in the audience's mind. One more time he spoke to Conrad's killer.

"Today the Rite of Sending established by Christ to His Apostles will indelibly mark the soul of Bishop Piorek as a descendant in the long line of succession of Christ's Apostles. He comes to us from a land where atheist rulers have persecuted Catholics far too long. Catholicism was founded in Poland ten centuries ago in this one, holy, catholic, apostolic Church. Only now is Poland able to see the day when Communism loses its sting and the Polish people are rising up to tell the world they will no longer be slaves to their anti-God Marxist ideologues. Would that it would be so now in our nation that we rise up against the tide of satanic lies, which enslave our nation with corruptible behaviors. Millions who believe those lies are destined to enter hell forever to suffer pain and torture of its demons!"

He was aware in his audience there were leaders with powers of persuasion able to affect changes in the American culture.

"God must be sending us a hidden message, today." He let that sink in stopping momentarily to look out and up into the great holy edifice watching waiting eyes for him to continue.

"What more can be said about Bishop Piorek than to say than a Polish Bishop and an American businessman helped sponsor his way to America. But here, Bishop-Elect Piorek's selection was the overwhelming choice of his fellow diocesan priests to be ordained for this office today. Though he was absent from them for a number of years they made their choice known to our Bishop.

"I have been made aware of the hundreds of years legend connected to a Bishop's Ring once worn by the martyred Bishop St. Stanislaw of Cracow, Poland. This ring has been a symbol of solidarity and protection of human rights since the day the martyred saint wore it when a brutally bad king beheaded the saint. Like venerated relics this ring has proved to be the cause of miraculous cures and changes down through the centuries. It is revered as a source of hope and once again it will be worn on the hand of a Polish born Bishop as a sign of conquering enemies. We can be grateful and humbled this holy ring is a sign of coming events planned by God.

"Poland as we know is in a turbulent crisis as it was in St. Stanislaw's day, when the sainted Bishop challenged a bad ruler's evil ways. The Communists had taken God out of the country. They allow people to attend Church, but not to build new churches. God is denied throughout all of Poland by the government ignoring his presence in the hearts and minds of the people. The return of the saint's Bishop's Ring sends a message that the Communists have been attempting to prevent, to the point of bribing and murder. We are all aware through our news sources of the killing of a Polish priest in Poland and dumping his body in a reservoir. That's the behavior of the enemies of God, who torture and kill.

"Should we wonder if there is another message behind the preservation of this ancient Bishop's Ring? Today when Bishop Piorek is ordained Bishop St. Stanislaw Bishop's Ring will be placed upon Bishop Piorek's hand. After Mass a reception will be held in Bishop Piorek's honor. We have been told he has been requested to meet at the Vatican with his Holiness, Pope John Paul II. Pope John Paul II is a former Archbishop of Cracow."

The Monsignor was ready to explain the Church's position on the Bishop's role taken from notes on Vatican Council II.

"And now for Bishop Piorek. The Second Vatican Council tells us the role of a Bishop is to work in concert with the Roman Pontiff subject to and never without the Pope as head of the Universal Church. The power of a Bishop the Council Fathers tell us is exercised only with the consent of the Pontiff.

"A Bishop is by his office a modern Apostle a member of a divinely instituted Church hierarchy. He is invested with the authority to govern a diocese and is a successor to the very men chosen by Christ as Apostles. Bishop Piorek today will be ordained to the hierarchy of the Church with the title of Auxiliary or Coadjutor Bishop. He will not be given a title to run a diocese but he will be granted the faculties necessary for safeguarding and rendering the work of the Ordinary of the diocese more effective and without detriment to the unity of the diocese." Then with a smile he dropped his oratorical voice and added, "He will be our number two man. He will have to try harder." Laughter erupted in the huge edifice.

"The Sacrament of Holy Orders we will witness today will confer the spiritual power to administer Confirmation and Holy Orders and ordain other bishops. As a successor to the Apostles the first duty of a Bishop is to teach and guard the purity of the Church's doctrines and to see to it that others receive the Gospel message. As the mother Church of all Christian faiths by its commission from Christ it speaks to safeguard the faith and morals of all who call themselves Christian. The second duty of a Bishop is to guard the morals of the faithful and maintain discipline among those entrusted to his care, which includes the reception of the sacraments and participation in divine worship. A Bishop has to visit parishes in his jurisdiction and he has to maintain a residence in the diocese. The last request seems only reasonable to expect. If he agrees to take the job shouldn't we think he wants to live among us?" Laughter erupted again. He continued when it stopped.

"By divine institution Bishops are linked with the Pontiff for the entire Church. They are ever conscious of a world such as in our own society where the Gospel has not been fully proclaimed. Here in our land we see people who have departed from the precepts of the Christian life because they are in an anti-God state of mind.

They will need a conversion of soul for them to enter heaven upon death!

"It will fall upon the shoulders of Bishop Piorek as his primary duty to take the seriousness of what the Church believes and teaches regarding the human person and his or her bodily life; the family and its unity and stability; the procreation and education of children; the civil society we live in. Bishops have to be a voice for God in crafting moral laws, teaching ethics to the professions, laborers, and enjoying some forms of leisure activities. As Christ's apostle, a Bishop's voice must be heard to point the divine way to live to please God, through many forms of art, our awesome technical capabilities, whether we live in poverty or affluence. In his own way he acts in a collegial effort with his fellow bishops." He raised his voice. "He must teach Christ's message with authority against the ungodly conspiracy which faces the Mystical Body of Christ, which we are now in, in this time in our country, in this century." The Monsignor stopped to give a reminder.

"The importance of this day is to remember Truth never changes. Time changes. Circumstance change. But truth is absolute. It remains the same in good and bad times. It remains the truth. The Apostles told the truth about the Resurrection of Christ. Caiaphas, the temple high priest heard it and ignored it."

He stopped to gather more thoughts to continue his homily.

"Remember the wars of liberation in Eastern Europe, China, Korea, Vietnam, Cuba and elsewhere. Historians will tell of a world where tens of millions of Christians became innocent victims brought on by Communism. Christians suffered as Christ suffered and died. Rulers of old like Caiaphas cooperated with evil just as Communists, Marxists, and atheists in our day deny God exists. Instead of offering mercy the enemies of God torture and kill. Instead of educating in the truth, they tell lies and half-truths. Instead of seeing their Creator as a miracle worker they go about the task of denying God a part in man's world. This is the world we live in. When they lie, people die!"

The homilist lifted his hand above his head. He said, "Truth! We have our own holocaust. UNBORN HUMAN LIFE! Forget the slogans! Common sense tells us inert human tissue will not grow of itself. We knew there is no human life without a heartbeat; no heartbeat without a soul sent by God. Science teaches us that at the moment of conception there is a detectable heartbeat and the beginning of life. When Stalin in 1929 found Soviet 'abortion-on-demand' policy lowered his empire's ability to grow he ended the ten-year abortion practice in the Soviet Union. A band of new Bolsheviks now conspire with Marxist ideology to destroy this nation. Paul, the Apostle, speaking to his converts in ancient, pagan Corinth, said,

"The body is not for immorality; it is for the Lord. And the Lord is for the body. God, who rose up the Lord, will raise us also by his power.... We are temples of the Holy Spirit, who is within us."

Monsignor O'Toole stopped, momentarily, and dropped his head, as if in contemplation. He recited a favorite verse:

Hidden from them, His Divinity,

Upon the Lake of Galilee,

He surprised His Apostles,

Who, fearing the storm asked,

"What manner of man is He?

Who quiets the wind?

And calms the sea?

"We are in peril as a nation. God can withhold His protective hand from us, His most blessed nation ever. Have not the furies touched us? Are tornadoes, floods, mountain and woodland fires, earthquakes, volcanic eruptions, riots, plagues, wars and holocausts destroying our sand foundations? The Apostles called on Christ when their boat was sinking? Our moral compass is lost and our boat is sinking! We must call on Christ to save us as a nation."

Monsignor O'Toole looked at Father John Piorek, as he was about to be ordained to become a Bishop, a descendant Apostle. His voice became velvety, mellifluous in tone, speaking directly to the man to become the new Bishop the Monsignor spoke eloquently, "In the Infinite Wisdom of God, John Piorek, God knows your heart and soul. He knows you to be a quiet humble man, who produces great things for the Body of Christ. You walk in the steps of Jesus, fearing no one to bring truth to those who hear but do not yet understand. You are a tireless missionary for Christ.

"Bishop John Piorek, as the inheritor of St. Stanislaw's legendary Bishop's Ring known for its miraculous powers, may you call upon this powerful saint and intercessor to help us save our people and nation for God and return it to holy purposes to build the Church and serve God and humanity. This Pentecost is a day of hope."

"Congratulations, 'Bishop' Piorek. May God always hold you kindly in the palm of His hand."

People applauded his Catholic celebratory sermon.

Monsignor O'Toole left the high pulpit where carved on the front in marble were the words, 'the Woman and her Seed' overlooked the shrine. John Piorek was about to become "Her seed," a modern day Bishop to serve God's hidden purposes in crushing the head of the Evil One.

The Mass continued with the second part with the Apostles Creed, the Prayers of the Faithful, and the Consecration called the mystery of "Transubstantiation" which Jesus Christ using bread and wine instituted as a Sacrament the Holy Eucharist at the Last Supper to become his Body and Blood, Soul and Divinity. Catholics believe the Eucharist (gift) contains the True Presence of Jesus Christ in both species forms.

In the third phase of the Mass long lines filled the shrine when the congregation came forward to receive Christ in Communion to be with Him to offer praise, thanksgiving, petitions and worship of Christ, the Son of God. During this period the three seminary choirs softly sang songs composed by St. Thomas Aquinas in the 13th century the most famous being "Panis Angelicus," (Bread of Angels).

During this celebration, kneeling before the Cardinal Archbishop of New York, John Piorek was blessed with the oils of his ordination. He was then vested with a miter and crosier to symbolize the apostolic mantle of authority granted to him. In a special ceremony the Pope's representative from the Vatican, the Apostolic Nuncio, placed the Bishop's Ring on the right hand of his ring finger.

In the audience, a killer, Thaddeus Sobleski waited in the reception line for his chance to meet Bishop Piorek.

Chapter 32

From the moment the Lieutenant and Magda left Monsignor O'Toole after they had visited him in his retirement home Morrison seemed preoccupied with making a plan in his mind for the capture of Conrad's killer, Thaddeus Sobleski. The car ride back to Queens the next day was quiet for both of them. Magda's thoughts were mostly about her children's future. Morrison fortuitously uncovered the killer's real name, "Sobleski". It was a big break in the case.

More than Magda would ever appreciate Morrison had to capture this killer. He needed to heal himself. When Monsignor O'Toole told the story of Maynard Bowles at dinner that night, and how he protected Father Lawrence's life from the killers, Morrison made sure he was going to be in contact with that fellow before the ordination of Bishop Piorek.

Morrison said, "Maynard, tomorrow at the church, there will be swarms of police, many of them will be in plain clothes at the Bishop's ordination. I have been in touch with the D.C. police to tell them that there is going to be a suspected killer who looks like the Hollywood actor who played 'Dirty Harry' in the movies."

Maynard laughed, "Dirty Harry? Everybody knows about Dirty Harry. 'Make my Day.' Pow. Pow. Pow."

"Maynard, this guy is a real killer. But he doesn't use guns. He injects poisons with strange looking syringes. I can't imagine what he might use. But tomorrow he will be in the reception line to greet your friend Bishop Piorek posing as a Diplomat from the Polish Embassy. The name on the invitation name is Thaddeus Sobleski.

Do you have that?" Morrison wrote down that name on a note pad he carried in his pocket and gave the paper to Maynard. "Keep that name. Memorize it. If you see a 'Dirty Harry' look alike stay close by. You don't look like the police. He wouldn't suspect you as being a police officer. Be Bishop Piorek's protector from this man, Maynard. Since we don't know what kind of weapon he will use keep your eyes on his hands at all times. If you see something strange going on, I'll be nearby. Give me a wink or some signal he can't see and we will move in on him. I don't think he knows what I look like. But there is a chance he does. The D.C. Police are ready to move in if they are given a signal. I'm depending on your signal. The suspected killer is very clever."

Maynard said, "Wow, this is just like the movies."

"Maynard, this is real. This man is out to kill the Bishop. And maybe someone else."

"I get you, Lieutenant. You want me to stick by this guy to see he doesn't have a trick up his sleeve."

"Tomorrow, when the people go into the Church, the usher will seat you directly behind Sobleski. It has all been worked out who sits where in the pews in your section. Remember keep your eyes on his hands! We don't want an incident. We don't know if he will carry a gun in the Basilica. There are no provisions for searching the invited guests. But there will be plenty of help nearby. You do not look like a cop with your Paul Bunyan beard. The police will know who you are. I've instructed them where you will be seated."

"But, what am I supposed to do?"

"Just grab him. I don't think even as big as he is he's going to be able to get away from you. We'll be there. Did you ever think about going into wrestling for a living?"

During the ordination ceremony instrumental music filled the Shrine during the Mass as the seminary choirs sang two Mozart selections, an Offertory Hymn, *Ave Verum Corpus,* and *Laudate Dominum*, as a Recessional Hymn, with the traditional Communion Hymn of *Panis Angelicus.* The most appropriate for the feast day was sung by a tenor. When the ceremony ended, the choirs combined to sing Shubert's rendition of *Ave Maria.*

A reception line began to form outside the Shrine to congratulate the new Bishop. Morrison kept his eye on "Thaddeus Sobleski" as people filed out of the church pews parallel to Maynard Bowles. They both saw him walk toward the public bathroom. Morrison's eyes flicked a silent message to have Maynard follow the trade envoy through the crowd. Subdued voices commented on the beauty of the ceremony they had just witnessed and Monsignor O'Toole's celebratory homily. Sobleski had not paid much attention to who sat behind him during the Mass. He would not have noticed Maynard but the "Kiss of Peace" ceremony of shaking hands with surrounding guests forced him to act in a congenial manner and turn to shake Maynard's hand. Sobleski was surprised there was a man taller than himself directly behind him.

In the bathroom Sobleski went to the wall urinal and reached into his pocket and pulled out a poison injection ring. He placed it on his ring finger of his right hand. At that precise moment, Maynard walked into the bathroom and walked over to the adjacent wall urinal. He looked at Sobleski and commented, "I never have been to anything like this before in my lifetime. I don't think I will again. That was really something."

Sobleski looked at him and smiled. But Maynard heard nothing. Out of the corner of his eye he saw Sobleski doing something with the ring on his right hand. The man appeared to be nervous. Sobleski was not certain if the man next to him could see that he was arming his weapon of choice with a poison serum. The plan was when he would shake the hand of the new Bishop the ring would inject a poison serum into the Bishop's hand. It would numb the Bishop's hand upon contact so that he would be able to slip the Bishop's Ring from his hand as they ended the handshake. Within minutes, the poison would kill the Bishop, but Sobleski would be out of the shrine and on his way.

Maynard washed his hands and left the bathroom to tell Morrison what he saw, while Sobleski remained at the urinal. Maynard walked away. Morrison called a quick meeting of the plainclothes policemen.

"This time, he is using a ring to do his dirty work. Our problem looks like this. If he uses his hands on someone, if my guess is right, that person is going to be in mortal danger of losing his life. We can't let him shake the Bishop's hand. Don't let this guy touch you. It could be deadly," was the last words said by Morrison when Sobleski walked out of the bathroom and entered the reception line moving towards the new Bishop.

Maynard moved to a position in the reception line behind Sobleski. Over the top of heads of those giving the new Bishop their best wishes he gave a raised hand signal of hello and smile to the Bishop. The Bishop returned a wave of the hand, which showed he had the Bishop's Ring on his hand. Quickly, the Bishop went back to speak with his well wishers. Sobleski witnessed the Bishop's response. Maynard stood talking with a stranger as if he was enjoying the whole event as the line progressed, moving Sobleski ahead of him closer to the Bishop.

Morrison could see that Maynard was blocking access for the plainclothes police to apprehend Sobleski. Then it hit Morrison that Maynard was not that familiar with the faces of the police and that he might interfere and actually end up preventing the snatch of the killer as the killer attempted to get to the Bishop. Morrison gave a signal to the chief of security for the D.C. Metro Police fearful that this was going to end up with another death on the floor with the Bishop's Ring being taken by Sobleski. Quietly, two plainclothes policemen moved just behind Maynard.

As he spoke to the woman before him Bishop Piorek looked up at the next person who was about to greet him. It was a man who closely resembled the killer's description. His eyes met Maynard's eyes with a glance that only the two of them knew. The woman walked away and Sobleski came forward with his hand outstretched toward the Bishop's. Maynard sprung from his spot and wrapped his long huge arms around Sobleski. Sobleski's arms were held against his own body. The plainclothes policemen moved in ready to wrap a set of handcuffs on Sobleski before he had a chance to move his hands towards anyone. Slowly, Sobleski's arms were drawn one by one, behind him by the plainclothes police and he was hand cuffed directly in front of a startled Bishop.

Maynard walked behind Sobleski. He grabbed the killer's hands and saw that the poison ring was still loaded and ready to fire off its poison. He grabbed Sobleski's hand and turned it inward toward his rear end. Maynard pushed the killer's hand into his own backside. No one noticed except one person, Morrison. Then he walked over to Bishop Piorek. Morrison heard him say, "Now that the police have him he won't be coming to bother you any more. They know how to take care of things. You know how Cousin Barney is at Shady Trail. Police have a way of doing what's right!" It was his usual sarcastic remark about law enforcement. Maynard wanted the police blamed should it come to that!

Just then Sobleski collapsed on the floor unable to speak and frothed at the mouth. He was a victim of his own ingenuity. The police called for an ambulance. Morrison reached behind Sobleski who was laying on the floor his eyes staring blindly into the sky. Morrison removed the poison ring from his finger and placed it in a small plastic bag. He always carried bags with him to collect evidence. He knew that there would be an autopsy of the body and that a poison compound would be found. Maynard's remarks to Bishop Piorek left the police as possible culprits for the killer's death if he failed to survive.

Morrison, after hearing of Maynard's attitude toward law enforcement based on cousin Barney's ways, and who heard Maynard tell that his cousin Barney "Couldn't do his business even if he was locked inside of an outhouse." Maynard did take care of things in his own way. Sobleski was not going to return to live another day, free to torment, nor free to fill the lives of others with fear. It was Maynard's form of justice which he learned going to war.

No one would want to prosecute a citizen for killing a killer, whose victim never knew he was a target of death. Morrison understood that kind of justice. If the police did not have a weapon and they were unable to prove that Maynard had one then Maynard like the killer who stalked Magda could go free. If no one from the police brought the poison ring into evidence, like unto like, the same rules applied to save the Conrad's killer, the lack of a weapon, should apply.

In an ironic twist of fate, Morrison thought over his dilemma of this evidence, and as he decided, this ring should never gain any recognition. This poison killer ring, could take on epic proportions, just as the Bishop's Ring had become, in the course of time. He would bury it in the waters of the East River of New York. There it would have a resting place with other unsolved mysteries, where only God knows the truth.

Bishop Piorek bent over the man lying on the floor, and whispered in Polish in his ear, hoping he could respond, and asked him if he could confess his sins. The eyes blinked once. He asked him if he was sorry for all of his sins of his life. He blinked his eye again. Fear filled his face. Bishop Piorek listened to his final words, and then raised his hand and gave Sobleski absolution from his sins. It was the only time Sobleski saw the Bishop's Ring. The killer posing in his alias as Janus Piotrowski died, without fame and fortune.

Morrison sat and looked at the papers on his desk. They were signed and ready for the Captain's signature. The Captain said, "I thought you'd stick around for another five with me. We could go out together." Morrison just shook his head from side to side, smiled, and said nothing. They shook hands and then hugged. It was good-bye and I'll see you some day soon. Morrison said with a smile, "When the first check comes in I'll come back and show it to you."

"Where you're going, you won't need that check."

Morrison responded, "Oh yea, who says?"

"Moe, have a good one. But, stay away from the beach."

Magda and her family helped bring a closing to the hidden mystery of the Bishop's Ring. She dreamed of a free Poland. It had to be more than the Bishop's Ring. The Polish people were prepared to restore the Church in their lives at any cost and the Polish Communist party bosses folded under the collapse of the Soviet Union.

Bishop Piorek had answers for her. When President Reagan and Soviet Premier Mikhail Gorbachov signed the ABM Treaty on December 8, 1987, it was not a matter of coincidence it was signed on that day. And again when Gorbachov chose to announce the end of Communism in Russia on December 25, 1989, against such a momentous declaration was not a matter of coincidence as most would shrug off. The Bishop's faith and reason allowed him to believe these two days are signs God want us to remember on the eternal calendar. The feast of the Immaculate Conception of the Blessed Virgin Mary on December 8th reminds Christians of her role in the defeat of Satan's evil through her seed who is the Christ. His birth celebrated on December 25th is a reminder God keeps his promises and does rule over the earth. Satan's anti-God role ended as all biblical bondages ended and slaves were freed after a seventy-year period. The Polish people were now free to form their own government and set themselves on a path of renewed religious freedom to worship Christ. Restoring the holy Bishop's Ring, he told her, to a Polish born Bishop is a sign of Poland's coming place in the world among free nations to enjoy their patriotic solidarity and human rights when God is called upon to protect them.

There were consolations to Magda's loss of Conrad. She would have a comfortable amount of money to begin a new life, and keep the design business going for the Churches. Someday her daughter could take over her wedding fashion business. Her son would have a job when he finished studying architecture. When he became licensed his name would be affixed to drawings. This certainly would make both parents happy.

Magda thought Conrad now lives in eternity. He would be remembered as one who preserved his faith with a constancy of belief. She hoped Conrad would meet the spirit of Bishop St. Stanislaw. He had given his life by protecting his Bishop's Ring.

The lights were on in the now retired detectives house. The drapes were drawn when a vehicle drove up and parked in front of his garage doors. The sun had set and the car lights were suddenly switched off. A woman climbed the front stairs to the porch over the garage. She could hear stereo music as she rang the doorbell.

Finally someone came to the door and looked at her.

"Bob. It's me. Magda."

"Come in Magda. By all means, come in. I was just out in the kitchen making a snack and watching some television."

"I've got a better idea. I know you like your music so I brought along a compact disc with a Chopin concert on it. I am Mrs. Chopin, remember?" She said with a smile. He returned her smile. "This compact disc is by an authentic Polish concert pianist, Marta

Sosinska. She is another Polish treasure. She is a Chopin expert. We could listen to her play the piano in a concert and talk and drink a little of this wine. We could talk and become friends. You have been so good to me, so helpful." There was a warm smile on her face.

Morrison asked, "You will be staying here, then, in America?"

Magda smiled, "Yes. I want to see my future grandchildren. Not too soon, I hope. My children do not know Poland. Their father is buried here. I must stay. The wedding dress orders I had to complete them. I had to bring some order to the design office. It took a while for me to make that choice. It's been a while I know. What did not take long for me to find out is that I always had a friend in you. The Bishop's Ring brought us together."

Morrison studied her face, "I think there is more to this than we will ever know. But I understand what you are saying to me. I think our deceased spouses know."

He picked up the compact disc and placed it in his disc player and turned up the sound. Then he went to the glass cabinet, and reached for two wine glasses and the corkscrew. They clinked their half full glasses, and looked into each other's eyes.

He said, "I know a Monsignor, who might be interested in listening to my idea of joining two people together because he already knows how they think." He said with a smile.

"And I know a Bishop who has a ring, who might like to bless rings, when we are ready to wear them."

"But first, before all of that," as he looked with open eyes upon Magda, "for beginners may I kiss you?"

"So what really happened to Father Lawrence, Monsignor?" Betty Ryan asked as she prepared a meal for the two of them. He understood the question beyond her simple question.

He responded "I don't think God will fault Father Lawrence for wanting to change St. Catherine of Siena's. He had the energy to do what I did not have, to be honest. God knows our limitations. I can't speak for his motivations. I don't know if he wasn't listening to God to make changes or if he really believed he deserved to be a Bishop. However, I kind of think the Lord would like to change the location of the Tabernacle."

"That still grinds you, doesn't it?"

The priest sat back smiling, in a thoughtful mood took his time to remark again. He became philosophical.

"This is the end of an era, Betty. We cannot ignore the Book of Revelations, the Woman clothed with the sun and her struggle with the Red Dragon. Restoring the Bishop's Ring is a small part of the heavenly signs going on all over the world. It's a narrow path to salvation! But thanks to the Marian apparitions, at Fatima, then Garabandal, and now in Medjugorje, Hrushiv in the Ukraine, Japan, the warnings we've received, we know God's promised chastisement is near unless humanity changes from its sinful ways. This matter of the Bishop's Ring is a hidden reminder for us to be converted to do our penances. In this world of apostasy, we will need to make the effort to be purified before God will accept us."

She said, "It always scares me to think about chastisement!"

He answered, "This century has been Satan's. I expect Satan will continue his hate of God with more conflicts in this world, but the Book of Revelations' prophecies about the Second Coming of Christ will be fulfilled. God will triumph over Satan. God keeps his promises."

"This, you deduce from what we went through about the Bishop's Ring?"

"No, but the signs are here. We have been given a knowledge and understanding of the ways of God. The Bishop's Ring being returned in this century is an act of love on the part of God. A sign He will triumph over evil. It's a sign, to convert, to repent, to ask to be forgiven for our sins. God wants us to avoid the heresy the Communists preached. He is a loving God who wants us to love Him and others He created. Unless we change, we will be chastised! Remember, God keeps his promises."

"You think the Second Coming of Christ is that soon?"

"No man knows except the Father when Jesus will return. Something tells me we are in for a supernatural sign from God. The Blessed Mother has been God's messenger for the last 2000 years. With all of her apparitions all over the world, She is preparing the way for the Lord's coming!"

Betty waited to hear more as the two drank tea.

Betty remarked, "I made Bishop Piorek's reservations for going to Rome today. Do you know what he said to me?"

"No, what?"

"He said he was going to offer the Bishop's Ring to the Pope, who was after all, Bishop of Cracow, once.

"The Pope already has his ring. Hmn! I wonder if a voice has been speaking softly to him. I just wonder! Could this be the end of the line for the Bishop's Ring? Does it make you wonder about the end of the line about other things?" Betty did not want to answer those questions.

"I have one for you, sort of a coincident. "Do you know the killer of Conrad Kaminski chose an alias, and Kaminski's son shared the same first name, Thaddeus? Now that should make you think."

"St. Jude Thaddeus. Apostle. One of the twelve! Patron of hopeless cases! In the last seconds of his life he was able to repent." He paused. "Yes, there is something hidden here. Imagine the power of this holy relic! To convert sinners, and protect human life! Isn't it amazing the killer was able to, in his last moments of breath, to confess his sorrow for his sins?"

"More, amazing to me was that Bishop Piorek's life was saved, protected, call it what you want!" She said.

"Ask Bishop Piorek if you can read the longer legend of the Bishop's Ring. It's been translated into English. Then you'll understand more fully what others went through in preserving the tradition of keeping the Bishop's Ring on the finger of a Bishop from Cracow."

"And Father Lawrence?"

"He'll emerge a better priest, a holier priest, a humbler priest, more obedient to the things of God, than the things of men. He benefits greatly from the experience."

"And, Quentin?"

"Pray for the mercy of God. We'll just have to wait for the day of Final Judgment to find out!"

Chapter 33

The serendipitous events, which led up to the John Piorek's escape from Communist Poland in his youth were not forgotten. Bishop Piorek's long memories of his youth were rising to the forefront of his mind. He found out his mother like so many other women tortured by the Soviet rulers in 1950 was forced to stand naked in a pool of water above her waist and starve until in weakness she dropped down and drowned as others had died along side her. His father was shipped to Siberia in a cattle car to live his life in suffering never to return. He knew the contempt Marxists had for human life and its willingness to destroy anyone or anything that would prevent them from gaining and holding power.

As a priest who heard thousands of confessions Bishop Piorek did not need to be reminded the lengths to which evil people will go to seek their revenge upon good people. In the aftermath of the Polish Secret Police Colonel Thaddeus Sobleski's death the news account of his dying beneath a kneeling newly ordained Bishop allowed Waldemir Wilk to obsess about the prize his boss failed to capture. From the news accounts, Bishop Piorek became the man of destiny who was given St. Stanislaw's Bishop's ring. Wilk knew money had to be connected to a payoff if his boss had succeeded. Where was that money?

Wilk and Zabinski pawed their way through their deceased boss's files in the office and at his home in Queens. They wanted to know in what bank account where the money was to be found to pay the authorized ransom price for the ring. Their plan was to forge documents and bank checks and give themselves a 50-50 split of their findings. If that was not possible, Wilk said he would finish what Sobleski failed to accomplish and sell the ring to a non-interested party who could sell it back to the Church.

Captain Antonnucci had not forgotten the Polish spy's promise to pay $750,000 for the Bishop's Ring to Quentin LaFayette. The NYPD provided Bishop Piorek with the names of secretary Wanda Zabinski and chauffer Waldemir Wilk. Bishop Piorek began to think the legend of the Bishop's Ring was continuing to be his problem. That's when he began to think about Rome to meet the Pope, a fellow Cracovian, who once was the Bishop of Cracow.

Bishop Piorek knew St. Stanislaw's Bishop's Ring survived all of these centuries for some great purpose. Poland was now free. But Bishop Piorek had his concerns. One killer was deceased. But the Bishop knew old causes do not die. He may still have willing enemies wanting to steal the Bishop's Ring to sell it to a willing buyer.

After finishing reading the obligatory daily divine office prayers every priest must pray at his St. Catherine of Siena residence, he knelt at his prie-dieu contemplating before the crucifix in his study those whom he would like to have join him on his journey to Rome. He called upon the Holy Spirit to help him make a correct decision. After completing his daily Rosary he returned to his desk to make a list of priorities, not the least of which was how, when and with whom he would travel this journey. He relied on his memories and the stories he remembered hearing of people who were connected and who protected the Bishop's Ring. Certainly His Holiness would be happy to meet them in an audience in the Vatican.

His mind drifted as he sat back with a pencil and yellow pad on a clipboard to make notes. He wasn't sure whom he would list to be worthy to add to the "legend" of the Bishop's Ring. But it could be a start of people he wanted to travel with him.

In 1939 Gabriel Takentur was on vacation with his parents in Cracow, Poland when he met Grigor Androwitz as a boy. Grigor initiated conversation with Gabriel and his father when he heard the Takenturs speaking in English at an outdoor café in the Public

Square. Proudly Grigor, the boy, told them he was an American and his father taught at Jagiellonian University. That meeting began to form a friendship when years later Grigor requested Gabriel's help for John Piorek's passage to study in America.

Gabriel told John Piorek his inherited wealth began when his mother's Irish immigrant father in his young years discovered oil in Western New York State more than 100 years ago. Gabriel put his own efforts for more than two decades to expand Gabriel Oil markets before and during World War II where the company's specialty oils were needed for steel cutting machines in the defense industry.

Post World War II demand for household products, autos, machinery and the demands for the rebuilding Europe kept Gabriel Oil expanding. His knowledge and expertise in European commerce led to his selection to an ambassadorship in the Eisenhower Administration. His appointment was based as his lifetime experience traveling in Europe where pre-World War II Communists inserted radicals to breakdown opposition to Cold War Marxist-Leninist ideologies. His former status of ambassador helped to gain a release for the future priest who came from Poland, which the then Bishop of Cracow had requested.

A smile came across the Bishop's face as he recalled when as an Ambassador, Takentur told the Communist Polish official "Let this young idealist leave your country where he can be lost in his dream world. Be rid of him so that his voice is never heard in a Catholic Church in Poland." The Communist official, who spoke one way, but believed another way, allowed young John Piorek to leave Poland and claim his actions were worthy of a medal to be able to send a potential priest away so that Poland would have one less priest to undermine the State. The tactic worked. Gabriel never said he bribed the Polish official. Gabriel would only say he used his "Leverage" to gain John Piorek's freedom.

In Gabriel Takentur's family John Piorek was accepted as an adopted member. Bishop Piorek's first choice for a travel companion to meet with the Pope was Gabriel Takentur. Takentur was a very fit man for his ninety years. He kept a regimen of exercise and eating habits that restored his body energy and muscle tone like that of a man thirty years younger than his actual age. Wealthy enough to give away millions to Catholic causes and support Gabriel Takentur gave John Piorek financial help in his student years to make him a life long friend.

His second choice to travel with him was Monsignor O'Toole, who guided him when he was a young cleric and who recommended him to Bishop O'Farrell for the position of Auxiliary Bishop.

He made a note to ask Monsignor O'Toole to put in a word for him with retired policeman Bob Morrison to ask the assistance of the NYPD to go to the appropriate authorities to use their persuasive powers to return any Polish funds used for clandestine activities to steal the Bishop's Ring to have them returned to the new Polish government.

Next on the Bishop's list was Magda Kaminski Morrison, and Bob her new husband. It was she who risked all and who suffered the most from the days of her youth. The loss of never seeing her parents again was the most difficult for her, even among the earlier intimidations and false charges filed against Conrad. Magda suffered quietly and with dignity until nearly drained of all hope of living free from her cruel former countrymen, her reward on this journey of faith remained rock solid.

Death was but inches a way if Maynard had not taken over to stop the man with his poison weapon. Certainly His Holiness would love to meet Maynard. He made notes that Maynard would need to plan to take vacation time, and yes, give him instructions about forming a proper conscience when it comes to the use of lethal weapons against humans.

Not wanting to go further, he called Gabriel Takentur at his home. "Gabriel, this is John."

"Good evening, Bishop. What can I do for you?"

"I would like to invite you to go with me to meet the Pope. It's for obvious reasons I want you to come along."
"Bishop, first I have to tell you something. I bought a plane last month. How is that for an old geezer like me?"

"Nothing you do Gabriel would surprise me."

"I bought the plane and hired the pilots. Gabriel Oil has joined the jet set. My sons put me up to it. It was on the market for a low price. A company went out of business when the owner died tragically. The price was low enough so we reconditioned the cabin to take out the gaudiness and any reminders of its past. Does the name Cutler Construction Company mean anything to you?

"Is that the plane that Maynard...?"

Gabriel quickly said, "It was. Yes I would love to go the Vatican with you. We can fill it up with your guests and off to Rome we go."

Bishop Piorek responded, "This is sudden."

"Sudden? At my age all opportunities are sudden! Maybe the Pope would like to hear about my father's interviews with Lenin and Stalin, and my bold challenge to Stalin when he became the Soviet Dictator."

"I'm sure he would like to hear about the man who enslaved Poland. In the meantime, I will make some calls to Monsignor O'Toole, to invite Magda and her sister Marta and their families. I would like to invite Maynard as well."

"Okay," Gabriel said, "I will bring my two sons and their wives. That should do it. Let me know when the plans are firmed up. It's sure to be exciting. Their kids are not living at home."

The Bishop responded, "It's all been exciting."

Leaving the United States would be his first trip out of the country since arriving to study to become a priest. The promise made by his Cracow Bishop to Seminarian Piorek was that he would be able to return to Poland someday.

But first, the new Bishop's release from obscurity into a world of recognition and responsibility toward his diocese, and his new parish was bewildering. There would be no nights to stare at the stars in the heavens with a protective friend like Maynard. Gnawing at his inner constitution was the sense the legend of the Bishop's Ring must be completed in its written form and when completed taken to its proper place in the Treasury of the Cathedral of Cracow. It belonged in no other place than in the same sacred area where the earthly remains of St. Stanislaw were placed. Of the Bishop's Ring final home he was not sure. That matter he would discuss with the Pope.

Chapter 34

Long before the Reformation the Treasury in the Cathedral in Cracow contained so many relics, artifacts and memories of days of Poland's struggle and glory. While neighboring kings and princes came to visit to give homage with jeweled religious objects, contending forces directed at Poland over centuries sought to steal its land in their attempts to overturn its religion. Poland's people have a strong sense of history and of blessing because it cherishes its Roman Catholic religious culture not the least of which is its belief in the true presence of Christ in the Holy Eucharist and the many miracles performed when the people and nation had been distressed. The atheist Communists for too many years in the 20th century subjected Poland to its slavish cruelty. And now after seventy years of Soviet bondage, God using normal means, convinced Soviet leader Gorbachev to declare Communism dead in the Russian motherland.

Bishop Piorek had come to the conclusion that someday the Bishop's Ring would be safe in the underground Treasury of Cracow's Cathedral, linked where one of Poland and America's Great War heroes, Thaddeus Kosciusko's remains were entombed. The Bishop knew the United States Congress in 1977 gave its heartfelt thanks for his part in the American Revolutionary War battles in helping to defeat British colonialism in America by placing a plaque on the wall above his burial sarcophagus. What better place for the Bishop's

Ring to remain than where its original owner's remains are held and venerated by the faithful?

The Bishop placed a telephone call to the Morrison's in Syosset. Magda answered. "Magda. This is Bishop Piorek."

"Good evening, Bishop."

"I can't get used to calling myself Bishop. It may take a few years. How are you doing? How is Bob?"

"We are both fine."

"I have been reading the Legend of the Bishop's Ring. But it's missing a conclusion. I know you and Conrad worked on details of your trials in safeguarding it, but now, the events of the recent time, is not recorded. I know Bob had a big hand protecting it for this time when I was chosen as its final bearer. I have given a lot of thought to the idea of what will happen to it when I die. At first I thought I would give it to His Holiness in Rome, but it belongs to Poland. Now I must ask you and Bob a question. Is he home?

"Bob, pick up the other phone, it's Bishop Piorek."

"Good evening, Bishop. It's so good of you to call."

"Hello, Bob. I was explaining to Magda I have been thinking about the final chapters for the Legend of the Bishop's Ring, and would be honored if the two of you would care to write about these days to be added to what Magda has contributed, so the book on the Legend is closed."

"Whew!" Bob responded.

"The reason I am asking is, the Legend and the Ring itself must take its place in Poland's thousand-year Catholic history."

"What will happen to the written Legend?" Bob asked.

"I thought you would ask. That has yet to be worked out. I have an elder gentleman, a friend," he hesitated, "I believe you met him at my ordination, Gabriel Takentur. Do you remember him?" They said they did.

"Very impressive man" Bob Morrison said. Magda added, "He told us how he met Conrad through our cousin Father Grigor. He told us a long story from there. We encouraged him to tell it. I know of the places he spoke about in Cracow, like churches and restaurants, landmarks. I long for the day to go back, to put flowers on my parent's grave. But I don't know if I will be safe doing it."

The Bishop listened and with happiness in his voice said, "I would like to invite the both of you and the kids, and your sister and her husband to fly to Rome to meet the Pope." Magda squealed with happiness. The Bishop waited until their excitement fell at least thirty decibels. "The plane is privately owned by Gabriel Takentur's company. The time of departure is not yet firm. You know our Holy Father loves to travel himself so we will have to wait for a firm date when we can be received by him."

Bob Morrison said, "Wow! We accept."

"Gabriel's two sons and their wives will be coming with us. I am inviting Maynard, and of course, Monsignor O'Toole." Then as an after thought he added, "Bob, can you contact your former boss tomorrow. I would like you to ask him if they followed up on what happened to the money the Communist were willing to pay for the Bishop's Ring. It would be better if that money sent back to Poland's new government. Converting dollars to zlotys that would be about three million zlotys they could use."

"I'll call him in the morning, and call you back when I have some details how it will work out." They continued to talk until the Bishop told them he had more calls to make.

Morrison called the Captain the next morning, and after some small talk, told him he had been invited to travel with the new Bishop to Rome and to tell him the Bishop's Ring case was not over. The new Bishop had a request that needed some attention. When the conversation ended the Captain sent Murphy out to get photos of people working at the Polish Embassy so as to match those photos with earlier ones taken. Morrison told him, "The chauffer and Sobleski's secretary are certain to know something, if they are still working there about the ransom funds which may still be held in an escrow account for Sobleski when he received and delivered the Bishop's Ring. The ousted regime in Poland is not going to reveal their dirty attempts to steal the ring."

Two days later a stack of photos were sent in the mail to Morrison. Earlier and present shots were compared. Wilk and Zabinski were still at the embassy. What Murphy did not know was that he was seen taking the pictures as the two parked the embassy limousine. Another matter was under the radar. Polish Communists sent their trained spies Wilk and Zabinski to spy on Sobleski. The two spies now knew the NYPD had not given up because Sobleski was dead. At the time they were photographed by Murphy the two had just returned from the bank where they cleared out the escrow account where the ransom money had been held. Could it be that the new government in Poland knew about the ransom money set aside for the return of the Bishop's Ring? The date of the transaction clearing would prove a dead Sobleski did not close the account.

Captain Antonnucci received passport information on the two spies and sent it to customs officials in the meantime in case the two embassy spies were ready to leave the U.S.A. Under the pretense of closing down the trade envoy section, Wilk and Zabinski worked in the embassy to bring their files home to Poland. In the event American customs were searching through computers to see if they left the country Wilk ordered a private jet aircraft and loaded it with spy collection data and carried forged Polish passports created in the embassy. Before telephone contact could be made to American officials of the whereabouts of Wilk and Zabinski, the two had successfully departed on a flight from JFK Airport headed for Poland with file cabinets filled with cash in US dollars.

Weeks had passed when Bishop Piorek received word from the Pope's secretary when the Pope would be available to receive them after his return from his most recent trip abroad. In the meantime, the word was out about Wilk and Zabinski and their false passports. Instead of going to Warsaw and stopping off in Poland's hotels the couple found a furnished apartment in Cracow and rented a small truck to unload their baggage and two file cabinets. The elderly woman who rented the apartment to them was happy to have the tenant rent and asked no questions.

Bishop Piorek's Group met at the St. Francis Hotel in Brooklyn. For him it was a return to a place he had been when he arrived in America and he wanted to go back. While their luggage was being loaded on to a bus to take them to Airport, Gabriel's Lear Jet was readied with prepared meals before departure. The group met early to hold an impromptu reception before departing for Rome.

Morrison was the one person who knew the least about Gabriel Takentur whose work and philanthropy in Catholic circles was often noticed. After the plane took off and all had settled for an over the ocean flight, the inquisitive Morrison wanted Gabriel to talk about his legendary risk taking journalist father. Gabriel loved his questions.

"My father, I am very proud to say was a journalist and well known in business and royal circles all over Europe. His commentary columns were widely read and his advice was sought quite often. He was an American who grew up in Philadelphia, went to Villanova and landed a job in London as a reporter, where my father's mother met my grandfather. They married and moved to America and landed in Philadelphia where my father was born. My father was working as a reporter in Philadelphia when he met he met my mother while she staying at a hotel with friends. They said it was love at first sight. My mother was a very beautiful green-eyed colleen. Few men are so lucky to find one like her."

Morrison gave a slight throat clearing as he looked over at Magda and back at Gabriel. Gabriel said, "You're lucky too!"

Morrison continued, "What started the connection with Cracow and the Bishop's Ring? I haven't heard an explanation."

"My father's connection had a connection with Cracow because it is a very cultural city, which supports writers, artists, sculptors, actors, musicians, playwrights, and people of similar crafts. It was a natural affinity for my father to want to be among his own kind, you know, creative people! Beside the city has so much religious and royal history. We should go there!"

"I'm looking forward to seeing where Magda lived once." Bob said.

Gabriel could see Morrison wanted to hear more. "My father followed his hunches, much like you did to protect the Bishop's Ring. He was religious, prayerful, and in tune with strong feelings. He was widely read in Europe and excellently paid. What I liked about our life there was that I had a chance to study in Europe and be in places making history. We were in St. Petersburg when the Russian Revolution broke out."

Morrison added, "I'll say he was lucky being a journalist!"

To which Gabriel added, "He followed his hunches and sought permission to leave London during World War I and ended up in Portugal to witness the Miracle of the Sun at Fatima in 1917. By anyone's account he was a very interesting man!"

Morrison continued, "Did he know about the Bishop's Ring?"

"That's a very good question. Possibly. I say this because he followed those kinds of stories. A beautiful holy icon filled with diamonds and rubies was stolen from the Cathedral in Kazan. So, when he had the chance, my father, in an interview with Lenin asked him if his revolutionaries had anything to do with its removal. Lenin denied anything to do with its loss. But we left Russia quickly when my father suspected he was poisoned during the interview. He wrenched in pain."

"Your father interviewed Lenin?" Morrison asked in awe.

"And Stalin as well. He met Stalin in Cracow a few years before the Russian Revolution at Café Jama Michalika. We'll go there. It's still going strong." Morrison continued to be amazed at Gabriel's life experience at the beginning of Communism and through the years of the Cold War.

"When John Piorek let his Bishop know he desired to be a priest, to save him from working in the coal or salt mines, Father Grigor contacted me and the rest is history. That is why it is so important that the finished "Legend" now becomes a written historical document preserving nearly a thousand years of Poland's journey in faith."

"This may be a foolish question Gabriel, but has anything ever been written about your father's or your days in the early days of Communism? I mean for a journalist it only seems ordinary he would have written some memoirs about his days when he spoke with Lenin and Stalin."

"Oh yes. My father chose to write a novel with a pen name at the end of his European career in journalism. It was a new thing then mixing real life people with fiction. He chronicled issues, which would not ordinarily be told in newspapers because newspapers editors would have been squeamish to insert spirituality into column space. You have to understand Europe in those days was a cauldron of Bolshevik deceit much like we have had since the days of Watergate." Gabriel became insightful.

Gabriel looked at Bishop Piorek and asked, "Are you sure you want to return your Bishop's Ring to the Cracow Cathedral Treasury? Poland may be free, but we are fighting another kind of battle here in America for the very soul of our nation. We need to be brought together in the unity St. Stanislaw represents. We need the solidarity of the Body of Christ members to stand up against the wiles of Satan's willing cooperators in their efforts to remove religion from the public forum. Give it some thought my dear friend and Bishop. When we get back home I'll look about for my father's book for you to read." Gabriel stopped to notice he had a larger audience and invited other to sit around them. He added his long view of the present times.

"I may be old but I can still think. History is being repeated. The anti-Christian hostility in our country's culture tells me atheists are still involved in dismantling the Constitution and destroying the U.S. They had their revenge upon Senator McCarthy and Richard Nixon, two fighters who exposed Communists working in the U.S. government. They use the same tactic that helped to bring down the Czar of Russia. Smear and smear until their lies take hold and they then sway people in their grab for power. These atheist deconstructionists wrap themselves in the American flag, put up front organizations to take away our freedoms and moral laws that have been part of the Judeo-Christian belief systems for four thousand years. They smear anyone who would object to their causes as being anti-American."

Maynard put his fist up and pulled it down with a smile on his face. Maynard knew about the Communist killing machines in the Vietnam era. Gabriel continued to speak of past history for his claim history is repeating itself.

"I remember the rabble rousers in St. Petersburg storming in the streets to bring down the provisional government that was in place after the Czar resigned. They undermined the Czar when Russia was fighting the battles of World War I. They chose power over patriotism. I see their hands in the riots in Detroit in the 1930's.

"During the 1930's Bolsheviks smeared Father Coughlin when his 40 million-listener radio audience heard the priest report

260

Bolsheviks were active in the Roosevelt Administration. Regular people working in Washington D.C. sent the priest letters telling him Bolsheviks were active in the bureaus of our national government. They attacked the priest with smears, but after World War II the country heard the truth. Under Secretary of State Alger Hiss was convicted as a communist, and ten thousand communists lost their federal jobs. Time, talent and truth proved the priest's allegations were true."

"Someone once called Watergate a bungled burglary. President Nixon had many enemies. I came to live among Marxist atheists in Europe. I know how they behave. They have no conscience. They break all of the Ten Commandments without fearing God. Smearing Nixon forced him to be defensive. He made mistakes for sure. But bringing him down by character assassination is like the same thing done to the Czar of Russia. It's a war fought without guns, one that is also forbidden by God, 'Thou shall not bear false witness against thy neighbor.' It just wasn't revenge upon Nixon. It brought doubt and fear upon the faith people had in our nation. It made us susceptible to more propaganda and lies. The unholy among us fail to recognize an injustice of such tactics. Freedom becomes a victim of their lies.

"Public discourse has never been the same since Watergate. Call them Marxist, Bolsheviks, Communists. The door was opened and we have nothing but hate speech against our cherished social structure, not the least of which began with removing the Christmas crèche and denial of Children to sing Christmas carols in the schools. In the land where freedom of speech and religion is the first of our freedoms, a small number of Marxists among us use the courts to deny the majority of us our sacred traditions. They want a godless society where anything goes. Who profits from the denial of God in our lives? Satan does!

"The Soviet Union fell from the weight of its own failures. God did not want it to succeed in promoting atheism. That is what the Miracle of Fatima was partially about. The Mother of God called upon nations to pray for the conversion of Russia, and to do penance for sins. The children she appeared to were given a vision of hell where sinners go after death. We Catholics affirm what they saw was true. We also know our country has lost so much control of human behavior which offends God because of the activists who argue in courts of the land for licentious licenses causing moral breakdown in society. It's the way it was in St. Petersburg in 1917 after the Communists gave license to 'no contest,' divorces, abortion on demand and promiscuity.

"We have come to learn there are people among us who work in our government, education field, judiciary, entertainment, media and political systems that are deeply committed to deconstructing our Judeo-Christian way of life. They just don't call themselves Communists but they are without the label. Cross them and they will make you pay the price."

Takentur looked around the lounged cabin and said, "My father took a safer path. He knew the Communists began infiltrating our country since 1919. Now they sit undeclared in the halls of Congress, on important committees able to deny us our rights and freedoms. Someday America may wake up. But then it may be too late."

Gabriel spoke to his two sons, "Maybe its time we have your grandfather's book reprinted. What do you think?"

They nodded thoughtfully, agreeing with their father.

The eldest son, Thomas said, "We can rename it. People should read it now to see where we have come from."

Gabriel responded, "So people will know the past before choosing their future that will surely lead them to bondage. It always happens when we leave God out of their lives."

Bishop Piorek said, "I would like to read your father's book when it is reprinted. The coincidence of my wearing of the Bishop's Ring still amazes me. Communism comes into existence and soon it enslaves people. I know it floats in like the tide drowning us without any barriers to stop it. Put on faith and action and we can defend ourselves." Gabriel's comments put as they were, could not be dismissed. "Perhaps I should rethink giving up the Bishop's Ring at this time. The things that I know to be true, such as:

"Morality is based on Revelation from God.

"Ethics is based on human philosophic reasoning.

"The Church teaches the Bible is the inerrant Word of God. Ethics based on human reasoning is capable of discerning truth, yet it often fails in accepting falsehoods as matters of expediency."

The Bishop reminded, "We are weaker when we permit our thoughts to control our actions. We are stronger when our actions control our thoughts. It was the lesson the Lord gave when he acted to carry out the prophecies of Isaiah 53, which was foretold eight centuries before in God's Revelation of the coming crucifixion of the Messiah, Jesus Christ."

Gabriel asked, "Are we ready for supper?"

Chapter 35

Waldemir Wilk drove Sobleski to Washington because his boss did not want his name to appear on an airline passenger lists. Wilk had not been privileged to know the real reason why his boss went to the ordination of the Polish immigrant who became a Catholic Bishop.

Following the ordination ceremony Wilk watched the reception line move forward that day when he saw his boss, Thaddeus Sobleski slowly approach the newly ordained Bishop. It wasn't until the bearded giant of a man behind Sobleski wrapped his arms around Sobleski that Wilk understood his boss came to the ordination not to express good wishes but to kill the new Bishop.

Wilk knew Sobleski was like a chameleon, changing his colors to suit his purposes. When he saw the Bishop kneeling over Sobleski in his boss's final moments, listening to what the dying man was saying while still dressed in his ordination robes Wilk knew his boss was given an opportunity to express sorrow for his sins. When the new Bishop raised his hand to make the sign of the Cross over the penitent sinner, Wilk understood his parents teaching him to love and forgive his enemies.

Back in New York City he told Wanda Zabinski what happened, and together they plotted to retrieve the money in the escrow account.

Waldemir Wilk and Wanda Zabinski made their escape out of New York.

In Cracow the two went to the Cathedral to find when the Archbishop celebrated his daily Mass. They were told Archbishop Adamowicz celebrates his daily Mass at his residence on Franciszkariska Street. They found their way to the Archbishop's residence, and without appointment managed to convince the gatekeeper they had a matter of great importance to discuss only with the Archbishop by showing him the inside of Wilk's leather valise. They were ushered in to an antechamber to wait until the Archbishop was free to see them.

When the smiling Archbishop opened the door to invite them into his office they were ready to unfold the story of their lives as loyal communists and were ready return to the Church of their youth. Their tale ended when Wilk opened his valise and dropped its contents upon the desk of the Archbishop, the neatly wrapped stacks of American $100 dollar bills. Wilk said, "There are more for you but I could not carry them here. This money belongs to the people of Poland. We thought it would be best turned over to the Church because the Church suffered so much at the hands of the Communists by denying support to the Church that the people would be given if the people were allowed to practice their faith. We realize we will die someday. We want God's forgiveness for our sins. If God will forgive the worst among us, we want his mercy as well."

For the time being, the Archbishop accepted responsibility for all of the money that had been in the special escrow account the Communist government set aside for the return of the Bishop's Ring until a proper disposition could be made the money belonged to the people of Poland. Having heard their stories he asked them if they would like to go to confession. The surprise question was an invitation to absolve away the evils of their past. Wilk remarked, "Even Sobleski was not going to give up his chance to enter heaven. We cannot refuse our chance to gain eternal life when God offers it through his priest."

In the Bishop's Office in Upstate New York, Betty Ryan while clicking keys on her computer keyboard was about to be surprised by a visitor. Jack Moran, a long forgotten high school classmate knocked on her open office door. Caught off guard she looked at him wondering who he was. When she heard his voice, it came to her she knew who he was. Could it be her boyfriend from high school?

Jack Moran was invited to her home that night. She had a new beginning. Jack never married. This time it was different. Jack retired early and came home to enjoy the rewards he earned from the world of business.

It really didn't take much for them to hug, kiss, snuggle and for Jack to propose marriage. He had no mountains to climb or rivers to cross. He was through doing the impossible. He wanted a loving wife, and she wanted a man who would love her. Jack considered himself lucky she was still available. Betty was ready to remind Jack how long she waited for him to return to her. Monsignor O'Toole promised he would marry them when he came back from his trip.

A special transport bus was waiting at the Airport for the Americans after they passed the inspection of Italian customs. The bus driver spoke English with a definite Italian accent charming the travelers as he pointed out the sites of Rome. All of their time, accommodations, and the audience with the Pope were prearranged. They would attend Mass in his private chapel, spend two hours with the Pope, and later have lunch with him in his dining room.

This was to be a special time for the Pope and the young man he sent to America to study to become a priest, who now shared a collegial authority with the Pontiff, and a share of the ministry given by Jesus Christ to his Apostles. Time on the schedule was set-aside for the both of them to have a private meeting.

Gabriel Takentur's remarks on the flight to Rome concerning the growing influence of Marxist, atheistic, and secular efforts to eliminate the religious culture of America awakened within Bishop Piorek a keener understanding of history being revisited. He had a mission with St. Stanislaw's Bishop's Ring to fight against bold atheists to be worthy to wear the ancient, holy relic ring. The time had come to discuss his concerns with the one person whom he knew would help him become enlightened.

The Legend of the Bishop's Ring had been completed, printed and bound in leather offering both English and Polish versions. Gabriel Takentur offered to take the group to Poland at the end of their Vatican visit so that the Bishop could take the Bishop's Ring and the leather bound Legend to Cracow's Cathedral on Wawel Hill, were they could become display items in the Cathedral's Treasury. Bishop Piorek was not so sure he wanted to give up the Bishop's Ring. He would discuss the matter with the Pope.

When the Pope walked into the library where the group assembled he carried with him two special envelopes. Bishop Piorek stood the closest to him when he arrived in the room. He handed him an envelope and the two walked away from the group where they could not be heard. The Pope signaled the Bishop to open the letter and read. After reading the Pope's personal congratulations to his ordination to the Episcopacy, the Pope wrote,

It was to be expected that the grave concerns the Blessed Mother of our Lord which she expressed at Fatima, Portugal in 1917 for the world to pray for the conversion of Russia, the evil that possessed that country came to an end officially on Christmas day in 1989 when the Soviet leader declare Communism dead on that day. Once again, in this century signs of the Blessed Virgin's work and presence have been made known in the world affairs of humanity.

When he read this paragraph, he looked up at the Pope and smiled, remembering him as Bishop of Cracow and telling him as a future seminarian of when her signs appeared during World War II. They all related to the prophecy in the Book of Genesis, Chapter 3, Verse: 15. He read on:

In the designs of Providence, dear Brother, there are no mere coincidences. Our small part in the return of the Bishop's Ring demonstrates God's will to end the suffering of the Polish People, to bring this chaos contrived by the devil to an end. Poland and so many other nations suffered at the hands of the brutal just as our Lord suffered in his crucifixion. Prayer and suffering are meritorious before the throne of God in this unbelieving world. When men stood together, and without fear, as with those who brought 'Solidarity' to life in Poland, and all others including the Kaminski's fought their evil enemy. They suffered to bring about this day when the Bishop's Ring has been returned to its proper place. May the Bishop's Ring be the source of miracles in your ministry in the United States. Your decision to have it placed in the Cracow Cathedral Treasury upon your death will then join with the Legend document as a fitting home on Wawel Hill.

After a few short words between them The Pope walked over to Magda and greeted her. She genuflected and kissed his Papal Ring. He gave her a warm greeting as he held her shoulders. Then she opened her envelope and read his letter to her written in English.

"My sincerest condolences to you for the loss of your very brave husband Conrad. He will be held high in Poland's esteem as one more martyr for a holy cause.

"It has been a long time since I sent you off to America with the Bishop's Ring and you have faithfully safeguarded it. You, yourself have had to suffer uncertainty and anxiety. I am asking our Blessed Savior to watch over you and yours all the days of your life. As a token of gratitude for your courage, I am giving you a gift this day for your role for so many years of faithful service to God.

"I presume you still have my Episcopal neck chain. You may keep it as a keepsake, as the only woman to whom I ever gave a ring!

"Devoted in Christ."

Magda looked at him with tears in her eyes and thanked him, and then began to laugh at his final words.

The Pope said to her in his typical humor, "Would you like this letter framed with my picture up in the corner and gold leaf art surrounding the outside? We have people who can do that here if you would like." His joviality and the group's laughter at his suggestion set a good mood for the time they could be together.

The Pope was in no hurry to end the two-hour audience he was having with Bishop Piorek's group. He cited the days when Poland in the grip of bondage was forced to do many things in secret and applauded Magda for her and her husband Conrad's courage to be the caretakers of the Bishop's Ring until Providence found the right person to be its wearer.

Each person involved in the return of the Bishop's Ring had a chance to tell a version of the complete story. Bob Morrison said he could not release the ring once he had it in his custody until he made contact with Monsignor O'Toole. He told the Pope he knew he had to pursue every avenue, but it wasn't until Magda recognized Conrad's killer by his real name Morrison said that the killer's façade was unmasked that they were prepared to capture him. And so it was as the Pope listened to each one's memories.

When they came to the part where Bishop Piorek heard the killer's confession, the Pope asked Maynard if he would like to go to confession to him. With that question each one in the group asked the Pope if he would hear their confession. He agreed. Maynard was first and when he walked back across the large room, he was both relieved and saddened. He was relieved when His Holiness offered him solace for his inner suffering because of those whom he killed. He was saddened because he agreed to lock up his weapons when the Pope asked him. He agreed to make peace with his cousin Barney and end their feud. The Pope encouraged him to study the Bible and the Catechism so that he could be useful to the Lord through Father Lawrence in other ways than with his armaments.

When the last member of the group Bishop Piorek completed his or her confession each knew they had been through a moving spiritual exercise of faith they would never forget. It was plain to the group that being in the presence of His Holiness was unlike anything they had ever experienced in their lives.

Their conversation turned to Poland and its war with atheism. Then with a smile on his face and self-deprecating humor, the Holy Father downplayed his lifelong efforts to undermine the atheist communists in his country by building an underground university so that Poland would have an educated class of people for the day when Poland was free from atheist bondage. The Holy Father reminded the group Christ promised to be with the Church he established until the end of the world.

The Pope encouraged the group to go to the Vatican Library to see the treasuries of civilization and the Sistine Chapel. The subject of seeing antiquity unfold before their eyes appealed to Magda, Bob and Maynard and Bishop Piorek, so Gabriel graciously accepted and arranged for all of them to take a city tour on a smaller tour bus.

When their time together had come to an ending, the Pope told them he would be with them for Mass in the morning in his private chapel.

After Mass, they met with the Pope for breakfast. It was their last meeting. In his final farewell he gave them his blessing for the rest of their trip. After expressing how they should "see" Poland, Gabriel decided they would not fly into Poland because of the risks to sabotage his Jet plane. Bishop Piorek decided before he left Italy for Poland he would return to America with his Bishop's Ring. He kept the decision a secret.

The Pope had made a private request of Gabriel to help the Sisters of the Nazarene in Cracow in their needs for van type transportation vehicles. The group could be housed at the Sister's convent where their luggage would be secure as they made their way on day trips to nearby towns and cities.

Considering all of the variances in the conversations being discussed, Gabriel decided to fly to Frankfurt, Germany to store his plane and start the trip to Poland based on papal security precautions.

Chapter 36

At the Frankfurt-Am-Main Flugplatz (airport) Gabriel, after renting space to store the airplane made arrangements to rent a medium size tour bus for the group and his two pilots. He who had known Poland before World War II and had subsequently returned due to his former diplomatic privilege status to experience for the last time in his life what the meaning of all that went into the restoration of the Bishop's Ring to the hand of a Polish Bishop. He wanted to savor the successful conclusion to the end of suffering of what only God could have achieved.

This time, once again, Poland was free. He looked forward to going back to Cracow, to sit at an open-air restaurant in the Rynek Gl'owny (Town Square) to observe the people who came to the Sukiennice (Cloth Hall), and remind himself that it was in this place where he met a young Grigor Androwitz, the boy whose destiny it was to become a priest and to share in the return of the Bishop's Ring. Of all the things he was able to achieve, Gabriel had a part in this work when he brought John Piorek to America. His support of John would become added fruit to his labors he would bring to the Lord in his moment of entering new life after his death. At his age, he thought about what he could harvest from his life that would bring happiness to God.

Gabriel Takentur took precautions. He carried his identities giving evidence of his former American bona fides during the Cold War. The group spent the night at an airport hotel. Gabriel, through

271

his business contacts knew that Ford Motors USA was going to build cars in Poland. He made a phone call to a local Ford dealership to set up the group's vehicles to travel to and through Poland.

In the morning, the sales manager of the local Ford dealership arrived early to pick up Gabriel, Maynard, and Bishop Piorek. In the matter of two hours, Gabriel rented a medium sized bus, bought vehicle insurance paying a heavy premium to the theft insurance rider to cover the bus. He bought a second, smaller van, and insured it so that the Sisters of the Nazarene convent would soon have their transportation needs met. The dealership agreed to supply a driver to follow their travel bus into Poland, where the Ford passenger van was to be delivered. At 10:00 A.M. the group headed out for the Polish border.

Magda, Bob and her children sat in the upfront window passenger seats across from the German driver. Across the aisle from Magda sat Marta and her husband. Magda held German and Polish road maps and looked for road signs. The Bishop and Monsignor O'Toole, sat behind the Morrisons while former Ambassador Takentur sat behind Marta and gazed out the windows and offered comments while Maynard seated across and seated behind him kept his eye on the countryside. Gabriel's two sons and their wives sat behind the others comfortably in the soft cushioned bus interior looking out tinted windows. Luggage was stored in the compartment below the passenger cabin. A useful compact toilet was in the rear of the bus.

Maynard felt very comfortable in his newly found surroundings of people who won their battle against Communism. It was a feeling he did not have coming home from his battles in Vietnam. He had a lot of questions to ask and Gabriel was all too happy to give his long view of history for answers.

"Maynard," Gabriel said, "All of Europe understood after decades of fighting against Karl Marx's philosophic 19th century viewpoints to change the world to atheism that Karl Marx knew what he was doing. He wrote despicable love poems to Satan. His claim not to believe in God yet believe in Satan is less than clever. Satan could not create the dirt Marx stood on. Yet, a secret kindred brotherhood has been following Marx's principles to this day, even in our own country, through his writings. They are the willing messengers of

Satan's vocal revolutionary minority to carry out chaotic tasks to keep people in bondage.

"God was so upset he sent the Blessed Virgin to France three times in the 19th century to give warnings and to affirm her Immaculate Conception. God put the apostates to the Catholic faith on notice where their future would be upon their death. The Bishop will tell you how miracles abounded as to the proofs in the existence of God. But still the Marxists persist and the un-churched buy into their lies." He looked into Maynard eyes and Maynard nodded his understanding.

"So that there is no misunderstanding there are bad people and good people in this world. Karl Marx was a paid toady for the conspiratorial group which fifty years earlier lead the French Revolution. They wanted Catholicism to die, to be done with. As a Jew he was a disgrace to all good Jews who lead good lives, who wanted to come to America or have their own country. But instead Marx was an inspiration to those who sought revenge or were filled with hate.

"The Marxists, my father would tell you if he was alive today, that they published four newspapers in Europe filled with Marxist propaganda. Their messages were to create discord all across Europe." He turned to his sons, and said, "Leon Trotsky, Lenin's number two man, was in New York publishing a propaganda fish wrapper and collecting money which he took back to Russia the spring before the Russian Revolution.

"The result of these Marxist actions someday would call for reactions. We know the rest. Bolshevik Marxists attacked Germany the day after the Armistice of World War I was signed at Versailles. The Marxists in that time lost their battle to win over Germany." Everyone in the bus was listening to this patriarchal group leader give his lesson of history views.

"Do you watch basketball Maynard?" Maynard nodded.

Gabriel said, "I'm old and happy to watch the college boys play the game. You know when a player deliberately commits a foul on his opponent hoping to get his opponent to respond, if the player who is not caught with his foul, and the person fouled is caught responding, it's the player who responds who get called for a foul, not the one who originally caused the fouled player to respond. True, right? Maynard again nodded, wondering where this was taking him.

"You see Hitler remembered the Marxist driven attempts in 1918 to take over Protestant Berlin and Catholic Munich, the cultural capitals of Christian religious beliefs. Hitler knew the enemy of Christianity from his earlier life in Austria. He heard these Marxists sell their souls in the city parks of Vienna where he lived before World War I. He knew their agenda was to take over the world. Hitler knew they succeeded in taking over Czarist Russia the largest country in the world. They did it without bloodshed, but with propaganda and lies. When they did, they began to starve and slaughter millions upon millions of people. Trotsky admitted to the world press they had done these things. He was proud of it. But Lenin gave him a talking to behind the barn. And secrecy about their horrors became policy.

"So, when Hitler came to power he later responded. Evil for evil! Even after the wars have ended Marxism is still telling its lies to the world. But then good people suffered for the conspired evils of the bad. The lesson is what Hitler did should never happen again. The Marxists were not charged with their foul play, Hitler, when he fought back he fouled out of Satan's game.

"In 1928 I was in Munich and heard what the people of Catholic Munich heard when the Communists introduced filthy jazz music to the little towns of the south of Germany. That was not all. They were very disruptive of local governments because huge crucifixes were displayed on road intersections as reminders to the Catholics of the Lord's suffering and death. They mocked and wanted Christianity taken out of public view. Again, Satan is served by their willing cooperation.

"Hitler lasted twelve years. Karl Marx's Communist manifesto is almost one hundred and fifty years old, carried on by the loyal soldiers of the kindred brotherhood. We are still hearing about Hitler's savagery to divert our attention from what is taking place underfoot. America has become fertile ground to plant evil trees to crucify more Christians in our time, because the anti-Catholic, anti-Christian cultural Marxists among us have embraced Marx's doctrines. Judeo-Christian Revelation was the source for forming our

National and State Laws. Power brokers and lobbyists now hold the positions across the spectrum of American life to deny our Christian faith's moral codes. There are no soldiers taking away our right to practice our faith. It's subtle! We hardly know its happening.

"But still Christianity and Catholic teachings are attacked constantly in our country to this day. Poland's freedom was paid for with decades of suffering because these Marxist atheists among us have denied the existence of Truth and Christ as the Son of God.

"I heard a priest once say, commenting on the Old Testament, God punished his people more than six-hundred times, and was angry with them for more than one-thousand times. Christ came to us to be with us to be the mediator so as to take on humanity's sins as an appeasement to save us from eternal destruction." Then in a quiet moment he muttered words from Holy Scripture, "God so loved the world he gave his only begotten Son…"

Gabriel knew when the group entered Poland they would see what Marxism wrought upon the Catholic country. Then they would appreciate and understand why in this time the Bishop's Ring reappeared.

Before the group was to enter former East Germany the bus driver suggested they stop in a shopping center off the autobahn to pick up food they might want to have as they journeyed into and about Poland. Not only did they buy food and drinks but storage containers where it could be kept for the times they would be traveling from city to city without taking extended mealtime breaks but in need of sandwiches, condiments, fruit and liquid drinks.

During the course of their early hours on the trip the group enjoyed seeing from the roadsides the fashionable expensive homes as they passed out of Frankfurt headed east. But the former East Germany still contained the vestiges of World War II with its starkly dirty gray buildings a reminder of days past when Marxists-Communists were in charge and God was denied a place in the Marxian utopia. They drove through the former Communist German Democratic Republic, stopping in Dresden, to see what was once a bombed out Catholic Cathedral the untouched ruin of atheist neglect destined by a vote of the majority faith of Protestants in the city to become something other than a reminder of its place where Heaven descended daily upon its altars in the celebration of Holy Mass. They were told a Catholic chapel would be built in the basement for those who wished to attend daily Holy Mass for the downtown dwellers and workers when construction begins to rebuild the ruins. The group continued on, passing through Gorlitz, and entered Poland in Zgorzelec, where they exchanged their US dollars currency for Polish zlotys.

Immediately, they began to see environmental neglect, the suffering poverty of fifty years of abandonment of land in the hands of slave masters. Legnica, their first stop over the border, still carried the scars of World War II. One large building near the town square, showed the contempt held by the Soviet masters on public display, a super sized open hole in the exterior of the building on an upper floor, produced by a mortar shell demonstrated the hate and suppression the Poles had to endure during the occupation of their country. The roads had not been resurfaced since World War II. The two traveling vehicles rolled up and down road, bouncing even on straight stretches.

Bishop Piorek looking out the van window said, "In the Lord's parable of the mustard seed, it appears there is a failed stewardship by the Communists here in Poland. There will be 'weeping and gnashing of teeth' as the Lord promised for those who allowed this destruction to take place in this land so gifted with resources."

The Bishop changed the subject. "I can see how Poland was sustained through prayer. As I watched the handful of elderly people kneeling before the caged altar in the Franciscan Church of St. Peter and St. Paul in Legnica where the monstrance containing the Blessed Sacrament was exposed. I saw adoring, praying souls who had much to do with saving Poland. They will find favor with God. That is the Poland I remember." The group remained silent for a short while. The Bishop continued to share his thoughts.

"I see this Poland and I see what can happen when the power of the few Marxists who can send their tanks and soldiers, and their," he hesitated saying, "what did Gabriel call them, 'toadies?' to rule over the multitude of a nation. It calls for an awakening of our faith in America in our challenging times. That is what we are faced with in America.

"I have been sitting here silent listening to Gabriel and telling myself he is correct. He knows the larger picture. He knows how Europe once a shining galaxy in Christian development has been transformed into an utopian swamp where people, who can read and learn about their faith, ignore their faith and show little or no fear of their eternal consequences." Emboldened by the moment, the Bishop continued.

"Marxism in America is not about tanks and soldiers. It is about ideas, which by their uniqueness are spiritual entities. Walls cannot stop them from entering a room or a nation. The kindred brotherhood Gabriel spoke of is fast at work in our nation. The Marxists, who deny Christ, expect a chair at the table to confront the truth with their lies, when truth, being Christ's Truth needs no other voice."

"It is reminiscent to me when in Holy Scripture Christ refused to go to his home town to perform miracles because the people there refused to believe in him and his teachings. There were those who walked away when he told them his flesh and blood would be food and drink; that he would abide in those who ate his flesh and drank his blood. Anyone who believes in the Incarnation of Christ as Christians do can believe Christ is the Voice in the Old Testament as the Word of God coming from a burning bush to Moses or present himself under the species of bread and wine as the Holy Eucharist."

Maynard spoke up. "Pardon me, Bishop. But not all Christians believe in the Holy Eucharist being Jesus' body and blood. Barney never did."

"Well Maynard, it wasn't always this way until the Reformation when separate groups chose to follow their own way. But with a division in the Church dogma, Sacred Tradition and Holy Scriptures did not change. The Church remained true to its teachings. St. Paul gave the warnings to the unfaithful, who disregarded Christ's teaching about the true nature of the Holy Eucharist.

"Tonight I will show you 1 Corinthians 11th Chapter, and Hebrews Chapter 6 Verse 6. But just remember we Catholics and other Christians have more in common through our baptisms in Christ.

"The Marxists and other non-believers like to exploit the differences between Catholics and Protestants. The Lord prayed for unity among us and let the Lord and our prayers be joined in unity with His "Will" to be done on earth as it is in heaven.

"The Marxist newspapers Gabriel spoke earlier about were the mouthpieces that caused discord and chaos in Europe. Today, in our country the Marxists are emboldened. They are part of what is called the American dream, but they depend upon the poor and unenlightened to carry their day as was done in Russia in the Czar's overthrow. While our country is conservative in its views, its news media is liberal. While Christ is abiding in us and in the hearts of other well meaning Christians, the liberal media decides what information it chooses to release, and often takes the side of those groups hostile to the Church Christ founded.

"It's the pattern of behavior the American public perceives which for the most part fails to trust the media and entertainment sources controlling our choices. It was that way in Russia, and Poland and now here in America on the national scene."

Monsignor O'Toole asked, "Dear Bishop, you speak like an Apostle. What did His Holiness say to you?"

Chapter 37

There are few roads in life that don't take a turn. The first night the group made their way to a very small village where they found a single woman and her elderly farmer father where they had turned their large farmhouse into a bed and breakfast. It had been recommended in Rome as a place to stay. The next morning she placed a very ample supply of food for their table.

The breakfast table conversation turned into a very interesting discussion. "Lech" was the name of the country's popular beer, and the name of the man in the 8th century who gave the name of "Poland" its name, meaning "People of the Land." Monsignor O'Toole, always one to connect the past to the present, suggested Poland's leader, Lech Walesa, presides over the "new and improved" Poland.

The group's journey continued east and dropping south headed for Cracow. They would not leave Poland without being changed by their experiences. They continued their way toward a destiny in Cracow.

On the outskirts of Wroclaw (Breslau) they entered a region where sixty-six mines produced the main energy for Poland. But along the way passed by Opole, Bytiom, Katowice, and finally came upon Cracow. Across the Vistula River before them, high on a hill was Wawel Castle and the Cathedral of St. Stanislaw. Magda had memories as if they were yesterday. The others compared the regions of Silesia to the states of New York and Pennsylvania, West Virginia, out to the Mid-West where so many Polish Americans settled to work in coalmines, and steel factories. Those Polish when they came to America brought their faith with them. There was so much to like from what they saw despite areas of land being neglected and polluted by Marxist edicts.

"Look this way," Gabriel said, "rusted machinery left behind. It shows contempt the Soviets had toward their lackey Polish bosses. For the Soviets, Poland was an economic jewel. Cheap labor produced coal, copper, salt, textiles, shipbuilding, oil, machinery, lead and zinc. I hate to say this but President Roosevelt should not have given in to his State Department to give Stalin the gift of Poland as a spoil of war. Poland was victimized first by Hitler then by Stalin. Like the Bishop said, it is the power of the Marxist minority among us even now, which denies us justice and makes the rules. They know it, but they would like to keep us from knowing it."

"What kept the Polish people from rising up?" Maynard asked him.

Gabriel responded. "Four Soviet divisions on the eastern border and nineteen Soviet divisions inside of East Germany's western border. Picks and hayforks against tanks and weapons! Legnica, where we passed through was headquarters for two Soviet Tank divisions."

Bishop Piorek added, "Yes, for all of their pressure upon my people, they were unable to destroy Polish faith. People refused to recognize or give the Marxist Poles true respect. Their unholy idealism denied us our religion. People fought back any way they could because they knew they had God on their side. It's different now in America. Our American Marxists hide behind organizations with patriotic names. But their agenda is the same as it was for Marx and Lenin."

Maynard asks, "Who are they Father, er Bishop?"

The Bishop looked at Maynard his friend of many years. "They are so obvious to me because I remember how Marxists operated in Poland. In Poland they indulged us with their shows of patriotism. But it was all façade. They took our history from us and tried to destroy our religious roots. Slowly the same is taking place now in America. I'm suspicious of educators and politicians who conspire to eliminate as something unimportant to schoolchildren their nation's grand history. It's worse when they lie about history and rewrite it! It goes on in America right now. What do we call it? Dumbing down!" Heads nodded in agreement, and that was another small departure.

The Bishop spoke again with intensity. "In my quiet hours in Shady Trail, I had time to observe the world and draw conclusions from my hidden space. Catholics and other Christians cannot remain indifferent to America's secular humanism. They must rise up like the Polish Solidarity movement. Americans need to break away from their television sets to have time to think and to do or else the Lord warns he will vomit us out of his mouth. Baptized Christians, united together can raise our voices and vote to break the powers of politicians and lobbyists who copy Marxist agendas to change our country. We Christians must pray first and defend our baptism in Christ. We have to remind everyone there will be a day for the Resurrection of the dead, Christ proved it. And he promised it would come for all to come to judgment."

All on the bus sat silently mesmerized by the inner depths of the priest they all thought they knew. As Bishop, he had a passport to a new life, to express in the open with the shared collegiality and authority of the Pope. His years of retreat to the mountain towns of Tennessee was not unlike Christ who sought sanctuary to pray and reinvigorate himself for the daily mission to show God's love for humanity and to awaken Jews first and then Gentiles to choose to save their eternal souls. He had begun to crystallize his thoughts as to what his mission would become. It began the day when Bishop O'Farrell asked him to be his Auxiliary Bishop. The Bishop made eye contact around the bus to make sure he was talking to all in the group as he knelt with one knee into his couch seat.

"American Marxists do not call themselves Marxists but they act the same as Lenin's Marxists. Would that Catholics and other Christians would behave like Poland's Solidarity movement and believe they had God on their side and unite in America. Would that all Christians would stand up with their baptized faith to stop the efforts of the anti-Catholic and anti-Christian bigotry by lobbyist groups whose agendas are designed to turn our nation into a godless, secular society, it would become if we all remain indifferent to God's holy will." Their eyes agreed.

"Satan, the first person to be 'Pro-Choice,' is behind this Marxist madness. The Soviets declare Communism finished. But it isn't. The Marxist ideas still exist and have taken up residence here in America where a military is not needed to hold them in check. Because we are an open society, for seventy years Marxists have invaded our most treasured universities transporting Marxist atheist doctrines into the minds of the gullible youth. Banking and financial institutions are not secure from corruption.

"America has experienced spies, treason, disloyalty, sabotage, bribery of willing officials, theft of secrets, theft of patents; the list goes on and on. And we sit back indifferent and happy with our freedoms while the anti-God crowd uses our freedoms to undermine our national will to remain a nation under God. Our freedoms could be vaporized in the split of a second because we are indifferent and ignorant of what the Marxist liars and thieves are doing and planning to do to our country. The Marxists attack the Constitution by turning it against itself by claiming rights never intended by the founding Fathers of this nation. As an immigrant I have studied the Federalist Papers."

The Bishop's monologue was new to Monsignor O'Toole.

"We need to go back to our Judeo-Christian origins. St. Paul writing in 1 Corinthians told how the ancient Israelites lost favor with God after they had been rescued from Egypt. He said Christ was the same God who called out to Moses from a burning bush on Mount Horeb, to tell Moses He was the God of Abraham, Isaac and Jacob. When Abraham asked God what he should tell the Israelites what his name was, God called Himself, 'I AM WHO AM.' By that holy name He was forever revered as the God of the Israelites." Some travelers nodded; they knew the Book of Exodus.

"To make his point, St. Paul said of the Israelites when they passed through the sea that they were under a cloud and all were baptized into Moses in that cloud. The Israelites ate the same spiritual food, the blood of a lamb, and all drank the same spiritual drink, for they drank from the spiritual rock that followed them. Paul said that rock was 'The Christ.' Still, God was not pleased with them, they went back to pagan behavior and they were struck down in the desert. Only one person who left Pharaoh's Egypt ever entered the

Promised Land. It was not Moses, as we would expect, but militant Joshua. If you did not know Joshua is another name for Jesus. The symbolism of Joshua taking the new generation born in the forty-year wanderings in the desert, now grown adults should not escape us.

"We are the people of the New Covenant with God. God sent a warrior to destroy the pagan cities that had once sprung up in the land he had given to the Israelites. He also let his people be defeated because of their pagan behavior. That time was then. The world has changed, but God has not.

"Pagan behavior has consequences. Those who gave us Marxism gave us paganism. Those who drag down our American society with pagan rituals the most grievous being killing the unborn do so as blood sacrifices to Satan. They are inviting the wrath of God upon all of us. God may be biding his time with us." Each member of the group looked at each other wondering what he was going to say next. He caught their puzzlement.

"Hear me out! The Marxist Government of Poland was like the Sadducees of Christ's time. The Sadducees of old did not believe in the Resurrection, yet they controlled the religious governing of the Jews. The Temple Sadducees sent their best to try to trip up the Lord to the point of mockery when they questioned his authority to teach what he was teaching. The Voice, which spoke from the burning bush to Moses at Mount Horeb, and Adam and Eve in the Garden of Eden, was the very same 'Voice', which spoke to the religious authorities of Jerusalem. The Sadducees were men who denied, angels, God's Providence, denied the spirit, immortality, of survival and resurrection. Christ told them they will die in their sins if they did not believe that 'I Am Who I Am.'" Because they refused to believe him when he said, 'Before Abraham was born, "I Am."'

"We are listening," Magda said.

"Just like the Marxist thinkers of our time. They belong to this world. They will die in their sins. Belief in Christ is a commitment to act on one's beliefs. It's all there in John's Gospel, Chapter 8. What did those who called themselves the sons of Abraham do when Christ revealed so much of himself and his connection to times of Abraham when Abraham was happy to see Christ's day, declaring himself to have existed before Abraham and to be the holy 'I Am?' They threw stones at him.

"Is that not what the anti-Catholic, anti-Christian detractors are doing when they deny the 'Truth' Christ teaches to maintain their power over the rest of us? The destruction of the fortress 'Marxism' that surrounded Poland has come down, like the prophecy revealed that those who did not believe in Christ would kill his followers."

Monsignor O'Toole looked at him with a quizzical look. The Bishop saw O'Toole's delight hearing him speak. "Yes, Bishop, you deserve to wear St. Stanislaw's Bishop's Ring. He too, fought for the faith against an evil king. Your evil king is Marxism. May God bless your work when you call for the end of our governmental Marxist rulers."

Bishop Piorek just nodded, quietly left to his thoughts.

This Polish immigrant now naturalized a citizen Bishop knew the American society's lack of action by the majority of Christian faiths were failing the "Temple Test" imposed by Christ when he became so outraged His holy anger drove the profiteers and peddlers from the holy grounds of Jerusalem's Temple. The profiteers had turned the house of God into a den of thieves. America, he came to believe was turning into a den of thieves and liars.

In his life in America the Bishop saw the changes taking place over the decades where decency, honesty, integrity, candor, and a host of other common sincerities were shrinking from the American culture. The increasing dangerous world actions of those committed to anti-Christian Marxist agendas are weakening the national social fabric. Elected, appointed, powerful evil influences in government were not unlike the times of Christ when all that was holy was being denied by the non-believing religious authorities. People in the positions of power and the marketplace were bolder, pushing their agendas outside the limits where the people could vote on changes, to where judges would serve as proxies to change America from its rooted laws based on Judeo-Christian Revelations from God.

America, he was often told was not the same place. Wars across the Pacific and Atlantic left behind bodies of the slain on bloody grounds and in deep seas those who fought for freedom and the love of God and country. Only those, who went to American cemeteries on foreign shores in Italy or France, knew the sacredness of their service to God and country in the defense of freedom.

This new Bishop knew down deep in his soul the horrors of regimes, which hate God and what they do to the innocent to make them suffer. He had only to think of his parents and how God placed him in his role to act as an Apostle. It was a daunting thought.

Bishop Piorek knew there were evil men in the world, willing to kill to deny Christ his place in heaven as the Savior of humanity. Christ died for no purpose if now in this world Catholics and Christians were indifferent or ignoring Christ's suffering on the Cross to pay for the sins of humanity by allowing the ungodly behavior and breakdown of society to persist. There was silence on the bus for the longest time after the two priestly prelates spoke. The mood was somber. The truth had been spoken. Small conversations continued. When they came together as a group there was full agreement.

Clearly the hand of God touched John Piorek for a purpose because God does all things with a purpose. An American moral society was on the decline. The two hundred year swing from freedom to bondage so prevalent in human history had already begun in America. He knew the truth: God allows wars to take place because of humanity's sins. Atheistic beliefs, licentious and lewd behavior was changing America. America was being fed evil by a narrow group of elitists whose views attacked enacted laws and invited dissent against church and government institutions. The powerful profiteers for death of the innocent unborn human life and peddlers of smut and violence had taken over the American temple grounds where once faith, hope, love, dignity, and other virtues once held places of honor.

The battleground to save America would have to begin with Americans on their knees as Americans had done before God and as the people of Poland had done for a millennium to keep their freedom.

These conversations continued until the bus driver, directed by Magda drove the bus into the driveway of the Convent of the Sisters of the Nazarene. The Vatican planned well. A smiling nun came out of the convent to meet the group and tell them they waited for their arrival and that their supper was waiting for them in the dining room.

Chapter 38

This was the day all of Bishop Piorek's friends had been waiting for since their trip began in the United States. They were going to St. Stanislaw's Cathedral on Wawel Hill located beyond the gates of Poland's former king Castle residence. Church and Kingdom, religious and government rulers co-existing in harmony on the same location!

The fortress was the undeniable social structure of the city sitting on a limestone hill, impressive and imposing as the Acropolis in Athens, the Capitol of Rome or the Kremlin in Moscow. Wawel Hill was made famous as the symbol of unity and tradition among back centuries before the castle was built. Below, a winding Vistula River, a water route passage south to north connecting cities, villages, farms, west, east and north to the great blue Baltic Sea.

Magda and Bob exited the bus and she walked quickly down a small slope to the bend in the river, where the both of them could look up at the fortress compound. "This is where it all began for me. Here, in there." She pointed to the Cathedral. "That is where my journey of faith began with Conrad. That is where we accepted the Bishop's Ring, to protect it until it was placed on the hand of a Polish Bishop." He listened to her speak softly. Bob said, "For me this is a spiritual reward for being selected, unknown to me then, to assist in the safe keeping of Bishop Piorek's Ring. You, my dear, are the bonus prize in this incomprehensible mystery of death and life." They turned around and walked back to the group waiting for them in the parking lot.

Archbishop Adamowicz had been contacted and arrangements were made for the travelers to visit the Cathedral and make preparations for Bishop Piorek to celebrate Mass at the altar of St. Stanislaw in the nave of Wawel Cathedral and place the leather bound "Legend" in the Cathedral Treasury located under the Cathedral. They were told where to park their bus off the Royal Castle grounds in a nearby-protected parking lot. For Magda and John Piorek this walk up the cobblestones path along side huge fortressed castle walls was a return to their young lives to relive their date with destiny. For both in their private moments it was a day of great joy and anticipation.

Archbishop Marius Adamowicz stood on the Cathedral's front steps with a man and a woman as the group finally arrived from the climb up the hill roadway and through the gated entrance adjacent to the Cathedral. Bishop Piorek recognized the Archbishop as a priest from his youth. Immediately he rushed up to him and knelt to kiss his ring.

Bob Morrison stared at the man standing next to the Archbishop and quickly left Magda to stand along side Bishop Piorek. Morrison recognized the man. It was Sobleski's chauffer, the man whose photo he had indelibly imprinted upon his mind. Morrison heard the Archbishop speaking in Polish to Bishop Piorek. Morrison turned and motioned to Magda to come.

Morrison asked, "What are the saying?"

Magda looked at Bob wondering why he asked. "They are talking about the man and the woman giving the Archbishop a lot of money."

Morrison said, "They are the two who cleaned out the Polish embassy's funds in New York. We have his picture on file." She looked at him astonished, knowing this could be one last attempt to steal the Bishop's Ring. Morrison moved her closer to the two Bishops as they privately conversed. Maynard, suspecting something was wrong moved over to the side of Bishop Piorek, when suddenly both prelates realized they were surrounded. Morrison told Bishop Piorek that the man standing with the Archbishop was Sobleski's driver.

Waldemir Wilk laughed since he understood English. "I know who you are, Mr. Morrison. I must admit I was a spy. Sobleski never trusted me to know what he was doing. His secretary, this woman, Wanda Zabinski, and I took the money Sobleski was using to bribe to get the Bishop's Ring. We took the money before the Communists found out he was dead. The Archbishop is holding all of that money. He will decide what will happen to it since it came from the labor of the Polish people who were deprived by the Communists to support the Church."

Morrison looked at Bishop Piorek who heard Wilk's answer. Bishop Piorek said to Morrison, "It's true what this man has said. Archbishop Adamowicz has just told me what these two people did."

Archbishop Adamowicz whispered to Bishop Piorek, "Both have confessed their sins to me. They are back in God's graces. Wilk saw you hearing Sobleski's confession. He told me he did not want to be a fool and deny himself a chance for heaven. She too had sins to confess."

The Archbishop stepped up on step and spoke to the group in English. "Today, you will tour the Royal Castle and St. Stanislaw's Cathedral. Wawel Hill has been the site of the kings of Poland from the mid-eleventh century to the early seventeenth century. You will have a guide who will tell you what happened in various centuries since them, and what kings served when. Fires in castles, marriages to royals of other nations, have had their influence upon the Royal Castle. The current Royal Castle is a mixture of 14th and 15th century Gothic. King Eric of Denmark lived here in what has been called the Danish Tower from the 15th century on. You will find a variety of stonework applied to the Castle coming from a mixture of cultures from central Europe and Italian Renaissance. But the rest we will let your guide describe in detail. They have fascinating stories about kings marrying Polish beauties. You will see a beautiful white marble sarcophagus of Queen Jawiga(Hedwig).

"Bishop Piorek and I have discussed the length of your tour and would like to celebrate Mass after it at 12:00 PM at the Shrine of St. Stanislaw. We will bless the Legend Book after Mass, we will all assemble in the Cathedral Treasury." The Archbishop laid down a plan.

"In the meantime Father Slovakia, who speaks English, will be your guide around the Cathedral to show you the chapels of saints, funerary tombs of kings, queens, Cardinals, Bishops, poets, and Polish warriors who fought for people's freedoms. One of our heroes, Thaddeus Kosciuszko fought for your American independence. He is buried in the crypt below. Your Congress recognized in 1977 his role in your Revolutionary War fighting for American freedom."

At noon, a group of diocesan seminary acolytes lead a procession of Bishop Piorek's fellow travelers, into the nave of the Cathedral where the very impressive silver sarcophagus ornately and richly sculpted, resided in the St. Stanislaw's Shrine. Three prelates, a Monsignor, an Auxiliary Bishop, and an Archbishop entered the railed sanctuary of the shrine. One seminarian held the "Legend" to be blessed with Holy Water.

This was the moment John Piorek anticipated ever since he was ordained an Auxiliary Bishop. Monsignor O'Toole was asked to read the Epistles in English in a foreign church in a Polish language private celebration. Magda's excitement all through the Mass could not be contained as she responded in Polish to the celebrant's recited prayers. While the Mass was being celebrated pilgrims and townspeople walked about the Cathedral praying and viewing in awe the wonders of what hundreds of years of faith had protected.

At the end of Mass, Bishop Piorek wanted to remain a few minutes in prayerful thanksgiving for the honor, which had been bestowed upon him as the inheritor of St. Stanislaw's Bishop's Ring. The atmosphere of the enclosed shrine was so peaceful that the group was content to remain as long as Bishop Piorek wanted to pray. Quietly, each remained in silent meditation, heads bowed, eyes closed. This was their moment too, in some way, contemplating events in their own lives.

Bishop Piorek rose from his prie-dieu and in a final rite of passage, moved to place his ringed finger against the saint's silver sarcophagus. When he did, an explosion of light enveloped the whole shrine like a cloud. Bishop Piorek could not tell if he was in a trance or sleeping through a dream.

Still within the clouded atmosphere, he was alone as clouds in front of him parted and before him stood very tall angels. Like a mirage, there appeared a small boy walking on puffy clouds off in the distance, walking forward towards him. As the boy came closer, a couple dressed as if they were bride and groom entered in his view. The boy came closer to them, and in his hands he held a gold ciborium.

Behind the boy, another figure vested in a hooded cloak covering his face. He approached the boy and stretched out his right hand and touched the boys shoulder. It was a signal. As he put his hand on the boy's shoulder Bishop Piorek noticed a wound in the center of his hand. It had to be, Bishop Piorek told himself, only one person, the Lord himself had come forward.

The boy held what appeared to be the Holy Eucharist. He recited the prayers John Piorek knew all too well when dispensing the Body of Christ. The vision grew larger and larger. And there receiving what appeared to be the Holy Eucharist, were two people whom John Piorek knew intimately. They were his parents, as they may have appeared on their wedding day!

Bishop Piorek began to cry, dropping tears down the front of his chasuble. In wonderment about what he was experiencing, he received an inner locution. He just knew this boy was a young St. Stanislaw, when the boy walked with the Lord in his youth to bring the Holy Eucharist to the sick and others. The couple received the Holy Eucharist and just as quickly as the event unfolded the clouds reappeared and this moment in another world disappeared.

Then and only then was Bishop Piorek able to withdraw his hand from St. Stanislaw's sarcophagus. He turned around and the group seemed to be oblivious as to what happened. There were no questions asked, except one, which asked him how he spilled water on his chasuble. It was then he knew they had not witnessed his moment in the heavens of eternal life. It was his private moment. Only when he would eventually meet the Lord after death would the Lord show his face to him.

The seminary acolytes lead the group out of the shrine, and lead the priests to the sacristy where they disrobed from their vestments. The group waited outside and when the priests came out a seminarian carried the blessed Legend Book down the narrow stairs to the Treasury crypt where the group had been earlier, to place the Legend Book in a glass covered reliquary cordoned off by ruby red ropes. Placards large enough for visitors to read from a distance were placed along side the St. Stanislaw's Bishop Ring Legend Book highlighted the value of the contents of the book.

No one could be happier with this event than Magda, for herself, and Conrad, and all others who participated in finally closing the last chapter of the return of the Bishop's Ring.

The group's journey was not over Magda reminded them as they walked about the Castle grounds. She wanted to show the group to see the rest of the historic complex beginning near the Sigismund Tower where a monument of "Tadeusz" Kosciuszko is mounted on his horse as a reminder of the great warriors of Poland who fought for independence for all people in Poland and America.

Magda had plans to go to the home of her birth where she and her sister, their American husbands could understand and appreciate all the love they had for Wieliczka. All could go into the mine and see the beauty the miners created over centuries in the place once was the home of the Bishop's Ring. From there, Gabriel directed their path to Auschwitz, a grim reminder of a horrid past, and see the cell where the saintly Franciscan priest, Maximillian Kolbe, offered his life so that a married man with a family would not be killed by the Nazis.

They continued on to neighboring cities and towns. Most impressive was Czestochowa where a true to life miraculous icon, the miraculous Shrine of the Black Madonna was enshrined. It is believed the original, which had been painted by St. Luke the Evangelist was later copied as a fifth century Byzantine icon of the Madonna and Child. Traced back to 1382, this copy was offered when a Polish Duke Wladyslaw Opalczyk founded a Pauline Monastery on a hill known as Jasna Gora.

The present painting is an exact copy of the painting completed by Cracovian painters in the 15th century after the Hussite's (Czech

Protestants) invasion and desecration of the painting in 1430. In the 17th century Sweden invaded Poland. But unlike most Polish towns, which were conquered, the defense of Jasna Gora was regarded as a miracle. The sanctuary became a religious and patriotic center, where for more than 600 years it has been a pilgrim center for the Catholic Faith in Poland.

Beyond their moments in Cracow and the inspirational return of the Bishop now wearing the holy relic ring, all members of his group enjoyed seeing the faith of the people being exercised wherever they went in a nation once smothered by evil men defeated in a struggle against God.

The group returned to Cracow, a city of so many miracles, the group visited the Church of the Blessed Virgin Mary in Rynek Glowny (Town Square) and the miraculous Corpus Christi Church. The Bishop's Ring journey of more than nine hundred years was now complete and they headed back to America renewed in faith and the love of God. The struggle against God failed. Magda completed the journey of faith for which Conrad had sacrificed his life that God would be served.

EPILOGUE

On the return flight to the United States, Bishop Piorek reread the Holy Father's letter given to him during the group's audience with the Pope.

"In the designs of Providence, dear Brother, there are no mere coincidences. For you were chosen to be the wearer of the Bishop's Ring was a part in God's overall all plan to end the suffering of our brethren. Poland and many other nations suffered at the hands of the brutal just as our Lord suffered in his crucifixion. Prayer and suffering are meritorious before the throne of God in this unbelieving world. Your parents, in their love for each other served God's purposes and joined with God to give you life so that God's purposes may be fulfilled."

The Bishop believed God worked a miracle through his hands. He had been given a vision of eternity with the joy of knowing his parents were in the presence of God. His moment was no mere coincidence! The meaning of this apparition was not lost on the Bishop. Whatever preceded the moment before placed the Bishop's Ring against the silver sarcophagus of St. Stanislaw, would not take away this moment when the will of God was to be fulfilled. His new faith journey had begun.

John Piorek was destined to be the final wearer of the Bishop's Ring. In gratitude he began reciting the Joyful, Sorrowful, and Glorious fifteen decades of the Rosary. The group joined him in prayer, high in the heavens above the earth.

As long as he lived and wore the Bishop's Ring there would be evils in the world yet to come. Heresies, false prophets, false gods would rise up against the Church and there would be willing cooperators guided by Satan wreaking havoc over human life: But as for the Church founded by Jesus, the promise he made would triumph in St. Matthew's Gospel, chapter 16: verses 18-20:

"...And I say to thee, thou art Peter (Rock), and upon this Rock I will build my Church, and the gates of hell shall not prevail against it. And I will give thee the keys of the kingdom of heaven; and whatever thou shall bind on earth shall be bound in heaven, and whatever thou shall loose on earth shall be loosed in heaven." Then he strictly charged his disciples to tell no one that he was Jesus the Christ. (Douay Version)

About The Author

Bill DeBottis was born in Syracuse, NY. He attended Catholic Schools from kindergarten to graduate school. He is a winner of a national Catholic High School essay contest. He served in the U.S. Army, 3rd Infantry Division in Germany. As a State Association Executive Director his writing assignments included speeches, promotional materials, publishing Newsletters and Magazine. Later, he published a company newspaper, created and presented material for corporate sales and management seminars. History and travel interests have taken him to 36 States, and 17 countries, including Poland. He served voluntarily on federal, state, county advisory committees; and his parish church for many years. He is married, has three children and four grandchildren. Enjoy this fiction novel. It's a spellbonding faith journey!

Printed in the United States
30770LVS00003B/49-276

9 781418 484453